HIGH SEDUCTION

"Ram, stop!"

"You don't want me to stop, Phoebe. You know I'll make it good for you. I'm the one man you can't deny your body. You belong to me."

Shaking her head vehemently, Phoebe wanted to dispute Ram's claim, but she knew it to be true. She couldn't think beyond the sensations buffeting her. She wanted to tell Ram he was the only man who had ever made love to her, but she wouldn't give him the satisfaction.

Phoebe didn't want to accept what she was experiencing with Ram, but his hungry mouth and inflamed passion reminded her how desperately she had once loved him and how vibrantly alive his loving had made her feel.

"What are you thinking?" Ram whispered against her lips. "What are you feeling?"

"Overwhelmed," Phoebe rasped. "And bewildered. That we are together again like this is incomprehensible."

"I don't see why it should be. I didn't leave you. If you recall, you left me. Is it difficult to believe I've been pining for you all these years?"

Phoebe gave a huff of disbelief. "You're a liar and a fraud, Lord Braxton."

SEDUCED BY A ROGUE

CONNIE MASON

LEISURE BOOKS NEW YORK CITY

A LEISURE BOOK®

April 2003

Published by

Dorchester Publishing Co., Inc.
276 Fifth Avenue
New York, NY 10001

ISBN 0-8439-5134-6

The name "Leisure Books" and the stylized "L" with design are
trademarks of Dorchester Publishing Co., Inc.

Printed in the United States of America.

Visit us on the web at www.dorchesterpub.com.

*I've dedicated many books to my husband,
but this one is especially appropriate. He knows why.*

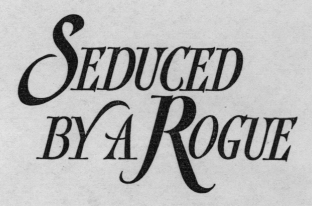

Prologue

"You want me to do what?" Ramsey Dunsmore, Earl of Braxton, was all but shouting at the man facing him across the desk.

"Seduce a woman. That's what you do best, isn't it?"

"I say, Fielding, you go too far."

Arthur Fielding, a middle-aged balding man of unremarkable height, removed his rimless spectacles and peered at Ram with keen blue eyes.

"Have you suddenly developed scruples, Braxton? The Foreign Office wouldn't ask this of you unless we thought you capable of carrying off this assignment. We need information, and thus far the woman has been uncooperative. But if you were to seduce her . . ." He left the sentence dangling.

"I stopped working for the Foreign Office years ago," Ram reminded him. "My spying days are over."

1

Fielding replaced his glasses and leaned back in the chair, his fingers tented before him. "Would it help to tell you the woman in question is a beauty? And that you were our unanimous choice for the assignment?"

Ram shrugged. "I'm sure there are others as capable as I am. Is she married?"

"No, but my sources tell me she has a lover."

"What kind of information are you looking for?"

"The woman's father is a noted Egyptologist and she's one of his assistants. They've been out of the country for several years."

Warning bells went off in Ram's head. *It couldn't be. It was just a coincidence.* "Go on."

"While collecting artifacts in a newly opened tomb in Egypt, they found a valuable amulet. It disappeared shortly thereafter, and the Egyptian government is demanding its return. Egyptian officials think the amulet was stolen and are threatening reprisals if it isn't returned. Newly arrived envoys from Egypt claim it's more than an artifact. The amulet is shaped like a golden starburst and crowned with an enormous ruby, and it's revered for its historical significance as well as its value."

Things were beginning to add up for Ram in ways he didn't like. "Let me guess. The Egyptologist is Sir Andrew Thompson and his daughter's name is Phoebe."

Surprise marched across Fielding's face. "You know them?"

The stark planes of Ram's face tautened. He hadn't spoken Phoebe's name since that fateful day four years ago, though she was never far from his thoughts. Forcing a calm he didn't feel, he tried to keep his voice emotionless as he said, "I know them."

"Then you can identify Miss Thompson when you see her."

"Unfortunately, yes. What exactly am I supposed to learn from Miss Thompson?"

"The whereabouts of her father, for one thing. He seems to have disappeared into thin air. The Egyptians believe Sir Thompson stole the amulet with the intention of selling it to a private buyer for personal gain."

"When did the Thompsons return from Egypt?"

"Miss Thompson arrived by ship four weeks ago. Three large crates of artifacts approved for deportation by the Egyptian government accompanied her. Sir Thompson boarded a ship two weeks after his daughter's departure. David Phillips, his assistant and Miss Thompson's lover, accompanied him."

He cleared his throat and continued. "Our sources reveal they arrived in England two weeks ago aboard the *Corinthian*; then Thompson mysteriously disappeared. We've been watching Miss Thompson's movements closely but cannot prove she's been in contact with him. Her only visitor thus far has been David Phillips."

"What makes you think I'm the man for the job?"

Fielding's eyes lit with amusement. "I have faith in your ability, Braxton. Though my experience is limited compared to yours, we both know seduction is a powerful tool. Use your legendary charm and sexual prowess to obtain information from Miss Thompson."

Painful memories hardened Ram's handsome features. "Find someone else."

"There *is* no one else. You're familiar with the workings of the Foreign Office and the dangers involved."

"Too bad Bathurst is married," Ram mused. "He would be perfect for the job. How about Viscount Westmore? His prowess with the ladies exceeds even mine."

Fielding waved his hand dismissively. "He won't do; he hasn't any experience with the Foreign Office. England is depending upon you to prevent an international incident. Can we count on you, Braxton?"

Ram's thoughts traveled backward in time. He didn't want to see Phoebe again, wanted nothing to do with her. The woman was cunning and manipulative; it didn't surprise him to learn she was a thief as well as a liar. If the Foreign Office said she and her father had conspired to steal the valuable artifact, he was inclined to believe it. But he wanted no part of any assignment that would bring him in contact with Phoebe Thompson.

"I'm afraid I'm going to have to—"

"Don't say no yet, Braxton," Fielding pleaded. "This is too important. England is counting on you to prevent communications from breaking down completely between England and Egypt. Why are you so skittish about accepting the assignment? Have you suddenly developed a conscience?"

He laughed. " 'Tis a well-known fact that you use your charms indiscriminately. All I'm asking is that you use them on Miss Phoebe Thompson. Once she tells you what we want to know, we will take it from there."

Ram was preparing to refuse for the second time when a devil's voice inside him asked, why not take the assignment? If Phoebe had helped her father steal the amulet, she deserved to be punished.

Seduced by a Rogue

Nothing would please him more than bringing about Phoebe's downfall.

A smile that didn't bode well for Phoebe Thompson curved Ram's lips. "Very well, Fielding. I'll do it."

Chapter One

Phoebe Thompson darted a glance over her shoulder but saw little through the encroaching darkness and evening fog. She wished now that she hadn't lingered to speak with the president of the Egyptology Society after the meeting. She'd been so happy to be discussing things she knew about with people of like minds that she had left the assembly later than she'd intended. Since the meeting hall was but a few short blocks from her home, she had elected to walk, but if a hackney had been available now, she would have hired it on the spot.

Gathering her cloak tightly about her, Phoebe lengthened her stride, trying to outdistance the chill creeping along the back of her slender neck. Someone was following her. Another government agent, she supposed. She should be used to it by now, but the feeling of being watched was discomfiting.

Where are you, Father? What have they done to

you? Phoebe silently lamented. Why wouldn't the Foreign Office believe she and her father had nothing to do with the missing amulet? She had been with her father and David the day the amulet had been found. It had been an awesome discovery, but they'd known from the onset that the Egyptian government would never let the valuable artifact leave the country. Its historical significance was invaluable.

Only someone who didn't know her father would believe he had stolen it.

Footsteps dogged Phoebe, and she quickened her pace. Someone was stalking her. Was it a government agent or someone more sinister? Where was the Watch when she needed it? Daring another glance over her shoulder, Phoebe saw a silhouette framed in the feeble glow of a streetlight. She began to run. Another block and she'd be home.

Phoebe nearly sobbed aloud when the dim outline of her house rose above the eerie mist she'd all but forgotten during her years in sunny Egypt. Fumbling in her reticule for her key, she had it firmly in her hand and ready to insert in the lock when a hand reached out from the fog and touched her shoulder.

The key dropped from her trembling fingers as she spun around to defend herself against this unknown terror.

"Hello, Phoebe. It's been a long time."

Phoebe paled and began to shake when she realized that her worst nightmare stood before her, looking as elegant and self-possessed as she remembered. Confident, arrogant, and more handsome than he had a right to be. Seeing him again reminded her of all the emotional baggage and guilt she'd carried around these past four years. *He* was the reason she had left England, the reason she hadn't returned.

"Braxton! You scared the wits out of me. How did you know I'd returned?"

Ramsey Dunsmore, Earl of Braxton, calmly retrieved the key Phoebe had dropped and fitted it in the lock. "I have my ways." He turned the key and pushed open the door.

Her voice held remarkably steady for a woman whose insides were churning. "Thank you. I can see myself inside."

"I think not."

Pushing past her, Ram walked into the foyer of the gray clapboard house Phoebe had let on Mount Street, a neighborhood cloaked in shabby respectability, a mixture of shops, lodging houses and unpretentious private homes. The neighborhood was the kind where people led quiet, uneventful lives, and Phoebe had hoped it would serve to keep her out of the public eye. Obviously not, for Ramsey had found her.

She followed him inside. "How dare you barge into my home without an invitation!"

"I dare many things, Phoebe," Ram drawled, "and apparently, so do you."

"If you're referring to our ill-conceived—"

"Think what you want."

"What are you doing here?"

"Close the door, Phoebe."

Phoebe slammed the door and whirled about to confront him . . . and lost the ability to breathe. Limned in the light from the lamp on the hall table, he was even more imposing than she recalled. Since her return from Egypt, she had learned a great deal about Lord Braxton and the Rogues of London from the gossip columns and was aware that Ramsey's indulgent lifestyle was leading him to perdition. Looking at him, however, brought back memories she'd tried hard to forget.

"Where are your servants?"

His question jerked her back to the present. "I have only day help. Our pockets aren't flush like yours. Father and I put all our resources into research."

"Don't you know it's dangerous to walk London streets at night? Where is your father?"

Phoebe suddenly found her fingernails fascinating. "He's . . . away."

"Where is your lover? He should have escorted you home."

Phoebe's dark brows drew together in a frown. "I have no idea whom you are talking about. Besides, what I do or don't do is none of your business. We're no longer . . ."

Ram sent her a mocking grin. "Aren't we? Are you sure?"

All vestiges of color drained from Phoebe's face. "After what I did I . . . I thought you had . . . taken care of the details."

Ram shrugged. "I saw no need."

"I'm sorry."

Bitterness rose like gorge in Ram's throat but he fought it down. "Rather late for that, isn't it?"

His expression must have been fierce, for Phoebe drew back as if struck. "You hate me."

"Can you blame me?"

"I . . . no, not really. I suppose it's too late for apologies."

His hard gaze delved into her eyes and held her trapped. She inhaled sharply when his gaze searched her face, seeking answers. "Way too late," he said.

"Why are you here? What do you hope to gain by stalking me?"

Ram's brows shot upward. "Stalking you? Hardly. You haven't changed much in four years, Phoebe. You're still as beautiful as I remember."

Her complexion, tinted gold by the Egyptian sun, contrasted vividly with her blue eyes and flowing dark hair. His gaze focused on her lush mouth and full lips, and unwelcome thoughts came unbidden to his mind. He remembered her taste, the shape and feel of her beneath his mouth and tongue and hands, and cursed himself for a fool. She meant nothing to him. He'd had four years to forget the humiliation he'd suffered at her hands. All he wanted from her now was information, and if he had to seduce her to get it, so be it.

Ram had no qualms about seducing Phoebe. He'd feel nothing, neither guilt nor remorse, for he wasn't the same man he'd been four years ago. He'd learned a great deal since then and he'd allowed no woman to get close enough to him to make a fool of him after Phoebe. Revenge was long overdue.

"We both know how you feel about me, so leave off with the compliments, Braxton," Phoebe said.

It wasn't difficult for Ram to summon the charismatic smile that charmed and beguiled women. Seduction was a game, one he and his friends Westmore and Bathurst had perfected.

Reaching out, he stroked her golden cheek, then drew his hand back as if burned. What in blazes was wrong with him? he wondered, staring at his hand. The tingling sensation extended from his fingers clear up his arm. Frowning, he thrust his hand into his pocket.

"Why did you do that?" Phoebe asked, touching her cheek.

"I wanted to see if your skin is as soft as I remembered."

Dismay widened Phoebe's blue eyes. "What are you after, Braxton? Am I still a challenge to you?"

Ram shrugged. "Not at all. I thought we should talk. Are you going to offer me a drink?"

"No. I'm tired and wish to retire. Besides, I can't imagine why you're interested in anything I have to say."

"You'd be surprised, Phoebe." He took a deep breath in preparation for the lies he was about to spin. Seduction had its own rules, and he had invented a few of his own along the way. If he could seduce Phoebe despite the bitterness in his heart, he would consider himself a master of seduction. He would truly have something to crow about to his peers, especially Westmore.

"Don't try to read my thoughts, Phoebe. Let's sit down and talk like civilized people. Deny it all you want, but you're mine. You'll always be mine."

Seizing the lamp with one hand and Phoebe's elbow with the other, he poked his head into a darkened room. When he saw it was the parlor, he guided her inside, placed the lamp down on a table, and drew Phoebe into his arms.

Her voice rose on a note of panic. "What are you doing?"

The heat of her body warmed his with unexpected results. He felt himself grow hard and thick, and he quickly set her away from him while he fought for control. He wanted to believe that Phoebe had nothing to do with his arousal, that he had responded because he was a male with highly cultivated sexual urges, but he knew better.

12

"Have you missed me, Phoebe?"

"Don't do this, Ram."

"I could use a drink. I don't suppose you have anything stronger than wine, do you?"

"If I give you a drink, will you leave?"

"Anxious to be rid of me? No, don't answer that. I know what you think of me. Now, about that drink . . ."

He watched Phoebe walk to the sideboard, her willowy figure still as enticing as he remembered, and innumerable questions formed in his mind. But his seduction had just begun; there would be plenty of time later to obtain the answers to her unforgivable behavior four years earlier. After he'd completed his assignment and walked out of Phoebe's life, he wanted her to be as devastated as he had been when she had walked out on him without benefit of an explanation.

"Will brandy do? Father enjoys a brandy before bedtime. Sometimes I join him."

"Brandy is fine." His narrowed gaze followed Phoebe as she lifted a bottle from a tray. "Where did you say your father was? If you think he'll return home soon, I'd like to wait and say hello. Did you ever tell him about us?"

Phoebe's shoulders stiffened, and Ram knew his question had hit a raw spot.

"Father is . . . out of town," Phoebe said.

Noting that her hand was trembling, Ram rose, took the bottle from her hand and poured a generous portion of amber liquid into two glasses. He handed her one. "You didn't tell him about us, did you?"

"No. I . . . didn't think it necessary."

"How soon do you expect your father to return? Maybe I should wait around and tell him myself."

Damn, what's wrong with me? I'm supposed to seduce Phoebe, not drive her away.

Phoebe's face crumpled, and Ram could have kicked himself for not curbing his anger.

"Say no more, Braxton. I already feel enough guilt over what I did to you." Her hand trembled as she lifted the glass to her mouth.

Ram took a large swallow of brandy, plucked Phoebe's glass from her hand and set both glasses down on the sideboard. Then he turned her into his arms.

"You're trembling. What's wrong? Can I help?"

"You're imagining things. Nothing is wrong. If I seem nervous, it's because I had hoped to avoid an encounter with you during my stay in London. I still don't understand how you found me."

Keeping sight of his goal to seduce Phoebe into revealing secrets, Ram curved his lips into a beguiling smile. Phoebe stirred in his arms and tried to pull away, but he wouldn't allow it.

"I found you—that's all you need to know."

"What do you want from me?"

Tongue in cheek, he said, "What I've always wanted, Phoebe—your love. Maybe this time I can win it."

"Liar! I was just a plaything to you, like all your other women. I'm sorry I didn't realize it before . . . before it was too late."

"You're wrong, Phoebe. You left before I could prove my love. I was willing to spend the rest of my life with you." *A lie, but it sounded good.*

Phoebe shook her head. "It's too late. The past can't be recalled. What's done is done."

"Are you saying you feel nothing for me? You loved me once." Watching her face for her reaction, he brought his hand up from her waist to cover her breast. She gasped but didn't pull away. "I can feel your heart thumping. Dare I hope it means you still care?"

She blinked, as if coming out of a trance, and shoved his hand aside. "Don't touch me like that. You have no right."

"I have more right than your lover. By the way, where is Phillips?"

"That's the second time you've referred to David as my lover, and I don't appreciate it. David is a good friend as well as Father's assistant. You always were jealous of him."

"It would appear I had every right to be jealous. He's the reason you ran away, isn't he?"

"You're wrong as usual, Ramsey. Release me."

He stared hungrily at her lips, plump and pink and inviting, and all his pretenses fled. Drawn by an invisible cord that seemed to pull him toward her, he lifted her chin and covered her mouth with his.

The kiss was more than he had bargained for, recalling memories he'd spent the past four years trying to forget. Phoebe was his past; he must be crazy to take pleasure in her kiss after what she'd done to him. And yet he couldn't deny the emotions she aroused in him, though not all of them were pleasant. Bitterness warred with desire, and bitterness won.

When he released her he felt keenly the loss of her warm body, the taste and feel of her. Hardening his resolve, he said, "Don't close your heart and mind to me, Phoebe. You wanted me once, nothing has changed."

"Everything has changed." Her eyes narrowed. "I find it difficult to believe you don't despise me. The fact that you're here talking to me is extraor-

15

dinary. You're up to something, Ramsey. What is it?"

"You're reading too much into my visit, Phoebe." His green eyes glinted mischievously. "Perhaps I wanted to see if that old spark still existed between us. It does, by the way. Or maybe I just want to speak with your father. He and I got along quite well, if you recall."

Phoebe felt no compunction to answer. The less said about her father, the better. She'd do or say nothing to jeopardize his life. Besides, seeing Ramsey again had unsettled her more than she cared to admit. Not much about him had changed. Despite the cynicism clearly visible in his green eyes and his mocking smile, he was as potent and provoking as ever. He still oozed charm and still had the power to seduce. Over the years she had learned to resist charming men. Besides, she had no time for Braxton now.

"Let me show you to the door, my lord," Phoebe said, brushing past him. "It's late and I'm alone. While you may have no reputation to protect, I do."

Phoebe reached for the doorknob at the same instant the brass knocker announced a visitor.

"Were you expecting company?" Ram drawled.

"No."

The rapping continued.

"Shouldn't you see who it is?"

Worry gnawed at Phoebe. Ram's appearance tonight was most unfortunate. "Yes, of course." Gingerly she turned the knob and pulled the door open, sagging in relief when she saw David Phillips standing on her doorstep. His bookish good looks and serious demeanor were welcome after Ram's overwhelming masculinity and daunting charm.

"What took you so long?" David asked as he

stepped over the threshold. "Are you all right? Have you heard anything further from . . ." His words trailed off when he saw Ram.

"Hello, Phillips," Ram said.

"What is *he* doing here?" Phillips choked out.

"It's good to see you, too," Ram said. "It's been a long time."

"Lord Braxton was just leaving, David," Phoebe said.

"That was your idea, not mine," Ram observed. He turned his head and said in a voice for her ears alone, "I thought you said he wasn't your lover."

Phoebe paled but quickly regained her composure. "Good-bye, my lord."

Ram strolled unhurriedly past Phoebe. "I'll return at another time to see your father," he said in passing. Phillips slammed the door behind him.

"What did Braxton want? How did he find you? It's not as if you travel in the same circles."

Still shaking from the encounter, Phoebe fought for the breath to answer David. Coming face to face with Ram again had stunned and confused her. She should have been the last person Ram wanted to see. She certainly had been trying to avoid him.

"I don't know what he wanted," Phoebe said truthfully. "I was walking home from the Egyptology Society meeting tonight, and there he was. It was almost as if he knew I'd be there. Where were *you*? I thought you planned to attend the lecture."

Phillips's gaze slid away. "I was delayed. You were already gone when I got there. You're not falling for that bastard again, are you? I thought you'd forgotten him. Had you married me when I first asked, you'd be too busy caring for our children to consort with a man like Braxton."

Bristling indignantly, Phoebe said, "I wasn't consorting with Braxton. He was on his way out when you arrived. Forget him. Have you learned anything further about Father? I can't stand not knowing whether he's dead or alive."

"We're not the only ones looking for him," Phillips reminded her. "The Foreign Office suspects him of stealing the amulet. Are you sure you don't know where it is? Hiding it is not helping your father, Phoebe, dear."

"I swear I know nothing about it," Phoebe reiterated. "How can you suspect Father of wrongdoing? You've known him for years. He's not the kind to steal valuable artifacts. His whole life has been devoted to the study of antiquities; he's not interested in monetary gain."

"I agree," Phillips concurred. He hesitated. "However, it's possible the amulet got sent to England with the government-approved artifacts by mistake."

"Father doesn't make that kind of mistake," Phoebe huffed. "I've gone through everything twice. Once alone and once with you, and we found nothing that wasn't supposed to be there. Why can't they leave me alone, David? All I want is to have Father back home safe and sound."

"We'll find him, Phoebe," David assured her as he led her to the parlor. "It would help if we had the amulet. Are you sure, absolutely sure, you haven't found it among the artifacts?"

Phoebe blinked away the tears forming in her eyes. "We can look again, if you'd like. The artifacts have been unpacked and are displayed on shelves in the study. Father intended to present them to the Museum of Egyptology."

"Don't give anything to the museum just yet," David cautioned. "We should wait for your father."

"But what if he . . . ? What if they . . . ? We have to find him, David. Perhaps I should show the notes I received from his kidnappers to the Foreign Office." She dashed away a tear. "I'm so frightened for him."

"We can't involve anyone in this," David warned, a note of panic in his voice. "Your father's life is at stake here. This has to remain between you and me."

Too upset to reply, Phoebe nodded. Her father meant everything to her.

"Does Braxton know what's going on?"

"With Father? I don't think so. I believe his appearance on my doorstep was a coincidence."

Pushing his fingers through his thinning blond hair, David said, "I don't like it. I can't forget how he duped you into believing he loved you, pretending you were the only woman in his life. If I hadn't warned you about him, you could have been terribly hurt. Thank God I intervened before it was too late."

It had already been too late, Phoebe reflected sadly. No one knew just how far things had gone before she'd realized her mistake and acted to correct it. David had been a stalwart shoulder to lean upon, but he didn't know the truth about her and Ramsey.

Taking her hand in both of his, David stared earnestly into her eyes and said, "I love you. You should have married me years ago. It's not too late, you know. Your father would be the first to congratulate us. Say yes and I'll purchase a special license tomorrow."

"I can't," Phoebe said. *For more reasons than you know.* "Not now. We need to concentrate on finding Father. Did you learn anything? Have you heard from the abductors?"

"Sorry, Phoebe, I've learned nothing of value since we last spoke. Your father and I walked down the gangplank together, just like I explained. I went to collect our baggage, and when I returned he was gone. Disappeared into thin air. I looked for him for hours, until darkness hindered my search, then came directly here, hoping to find him with you. By that time you had received the note advising you of his abduction."

"I know, I know. We've been through all this before. I don't know what to think anymore. The kidnappers are becoming impatient, and so is the Foreign Office. They want the amulet and refuse to believe I don't have it."

"We'll keep looking for it," David promised. "You're tired. I'll come back tomorrow. Meanwhile, get some rest and try not to worry. And if Braxton returns, tell him nothing. Don't even let him in the house. He will only hurt you again."

He kissed her forehead. "Good night, dear. Don't bother seeing me out. I know the way."

Phoebe squared her shoulders and nodded. She had to be brave for her father. Thank God for David. He'd been her strength and her solace, but no matter how badly she wanted to love him, she couldn't. Despite David's numerous proposals, she continued to refuse him. She would have done David an injustice had she married him. Her acceptance of his proposal would have been for all the wrong reasons.

Although David was handsome in a bookish sort of way, dependable and steady, every time she looked at him, she compared him unfavorably to Ram. Four years had done nothing to dim Ram's image. While David was thin and wiry, Ram was powerfully built and virile. David's thinning blond hair and brown eyes paled in comparison to Ram's vibrant gold-shot brown hair and green eyes. The biggest difference between them, however, was that David loved her while Ram couldn't possibly care for her after what she'd done to him.

Ram was waiting in the shadows beside Phoebe's front door when David Phillips left the house. Ram's fierce expression eased somewhat when he realized Phillips hadn't been inside long enough to bed Phoebe. He wasn't sure why he even cared. He wanted to hate Phoebe, but couldn't. Forgiving her, however, was impossible. He couldn't find it in his heart to relent. Yet his feelings had to remain ambivalent while he seduced her. He had to be charming and believable, else she'd become suspicious before he got the information he needed from her.

Ram stepped from the shadows to confront Phillips. The other man started violently but stood his ground.

"Still here, Braxton?" Phillips said. "You're wasting your time. Phoebe wants nothing to do with you."

"I wouldn't be too sure of that if I were you."

"What are you doing here?"

"Waiting to see how long you'd remain inside. What's wrong? Did the lady have a headache tonight?"

"You have a nasty mind, Braxton. I know all about you and your unsavory reputation. I'm glad I stopped Phoebe from making the biggest mistake of her life. She cares nothing for you."

Ram gave him a wolfish grin. "Doesn't she? Why

hasn't she married you? If I recall, you were quite eager to make her your wife."

"What is it you want?"

"I heard Sir Thompson had returned from Egypt and thought I'd pay him a call. Phoebe said he was out of town. Do you know where he went?"

"I'm not Sir Thompson's keeper," Phillips said, shoving past Ram. "Don't meddle where you're not wanted. Good night, Braxton."

Ram watched Phillips stride down the street, his curiosity running rampant. How much did Phillips know about the amulet and Thompson's disappearance? Ram was convinced it was more than Phillips was letting on. Also, it was apparent that Phoebe knew more than she was admitting. Something strange was going on, and it was up to him to find out.

His mood contemplative, Ram walked into Brooks's a short time later. He saw Lucas, Viscount Westmore, talking to the Earl of Ashcombe and headed over to join them.

"You look like you could use a friend," Luc said in greeting. "Something bothering you, Braxton?"

Ram forced a smile. Though Luc was his best friend, he couldn't tell him about his investigation into the missing amulet, for Fielding had sworn him to secrecy. Many people knew he had worked for the Foreign Office during the war, but no one was aware of his current status with the department.

"Nothing that a few drinks and a woman won't cure," Ram said. "Dinner first, then Madam Bella's. How does that sound?"

"Leave me out of this," Lord Ashcombe said. "My wife invited dinner guests tonight and I'm expected to attend. Damn unfortunate business, marriage. Don't know why my parents talked me into getting leg-shackled."

"There goes another disgruntled husband," Luc chuckled as Ashcombe ambled off. "Speaking of husbands, have you heard from Bathurst recently?"

"He and Olivia have settled in at Bathurst Park. I don't expect them to bring their twins to London any time soon. From what I gather, they're disgustingly happy in the country."

"To each his own," Luc said. "Thank God we're smart enough to escape the parson's trap."

"Amen," Ram muttered. "Shall we repair to the dining room?"

"I heard you'd taken up with the newly widowed Lady Celeste. I suspect she's ecstatic to be rid of her elderly husband. Watch yourself, Braxton; she's undoubtedly looking for a new husband."

"She'd be wise to look elsewhere," Ram said. "I'm not marriage material and never will be."

Thanks to Phoebe, Ram thought. She had singlehandedly destroyed his belief in marriage and fidelity. At one time Phoebe had meant everything to him. Unfortunately, Phoebe hadn't felt the same way. She had played him for a fool, and now it was her turn to become the victim.

"Are you sure you're all right?" Luc asked as he and Ram entered the dining room and seated themselves at a table. "Want to tell me about it?"

Ram thought about it for a moment, then asked, "Have you ever seduced a woman you didn't like?"

"Good God! Why would I do that when there are plenty I do like?" His eyes narrowed. "Is that what you're planning?"

"It's complicated, Westmore. But yes, I suppose that's what I'm going to do."

"The reason being . . ."

23

"I can't tell you."

"Is she young and beautiful?"

"Yes to both."

"The mystery deepens. I'm surprised to learn there's a woman you don't like. You haven't been particularly selective in the past, old chap. Since the woman is a beauty, you should have no problem getting your juices flowing. May I ask why?"

"No, not yet, but you'll be the first to know what I'm about when the time comes to confide in someone."

Luc's dark brows shot upward. "That sounds ominous, Braxton. Care to tell me the woman's name?"

Ram shrugged. "If I'm openly courting the woman, her name won't remain a secret for long, so I can tell you that much. It's Phoebe Thompson. Her father is Sir Andrew Thompson, an Egyptologist of some renown. You may have heard of him."

"I say, old boy, you surprise me. How long have you known the lady, and what did she do to make you dislike her?"

"I've known Phoebe and her father longer than I care to acknowledge. Our last parting wasn't particularly happy, and that's all I'm going to say. Shall we order? I'm starving."

Ram tried not to think of Phoebe as he perused the menu. He didn't want to recall how right she felt in his arms or the lush softness of her mouth. The only thing he wanted to think about was how sweet revenge would taste.

Chapter Two

A noise startled Phoebe awake. She had retired with a troubled mind after the Earl of Braxton's visit and had just gotten to sleep when a muted crash from below awakened her. Her heart pounding wildly, she rose, donned a dressing gown and peered into the hallway. The lamp on the hall table had gone out, leaving deep, disturbing shadows where none should have been. Phoebe retreated into her room, carefully closing and locking the door behind her.

With shaking hands she found a sulfur match and lit the lamp on her nightstand. Diffused lamplight spread throughout the room. Relief shuddered through her when she saw that she was alone. If intruders had broken into the house, they had not yet reached the upper floor.

That blasted amulet! Phoebe thought. She wished her father had never found the priceless artifact. Another muffled sound from below firmed Phoebe's resolve and lent her the courage to investigate. She wasn't about to let an intruder rifle through her personal belongings. Besides, if the intruder didn't find what he was looking for below stairs, he'd probably search the bedrooms next.

The poker resting beside the hearth caught her eye and she picked it up, the comforting weight bolstering her courage. Fearing the light would alert the intruder to her presence, she extinguished the lamp and placed it on the table. Then she unlocked the door and stepped into the hallway.

Praying that none of the treads squeaked, Phoebe gripped the poker and slowly descended the stairs. She reached the bottom landing with only one giveaway squeak and paused to get her bearings. She saw a faint light coming from beneath the closed study door, and her heart began a frantic tattoo.

She reached for the doorknob, eased the door open, and poked her head through the opening. What she saw froze the blood in her veins. The artifacts she had so lovingly cataloged and placed on shelves were in disarray, and the desk had been ransacked, its drawers gaping open and papers strewn about. But even more frightening was the man dressed in black who appeared to be searching for loose bricks above the mantel.

As if sensing Phoebe's presence, the man whipped around to confront her. His lower face was masked by a scarf, and a knit cap was pulled down low over his forehead and over his ears, making identification impossible.

"Who are you?" Phoebe cried, wielding the poker like a sword. "What do you want?"

"Where is it?" the man asked in a raspy voice.

"If you don't leave now, I'm going to call the Watch."

The intruder laughed, the harsh sound sending shards of fear down her spine. But to her credit, Phoebe didn't flinch.

He took a menacing step forward. "That poker don't scare me, lady. Where is it?"

"I don't know what you're talking about. I'm calling the Watch."

Swinging the poker in a wide arc, Phoebe edged backward toward the door. The intruder bolted, startling her as he shoved her aside and raced out the door. Unprepared for the assault, Phoebe went flying, hitting her head on the edge of the door as she fell. Blackness consumed the edges of her awareness, and she knew no more.

Ram knew it was too early for social calls but he had awakened this morning with a feeling that something was amiss. Since his own household seemed to be running smoothly, his thoughts turned to Phoebe and his plans for her seduction. While Dudley, his valet, shaved and groomed him, Ram pondered the tactics that might work best with Phoebe. No two women were alike, he'd found; each one required special handling. Some responded best to subtle seduction, while others preferred more direct methods.

In view of their previous relationship, Ram knew he would have to tread lightly where Phoebe was concerned. A heavy-handed approach would rouse her suspicions and make her skittish.

After breakfast, Ram ordered his carriage brought around and drove toward Mount Street. He knew something was wrong the moment he pulled up before Phoebe's house. The door was open, and members of the Watch were searching the immediate area.

"What happened here?" Ram asked, stopping a man who had just exited the house.

"A break-in, milord," he said.

"Was anyone hurt?"

"The lady of the house was injured. The surgeon is with her now. Are you acquainted with Miss Thompson?"

Spitting out a curse, Ram didn't answer as he rushed through the open door. The housekeeper stopped him as he sprinted toward the stairs leading to the bedrooms.

"Here now, where do you think you're going?" the woman asked, giving Ram a look that would have felled a lesser man.

"Who are you?" Ram asked.

"Mrs. Crowley, the housekeeper. Who are you?"

"The Earl of Braxton, a friend of Miss Thompson's. Can you tell me what happened?"

The housekeeper's plump face sagged in concern. "I knew it wasn't right for Miss Phoebe to be in the house alone. I can't imagine what her father is thinking. He should be here with her."

"I agree, Mrs. Crowley," Ram said impatiently, "but that doesn't answer my question."

"The door was open when I arrived early this morning. Then I found Miss Phoebe lying unconscious on the floor," Mrs. Crowley explained. "She had a lump the size of Westminster Abbey on her head. I got her into bed and summoned the surgeon. He's with her now."

"Does Miss Thompson know who did this to her?"

"She mumbled something about a thief. Poor

brave lass. She still had the poker in her hand when I found her."

"I'll wait to hear what the surgeon has to say, if you don't mind," Ram said in a voice that brooked no argument. "Do you know if anything was taken?"

"The only room disturbed was the study, and I can't imagine anyone wanting those dusty old relics. I don't know if anything was stolen; you'll have to ask Miss Phoebe."

"Thank you, Mrs. Crowley. You've been a big help."

"Good day to you, milord."

Left to his own devices, Ram wandered down the hallway to the study. Shaking his head in dismay, he surveyed the mess the thief had made. Papers were scattered from one end of the room to the other, and statuary, urns and various artifacts were lying askew on shelves. A few had been smashed beyond recognition.

"What's going on here?"

The voice from the doorway spun Ram around. "Phillips. Join me. Perhaps together we can make some sense of this."

David Phillips picked up a shard of broken pottery and shook his head. "Who would do such a thing?"

"You tell me. Is there anything of value in these artifacts?"

"No. They are worth nothing save to historians, who value them for what they reveal about ancient times. How badly was Phoebe hurt?"

Ram went still. He didn't recall saying anything about Phoebe being injured. He relaxed somewhat when he recalled that either the housekeeper or the Watch could have mentioned it.

29

"I don't know yet. The surgeon is still with her."

"What are you doing here? I thought Phoebe made it clear she didn't want to see you again."

Ram sent Phillips an oblique look. "So she did. Shall we clean up this mess?"

"Ah, there you are, Lord Braxton. The housekeeper said you wished to see me."

"You must be the surgeon," Ram said to the thin, somberly dressed man standing in the doorway. "How is Phoebe?"

"She's going to be just fine, milord. A day or two of bed rest and she'll be right as rain. She has a nasty lump on her head, but I detected no signs of a concussion. If you'll excuse me, I have other patients to see."

"Send your bill around to Mr. Proctor, my solicitor," Ram instructed as the physician took his leave.

"Now see here, Braxton," Phillips argued. "Phoebe isn't your responsibility."

"I'm making her my responsibility," Ram said as he strode out the door.

"Where are you going?"

"To see Phoebe."

Phillips caught his arm. "Oh, no, you're not. You heard the surgeon. Phoebe should rest. You're nothing to her. There's no reason for you to visit her in her bedroom."

Pretending to back down, Ram allowed Phillips to guide him out. He stopped to speak briefly with the Watch before climbing into his carriage and taking up the reins. But once Phillips was out of sight, he leaped down from the driver's box and returned to the house.

Ram walked through the unlocked front door, carefully latched it behind him and hurried up the staircase. He looked into two vacant bedrooms before he found Phoebe. Lying in the center of a large bed, she appeared to be sleeping. He tiptoed closer, surprised at how small and fragile she looked beneath the blanket.

"Is that you, Mrs. Crowley? I'm sorry to be such a bother, but could you please fetch me a glass of water?"

Spying a pitcher of water on a nearby table, Ram filled a glass and carried it to the bed. Phoebe's eyes remained closed as he placed an arm beneath her shoulders and lifted her so she could drink. When she had drunk her fill, she sighed and opened her eyes.

"Thank you, Mrs. . . . You! You're not Mrs. Crowley."

"I should hope not. How do you feel?"

"Why do you care?"

"I know I shouldn't, but I do."

She grimaced and massaged her temples. "My head hurts. Go away."

Ram perched on the edge of the bed, his expression grim. "I don't want to upset you, but there are things I need to know. Did you see the intruder? Can you identify him?"

"I didn't see his face, nor did I recognize his voice. I think he deliberately tried to disguise it."

"What in God's name made you confront him? Why didn't you stay in your room? Or run out the door? Mrs. Crowley said you had a poker in your hand when she found you."

"I don't know why I did what I did," Phoebe said.

"Do you keep valuables in the house?"

"No. There is nothing of value in the house."

Ram searched her face. Was she lying? "Why

31

won't you let me help you? Something strange is going on here."

"You're imagining things."

An indignant voice forestalled Ram's reply. "Lord Braxton! What are you doing in Miss Phoebe's bedroom?"

Pasting on a charming smile, Ram rose to greet the housekeeper. "I wanted to see for myself how she fared."

"She'll be fine if a body will let her rest. Be off with you, milord," Mrs. Crowley huffed, shooing him out of the room. "You shouldn't be here. It isn't decent."

"I was just leaving," Ram said. "Might I have a private word with you?"

Concern furrowing her brow, Mrs. Crowley followed Ram into the hallway. "I don't want Phoebe to be alone tonight, or any other night until her father returns," Ram said. "I'll make it worth your while if you move into the house with Phoebe. I'll double your salary, if that's agreeable to you."

"My word," the housekeeper said, apparently overwhelmed by Ram's generous offer. "I would have stayed without the raise in salary. But I do thank you. I can use the blunt."

"Good. Don't tell Phoebe what we've just discussed, I'm afraid she wouldn't approve."

"You can count on me, milord. I never did think it was right for Miss Phoebe to stay on here alone. I never met her father, but when I do I intend to give him a piece of my mind. What could he be thinking? And that Mr. Phillips! He's no protection. Trouble is, Miss Phoebe has a mind of her own and ignores a body's advice. That's what comes of living in a heathen country all those years."

"How well I know," Ram said, rolling his eyes

heavenward. "Good day, Mrs. Crowley. I'll return tomorrow to check on Phoebe. If Mr. Phillips comes around, I suggest that you tell him Phoebe isn't up to company. I doubt he'll push the issue."

"What did he want?" Phoebe asked when Mrs. Crowley returned.

"He just wanted to make sure I'm taking good care of you," the housekeeper replied.

"It's none of Lord Braxton's business," Phoebe said.

"I won't be going home tonight, Miss Phoebe. You shouldn't be alone after what happened. Are you ready for some hot broth?"

Confused, Phoebe stared at the woman, who seemed to jump from one subject to another. "Broth? Yes, of course, but about your staying. I can't afford full-time help and—"

"Never you mind, dearie. It's all settled. Close your eyes and get some rest while I fetch the broth."

Phoebe closed her eyes but she didn't go to sleep.

Ram stormed into Fielding's office and slammed the door. Startled by the unannounced intrusion, Fielding set the papers he was perusing aside and scowled up at Ram.

"What's wrong, Braxton? How did you get past my secretary?"

"I didn't give him a chance to stop me, and there's plenty wrong. Did you instruct your agent to hurt Phoebe Thompson?"

"What the devil are you talking about?"

"Are you denying that your agent ransacked Phoebe's house last night?"

Fielding lurched from his chair. "Of course I deny it. Why would I send another agent when I've

33

got you? Sit down and tell me what happened."

Ram began to pace, too riled to sit. "Someone broke into Phoebe's house last night. Apparently, she walked in on him and suffered an injury."

"The thief was after the amulet," Fielding surmised. "We're not the only ones who want it, which proves my theory that Miss Thompson and her father either have the amulet in their possession or know where to find it. Did you make any progress with the woman?"

"She's definitely involved, but I don't know how. Phoebe is frightened of something or someone and refuses to discuss her father. She and David Phillips seem exceptionally close, he may know more about the amulet than he's letting on."

"How badly was Miss Thompson hurt?"

"She'll be fine. The surgeon said she suffered a nasty bump on the head. But I still don't like it. She's alone in the house at night and a vulnerable target."

"Hmmm," Fielding said, eyeing Ram curiosly. "I never expected you to have a personal interest in Miss Thompson when I recruited you for this job. Perhaps I should assign another agent to the case."

Ram didn't agree. If anyone was going to seduce Phoebe, it had to be he. A stranger couldn't possibly know where she liked to be touched, which caresses drove her wild. Another man wouldn't have the incentive he had to seduce her. Seduction had always been a game with him, but this time he had ample reason to put heart and soul into it.

"Phoebe and I have a history together, but my feelings are no longer engaged. This is strictly an assignment to me. Once I have the information you need, I'll happily walk away."

Fielding grinned. "That's exactly what I wanted

to hear. It worries me, however, that someone besides England and Egypt wants the amulet. Unknown forces are working against us, and I don't like it. If we don't return the amulet to the Egyptian government, an international incident with far-reaching consequences is likely to occur.

"You must exert more pressure on Thompson's daughter. We have to know where he is and what he's done with the amulet." He fell silent, then asked, "You don't suppose the thief found the amulet, do you?"

"I doubt it. Phoebe interrupted his search."

"The break-in puts a new light on our investigation," Fielding said thoughtfully. "A third party wants the amulet, and we have to beat the would-be thief to it. Carry on with your seduction, but watch your back."

"And Phoebe's back," Ram muttered. He wanted revenge for the callous way she had left him, but he didn't want her physically harmed. There were other more subtle methods to repay her for the hurt she had caused him.

"I'll report back to you when I learn anything new," Ram said as he headed out the door.

"Good luck. England is counting on you," Fielding called after him.

The day following the break-in, Phoebe felt well enough to leave her bed. She wanted to put the study to rights and refused to let Mrs. Crowley do it. She needed to catalog the broken items and assess the damage herself.

That blasted amulet was nothing but trouble. She sincerely hoped the Foreign Office found it and returned it to its rightful owner soon. It was ridiculous to think her father had had anything to do with its disappearance; she couldn't help wondering why anyone would think he could do such a thing.

Phoebe picked up a shard of pottery from the floor and nearly wept when she saw it was from a vase dating back to Egypt's earliest times. She carefully gathered up all the shattered pieces and placed them reverently on the desk for her father to inspect when he returned.

If he returned, she thought despondently.

"Miss Phoebe, I found this note on the doorstep when I went out to sweep the stoop."

Fear etched Phoebe's features as she whirled to stare at the scrap of paper in Mrs. Crowley's hand. "Thank you, Mrs. Crowley," Phoebe said, reaching for the note with trembling fingers.

"Are you all right, dearie? You're pale as a ghost. Perhaps you should have remained in bed another day."

Phoebe summoned a wan smile. "I'm fine. I just need . . ." A loud rapping on the door interrupted her sentence. "Would you see who's at the door?"

After Mrs. Crowley left, Phoebe unfolded the note and read the message. She read it through twice, wadded it in her hand and tossed it into the wastebasket. Then she staggered into the nearest chair, where David Phillips found her a few minutes later.

"Phoebe, what's wrong? You look dreadful. Are you unwell?"

Phoebe shook her head. She wanted to tell David about the note, but something warned her against it. He'd probably insist on going with her tonight. The note instructed her to be at Vauxhall Pleasure Gardens at nine o'clock this evening and to leave the amulet in the urn at Caesar's feet in the Roman Pavilion. She was to go alone.

"I'm worried about Father." Tears leaked from the corners of her eyes. "I know nothing about that blasted amulet. What if they kill Father?"

David dropped to his haunches and took Phoebe's hands in his. "They won't kill him. Think, dear. I know your father packed some urns and statuary in the trunk of personal belongings I had delivered here. Did you find the amulet after you unpacked it?"

"No," Phoebe denied vehemently. "I merely cataloged the artifacts and placed them on shelves. We've been over this before, David."

"I see you're straightening the room."

"Two vases were completely destroyed. I saved the pieces for Father to inspect."

"And you found nothing?"

"David, please. You know neither Father nor I would do anything illegal."

His gaze slid away from hers. "Yes, of course."

She rose abruptly. "I can't take this! I'm going to the authorities. Father's life is at stake; it's time to seek help."

David grasped her arm and urged her back into the chair. "You're understandably upset, and I don't blame you, but you're not thinking clearly. What if the intruder was a government agent? The Foreign Office cares nothing about your father. You'd be better served to cooperate with the kidnappers. For your father's sake, give them what they want."

"David, what do I have to do to convince you I don't have the amulet? Don't you think I would have cooperated when Father disappeared? All I have of him is the trunk that arrived from the ship." She gestured to the shelves behind him. "You're welcome to inspect the artifacts again, but you won't find anything that's not supposed to be there."

While David wandered over to the shelves to examine the rows of vases, urns and statuary, Phoebe's thoughts returned to the note. Even though she didn't have the amulet, Phoebe intended to go to Vauxhall Gardens tonight and confront her father's abductor.

"You're right," David said, turning away from the shelves. "There's nothing here. I don't understand."

"What don't you understand?"

"Never mind. It's not important. You'll be alone in the house tonight. Shall I stay with you?"

"I won't be alone. Mrs. Crowley will be here."

"I thought she was day help."

"She wants to stay. Truthfully, I'm glad for the company."

"Yes, well, excellent. You'll be in good hands, then. Send a note around to my lodgings should you learn anything, anything at all."

"Of course. Good-bye, David. Thank you for being my rock during these difficult times."

Phoebe saw David out and returned to the study to finish putting the room in order, but her heart wasn't in it. It was difficult to keep her spirits up when she lacked what was needed to save her father's life.

In order to reach the meeting place in time, Phoebe had decided she would leave at eight. What she hadn't counted on was Mrs. Crowley's disapproval. The housekeeper wasn't happy about Phoebe's decision to go out alone after dark. It had been a long time since she'd had to explain her actions to anyone. That thought brought on another.

Ramsey Dunsmore, the Earl of Braxton. During

the four years they had been apart, she hadn't forgotten him. The way he looked, the scent of him, his uniqueness among men. Had she been the only woman in his life, she would have been the happiest woman alive, but thanks to David, she'd learned the truth about Ram in time to salvage her self-respect.

Mrs. Crowley's disapproval didn't stop Phoebe from donning her cloak and leaving the house at precisely eight o'clock. Finding a hackney was as difficult as she had expected, but one finally picked her up at half past the hour. Leaning back against the squabs, Phoebe rehearsed the words she intended to say to her father's abductor. She'd cry, beg, promise anything to free her father.

Phoebe knew little about Vauxhall Gardens except that it was considered slightly disreputable. It was a kind of gaudy year-round festival, a place to see and be seen, a place where spirits were rowdy, morals were loose and courtesans mingled with the *ton*.

Phoebe felt the excitement the moment she stepped down from the hackney and strode through the entrance and up the Grand Walk, where couples strolled arm in arm and doxies paraded among them. Pulling her hood as low over her forehead as it would go, she walked past the artificial Gothic ruin and the Cascade, hoping the walkway would lead her to the Roman Pavilion.

Ram strode up to Phoebe's front door and rapped sharply. As soon as Mrs. Crowley opened the portal, he stepped inside.

"Good evening, Mrs. Crowley. If Miss Thompson has recovered from her injury, I'd like to see her."

The housekeeper wrung her hands, her concern apparent. "She's not in, milord."

Ram sent her a startled look. "Not in? Where is she?"

"I don't know; she didn't tell me where she was going. I didn't like it and told her so, for all the good it did."

"Was Phillips with her?"

"She was quite alone, milord."

"Did you notice anything strange? Did anything out of the ordinary happen today?"

Mrs. Crowley thought a moment, then said, "Miss Phoebe received a note this morning. I found it on the doorstep."

Ram tensed. "A note? Do you know whom it was from?"

"I couldn't say, milord."

"Where was Phoebe when she read it?"

"In the study, milord."

"Do you mind if I take a look around?"

"Not if you think it will help. I don't like her going off alone. London can be a dangerous place at night. I thought the note might have been from her father. I know she's been worried about him."

Ram didn't reply as he strode to the study. He made a cursory inspection of the desk and floor around it and found nothing. Then his sharp gaze spotted a crumpled paper in the wastebasket, and he bent to retrieve it. Smoothing it out, he read the brief message and cursed beneath his breath. He stuffed the note in his pocket and went off to find the housekeeper.

"Don't worry, Mrs. Crowley," he said when he located her in the kitchen. "I know where Phoebe went and will have her home in no time."

As Ram rode toward Vauxhall Gardens, he came

to an unsettling and unwelcome conclusion: Phoebe did indeed have the amulet. Why else would she follow the note's directions? The longer he considered his theory, the more the mystery deepened. The pieces of the puzzle just didn't fit. The Foreign Office believed Sir Andrew Thompson had disappeared with the amulet in his possession. But if the note was to be believed, Sir Thompson's disappearance wasn't voluntary and it was Phoebe who actually had the amulet. What a coil.

Phoebe arrived at the Roman Pavilion and hid amid the foliage to wait and watch. Several couples drifted past as they wandered toward the entertainment that was taking place at the bandbox. Music wafted to her on the warm breeze, but she was too distracted to notice. When no one else appeared, she left her concealment and approached the statue.

"Give me the amulet!" a rough voice said.

Startled, Phoebe peered behind the statue, where the voice had come from. Her legs trembled when she saw the outline of a figure cloaked in shadows. She knew, however, that now was not the time for her courage to fail.

"I don't have it. I never had it. Where is my father? Is he well?"

"For the time being," the man rasped. "His well-being depends on your cooperation."

Her voice held a note of panic. "Why won't you believe me? If I had the amulet, I'd gladly give it to you in exchange for my father's life."

"We think you know where it is," the man hissed.

"What? That's not true."

"Your father told us differently."

Anger bolstered her courage. "What did you do

41

to him to make him lie? I'm going to do what I should have done long ago. I'm going to the authorities."

As she turned to leave, she was seized from behind, her breath nearly cut off by the arm clasped tightly around her neck. Gasping for air, she fought unsuccessfully to free herself.

"Take warning," the man growled into her ear. "I'll kill your father if you fail to produce the amulet. Find it!"

Blackness was closing in fast. Then the pressure eased, and Phoebe heard pounding footsteps floating to her on the wings of unconsciousness.

Chapter Three

Ram hastened along the Grand Walk, thankful for the swaying paper lanterns that illuminated the path and paying scant heed to friends hailing him as he rushed past. Since Vauxhall Pleasure Gardens were familiar to him, he knew exactly where the Roman Pavilion was located. When he passed the artificial Gothic ruin and the Cascade, he broke into a run, heeding the painful warning in his gut that danger stalked Phoebe.

Panic gave wing to his feet when he saw Phoebe struggling with an unknown assailant near the statue of Caesar. Shouting her name, he raced to reach her. Terror overwhelmed him when he saw her slump in her assailant's arms. His shout of outrage caught the man's attention, and he thrust Phoebe away from him. She spiraled to the ground as the man took to his heels.

Ram let the man escape; he was more concerned

about Phoebe than her assailant. Dropping to his knees, he lifted her head and studied her face in the wavering light from an overhead lantern. She was pale, too pale, but seemed to be breathing normally. She was beginning to stir when he noticed the bruises on her neck. Anger emanated from him in great waves. That anyone would touch Phoebe in such a vile manner was despicable.

"Phoebe, speak to me. Are you all right?"

Phoebe opened her eyes and tried to speak, but the words were so distorted, Ram could scarcely make them out. After several tries she managed to say, "My throat hurts."

Lifting her carefully, Ram carried her to a nearby bench. He left her briefly to glance inside the urn at Caesar's feet. Nothing. Either Phoebe's assailant had already taken the amulet or Phoebe still had it. He returned to the bench and sat down beside her. "What happened? What are you doing here alone?"

"I . . . was enjoying the gardens when a strange man accosted me," she lied.

Ram gave a snort of disbelief. "Come now, Phoebe, I know you better than that. You're lying. What are you *really* doing here?"

"I just told you."

"I'm taking you home. Can you walk?"

"I'm fine."

"You don't look fine. You've some nasty bruises on your neck. What did the bastard want?"

Silence. "Money," she said after a long pause. "Yes, that's what he wanted. He became angry when I had nothing to give him."

"I see," Ram said without conviction as he helped Phoebe to her feet and guided her along the Grand Walk. They had just reached the Cascade when they ran into Viscount Westmore strolling toward them with his arm around a saucy courtesan.

"I say, Braxton, fancy meeting you here," Luc said. His sharp gaze settled on Phoebe. "Who is your friend?"

"Westmore, good to see you," Ram said. "I'd like to present Miss Phoebe Thompson. Phoebe, this is my good friend Viscount Westmore."

Luc and Ram exchanged meaningful glances. "Ah, I see," Luc said. "That Miss Thompson." Before Phoebe could wonder at his words, Luc introduced his companion to them.

"I'm in need of a carriage," Ram said without preamble.

Luc's hazel eyes gleamed with curiosity. "You're in luck, Braxton. My carriage is parked at the curb outside the entrance."

"May I borrow it? Miss Thompson had a slight accident near the Roman Pavilion and needs a conveyance more comfortable than my horse."

"Of course," Luc said. "I know you wouldn't ask if it wasn't important." His gaze, ripe with speculation, rested on Phoebe. "Is there anything else I can do for you?"

"You've already helped immensely," Ram replied, guiding Phoebe past Luc and his ladybird. "If I don't return, feel free to ride Duke home. You'll find him tethered near the entrance. I'll catch up with you tomorrow."

Ram found Luc's carriage with little difficulty. He knew it well from the times they had shared rides to society events and other less respectable entertainments.

"Up you go," Ram said, grasping Phoebe's slim waist and lifting her onto the padded leather seat. Walking around to the other side, he vaulted into the driver's bench and picked up the reins.

"Are you sure you're all right?" Ram asked worriedly. "You haven't said a word since we left the Roman Pavilion. If you feel like talking, why don't you start by telling me what you were doing at Vauxhall Gardens without an escort? Don't you know the only women daring enough to venture into the gardens alone are prostitutes?"

"I . . . didn't know. I've never been there before. Many things have changed since I left England."

"If you wanted to visit Vauxhall and lacked an escort, why didn't you ask me?"

"I'm not your responsibility," Phoebe rasped. "Besides, my throat hurts and I'm in no mood for lengthy explanations." She slanted him a curious look from beneath shuttered lids. "Thank you for coming to my aid. How did you know where to find me? Or did you just happen to be strolling in Vauxhall Gardens tonight?"

"Here we are," Ram said, pulling up before Phoebe's house. "I'll tell you how I knew where to find you once we're inside."

"I'm tired, Ram."

"Not too tired to hear what I've got to say, I'll wager."

Ram lifted her down and accompanied her to the front door. "Do you have your key?"

Before Phoebe could retrieve her key from her reticule, Mrs. Crowley flung open the door. "Thank God you found her, milord. I've been that worried. I've been watching through the window for your return."

"I'm sorry I worried you, Mrs. Crowley," Phoebe croaked.

Mrs. Crowley's eyes widened. "What happened to your voice? I knew it! You caught a chill in the

night air. Go straight up to bed and I'll bring you
a nice hot toddy."

"Please don't fuss, Mrs. Crowley. I'm a little
hoarse but I feel fine."

"I can vouch for Phoebe's state of health," Ram
said. "Why don't you retire? I promise not to keep
Phoebe up long."

"Are you sure? Will you take tea with Miss
Phoebe before I go off to bed?"

Ram slanted a glance at Phoebe and decided a
cup of hot tea would be just the thing for her
bruised throat. "Very well, tea it is."

Mrs. Crowley hurried off, leaving Ram and
Phoebe alone in the parlor. "Sit down, Phoebe,"
Ram said. "You look ready to collapse. You've had
a harrowing experience tonight, and I'm not satisfied with your explanation. It will keep, however,
until Mrs. Crowley takes herself off to bed."

The tea trolley arrived amid a strained silence.
After Mrs. Crowley poured, she bade them good
night and discreetly retired. Ram handed Phoebe
her tea and sipped his own, noting the way she
winced as she swallowed.

It serves her right, Ram thought uncharitably.
Phoebe should have sought help instead of rushing
off on her own.

"You never said how you knew I'd be at Vauxhall
Gardens tonight," Phoebe said.

"I didn't," Ram lied. "When I stopped by tonight
to see how you were faring, Mrs. Crowley told me
you had left the house. She wasn't happy about it,
and neither was I. But knowing how independent
you are, I decided it was none of my business and
continued on to Vauxhall Gardens to watch the
fireworks. As I was strolling, I saw a woman being

accosted by a man, and being an upstanding citizen, I flew to her defense."

"You didn't know it was I?"

"Not until I frightened the man away and knelt down beside you."

Phoebe looked confused but didn't press him.

Ram decided it was best to let the subject drop and get on with his seduction. But it wasn't until he raised Phoebe's chin and looked into her eyes that he realized he wanted to kiss her for reasons other than duty. As long as he remembered that Phoebe was in his past, that duty to country came first, he saw no harm in enjoying the seduction. The information he coaxed from Phoebe could be as valuable as the lesson she'd learn when he left her.

"You're as beautiful as I remember," Ram whispered as he drew her gently into his arms. He kissed her temple, her cheek, the tip of her nose. "Do you recall how it was between us?"

"I spent four years trying to forget," Phoebe murmured. "How many women have you bedded since I walked out of your life?"

Too many to count. "How many men have *you* bedded?" he shot back.

"My answer would surprise you."

Ram grinned. "So would mine."

Phoebe searched his face, the wicked glint in his green eyes warning her to be on guard. She'd seen that look before and had been seduced by it once, but not again. No, never again. Ram's reputation as a womanizer and rogue was public knowledge. She had no idea why he seemed interested in her again after their bitter parting, but every instinct warned her that no good could come of it.

Her gaze rested on his mouth; without volition, memories came rushing back. Were his lips as soft as she remembered? At one time she couldn't get enough of his kisses. He had filled her senses, sated her body and made her feel loved. Unfortunately, she wasn't the only woman who believed Ram's treacherous lies. If not for David, she never would have found the courage to cut Ram from her life before he grew tired of her and found another to take her place. She hadn't wanted to believe it, but David had convinced her it would happen once Ram got what he wanted from her.

Phoebe's thoughts ground to a halt as Ram caressed her cheek with the back of his hand. His fingers felt warm as they teased her jawline, and she nearly jumped out of her skin when his fingertips rested on the sensitive pulse at the base of her throat.

"You're going to wear those bruises for a long time," he said.

"It could be worse," Phoebe rasped hoarsely. *I could have lost my life instead of my voice.*

He traced the bruises with his fingertips, then surprised her by placing his lips over them and gently licking.

"Does that feel soothing?"

She pushed feebly against his chest. "You must stop, Ram."

He raised his head. "Why? I recognize that look in your eyes. You want me to kiss you. We both want the same thing, Phoebe. Why fight it?"

He tipped her chin upward; his lips hovered so close, Phoebe felt the enticing whisper of his breath against her cheek. His eyes had turned a misty green; she couldn't look away. His compelling gaze was as potent as she remembered. When Ram set his sights on a woman, she became the focus of his world . . . until another came along. Phoebe tried to remember that as his hands urged her closer against him and his tongue licked along the seam of her lips.

This must stop! Phoebe couldn't endure the magic of Ram's kisses or survive the magnetism that drew women to him like moths to a flame. But before she could marshal her willpower, Ram's lips closed over hers. His skillful kiss sucked the very breath from her lungs. The reality of his taste moved her far more powerfully than the memory of it.

"Open to me, Phoebe," he whispered against her lips.

"No."

But even as she said it, her lips parted and she felt his tongue probing her mouth. The moment his tongue touched hers, a flame burst into being inside her, sending liquid fire through her veins, clear down to the sensitive region beneath her belly. She sighed as his hands sought her breasts, their warmth seeping beneath her skin. The raw passion his touch evoked overwhelmed her.

Was it his passion or hers she felt so strongly? She wasn't sure and didn't want to think about it.

As if in a dream, she felt herself being lowered to the sofa, felt the hardness of Ram's body pressing her into the cushions. She summoned a protest but lost the ability to speak when his hand skimmed beneath her skirts and up the inside of her leg. Struggling to free her mouth from his persistent kisses, she managed a desperate, "Ram, stop!"

"You don't want me to stop, Phoebe. You know I'll make it good for you. I'm the one man you can't deny your body. You belong to me."

Shaking her head vehemently, Phoebe wanted to dispute Ram's claim, but she knew it to be true.

A gasp left her lips when his hand moved higher and he caressed the soft petals of her sex with the tip of his finger.

"I want you, Phoebe. I don't care if you've taken Phillips as your lover—we can still take up where we left off." His finger slipped inside her. "I can feel you quivering." The intensity of his gaze burned a path along her skin. "You feel . . . tight."

Phoebe couldn't think beyond the sensations buffeting her. She wanted to tell Ram he was the only man who had ever made love to her, but she wouldn't give him the satisfaction.

Phoebe didn't want to accept what she was experiencing with Ram, but his hungry mouth and inflamed passion reminded her how desperately she had once loved him and how vibrantly alive his loving had made her feel.

"What are you thinking?" Ram whispered against her lips. "What are you feeling?"

"Overwhelmed," Phoebe rasped. "And bewildered. That we are together again like this is incomprehensible."

"I don't see why it should be. I didn't leave you. If you recall, you left me. Is it difficult to believe I've been pining for you all these years?"

Phoebe gave a huff of disbelief. "You're a liar and a fraud, Lord Braxton."

Unfazed, he grinned. "Your kisses taste like heaven. Will your father approve of us being together again? Where is he, by the way? Do you expect him back soon?"

The mention of her father was like a splash of cold water to her numb senses. Why was Ram interested in her father? Did he know about the amulet? She studied him from beneath lowered lids, but his closed expression told her nothing.

"There is no *us*, Ram. At one time I believed in happily ever after, but I was young and naïve then."

"Your father always liked me. Tell me where to find him and I'll ask him myself if he approves of us being together."

"Father is visiting friends in the country," she lied. "He wants whatever will make me happy, and that's not you. Your reputation precedes you."

He ignored her last remark. "You must miss your father. I'm ready for a vacation from the London scene—perhaps we should visit him together."

"Father's health was failing when he returned from Egypt. What he needs most right now is solitude."

Ram seemed disinclined to agree. "Seeing his daughter should cheer him. We could leave tomorrow, if you'd like."

"Why are you being so persistent about this? I'm not taking you to Father or telling you where to find him, so stop pestering me."

"Look at me, Phoebe. I'm a man of vast experience. I could get whatever information from you I wanted."

She gazed into the smoldering depths of his green eyes and realized the truth of his words. She had let him kiss and caress her tonight when every instinct told her she was treading in dangerous waters. A rogue like Ram could coax a virgin out of her petticoats in the blink of an eye. He could even persuade a woman to . . . No, she refused to remember how hard she had fallen for Lord Ramsey Braxton.

Curiosity made Phoebe ask, "What makes you think I have information that would interest you?"

"I'm interested in everything about you," Ram said breezily. "But right now I'd rather kiss you."

His arms tightened around her; Phoebe wriggled free. "I'm not going to let you into my life again, Ram. I appreciate what you did for me tonight, but nothing good can come of renewing our relationship. I suggest you take legal steps to make our break a permanent one."

"I'm not taking no for an answer, Phoebe," Ram said. "Your father is gone, and danger seems to be stalking you. What kind of man would leave you alone and unprotected?"

"A smart one," Phoebe suggested. "I can take care of myself. And I have David."

"Phillips wasn't around when you needed him tonight," Ram taunted. "Why did that man accost you? What are you mixed up in? Trust me, Phoebe. I want to help."

Trustworthiness wasn't Ram's strongest attribute, Phoebe thought uncharitably. Rake, seducer of women, and liar better described the debauched Lord Braxton. It occurred to her that he wouldn't be here if he didn't want something from her, something besides a casual sexual encounter or a renewal of their relationship.

"You can help by leaving me alone," Phoebe advised. "Don't meddle where you're not wanted. You'll only make things worse. Innocent people could be hurt."

Ram sat on the horns of a dilemma. Instinct told him Phoebe didn't have the amulet, had never had it, but common sense warned him against trusting her again. Phoebe had dealt a terrible blow to his pride, and as far as he could tell, she hadn't changed her ways. Seducing her wasn't going to be as easy as he'd thought. She was too distrustful of him. Nevertheless, he had no intention of letting Fielding down. If he failed to produce the amulet, an international incident would result.

"What will I make worse? Who will be hurt? You're talking in riddles."

Phoebe rose and walked to the door. "Good night, my lord. Please don't call again."

Ram followed her to the door. "You can't brush me off that easily, Phoebe. Would you like to attend the opera with me? I know you'll enjoy it. Say yes."

It had been years since Phoebe had attended the opera. The last time had been with her father on their most recent visit to London over five years ago. She remembered it because she had seen Ram for the first time that night. A young beauty was clinging to him like a leech. She'd thought him the most handsome, debonair man she'd ever seen. She didn't meet him in person until six months later, when she and her father visited a backer in their Egyptian venture whose lands bordered Lord Braxton's ancestral estate. Ram had attended a ball given in her father's honor, and she'd fallen instantly in love with him. Ram had seemed as enthralled with her as she was with him. What a fool she'd been to believe that she was the only woman in his life.

"The opera isn't a good idea, my lord," Phoebe said. "You're far above my touch."

Ram's elegant brows shot upward. "I'm well within your reach, my dear, whether you wish to remember the closeness of our relationship or not. I'll pick you up at eight o'clock."

Fuming inwardly, Phoebe opened the door, inviting Ram to leave. She should have known he had mischief in mind when she saw the wicked grin curving his lips, but she had forgotten how devilishly determined he could be. Grasping her waist as he passed her, he swung her around and brought her against him, until every part of her touched every part of him.

She felt the tumultuous bulge of his sex pressing between her legs, the hardness of his chest against her breasts, and the long muscles of his thighs molding hers. And his mouth . . . His kiss tasted like sin as his hands grasped her buttocks and lifted her off her feet, bringing her more firmly against his arousal.

"Put me down!" Phoebe ordered, fighting for breath.

Laughing, Ram swung her around, sending her skirts flying before releasing her. "Your body remembers mine, sweet Phoebe. Pleasant dreams." Then he was gone.

Slamming the door behind him, Phoebe leaned against it for support, still shaking from their volatile encounter. Damn him! How dare he walk into her life and turn it upside down? She'd made it abundantly clear the day she walked out on him that she wanted no part of his scandalous lifestyle. Until Ram reentered her life, she hadn't regretted her decision, for she had convinced herself that she had escaped a world of heartache.

She'd been so young, so utterly captivated and so in love that she hadn't wanted to believe the harsh truth. Thank God she'd had the courage to leave Ram and board that ship with David. But all that was water under the bridge now. She couldn't allow Ram to divert her from what was important: finding her father and returning that cursed amulet to its owner.

Ram left Phoebe's house in a pensive mood. If he didn't know Phoebe to be untrustworthy, he could almost believe she knew nothing about the amulet.

He was convinced, however, that something very strange was going on with her father. Maybe Sir Andrew Thompson had stolen the amulet and maybe he hadn't. Ram would never know until Sir Andrew reappeared and proved his innocence.

Ram's thoughts turned to the man who had assaulted Phoebe tonight in Vauxhall Gardens. Apparently, someone wanted the amulet badly enough to harm Sir Andrew and threaten his daughter. Who else knew about the valuable artifact? David Phillips, certainly. But he was Thompson's assistant and Phoebe's lover, why would he wish her harm? Nothing made sense. Perhaps Fielding would have some ideas.

Ram drove Westmore's carriage through the streets to Vauxhall Gardens, hoping to find his friend and convince him to accompany him to Madam Bella's. Kissing and caressing Phoebe had made him randy as a goat. He hadn't thought it would be so difficult to seduce Phoebe and glean the information he needed, but he hadn't counted on her stubbornness. He smiled grimly, more determined than ever to have Phoebe in his bed.

Ram found his horse still tethered where he had left him, which meant Westmore would be waiting for him at the bandstand. Parking his carriage in a vacant spot, Ram stepped down and walked toward the music drifting to him on the gentle night breeze.

The crowd around the bandstand hadn't thinned, but Ram easily spotted his friend standing to the left of the bandstand, a head taller than anyone else. Ram ambled toward Westmore, noting with amusement that his friend seemed quite taken with his ladybird. One hand was boldly exploring her shapely bottom while the other dipped into the low neckline of her bodice.

"Still here, I see," Ram said, clapping Luc on the shoulder.

Luc greeted Ram with a smile. "Thought I'd wait around and see if you turned up. You must be losing your touch, old boy. Wouldn't she have you?"

Ram ignored the question. "Might I have a word with you in private?"

Luc tucked a coin between the prostitute's ample breasts, patted her bottom and sent her off. "I'm all yours, Braxton. What mischief are you up to now? Miss Thompson isn't your type, but that's no reason to dislike her. Have you seduced her yet? Don't keep your best friend in the dark."

"Are you *up* for Madam Bella's?" Ram asked, grinning at his double entendre. "I thought I'd try Lulu tonight if she's not already engaged. I'll tie Duke to the carriage and explain everything to you on the way."

"I'm always up for Bella's," Luc laughed. "Come along, my friend. I'm anxious to hear what mischief you've gotten yourself into now. Too bad Bathurst isn't around; I'm sure he'd enjoy your tale as much as I'm going to."

Once Ram was settled in the carriage beside Luc, he nearly changed his mind about telling Westmore what was afoot. But he and Westmore and Bathurst had shared so many confidences, it was second nature to confide in his best friend and fellow rogue.

"Well, I'm waiting," Luc said. "Why don't you like Miss Thompson, and why are you trying to seduce her? Never say you're altar bound, old boy. I'd hate to be the last rogue left in London." He gave a careless shrug. "But if I am, I'm sure I can make do."

"Do you recall my telling you I worked for the Foreign Office while you and Bathurst were fighting on the Peninsula?"

"Good Lord, you're not involved in some kind of intrigue, are you?"

"In a sense."

"I thought you gave that up after the war."

"I did, but the Foreign Office asked me to take on a special assignment, one involving Phoebe Thompson and her father."

"Nothing dangerous, I hope."

"No danger involved. I'm to do what I do best."

Luc shot him an amused look, then burst out laughing. "Why does the Foreign Office want you to seduce a gently bred young woman? We both know virgins are off limits to us."

"That didn't seem to bother Bathurst," Ram said dryly. "Besides, what makes you think Phoebe is a virgin?"

Luc's dark brows shot upward. "Do you know something no one else does? Sounds as if you and Miss Thompson are more than mere acquaintances. Something tells me you accepted this assignment for personal reasons."

"All I can tell you is that I knew Phoebe long before I was asked to take on this assignment."

"What exactly is it the Foreign Office wants from the woman?"

"Information. They want to find her father. Sir Andrew Thompson has disappeared."

"Ah, yes, the Egyptologist. Not exactly my field of expertise, but I believe I have heard the name mentioned a time or two. So you're to seduce his daughter. Interesting. Anything else you care to tell me?"

"Not at this time. I've already told you more than I should have."

"Obviously your seduction hasn't succeeded, else you wouldn't be so hot to visit Bella's."

"Phoebe is skittish and needs special handling. Our former relationship didn't end well—that's all I'm going to say."

"Ah, here we are," Luc said, reining in before Madam Bella's establishment. "Shall we go inside?"

A tall, distinguished servant opened the door, and they entered the decadent elegance of Bella's drawing room. Several of Bella's girls strolled about the room in artful dishabille. Ram spotted Lulu immediately and would have strolled over in her direction had Bella not appeared to greet him and Luc.

"Welcome, Lord Braxton, Lord Westmore. I'm pleased to know I can still count on the two remaining rogues of London to visit my establishment. What is your pleasure tonight?"

"Lulu appeals to me tonight," Ram said. "Is she available?"

"For you, she is," Bella beamed. "What about you, Lord Westmore? Whom do you fancy?"

Luc sent Bella a smoldering look. "Are *you* free? I know you favored Bathurst, but since he's no longer available, I thought I might do."

"It just so happens I am free," Bella said, threading her arm through Luc's.

Ram watched them walk off, then turned to Lulu. As he wended his way around the room, something strange happened. His steps slowed and the sexual tension resulting from his encounter with Phoebe drained from his body, leaving him curiously uninterested in Lulu.

Lulu's red hair was too brash and her painted face seemed coarse and vulgar. Her breasts were too large and the sheer peignoir she wore was tastelessly revealing. The triangle shielding her sex was black, not red like the hair on her head, and his thoughts turned abruptly from Lulu to Phoebe.

Why did Phoebe have to intrude where she wasn't wanted? Ram silently groused.

He had come to Bella's to forget the dark-haired vixen and appease the lust she had provoked. Yet, impossibly, he was recalling how Phoebe looked naked, how she felt in his arms, and how eager he had been to make her his. Four years melted away as if they were nothing.

He had been her first lover. She had been as hot for him as he was for her. But there had been only one way she'd let him have her. And fool that he was, he had let his cock rule his head and done the unthinkable. It had seemed so right at the time; he'd actually thought himself in love.

He didn't realize he had stopped walking and was standing in the middle of the room until he glanced up and realized he was drawing attention. Self-consciously he willed himself to move. A half dozen steps took him to his destination.

Lulu greeted him with a smile that held a wealth of sexual promise. Sidling close, she pressed her breasts against his arm. "Shall we go upstairs, milord? I promise you won't be sorry."

Ram was already sorry. He couldn't imagine why Lulu had appealed to him. She was nothing like Phoebe. That thought stopped him in his tracks. Where had it come from? Since when had he compared other women to Phoebe?

Since Phoebe had reappeared in my life.

"Another time, Lulu," Ram said. "I suddenly remembered a previous engagement."

Turning on his heel, he beat a hasty retreat.

Chapter Four

David Phillips arrived at Phoebe's door early the following morning. Mrs. Crowley showed him into the study, where Phoebe was going over her father's notes. She had found them in his trunk and hoped they might provide information about the amulet.

Phoebe summoned an impatient smile for David. "Good morning, David. What brings you out so early?"

"*He* was here last night, wasn't he?"

Phoebe blinked. "To whom are you referring?"

David's chin jutted belligerently. "Braxton. What was he doing here? Haven't you learned your lesson where Braxton is concerned?"

It occurred to Phoebe that David couldn't possibly know Ram was here unless . . . "You were watching the house!"

David gave a nervous twitch of his shoulders.

"I'm concerned about you. I passed by last night to make sure you were all right. That break-in worried me. I saw Braxton leaving and didn't like it one damn bit."

"Why didn't you make your presence known? You shouldn't have been sneaking around."

"I felt betrayed by your willingness to involve yourself with Braxton again. As close as we've been these past four years, I would have thought you'd come to me for comfort."

Phoebe blew out an exasperated sigh. "I didn't go to Braxton for comfort. If you must know, he rescued me from a dangerous situation last night. I was accosted at Vauxhall Pleasure Gardens."

"You were in no danger," David scoffed.

A chill slid down Phoebe's spine. "What makes you say that? You weren't there. You couldn't possibly know what happened."

"Vauxhall Gardens is a public place. If you were attacked, it was probably a pickpocket in need of blunt. You just happened to be handy."

"My assailant was quite clear about what he wanted. It was the amulet," Phoebe informed him. "I received a note instructing me to bring the amulet to Vauxhall Gardens and leave it in the urn near Caesar's feet in the Roman Pavilion."

"Why didn't I know about this? You deliberately withheld information from me." His eyes narrowed. "Did you leave the amulet in the urn?"

Phoebe rolled her eyes. "Really, David, I couldn't leave what I don't have. I didn't tell you because I knew you wouldn't let me go alone, as the note directed."

"Of course I wouldn't have let you go alone," David said. "What happened?"

"I went to Vauxhall and confronted the abductor, demanding Father's release. He attacked me when I told him I didn't have the amulet. Thank God Braxton came along when he did."

"Quite a coincidence," David drawled. "Does he suspect anything?"

"He knows something is troubling me and is looking for answers."

"Don't tell him," David cautioned. "We'll find the amulet and give the kidnappers what they want."

Phoebe gave him a strange look. "What makes you think Father stole it?"

"It's just a hunch," David hedged.

Phoebe shook her head in vehement denial. "I refuse to believe Father is a thief."

David shrugged. "Perhaps you don't know your father as well as you think."

"I know my father better than anyone," Phoebe maintained. "My greatest fear is that the kidnappers will become impatient and hurt him."

"A thought occurred to me while I was on my way here," David said. "Have you searched beneath the lining of Andrew's trunk?"

"No, I saw no need. After receiving that first note demanding the amulet in exchange for my father, I searched through Father's belongings and put everything away." Her shoulders slumped. "There was nothing but clothing, a few artifacts, and personal items in the trunk."

"Are you sure?"

"Positive."

"Do you mind if I take a look?"

Phoebe bristled. "Yes, I do mind. What in the world is wrong with you, David? Don't you trust me? I know you're as worried about Father as I am but you're being ridiculous. There was nothing outstanding in that trunk."

"Sorry, darling, of course I trust you. I want you for my wife, don't I? Why are you being so stubborn about marrying me? I don't understand you at all. There is nothing to stop us from marrying."

If you only knew, Phoebe thought. "Had I wanted to marry you, I would have done so long ago," Phoebe said gently. "Seriously, David, if Father doesn't show up soon, I'm going to the authorities with what I know. I pretended ignorance when those men from the Foreign Office questioned me but things have changed. I believe they should know what's going on."

"Give me another week to find Andrew," David said. "If I turn up no new information, we'll go to the authorities together. Meanwhile, have nothing further to do with Braxton. He's up to no good."

He kissed her lightly on the lips. "I have to go now. Will you be all right alone? No more wandering off by yourself, do you hear?"

"I'll be fine, David. I won't be careless again."

"Would you like some tea, dearie?" Mrs. Crowley asked after David left. "Are you hungry? You hardly ate any breakfast."

"No, thank you, Mrs. Crowley," Phoebe said distractedly.

"Well, then, I'm off to the market. I'll be back in time to fix you a nice lunch."

Phoebe returned to the notes she was perusing but her heart wasn't in the task. Her thoughts kept returning to Ram . . . to that last day . . .

The sun was high in the sky when Phoebe rose from bed and dressed. Pausing in the doorway, she smiled lovingly at Ram, who was still sleeping deeply, then tiptoed down the stairs to the kitchen.

Last night had been the most wonderful, fulfilling night of her life. Ram had delivered everything he had promised and given her a night to remember. She hadn't been frightened at all. He'd made it so remarkably rewarding, so perfect, she couldn't have asked for a better initiation to sex.

Her body still thrummed from their loving. She ached, but in a good way. She loved him so much, and he had proven his love by giving her the one thing she had asked of him. Though exhausted, she couldn't wait until they came together again. She wanted his kisses and caresses, craved his touch, couldn't wait to repeat all the sinful, decadent, amazingly arousing things they had done last night.

Humming a wordless tune, Phoebe brought out pots and pans to prepare something special for Ram's breakfast. The cook had already been let go and there was no one in the cottage but her and Ram. Had Ram not made her dream come true, she would be traveling to Liverpool today with David Phillips to board a ship that would take her to Egypt to join her father. Phoebe chuckled to herself when she imagined her father's reaction to the letter she intended to write and entrust to David before he left.

Of course David wasn't going to be happy about her decision to remain in England with Ram. He'd been warning her about Lord Braxton since he became aware of their growing affection. He'd done everything in his power to turn her away from Ram.

Over the rattling pots, Phoebe heard someone rapping on the front door.

David.

Phoebe opened the door to her father's assistant

and stepped outside to speak to him so as not to awaken Ram.

"I just wanted to make sure you're all packed and ready to leave."

"I'm not going, David."

"What? Of course you're going. Your father is expecting you."

Dragging in a sustaining breath, Phoebe said, "I'm staying here with Lord Braxton."

"I won't allow it!" David blasted. "Where is your self-respect, your pride?"

"Where it belongs. Don't fuss so, David. Father will be pleased I've found a man to love."

"Braxton wants but one thing from you, Phoebe. I pray he hasn't compromised you, for your father would never forgive me for allowing you to go astray."

"I'm of age, David. No one can tell me what to do."

"Do you know where Braxton was last night?"

Phoebe smiled dreamily. "Yes, as a matter of fact, I do."

"What about the night before that?"

Phoebe frowned. The night before last Ram had said he'd had business to conduct and couldn't see her. "No, but I suspect you're going to tell me."

"I'll not only tell you, I'll show you." *Grasping her hand, he pulled her down the steps and through the front gate.*

"David, where are you taking me?"

"You'll see. It's not far."

Indeed it was not. The village in which she and her father had been living was small, the houses and shops clustered close together. When they reached the Bull and Heifer, the village's only inn, David pulled her inside and led her into the tap-

room . . . where her dreams of happily ever after had been shattered.

Lowering her head into her hands, Phoebe remembered how she had felt when the saucy barmaid coyly admitted that Ram was one of her regular customers, and that he had been with her just the evening before. Furthermore, he came to her whenever he visited his country estate. Then she went on to praise Ram's sexual prowess. Phoebe hadn't wanted to believe Ram had lied, but by the time David had taken her to visit a young widow who admitted to having an ongoing affair with Ram, Phoebe's disillusionment had been complete. Phoebe had known Ram's reputation was far from pristine, but he had sworn he wanted no one but her.

David had convinced her that Ram only wanted to take her maidenhead. That once he'd had her he would abandon her.

So she had abandoned him first.

Shattered, she had promised David she would leave with him immediately. Ram was awake when she trudged up the stairs to collect her belongings. Her last conversation with him was still imprinted in her mind . . .

"Where did you go?" Ram asked sleepily. "Come back to bed, love. I have so much to teach you and you're such an eager student."

"Bastard!" Phoebe hissed. "I thought you loved me."

Ram was suddenly wide awake. "Where did that come from? Did I do something to make you angry? You told me last night that I was wonderful, that you'd never been happier."

She pulled her packed bag from beneath the bed.

69

"That was last night, before I learned what you're really like."

Ram sent her a puzzled look. "Have I missed something?"

"No, I did. I'm leaving to join Father as planned."

"Like hell! You're mine now. You can't just up and leave."

"I can and I will. Take whatever legal action is necessary, just don't try to stop me."

She could tell he was raging inside and needed to get away before he became violent.

"It's Phillips, isn't it?"

"No, it's you. Good-bye, Ram."

"Go, damn you! Get out of my sight! I never want to see you again. If you loved me, you'd trust me."

Her eyes burned with unshed tears. "Then I suppose I don't love you."

She had walked out of Ram's life and never looked back. But everything had changed. Though she tried to deny it, her heart had been broken. She should have known that to a man like Braxton women were nothing but playthings, to be used and discarded with no more thought than he'd give to a worn pair of boots.

The tears she'd so bravely withheld trekked slowly down her cheeks, splashing onto her folded hands. She wanted to be strong for her father, but it was becoming increasingly difficult to maintain her composure. Lord Braxton's perceptive nature and his ability to probe beneath her calm façade were disturbing. So was David's objection to approaching the authorities.

The way things stood now, government agents were questioning her, Ram was butting into her business, and David was admonishing her to remain silent. To make matters worse, an unknown enemy was stalking her. Phoebe knew herself to be a strong woman, but how could she continue as if nothing was wrong? Why was David so adamantly opposed to bringing the authorities into the mix? Why had Braxton shown up at her door, pretending interest in her when he had every reason to hate her?

It suddenly occurred to Phoebe that she should begin solving those mysteries by learning what Ram wanted from her and why he was being so attentive. He was up to something, but what?

Phoebe went into the kitchen to brew herself a pot of tea. While waiting for the water to boil, she sat at the table and considered her options.

Waiting for something to happen was nerve-wracking. Her father had been missing for weeks and she had no idea if he was still alive. Dissecting the situation further, Phoebe knew that three different factions wanted the amulet: the government, Egypt, and an unknown party. Was Braxton somehow involved?

Phoebe's thoughts returned to Ram as she poured boiling water into the pot and waited for the tea to steep. David had warned her to keep away from Ram but every instinct told her that Ram would help if she confided in him. First, however, she had to discover what he was about and why.

Phoebe wasn't stupid. Ram was trying to seduce her for a reason. Did it have anything to do with the amulet? With any luck she'd find out tonight. Despite David's warning, she was going to attend the opera with Ram. Two could play at seduction and she intended to beat Ram at his own game. She needed to know the reason behind his sudden interest in her. The only thing she was sure of was that he didn't love her.

Ram reported to Fielding that afternoon. The moment the door closed behind him, he lit into the agent. "Phoebe was attacked again last night. This has to stop, Fielding! Call off your agents. I'll get that damned amulet for you without anyone being hurt."

"I told you the last time you accused me of interfering that my men have been taken off the case. Hurting Miss Thompson is not our intention. We want the amulet and whoever stole it."

"I'm convinced that Phoebe is innocent."

"That leaves her father," Fielding mused.

"Sir Thompson is being held against his will by unknown assailants who want the amulet as badly as you do."

Fielding's eyes narrowed. "How do you know that?"

"Phoebe received a note instructing her to bring the amulet to Vauxhall Pleasure Gardens last night. I saw the note myself and it was no hoax. She went to confront the kidnappers and demand her father's release, and she suffered for it. I chased her assailant off before she suffered serious damage, but it was a close call."

"Do you think they meant Miss Thompson harm?"

Ram grew thoughtful. "I think they're serious. Perhaps they intended to abduct her in order to force her father's hand. I know Sir Thompson. He'd give them the amulet if he thought his daughter's life was in danger."

"Do you really think Thompson is being held

against his will? Consider this. What if he went in to hiding with the amulet and claims he is being held prisoner in order to throw us off the trail?"

Ram rubbed his jaw as he considered Fielding's words. "Anything is possible. I'm hoping I'll have the truth soon."

"Excellent. The Egyptian emissaries are becoming impatient. The Crown is counting on you, Braxton. How is the seduction coming? Is Miss Thompson proving stubborn?"

"I'm taking Phoebe to the opera tonight. I should have some answers for you tomorrow. Our rather turbulent history together is making this more difficult than I anticipated, but I won't fail you."

Mrs. Crowley helped Phoebe dress that night. Upon her return to England, Phoebe had purchased two gowns to replace those hopelessly out of date. Only one of the new gowns was suitable to be worn to the opera. The vibrant lavender silk had a low scooped neckline, fitted waist, billowing skirt and short puff sleeves. Though Phoebe thought the neckline somewhat indecent, the mantua maker had insisted that it was modest compared to today's fashions. Phoebe loved the color and thought it contrasted nicely with her sun-kissed skin and dark hair.

Mrs. Crowley helped Phoebe pile her hair high atop her head in an elegant style that emphasized her slender neck. As a crowning touch, the housekeeper tucked an ostrich feather into the shining mass. "You look lovely, dearie," Mrs. Crowley cooed. "Lord Braxton will be pleased."

"Thank you, Mrs. Crowley," Phoebe said as she pulled on her long opera-length gloves. "You needn't wait up for me. I can manage on my own tonight."

"In that case, would it be all right if I spent the night with my daughter?" Mrs. Crowley asked. "She's expecting, you know, and having a hard time of it. I planned to visit her tonight and return before you arrived home, but if you don't need me, I'd like to stay the night."

"It was so good of you to agree to spend your nights with me; how can I deny your request? Have a good visit."

"That I will. Oh," Mrs. Crowley said when the sound of someone rapping on the door resounded through the house. "There's Lord Braxton now. I'll let him in, dearie."

Ram waiting impatiently for someone to open the door. He hadn't seen Phoebe since yesterday and was eagerly looking forward to tonight. Encountering her again after all these years had reminded him of what had attracted him to her in the first place. Though he had bedded women more beautiful than Phoebe, there was something compelling about her that pulled at his heart.

Ram summoned a smile for Mrs. Crowley as she opened the door to him.

"Miss Thompson will be down directly, milord. Would you care to wait in the parlor?"

"I'll wait right here if you don't mind," Ram replied. He wanted to see Phoebe when she walked down the stairs. He'd never seen her in anything fancy and knew the wait would be worth it. If anything, Phoebe had grown more beautiful over the years. At twenty she had been lovely, at twenty-six she had matured to her full potential and was breathtaking.

"Here she comes now," Mrs. Crowley said, beaming. "Isn't she a vision?"

That description didn't do Phoebe justice. She looked the height of elegance, fitted out in the latest fashion with her hair styled to enhance her natural beauty. He studied the ostrich feather perched atop her dark curls and decided it suited her. Then she started down the stairs and the breath caught in his throat. She didn't walk, she floated. Funny, he'd almost forgotten her gracefulness.

Ram stepped forward when she reached the foot of the stairs. "I'm glad you decided to accept my invitation. You're breathtaking." Taking her hand, he pressed his lips to her fingertips. "Do you have a wrap?"

Mrs. Crowley reappeared with a velvet cloak over her arm. Ram took it and placed it over Phoebe's shoulders. "Shall we go? I don't want to miss the curtain."

Ram ushered Phoebe through the door and handed her into his coach. "The Opera House, Wilson," he directed his coachman. Then he climbed in beside Phoebe and gave her his most beguiling smile. "You're rather quiet tonight. Are you all right? You appear on edge."

"I'm fine, my lord. I'm wondering if this is a good idea and curious as to why you're being so friendly. It doesn't make sense, Ram. Obviously neither of us has changed in four years, it's only natural that I should wonder about your motives for renewing our . . . relationship."

"How do you know I haven't changed?"

"I can read, my lord. The newspapers and gossip sheets have a field day with your amorous exploits. You haven't changed your ways. If anything, you've become more debauched. You and your friends

Bathurst and Westmore made quite a name for yourselves in the four years I've been away."

"Bathurst is married, you can no longer count him among our rank. Perhaps it's time for a change. Maybe I envy Bathurst's happiness. One woman seems to be enough for him, what makes you think one woman won't satisfy me?"

"Perhaps there is a woman who can satisfy you, but it isn't me. You've already proven that."

"You're wrong, Phoebe. I don't know what sent you fleeing that morning, but I'm willing to bet David Phillips was behind it."

Phoebe glanced out the window, unable to face the accusation in Ram's eyes. "It no longer matters. Too much time has elapsed for us to take up where we left off."

"We'll see," Ram said cryptically. "Nothing can change our relationship to anything other than what it is. Let's just relax tonight and see where the evening takes us."

"Nowhere," Phoebe said tonelessly.

"Ah, here we are," Ram said as the coach pulled up behind a line of coaches waiting to discharge their passengers.

"I don't feel comfortable about this," Phoebe ventured. "People will talk. They'll know I'm not one of the *ton*. I can well imagine the gossip we'll create."

Ram laughed. "Let them talk. I told you once it didn't matter that you were a commoner and that hasn't changed. I don't hold to convention."

The coachman opened the door and pulled down the stairs. Ram stepped out first, then handed Phoebe down. Tucking her hand beneath his arm, he guided her into the opera house.

* * *

Awed by the grandeur, Phoebe gazed at the splendor unfolding before her eyes. Above them, crystal chandeliers sparkled like diamonds in the light from hundreds of candles, and the velvet hangings at the windows provided a vibrant background for the peacock brilliance of the clothing worn by the ladies and gentlemen milling about in the lobby.

Was there a hush following their entrance or had she imagined it? Phoebe wondered. Were people staring at her? Or was it Ram attracting all the attention? Most likely Ram, she decided. There wasn't a woman present immune to his compelling presence. Women were drawn to him like bees to honey.

Placing his hand on her back, he urged her toward the stairs. "Shall we find our seats? I keep a private box, so we'll be able to watch the opera in comfort."

"People are staring at us," Phoebe hissed.

"They're jealous of your beauty," Ram assured her.

"Lord Braxton, where *have* you been keeping yourself?" Phoebe glanced at the lady who waylaid them on the stairs and sighed with resignation. Women couldn't resist Ram. Tapping Ram playfully on the shoulder with her fan, the woman said, "Naughty boy. I missed you at the Hampton's ball last night. I had such grand plans for us."

"Lady Frampton," Ram said cordially. "Allow me to present Miss Phoebe Thompson. Phoebe, this is Lady Sylvia Frampton."

Sylvia Frampton, a blonde beauty with voluptuous breasts disdained the hand Phoebe offered, her contemptuous gaze dismissing Phoebe out of hand. "She's not your type, Braxton. Is she your latest mistress?"

"Behave, Sylvia," Ram warned. "Miss Thompson is an old and dear friend. Her father is Sir Andrew Thompson, the renowned Egyptologist."

"Need I say more?" Phoebe said after Sylvia ambled off. "You'll never change, Ram. It's not in your blood. Never say Lady Frampton isn't one of your lovers."

"I won't deny it, Phoebe. You left me quite bereft and distrustful of women. The only way to forget you was to stumble from one affair to another. Your betrayal devastated me."

Phoebe's chin, already held at a defiant angle, rose even higher. Thank God she was a practical woman. She'd put her own silly dreams about Ram in the past where they belonged. She'd taken charge of her life, abandoning foolish hopes and dreams that could never come true.

Phoebe waited until Ram seated her in his box before answering. "I can't picture you as being devastated, Lord Braxton. Embarrassed, perhaps, but I'll wager you had plenty of female companionship to help you forget." She turned away from him. "The curtain is going up and I intend to enjoy the opera."

Phoebe did enjoy the opera, immensely. The singing was superb and the story fascinating. The intermission came before Phoebe was ready.

"Would you like some refreshment?" Ram asked. "We could go to the lobby and stretch our legs, or I could bring you something."

"Bring me something," Phoebe replied. She'd been stared at enough tonight. "I'll wait here. Anything to quench my thirst will do."

"I'll be right back," Ram promised.

Phoebe settled into her chair to await Ram's return. She couldn't blame other women for admiring him, for he was worthy of their admiration. Dressed fashionably in long dark trousers, cutaway coat and violet brocade vest, he was the epitome of elegance. No man had a right to look as handsome as Lord Braxton.

"Oh, I say, I thought I'd find Braxton here."

Whipping her head around, Phoebe recognized the handsome and debonair Lord Westmore. "He just stepped out. He should return shortly, if you care to wait."

"You're Miss Thompson. I'm Westmore. We met in Vauxhall Pleasure Gardens."

"Yes, I recall our meeting. You're Braxton's friend and fellow rogue."

"Guilty on both counts," Luc drawled. He gave her a wicked grin. "If you should tire of Braxton, my dear, don't hesitate to call on me."

"Westmore, stop flirting," Ram said from the doorway. He handed Phoebe a glass of lemonade. "Now that you've greeted Phoebe, you may leave."

"Is that any way to treat a friend?" Luc teased.

Ram ignored the question "Are you here alone tonight?"

"No. I'm with the Carlton party. Lady Carlton needed an escort. Her husband is out of town, you see."

"Only too well," Ram said.

"I came to extend an invitation. Will you attend the races with me tomorrow?"

"Sounds like a good idea," Ram said.

"Miss Thompson, it's been a pleasure seeing you again," Luc said as he took his leave. "Until tomorrow, Braxton."

"He seems rather pleasant for a man with a reputation as wicked as yours," Phoebe mused after he left.

"Don't believe everything you read or hear," Ram said with a hint of amusement. "Forget Westmore and concentrate on me . . . on us."

The last aria passed in a blur as Phoebe's mind wandered. Somehow she needed to draw the truth from Ram. He wouldn't be with her if he didn't have an agenda. Thunderous applause pulled her from her dark thoughts.

"Shall we leave before the mass exodus begins?" Ram asked.

"By all means," Phoebe said, rising.

They managed to make it down the stairs and into their coach without incident. As the coach rattled off through the dark night, Phoebe planned her strategy to draw the truth from Ram. Little did she know that Ram had plans of his own, plans that placed Phoebe in his arms and bed very soon.

Chapter Five

"I'll escort you inside," Ram said as the coach pulled up to Phoebe's door. "Is Mrs. Crowley waiting up for you?"

"Mrs. Crowley is spending the night with her daughter," Phoebe said. "I told her I wouldn't need her tonight."

Ram didn't like the idea of Phoebe being alone. Damn, why had he taken this assignment? Someone wished Phoebe ill, and he had no recourse but to protect her. The sooner he learned the whereabouts of the amulet, the faster he could remove Phoebe from his life. He hadn't known what he was getting into when he'd accepted the assignment. Their antagonistic parting four years ago had left him disillusioned and bitter, but to his surprise, being with Phoebe again had blunted his desire to punish her. He still wanted to seduce her, and fully intended to, but the only hurt she would suffer would be his leaving her as she had left him.

Ram assisted Phoebe down from the coach and accompanied her to the door. As Phoebe searched her reticule for the key, a prickling sensation raised the hair on his nape. His gut told him something was wrong, very wrong. Grasping Phoebe about the waist, he shoved her behind him and turned the doorknob. The door swung open.

"The door wasn't locked!" Phoebe exclaimed. "Mrs. Crowley wouldn't leave it open." She tried to push past Ram, but he kept her safely behind him.

"Get back in the coach."

"No. I'm going inside with you."

"Phoebe—"

"This is my house, Ram."

Ram blew out an exasperated sigh. "Very well, but stay behind me. Whoever broke in is probably gone now, but I'm not taking any chances." The lamp Mrs. Crowley had left burning in the hall had gone out, creating a black void.

"Are you armed?" Phoebe asked.

"Not tonight."

Ram found a sulfur match in his pocket, lit the lamp and ushered Phoebe into the parlor. Nothing appeared out of place, and he moved on to the study. Finding nothing amiss, he continued into the kitchen and Mrs. Crowley's room at the back of the house, with Phoebe hard on his heels.

"Everything looks fine to me," Phoebe said. "Maybe Mrs. Crowley *did* forget to lock the door."

"Let's look upstairs," Ram said, "though I'm inclined to agree with your first assessment. Mrs. Crowley is too conscientious to leave the door unlocked."

Cautiously, Ram preceded her up the staircase. "How many bedrooms are up here?"

"Just two, mine and Father's. Mine is on the right, Father's on the left."

Both bedrooms had been torn apart. Nothing had been left unturned or unopened. The mattresses had been ripped from the bed and tossed to the floor, and clothing was strewn about the room. The trunk that had held Sir Thompson's belongings had been literally ripped apart.

"Oh, my God," Phoebe whispered.

"Who did this, Phoebe?" Ram asked harshly. "Are you ready now to confide in me?"

"I don't know who did this."

Phoebe appeared so shaken, Ram decided not to press the issue until she calmed down. He struck a match to the candle on the nightstand. "Stay here. I'll be right back."

"Where are you going?"

"To take a look outside. The intruder might have left evidence behind."

"Be careful."

Ram found no clues to the intruder's identity inside or outside the house. He did, however, send his coach home without him and made sure the windows and doors were locked. He returned to Phoebe's bedroom and found her sitting just as he'd left her. She leaped to her feet when she saw him.

"I heard your coach driving off and thought you'd left."

"I'm not going anywhere tonight, Phoebe. Are you all right?"

She nodded distractedly. Then, as if she realized what he'd just said, her eyes widened. "What do you mean you're not going anywhere tonight?"

"I'm not leaving you alone after what just happened. Why don't you brew a pot of tea while I set the room to rights? I locked the doors and windows before coming up, so you should be safe down there by yourself. I'll join you shortly."

Phoebe picked up the candle and headed out the door. "I'll . . . be fine."

Ram made short work of cleaning up the mess; he folded Phoebe's garments neatly and replaced them in the clothes press. Then he moved on to the second bedroom before joining Phoebe in the kitchen.

"What are you hiding from me, Phoebe?" Ram asked as he lowered himself into a chair.

Phoebe poured tea into two cups and sat down across from him. "It's none of your concern, Ram."

"I want to help."

"I can handle it myself."

"You're not doing a very good job of it. In the past few days you've been accosted in a public place and had your house ransacked twice. What do you have that someone wants?"

Phoebe placed her cup carefully on the table and rose. "I'm tired; you a long walk home. I suggest you leave."

Ram shoved his chair back and stood. "I'm not leaving. You need protection, and who better to provide it than me? You're too unnerved to sleep. Come into the parlor with me. We need to talk."

He picked up the lamp with one hand, grasped her elbow with the other and guided her into the parlor. He seated her on the sofa, placed the lamp on a table and sat down beside her. His arm came around her and he settled her against him.

"You're trembling. Relax, you're safe now."

Phoebe gave a shaky sigh. "I'm not a coward,

84

Ram, but this matter has gotten out of hand."

"Tell me about it."

"Why do you care? If you weren't after something, you wouldn't be here with me now."

He found her hand and placed it over the bulge in his trousers, his voice low and husky as he rasped, "I'm indeed 'up' to something. Can you feel what I'm 'up' for? When I heard you were in town, I had to see you again. And once I did, all the feelings I'd suppressed returned. I realized that time had changed nothing. I still want you as much as I ever did."

Phoebe's mouth opened wordlessly as her fingers curled around his sex. Not a moment too soon, her wits returned and she withdrew her hand as if burned. "Why are you doing this? What do you want from me?"

He caressed her cheek. "What makes you think I want anything other than this?" His hand wandered to her breast. "You're a lovely, passionate woman, Phoebe. I haven't forgotten how good we were together."

Phoebe's skin burned beneath his touch. Ram wasn't the only one who hadn't forgotten the one night of passion they had shared. The ecstasy she'd experienced with Ram had remained in her thoughts despite her resolve to forget him. Why did he have to walk into her life again and bring back those forbidden memories?

"How can you expect me to believe you still care for me?" she challenged. Her eyes narrowed suspiciously. "Did someone send you to spy on me?"

"We're bound by ties that cannot be severed," he reminded her. "I still account myself responsible for you. If you're in danger, I want to know why. Why won't you confide in me? I'm not stupid. I

Connie Mason

know these mysterious attacks upon your home and person are connected to your missing father. Are you and Sir Thompson involved in something illegal?"

Phoebe's lips thinned. "I don't want to talk about Father."

"What *do* you want to talk about?"

"Nothing."

A slow grin curved his lips. "I agree. Talk is *de trop* at a time like this." His hand pressed more firmly against her breast, his thumb rubbing back and forth across the stiffening peak of her nipple.

Inhaling sharply, Phoebe closed her eyes and surrendered to the feelings coursing through her. The familiarity of Ram's hands on her body made her feel vitally alive, but it was wrong. Their relationship had ended four years ago in all ways but one.

Phoebe searched for the courage to resist and found it. "Stop this, Ram. Now!"

"I don't think so, Phoebe. I'm going to kiss you."

The protest died in her throat as Ram's mouth seized hers in a bold kiss that turned her blood to liquid fire. When he pushed his tongue into her mouth, she had to stifle a cry of joyful welcome. Her body tingled, her blood sang, and anticipation warmed her. She shouldn't feel like this . . . didn't want to feel anything, but the rush of pleasure was too heady to deny.

Even though Phoebe suspected Ram had an ulterior motive for seducing her, she couldn't find the willpower to put an end to it. She had allowed David Phillips to kiss her, but his kisses had left her cold. She'd felt nothing but friendship for David, which was why she had refused to marry him after leaving Ram. As it turned out, her refusal had been

86

a wise choice, for Ram hadn't put a period to their relationship as she'd expected.

Phoebe's thoughts scattered when Ram's mouth left hers and began a sensuous journey over her throat. She wasn't aware that he had pulled down her bodice until she felt his tongue flick over the upper reaches of her breasts and the cleft between them. Then she felt a tug on her corset strings and stiffened.

"Let's get you out of this contraption," Ram whispered hoarsely.

Phoebe blew out a startled gasp when he scooped her up into his arms and headed for the stairs. "What are you doing?"

"Taking you to bed. A hasty coupling on the sofa isn't what I had in mind. I'm going to love you properly, Phoebe. I want us both naked when we join, and afterward I want to be the only lover you'll remember."

You're the only lover I've ever had, Phoebe wanted to scream. Instead, she said, "This isn't right, Ram."

"This is more than right. I'm the only man with the legal right to make love to you."

Hearing the truth unsettled Phoebe. Legally, Ram could make love to her whenever he pleased. But morally it was wrong. Yet Phoebe couldn't deny she wanted the comfort he offered. She'd been so on edge lately, so utterly lost and frightened, that Ram was like a safe harbor in a turbulent storm. She needed someone to shelter and protect her, to soothe her troubled heart. Letting Ram make love to her wasn't a permanent solution to her problems, but for one night she wanted to forget her troubles.

When he reached her bedroom, Ram shoved the

door open and carried her inside. Then he set her on her feet and began to undress her with swift expertise. Phoebe couldn't help wondering how many women he'd undressed, but quickly shoved the disturbing thought from her mind as Ram removed her dress, released the tapes on her petticoats and turned her around to work on her corset strings.

She heard Ram huff an impatient sigh; then the garment loosened and slid to the floor. Swinging her around, he stared at her, his hungry gaze glittering with admiration.

"You're even lovelier than I remembered."

Reaching out, he touched her nipple. She felt it rise and harden beneath his touch. A cry left her lips when he bent and took it into his mouth, bathing it with his tongue. Arching into his bold caress, she felt the ground tilt beneath her feet and clung to him; he was her lifeline to reality. Then reality fled when Ram dropped to his knees and licked a trail of fire down her stomach, his tongue dipping into the dark triangle between her legs. Clutching her buttocks, he pressed her against his mouth, his tongue parting her, then slipping inside the moist petals of her femininity.

She gasped out his name and would have collapsed had Ram not maintained a firm grip on her. She was shaking like a leaf when he swept her into his arms and placed her on the bed. His gaze locked with hers as he began to undress. She wanted to look away from the compelling sight of broad shoulders, slim hips and tautly muscled legs but could not. Nor could she stop her gaze from drifting down to his sex. Stunningly thick and hard, his erection was worthy of admiration.

It seemed impossible that a man who had every

reason to hate her could become aroused so easily, until she recalled that rogues needed little provocation to initiate sex. A willing woman and a bed were all it took for a rogue to summon passion. She'd learned that lesson long ago and had vowed never to fall prey to men like Braxton again. She wasn't the innocent virgin she had been four years ago. Because she knew Ram was using her for some unknown reason, she felt no guilt for using him.

She needed Ram, needed his comfort, his body, the feeling of being wanted. Tomorrow she would likely hate herself for succumbing to his charm, but tonight she wanted to be close to someone.

Close to Ram.

Besides, Phoebe needed to know what Ram wanted from her and intended to get to the bottom of his sudden and unwarranted attention. Once she found out, she'd follow David's advice and banish Ram from her life . . . again.

"What are you thinking?" Ram asked as he lay down beside her and pulled her into his arms.

"I was remembering something David told me."

A curse flew from Ram's lips. "Forget that bastard. Phillips will never get near your bed again. I'm the only man with that right."

As if to reinforce his words, he tilted her face up to his and kissed her with a fervor that stole her breath and sent her senses reeling. Just when she thought she'd expire from lack of air, he broke off the kiss. Raising himself up on his elbows, he gazed down at her, his eyes dark and intense.

"Have you forgotten Phillips yet?"

"Who?"

Forgetting David wasn't difficult when she was in Ram's arms. She gazed up at him. His eyebrows were utterly black, steeply arched and elegant, but his face was a study of stark, hungry planes and passion-glazed eyes. He was even more compelling than she recalled.

Grinning, he caressed her breasts with strong, clever fingers that sent a frisson of excitement scorching through her veins, igniting a fire in her loins. Then he replaced his fingers with his mouth, sucking and licking her nipples into hard nubs. A moan flowed from her lips. She had almost forgotten how exciting passion could be; what had made her think she could live without it? Ram was quickly proving how wrong she had been to deny herself.

She nearly burst into flame when he shifted, parted her legs with the breadth of his shoulders and kissed a trail of fire to the sensitive place between her thighs. The burning grew hotter, unbearably so when he opened her with his fingers and teased the throbbing nub of her womanhood. Without mercy he slashed his tongue up and down her tender slit. Desperation sent her arching against his mouth, her fingers tangling in his hair to bring him closer. Then suddenly he was gone. Disappointment clawed at her as he moved slowly up her body.

"No! Don't stop!"

She realized she was begging, but she couldn't help herself. Then he lowered himself atop her, until every part of him touched every part of her, and she knew he wasn't going to abandon her.

"Don't worry, I won't leave you. I want to be inside you when you find release." He nudged her legs apart and settled between them. "Take me in your hand."

She hesitated but a moment before curling her fingers around his burgeoning sex. Caressing it with trembling fingers, she felt it stir and grow and harden. She had forgotten a great deal about Ram during the years but not his strength, nor his virility, nor his sexual prowess.

"Put me inside you."

She trembled, suddenly afraid of the way she felt . . . afraid and uncertain of the power he exerted over her, the strong feelings he evoked. How foolish of her to believe that making love with Ram meant nothing except momentary gratification and a means to learn the truth about his reappearance in her life.

"Phoebe," Ram rasped. "Put me inside you now."

When Phoebe hesitated, Ram drew back and thrust himself inside her, sliding full and deep into the hot, velvet-smooth crevice between her thighs. Phoebe's lips parted, but no sound emerged. Ram could tell by her expression that he had hurt her. She was tight, too tight. If he didn't know better, he could almost believe there had been no lovers after him, but even Fielding had known that Phillips was her lover.

Then all thought ceased as his hands swept down to catch her buttocks in his hands, lifting her, binding her to him in the most elemental way.

Phoebe was shocked at the pain of Ram's entry. Since she wasn't a virgin, she hadn't expected discomfort. Then her body gave way, closing tight around his rigid flesh as he buried himself to the hilt.

"Look at me, Phoebe."

Ram's ragged whisper compelled compliance, and she gazed into his face. His features were twisted into a grimace of tightly leashed restraint. The cords of his neck protruded, and his eyes were all aglitter as he thrust and withdrew, the pounding of his hips quickening to match the rhythm of her racing heartbeat. A flame caught inside her. She felt utterly possessed. Consumed. Engulfed in a raging inferno. Drowning in sensation, she clutched his shoulders and arched her back . . . seeking . . . wanting . . .

"Come with me, Phoebe."

A shudder ripped through him. The feel of her fingers digging into him, her in-drawn breath at each plunge of his body into her drove him harder, faster, deeper. A storm was building inside him, but he held it in check, waiting for Phoebe to join the maelstrom. When he heard her cry out and felt her contract around him, he unleashed the full force of his passion, penetrating her again and again until he exploded, spewing his seed hotly into her womb.

Surrounded by the arousing scent of spent sex, Ram rested his forehead against Phoebe's until he could summon the energy to move. The quick, harsh intake of his breath punctured the silence as he rolled away and settled down beside her. When he turned her toward him, he was pleased at how easily she snuggled into his arms.

He caressed her cheek. "That was . . . I'd almost forgotten." A troubled pause ensued. "You're so quiet. Are you all right?"

Her eyes were closed; a dreamy expression softened her face. "Hmmm?"

"Phoebe, can you hear me? Tell me what you're feeling?"

When she opened her eyes, Ram was surprised to see the shimmer of unshed tears. "I'm frightened," she whispered.

"Of me?"

"You're part of it."

Suddenly Ram realized it was time to broach the

subject he'd been skirting for days. "Tell me about the amulet, Phoebe. Did your father steal it?"

The sharp intake of her breath told Ram that he had gone too far too fast, but it was too late to retreat. He could only go forward now.

Her questions came fast and furious. "What do you know about the amulet? Who are you working for? Are you one of my enemies? I'm aware that your reason for seducing me had little to do with your desire for me."

"Don't delude yourself, Phoebe. I *did* want you. I still do, but like everything else, our needs and desires come with a price. Mine is the truth, so you may as well tell me what I want to know."

"Who are you working for?"

"The government. Why didn't you tell the Foreign Office your father had been abducted when you were questioned?"

"I was warned not to. Do you truly believe I would jeopardize my father's life?"

His expression implacable, Ram said, "You've given me no reason to trust you."

Phoebe reared up on her elbows. "How dare you insinuate I'm untrustworthy! You're the one who promised love and fidelity. I was a fool to believe you would honor those vows."

"This isn't about us, Phoebe. This is about diplomatic relations between England and Egypt. The Egyptian government wants the amulet returned. If it's not, the incident is likely to become an embarrassment to the Crown."

Phoebe sat up, pulling the sheet around her to cover her nakedness. Unconcerned about his nudity, Ram scooted up, resting his back against the headboard. "Tell me everything, Phoebe."

Eyes narrowed, Phoebe considered Ram's request. Just as she had suspected, getting information about the amulet had been his sole reason for seducing her. She recalled now that he had worked for the Foreign Office during the war, but when she'd met him he had already left the service.

"David said we shouldn't involve anyone else in our problems if I valued Father's life. We've been given specific orders to tell no one."

"I see," Ram mused. "I assume Phillips knows everything."

"Of course. He's been my rock and my salvation. I don't know what I would have done without him."

Ram's brows shot upward. "Really." His dark gaze swept over her with penetrating intensity. "*Do you have the amulet?*"

Phoebe's cheeks reddened with anger. "Damn you! Don't you think I'd give the amulet to my father's abductors if I had it? I would never endanger Father's life for a mere bauble. Furthermore, I refuse to believe Father stole it."

Phoebe was shocked when Ram said, "I believe you, and I want to help. Start from the beginning and tell me everything."

Phoebe had no choice but to comply. She knew David would be livid when he learned she'd told Ram, but his disapproval no longer mattered. Ram might not be faithful, but she knew she could trust in his loyalty to his country.

"Father, David and I were together inside the tomb when we opened the coffin. We knew immediately we had discovered something of importance when we saw the starburst amulet around the neck of the mummy. The ruby at its center was flawless and as large as a bird's egg."

"Did anyone else see it?"

"There were several Egyptian workers with us at

the time. Father knew from the beginning the amulet belonged to the Egyptian government and had no designs upon it. I know for a fact it wasn't among the artifacts I packed to take back to England with me. I assumed that either Father or David saw it turned over to the correct authority."

"Why did you leave Egypt before your father and Phillips?"

"Father wanted me to return with the bulk of the artifacts and rent a house in London in preparation for his return," Phoebe explained. "I was to have the artifacts catalogued and ready to donate to the Museum of Egyptology when he arrived."

"And you have no idea who abducted your father?"

Phoebe wrung her hands. "Don't you think I'd do something about it if I did? I was stunned when government agents appeared on my doorstep to question me about Father and the amulet. They think Father stole it and intends to sell it to a private collector. What nonsense! Father would never do such a thing."

"You should have told me this days ago. It would have saved us both a lot of trouble."

Phoebe bristled. "You should have told me what you were up to. Had you been truthful about what you wanted from me, you could have skipped this seduction."

Ram sent her a veiled look. "Now that explanations are out of the way, tell me why you walked out on me four years ago."

"Why revisit old hurts?" Phoebe said. "We've both got the information we sought. You can report to your superiors that my father doesn't have the amulet, and I can return to the business of finding his abductors."

She started to rise. Ram reached for her. "It's not that simple. You're treading on dangerous ground, Phoebe. You have no idea the peril you're in. Whoever wants that amulet will stop at nothing to get it."

"I'm aware of that, but what choice do I have? If neither the Egyptian government nor my father has the amulet, then who does?"

"What about Phillips?"

"David? Absolutely not! He wants to see Father's name cleared as badly as I do. His help during this trying time has been invaluable. I couldn't have managed without him. We're working together to find Father."

"With little success," Ram said dryly. "Do you love Phillips?"

"He's been a great comfort to me," she said, avoiding a direct answer.

Ram rolled his eyes. "I'll bet, but that's not what I asked. Do you love him? You must have deep feelings for him if you've let him bed you."

"Think what you want about David and me. You will anyway. I could have had a dozen lovers after we parted."

"I was the first," Ram reminded her.

And the last, Phoebe thought with silent indignation. "Why are we even discussing this?"

"Damned if I know. Perhaps my male ego is still reeling at your callous disregard for my feelings. Maybe I need a reason for being abandoned without an explanation."

Phoebe gave a bitter laugh. "That's ludicrous coming from an unprincipled rake who changes women as often as he does his shirts. Shouldn't you leave? It's a long walk back to your townhouse."

"I'm not leaving, Phoebe. After the break-in tonight and the attacks upon your person, leaving you alone without protection is out of the question." He pulled her down beside him and snuggled her against him. "Get some rest. I'm a light sleeper. I'll hear if someone tries to break in again."

"Really, Ram, this isn't necessary."

"It is to me."

Phoebe had to admit she did feel safe with him. Though she distrusted him with her heart, she felt she could rely on him to protect her. He seemed to exude power and confidence. Relaxing against him, she closed her eyes and waited for sleep to claim her.

Ram had no intention of sleeping. He had too much to think about. Vital pieces of information were lacking, confusing the issue of Sir Thompson's abduction. He'd been aware from the moment they'd found the front door unlocked that there hadn't been a break-in in the true sense of the word. The door had either been left open deliberately or accidentally . . . or someone other than Phoebe had a key.

It was possible that Mrs. Crowley had forgotten to lock the door, but he thought it highly unlikely. Then there was Phillips. Had Phoebe given a key to her lover? Could Phillips have taken the amulet? Ram shook his head. That didn't make sense. If Phillips had the amulet, why had Sir Thompson been abducted? Phillips would have no reason to terrorize Phoebe and demand the amulet if he had it in his possession. The mystery deepened. If neither Phoebe nor her father had the amulet, then who did?

Ram didn't realize he was fidgeting until Phoebe stirred and said, "Can't you sleep? Perhaps you'd be more comfortable in Father's room."

"I have a great deal to think about."

"I can't sleep either. There's too much on my mind. I haven't had a good night's sleep since Father disappeared."

"As long as we're both awake . . ."

While his mind counseled constraint, his body responded eagerly as his arms tightened around her. Her skin was warm and her body fragrant with the highly arousing scents of woman and sex. Not even a saint could resist such a seductive combination, and Ram was no saint.

He'd thought of Phoebe often during the past four years, mostly with enmity, but it was difficult to maintain that same degree of hatred while she was curled trustingly in his arms. He wanted to make love to her again. He wanted to kiss her and touch her and put himself inside her. When his assignment ended and he walked away from her, he wanted her to remember him above all the other men in her life.

"I want to make love to you again, Phoebe. Do you have any objections?"

"Would it matter?"

"There's nothing wrong in satisfying our needs. You're a grown woman who obviously knows her own mind. You're beautiful and desirable and in my arms. Denying our passions would be dishonest."

"As long as you know that making love with you tonight means nothing to me," Phoebe said.

"At least we're in agreement. We're merely two people taking pleasure in one another."

Then she was caught fast in his embrace, their lips fused in a hot, devouring kiss that drained from her what little resistance remained. His hands squeezed her breasts together so that her nipples thrust upward, pink and erect, and she heard a low moan rise up from his throat. Then his mouth closed over one stiffening peak, suckling her hard and long before moving on to the second. She felt the tugging all the way to her throbbing core.

Then he shifted and rose over her. Flexing his hips, he thrust deep and hard. With his loins pounding against her and his tongue plundering her mouth, she reached for paradise.

They found it together.

Chapter Six

Phoebe was still sleeping when Ram left her bed following a sleepless night. Dawn was but moments away and he didn't want Mrs. Crowley to find him with Phoebe when she returned. Ram washed and dressed and went downstairs to the kitchen, wishing he had a razor to shave his bristly chin. He was startled to find that the housekeeper had arrived early and was bustling about in the kitchen.

He tried to back out of the room and leave quietly, but Mrs. Crowley turned and saw him. Her mouth rounded and her eyes nearly left their sockets. Several minutes passed before she could speak.

"Lord Braxton! What are you doing here? 'Tis unseemly that you should be here so early in the morning." Her hand flew to her chest. "Never say you spent the night! Where is Miss Phoebe?"

Thinking fast, Ram said, "This isn't what it seems. When I brought Phoebe home from the

Connie Mason

opera last night, we found the front door open and the upstairs rooms in disarray. I couldn't in good conscience leave her alone."

Mrs. Crowley gasped. "You found the door open? I distinctly remember locking it when I left. You don't think I—"

"Not at all, Mrs. Crowley. Now you understand why I didn't feel comfortable leaving Phoebe alone."

"I shouldn't have left the house unprotected," the housekeeper lamented. "Since Miss Phoebe had gone out for the night, I thought it a good time to visit my daughter. The poor lass is having a difficult time with her pregnancy."

"Does anyone else have a key to the house?" Ram asked.

"There's only one other key. It's hanging right here beside the . . . good Lord, it's gone!"

"Are you sure you haven't misplaced it?"

"It was here the last time I looked, milord."

"When was that?"

She wrung her hands. "I . . . can't say. I just assumed it was there like always."

"Don't blame yourself, Mrs. Crowley. It's not your fault it's missing. If we keep this between you and me and Phoebe, no one will ever know an impropriety exists."

"Oh, dear," the housekeeper fretted. "Poor Miss Phoebe. Strange things are happening. I'm so worried about her." She clucked her tongue. "All these break-ins are bewildering. What could they want? Surely not those old vases and statues. Where is Miss Phoebe's father when she needs him?"

"I'm going to ask another favor of you, Mrs. Crowley," Ram said. "I'm moving Phoebe to my townhouse, and I want you to come with us."

"Is that wise, milord? There's bound to be talk. Mr. Phillips isn't going to like it. I was under the impression he had offered for her."

Ram hesitated, then said, "Phillips has no say in what Phoebe does or doesn't do. For your information, Phoebe and I are—"

"Lord Braxton!"

Phoebe stood in the doorway, her eyes wide with horror. "Don't say anything you're going to regret later."

Ram sent her an exasperated look. "Mrs. Crowley deserves the truth."

"The truth is that you stayed with me because I needed protection. It was very gallant of you, and I thank you."

"Don't worry, dearie," Mrs. Crowley said. "I won't say a word."

"Mrs. Crowley, would you please go upstairs and pack Phoebe's belongings?"

"Where am I going?" Phoebe asked as the housekeeper disappeared through the door.

"You and Mrs. Crowley are moving to my townhouse. You're not safe here."

"What? Absolutely not!"

"You have no choice in the matter, Phoebe."

"What about the artifacts? Father spent years collecting them and obtaining permission to ship them to England. I can't run off and leave them unprotected."

"Didn't you say they were to go to the Museum of Egyptology?"

"Of course, but—"

"Then that's where they shall go. I'll fetch some men, and you can oversee the packing yourself. Once the artifacts are seen to, you'll come with me."

Phoebe's spine stiffened. "I'm not going anywhere. David will be scandalized if I move into your home."

"I don't see Phillips doing anything to protect you," Ram argued. "I mean it, Phoebe. You're coming with me whether you like it or not. I'll place Mrs. Crowley on my payroll if she chooses to come along. If not, she'll be given a generous severance and references."

"You can't tell me what to do."

"I can and you know it. Wilson should have returned with my coach by now, so I'll take my leave."

Phoebe looked so unnerved, Ram had to harden his heart against her. The attraction that had first drawn them together and the fire she ignited in him would blaze up anew if he wasn't careful.

Seething with anger, Phoebe stormed up to her room after Ram left. He couldn't tell her what to do, could he? What was he going to tell people when they learned he had installed her in his home? Certainly not the truth. They might think she was his mistress, except mistresses were usually kept in separate houses purchased by their lovers. What was she going to tell David?

Damn Braxton for interfering in my life.

Mrs. Crowley looked up from her packing when Phoebe entered the room. "Shall I pack everything, dearie?"

"This is ridiculous, Mrs. Crowley. Lord Braxton has no right to tell me what to do."

"I think he means well," the housekeeper offered. "What's been happening in this house is frightening. You should summon your father immediately. I'm sure he wouldn't want you to be alone."

"Father is . . . ill," she improvised, "and recuperating in the country. I don't want to worry him."

"I'm to accompany you to Lord Braxton's home. Is that what you wish also?"

"If I do go, and I'm not saying I will, I would be pleased to have you with me. I'm sure Lord Braxton will find a place for you in his household."

"I wouldn't dream of letting you go alone, dearie. Someone has to look out for you. Besides, finding new employment won't be easy for someone my age. As long as I'm employed, I won't become a burden to my daughter and her husband."

Ram returned two hours later, accompanied by three men with a cart, who helped Phoebe pack the artifacts in the cartons she had stored in a shed behind the house. Once the cartons were packed, they were loaded in the cart and taken to the Museum of Egyptology for display.

Phoebe watched the cart leave with mixed feelings, but she knew it was the most practical solution for her problem. Several precious artifacts had been damaged during the break-ins, and she feared more of them would be destroyed if they were left in the house.

"I hired Bow Street Runners to keep an eye on things here," Ram said. "The house has been ransacked twice; I don't believe there is anything left that's worth stealing, but I know you'd feel better if someone was watching the place. Are you ready to leave?"

Phoebe's chin firmed. "I'm not going with you, Ram. We can't return to the past, and I don't see a future for us. You live the life you've always wanted, and I've learned to accept that I was meant to be alone."

Neither Ram nor Phoebe seemed to realize they

were standing on the doorstep arguing in public. "Mrs. Crowley has agreed to accompany us," Ram said, ignoring her outburst.

The scattering of loose stones alerted them to another presence. "Where are you going, Phoebe? What's *he* doing here?"

Ram cursed beneath his breath as Phoebe greeted David Phillips with a smile. "It's a long story, David."

"I'm willing to listen," David said, glaring at Ram.

"The house was ransacked last night while Lord Braxton and I attended the opera."

"You went to the opera with Braxton? Really, Phoebe, where are your brains?"

"Where they belong," Ram growled. "I didn't see you here when she needed you. I'm placing Phoebe under my protection."

"Like hell! You have no right. Phoebe and I are as good as engaged. I'd move in with her myself if I thought it wouldn't damage her reputation."

"Stop arguing!" Phoebe shouted. "Both of you go away and leave me alone."

"Not yet," Phillips retorted. "I want to know what Braxton is doing here after I expressly forbade you to see him."

"I spent the night with Phoebe," Ram replied without batting an eyelash.

A moan of dismay escaped from Phoebe's throat. She wanted to crawl into the woodwork. "Ram, how could you?"

Phillips looked angry enough to spit nails. "My God, Phoebe, are you mad? Do you enjoy being used? Were I a swordsman of Braxton's equal, I would challenge him."

"I'm fairly good at fisticuffs," Ram drawled. "I'd be happy to take you on."

"Stop acting like children!" Phoebe ordered. "This is preposterous. I'm old enough to know my own mind. Go away, Lord Braxton. And you, too, David. I've had my fill of both of you."

"You need me, Phoebe. So does your father," David pointed out. "Don't become a victim of Braxton's lies. He devours innocent women like you."

"Leave off, David. I know what Lord Braxton is like. If you'll both excuse me, I have things to do."

Mrs. Crowley appeared at Phoebe's elbow. "Your bags are packed, Miss Phoebe."

"Please unpack them, Mrs. Crowley," Phoebe replied. "I'm not going anywhere."

"Phoebe," Ram growled.

Mrs. Crowley retreated into the house. "I'll be in the kitchen while you decide."

"The artifacts are gone, so I see no reason to leave my home," Phoebe said after the housekeeper left.

"The artifacts are gone?" Phillips gasped. "What happened to them?"

"Lord Braxton arranged for them to be taken to the Museum of Egyptology," Phoebe explained.

"I suppose that makes sense," Phillips admitted. "But where, pray tell, are *you* going?"

"Phoebe and Mrs. Crowley will be residing at my townhouse for the time being," Ram said. "Phoebe needs more protection than you're providing."

"I won't allow it!" Phillips blasted. "The scoundrel is taking advantage of your vulnerable state, Phoebe. Once he's finished with you, he'll discard you. Surely you don't believe that garbage about protecting you, do you?"

Phoebe had had more than enough of this bickering. She'd never had any intention of removing herself to Ram's house. She was neither fragile nor without courage. Resolve stiffened her spine. Despite Ram's determination, she was rigidly opposed to letting him control her life. As for David, his jealousy was intolerable. She'd never encouraged his suit, no matter how often he'd asked her to marry him.

Without a word to either man, she spun on her heel and entered the house, slamming and locking the door behind her. Several moments passed before either of the two combatants got over the shock of Phoebe's abrupt departure.

"Phoebe! Open up," Ram said, pounding on the door. "You're only postponing the inevitable."

Phoebe chose not to answer.

"I'll come back later," David called out after Ram failed to raise a reply, "when you're in a more receptive mood. I have news about . . . well, you know. Keep your doors locked at all times and don't let Braxton get near you. He's a predator."

Peeking out the window, Phoebe was pleased to see David mount his horse and ride off. That left only Ram to deal with, and if she ignored him, perhaps he would go away.

"I'm not going away," Ram called through the door, dashing Phoebe's hopes. "This ruckus is beginning to draw attention. How much do you want the neighbors to know about your business?"

Damning Ram for his persistence, Phoebe unlocked the door, swung it open and grasped his lapels, propelling him inside. "Are you crazy? I don't need this kind of notoriety. You got what you wanted last night. Why are you still here?"

"You know why. It's not over between us. It's not just about sex, Phoebe, and you know it. My original plan was to seduce you, get the information I needed from you and abandon you like you did me."

"You didn't seduce me, Ram," Phoebe retorted hotly. "I seduced you. I needed to know what you were after, and now that I know, we can part without regrets."

Ram roared with laughter. "*You* seduced *me*? What rubbish. I've been trying to seduce you since the day I turned up at your door. That was no accident, you know. I was simply following orders. Had I a choice, I would have avoided you like the plague."

His words hurt more than she was willing to admit. But she couldn't blame Ram for hating her.

"That's my point exactly," Phoebe pointed out. "You have the information you needed, so there is no reason for us to continue a relationship neither of us want."

"The amulet is still missing. Have you forgotten your father? You are no closer to finding him than you were a month ago. You need my help. I'm in direct contact with the Foreign Office. They'll put all their resources to work to find your father if you cooperate."

Phoebe shrugged. "Why? Father doesn't have the amulet."

"Maybe not, but he might have information the Crown needs."

Phoebe considered his words before coming to a decision. "I can't. If Father's abductors learn I've gone to the authorities, they'll kill him."

Ram thrust his fingers through his hair in a gesture of impatience. "Very well, have it your way. You and I will work together in secret to find your father. There are conditions, however. You're not

Connie Mason

to confide in Phillips and you'll let me know when you receive another communication from the abductors. And you're not to go out alone."

"Your first two conditions are reasonable, but the last one is absurd. I refuse to become a prisoner in my own home."

"Then you leave me no alternative."

Phoebe was about to ask what he meant when Mrs. Crowley rushed into the foyer, followed by a thin young man with a wild thatch of black hair sticking out from beneath a knit cap.

"Miss Phoebe, something terrible has happened," Mrs. Crowley wailed. "This is Dan, my daughter's husband. Molly is having pains, and the midwife fears she's losing the baby. It's their first, and poor Dan is beside himself. I hate to leave you in a lurch, but my Molly needs me."

"You must go to her," Phoebe said. "Stay as long as necessary. I'll keep your position open for you."

Mrs. Crowley brought Phoebe's hands to her lips. "Thank you, thank you. You don't know how much that means to me."

"If you have need of anything, anything at all, please feel free to contact me at my townhouse on Park Lane. Number twenty-four," Ram said. He pulled a gold crown from his pocket and pressed it into the housekeeper's palm. "This should help until you can return to work."

"Oh, my lord! Indeed it will. Dan has been out of work since Lord Amherst inherited his father's title and sold off the old earl's stables to raise money for the estate. Dan was head groom."

Ram stared intently at the young man and liked what he saw. "If you're interested in removing your family to the country, Dan, I can use another groom

110

at my country estate. A small cottage goes with the post."

Dan's haggard face lit up. "Molly loves the country, milord. Moving might be a hardship right now, but I'd be happy to accept the post if it's still open once Molly is on her feet again."

"I'll make sure it's kept open for you," Ram said. "Let me know when you're ready to take up your duties."

Dan doffed his hat; then he and Mrs. Crowley took their leave. Her eyes wide with disbelief, Phoebe stared at Ram. "You surprise me. I didn't think you had a heart."

"I don't. I gave my heart to you and you destroyed it. But that's beside the point. Mrs. Crowley is gone and you're alone now. Remaining in this house is no longer possible."

He grasped her arm and urged her toward the door. "Wilson will fetch your bags."

Phoebe dug in her heels. "Wait, Ram! There has to be another solution. I thought you were beginning to see things my way."

"That was before Mrs. Crowley left."

Patience was not one of Ram's better qualities and he was becoming extremely short-tempered. "Your stubbornness is growing tiresome. No matter what you think, I'm still responsible for you and will do my utmost to protect you."

A squawk of surprise left Phoebe's lips as Ram swung her up into his arms. "Put me down. What are you doing?"

"Taking matters into my own hands. You can't be trusted to stay out of trouble."

Flinging open the door, he carried her to his coach and tumbled her inside as a stunned Wilson looked on.

"Please fetch Miss Thompson's bags and place them in the boot," Ram instructed the coachman. "You'll find them in the foyer."

"You always were an overbearing oaf," Phoebe muttered. "Very well, I acquiesce under protest. I have a condition of my own, however. There will be no intimacy while I'm under your roof."

Ram grinned. "Are you sure that's what you want?"

"Very sure." She sent him an exasperated look. "How do you intend to explain my presence in your home? Am I to be your ward? Or a long-lost relative? Shall you introduce me as your mistress?"

Ram sent her a long, thoughtful look. "Perhaps it's time for the truth."

In a sparsely furnished cottage located in a small village a short distance from London, an elderly man lay on a cot, shivering and feverish. His hands shook as he pulled the worn blanket up to his neck and stared at the figure looming over him.

"You again. What do you want?" he asked weakly. "Why are you terrorizing me?"

"You know what I want, Thompson," the man said in a grating voice. "Where is it? A search of your house turned up nothing. Why did you lie to me? My employer is growing impatient."

"I'm ill with malaria. I don't remember what I said. I can't think straight. What do you want from me? Let me go. My daughter needs me."

The man laughed. "Your daughter is being looked after."

Sir Andrew Thompson attempted to sit up. "What have you done to Phoebe?"

The man pushed him down with the heel of his hand. "Nothing . . . yet. Shall we discuss the amulet? Does your daughter know where you've hidden it?"

Thompson was shaking so hard, his teeth were rattling. "The amulet," he repeated. "I . . . I don't recall. My head hurts and I can't think."

"Damn you! I don't get paid unless I get answers from you."

"I need . . . medicine. Please help me." His voice drifted off as unconsciousness claimed him.

A second man entered the room and stared down at Thompson's still form. "Did he say anything, Watts?"

"Nothing that makes sense. He says he's sick and needs medicine."

"He's not getting anything until he talks. Once the amulet is in my possession and I'm on my way across the channel, you can release him. But he's not leaving this room until he tells me what I want to know. Maybe we need to exert a little more pressure. I'll think about it and get back to you in a day or two."

Watts saw his employer to the door, then turned back to his charge. "You're in for it now, old man," he muttered. "I'm glad I'm not in your place."

Braxton's butler opened the door and stood back as Ram swept Phoebe into an elegant foyer that spoke eloquently of his wealth.

"Porter, Miss Thompson will be staying with us for an undetermined length of time. Wilson is bringing in her bags. Direct them to the suite adjoining mine and see that it is made ready for her. And ask cook to prepare tea and serve it in the study."

"Certainly, milord," Porter said without batting an eye. "Welcome, Miss Thompson."

"That was rather awkward," Phoebe said as Ram steered her into the study. "What must your servants think?"

"They're not paid to think," Ram said with typical male arrogance.

"Servants gossip. Nothing gets past them. Even those loyal to their employers talk among themselves. How many times have you brought a woman into your home to spend more than an occasional night?"

"Never," Ram said indignantly. He stroked his chin, his expression thoughtful. "You're forcing my hand, Phoebe."

A frisson of fear slid down Phoebe's spine. "What do you mean?"

"Ah, here's Porter with our tea. Porter, I made a mistake. I should have introduced Miss Thompson as my wife, Lady Braxton."

Porter was so startled, the cup rattled in his hand, spilling tea in the saucer, something that would never have happened under normal circumstances.

"Your wife, milord? You're married? When did you . . ." He caught himself before blurting out something he might regret later and bowed formally. "May I be the first to offer congratulations?"

"You may indeed. Thank you, Porter, you may go now. I'll introduce Lady Braxton to the rest of the staff later."

"How dare you!" Phoebe exclaimed. "You've really done it this time. What did you hope to gain by introducing me as your wife?"

"A measure of safety for you. The people who abducted your father aren't playing games, Phoebe. They've gone to great lengths to get the amulet."

"I fear your words will come back to haunt you," Phoebe warned.

"Is someone being haunted?" a deep male voice asked from the doorway. "Am I intruding? Porter let me in. He seemed rather out of sorts."

"Westmore! Come in and join us," Ram invited.

Luc sent Phoebe a fetching smile. If he thought it strange to find Phoebe visiting a bachelor's home without a chaperone, he was too polite to mention it. "Miss Thompson, how nice to see you again. Are you sure I'm not intruding?"

"Not at all," Ram assured him. "In fact, your timing couldn't be better. As my best friend, you should be the first to be properly introduced to Phoebe."

"Ram, don't do this," Phoebe pleaded.

"Where is your mind, Braxton? Miss Thompson and I have already met."

"I believe you met *Miss Thompson*," Ram said. "Now I'd like to introduce you to my wife, Lady Braxton."

Luc's mouth dropped open. "Your . . . wife?" He guffawed loudly. "You're pulling my leg. You had me going there for a moment. No one knows better than I how religiously you've avoided the parson's mousetrap."

"It's the truth, Westmore."

As if his legs refused to hold him, Luc flopped into a chair. "When were you married? You never mentioned a word about it to me." He peered closely at Phoebe, then directed a disapproving frown at Ram. "Good God! I assume Miss Thompson . . . er . . . Lady Braxton is increasing. How unlike you to despoil an innocent."

Gripping the arms of the chair, Phoebe shot venomous daggers at Ram. "I cannot bear this. Please

115

excuse me." Drawing her dignity about her like a cloak, she rose and made a hasty exit.

"Porter will show you to your rooms," Ram called after her.

A curt nod of her head was Phoebe's only acknowledgment that she had heard Ram.

"What the hell is going on?" Luc demanded. "I can't believe you'd marry a woman you scarcely know. Besides, she's a commoner."

"I've known Phoebe a long time—several years, in fact."

"Why haven't you mentioned her before? Why have I never seen you together?"

"As I explained before, Phoebe and her father have been out of the country. They just recently returned."

"Am I to believe you fell desperately in love, swept Phoebe off her feet and married her within a period of a few weeks? Why not just make her your mistress? I can't believe you're following in Bathurst's footsteps. Did you learn nothing from his downfall?"

"I may as well tell you the truth," Ram said on a sigh. "Phoebe and I were married four years ago, long before I met you."

"That's the most ridiculous thing I've ever heard," Luc retorted. "Let me get this straight. You married Phoebe four years ago and she's been out of the country until just recently. What kind of marriage is that, and why the secrecy?" His eyes narrowed. "You don't look or act like a couple in love. Something strange is going on here."

"Stranger than you think," Ram allowed. "Phoebe and I are indeed husband and wife. Humiliating as it is to admit, she left me the morning after our wedding night."

"And you remained married to her? Desertion is grounds for annulment."

Ram shrugged. "I saw no need, since I never intended to take another wife."

"What if Phoebe wanted another husband?"

"I really didn't care. She'd be the one breaking the law, not I. I've felt nothing but resentment for Phoebe since the day she left me to join her father in Egypt."

"This is bizarre," Luc maintained. "I'm surprised you're taking up with her again after such a bitter parting. You should have refused to accept the assignment with the Foreign Office."

"I thought about it, but I had an agenda of my own."

"Never say your personal objective is an act of vengeance. Not like you at all, old boy."

"That's precisely what I intended, but matters have taken an unusual turn. Fielding suspects Phoebe and her father of stealing a valuable amulet the Egyptian government wants returned. Questioning Phoebe got them nowhere, and her father has mysteriously disappeared. I was supposed to seduce Phoebe to gain the information Fielding wants. You can't imagine how shocked I was when I was asked to seduce my own wife."

"Estranged wife," Luc reminded him. "I imagine Phoebe's shock was nearly as great as yours, especially if you parted on less than friendly terms."

"Just so. But the game changed when an attempt was made on Phoebe's life and her house was broken into. No matter how much I resented her for what she did to me, she is still my wife and in need of my protection."

Luc grinned. "You've really made a cake of yourself, haven't you? I can't wait to see how it all turns out. Have you located Phoebe's father yet?"

"He's still missing. His abductors are threatening to kill him if Phoebe doesn't give them the amulet."

"Does she have it?"

"I'm convinced she doesn't. It's missing along with Phoebe's father."

"What a muddle. Can I help?"

"Not now. I'll let you know. My first priority is keeping Phoebe safe and finding Sir Thompson, if he's still alive."

Luc sent Ram an assessing glance. "How deeply are you involved with Phoebe? What happens when this is over and done with?"

"Phoebe and I will go our own ways," Ram said without hesitation. "It's what we both want. But introducing her to society as my wife is the only way to protect her reputation as well as her person. We may not like each other, but bringing her into my home will assure her safety."

"If you say so," Luc said, looking dubious. He surged to his feet. "I have to go. Keep me informed."

He paused in the doorway. "By the way, have you seduced Phoebe yet?"

Ram sent him an enigmatic smile. "That, my friend, is none of your business."

Chapter Seven

Angry steps took Phoebe from one end of the spacious room to the other. Ram was making her life even more difficult than it had been. The final insult had come when Ram claimed her as his wife. Had she wanted to be his wife, she would have remained with him four years ago. What was he thinking? What was he feeling? He kept his emotions too carefully guarded for her to guess.

Phoebe realized too late that she shouldn't have let Ram make love to her. She'd made a muddle of things, as usual. Even more disturbing, she'd *wanted* Ram to make love to her. Why? To prove that Ram held no sway over her emotions? If so, the experiment had failed miserably.

Phoebe sensed Ram's presence before she saw him. He cleared his throat, and she turned toward the sound. He was standing in the doorway separating their rooms, leaning against the doorjamb, arms and legs crossed in a display of male arrogance that set her teeth on edge.

"I didn't hear you knock," she said coolly.

"Why should I? I'm your husband; it's not unusual for a husband to enter his wife's rooms unannounced."

His voice sounded low, husky, intimate, as though he'd just whispered something deliciously sensual. It conjured up memories of sweat-soaked bodies, kisses, caresses and the smell of sex.

She shook those forbidden images from her head and fought for sanity. "Your misguided need to protect me has caused havoc in both our lives. What happens now, Ram? Will you introduce your commoner wife to society? Or will you continue your wicked ways and pretend I don't exist?"

"Had I wished you didn't exist, I wouldn't have claimed you. There may be a bit of scandal associated with our 'sudden' marriage, but the gossip will pass like everything else. I'm hoping that whoever is threatening you will cease once it's clear that I am your husband and protector. I sent an announcement of our marriage off to the *Times*. Tomorrow morning all London will know that the Earl of Braxton has taken a wife."

Ram's words sent shock waves racing through Phoebe. "How is that going to help my father? You may have just written his death warrant."

"I promised to return your father to you unharmed, and so I shall."

"How? Talk is cheap," Phoebe scoffed. "David has been looking for Father without success since he disappeared. How do you expect to succeed when he could not?"

"Have you no faith in me?"

"None whatsoever," Phoebe declared. "You can't be trusted, Lord Braxton."

Propelling himself from the doorway, Ram moved into the room, reminding Phoebe of a wolf stalking a rabbit. She stood her ground, refusing to be intimidated, if that was his purpose.

"You have no choice, Phoebe. I'm your only hope of finding your father. Your lack of faith in me is unjustified."

"Say you're successful and find my father. What happens then? Will you return to your former life and let me return to mine?"

A frown darkened Ram's brow. "Of course— that's what you want, isn't it? I must have been mad with lust all those years ago when I acquiesced to your demand that we wed before consummating our relationship. Our brief marriage turned me against matrimony forever. I'm older and wiser now, and no fonder of marriage than I was when we wed. Finding willing women has never been a problem for me."

Ram found that telling half-truths was far easier than admitting how badly Phoebe's leaving him had hurt. He'd been so deeply in love with her he had married her with the intention of remaining faithful. He still had no idea what had made her run away, but he was willing to bet David Phillips was behind it. After Phoebe left him, he had blazed a carnal swath through the *ton*, enjoying the sexual favors of women the complete opposite of his virginal wife. He had broken hearts, strained marriages and corrupted countless women without a care for their feelings, and would continue to do so long after he and Phoebe parted.

Over the years his bitterness and disillusionment had grown, until he began to look upon women as warm bodies capable of giving pleasure and little else. He was a man of vast experience, possessed of strong sexual desires, and he never declined what was offered him. But whenever he became too enthusiastic about a woman, he had only to remember Phoebe to return to sanity.

Faithless Phoebe. Had she loved him, she would have discussed her doubts and fears with him and given him a chance to explain. Running off was the coward's way, and he'd expected better from her.

"I know all about your women, my lord," Phoebe sniffed. "Once my father is found, I won't hamper your licentious lifestyle. After all, two nights together hardly constitute a marriage. You should get that annulment you failed to obtain four years ago. We've never actually lived as husband and wife."

"We had a wedding night," Ram reminded. "And we had last night. What if my seed is already growing inside you?"

"Have no fear, Braxton. In the unlikely event I am increasing, I absolve you of all responsibility. I have no expectations where you're concerned, Braxton. You need never acknowledge our child should there be one."

Instead of easing Ram's mind, Phoebe's words created a seething anger inside him. What made her think he wouldn't acknowledge a child of their union? Did she think him so debauched that he'd deny his own blood?

He reached Phoebe in two long strides. Grasping her shoulders, he gave her an ungentle shake. "No child of mine will be illegitimate or raised in obscurity. I still have possession of our marriage papers, and if you try to disappear with a child of mine, I'll find you and take our child from you."

"Stop it, Ram! Why are we even discussing this?

There's never going to be a child, because we will never make love again."

His green eyes became hooded; a sensual smile stretched his lips. "Are you sure? Making love is what married people do. While you're in my home, you will abide by my rules."

What in blazes is wrong with me? Ram chided himself. Phoebe wanted nothing to do with him; why couldn't he accept that? *Because you want more than Phoebe is willing to give,* a voice inside him whispered. Making love to her last night had awakened a dormant devil in him. Once was not enough. Phoebe hadn't been reluctant to make love last night; why should she complain about doing it again . . . and again? Ram thought it a fair exchange for her father's life.

"Why are you being so unreasonable?" Phoebe asked.

He stared at her lips, mesmerized by their lush fullness and rosy color, suddenly, inexplicably, desperate to taste them. Her unique scent filled the space around him, stimulating his senses. "Is it so unreasonable to want one's wife?"

"It is when you consider our history. We're together for one reason, Ram. To rescue my father and return the amulet to its rightful owner."

His arms came around her. "Are you sure, Phoebe?" His hoarse voice betrayed his arousal. She gasped and tried to pull away when she felt his hardened length pressing determinedly against her. "I know you haven't forgotten me during our years apart. You can't deny you wanted to make love with me last night. Have you no regrets about leaving me? Have you never wondered what I was doing, whom I was with?"

Phoebe dragged in a sustaining breath and lied

through her teeth. "There are many things I regret, but leaving you is not one of them. Please, Ram, you're confusing me. I can't think straight when I'm in your arms."

He grinned. "Do you know what you just admitted?"

"No . . . yes . . . I don't know."

He caressed her cheek with the back of his hand. "So smooth, so soft—you're more beautiful than I remembered. The young woman on the verge of womanhood I married has lived up to her youthful promise. You're everything I'd hoped you'd become."

"Sweet words coming from you are meaningless," Phoebe returned. "You made me a woman, but the courage to live my life without you came from within myself."

When Phoebe's gaze fastened on his lips, Ram wanted to give a triumphant shout. She wasn't as immune to him as she'd like him to think. His eyes gleamed mischievously. "Kiss me, Phoebe."

"No."

"You know you want to."

With his hard body pressed intimately against hers, Phoebe couldn't find the breath to deny his words. She didn't want Ram. She *didn't*! If she let him seduce her again, she would lose the independence she'd fought so hard to attain. Last night had happened because she'd allowed it. They'd both wanted information and they both had gotten what they wanted.

"Kiss me, Phoebe."

His lips were full, moist; she knew they were as soft as they looked. At one time his kisses had thrilled her; she couldn't get enough of them. Gazing into the torrid depths of his eyes was like falling into a volcano on the verge of erupting. Her skin burned, her blood thickened. It took every ounce of willpower to deny him what he wanted.

"You're a coward, Phoebe. What are you afraid of?"

"I'm afraid of nothing," Phoebe said without conviction.

"Prove it."

"Damn you!" Grasping his collar, she yanked him close and pressed her lips to his. She released him just as abruptly, smirking in satisfaction when she saw the stunned expression on his face.

"You call that a kiss? Come now, Phoebe, I taught you better than that."

His hand curled around her nape, using gentle coercion to bring their mouths together. The moment their lips brushed and melded, Phoebe knew Ram had won. Without volition, her arms circled his neck and her mouth opened to admit his probing tongue. Slanting his mouth over hers, he deepened the kiss. Her breath hitched and her legs trembled as pleasure invaded her senses. Ram was doing it again. Making her body want him when her mind utterly rejected him.

He broke off the kiss and stared at her. "I think I've proved my point." He turned to leave.

"Where are you going?"

His elegant brows arched upward. "I can stay if you'd like, but we both know where that will lead."

Her chin jutted pugnaciously. Intimidation didn't work with her. "You promised to find my father. I'm curious as to what you're going to do about it."

"After I report to Fielding, I'm going to follow some leads."

"Have you something specific to go on?" Phoebe

asked enthusiastically. "Why didn't you tell me?"

"I will if it proves out. Get some rest while I'm gone. Neither of us got much sleep last night. You're the mistress here now. Use the bell pull to order whatever you want. I'll see about hiring a maid for you while I'm out."

When he turned to leave, Phoebe grasped his sleeve. "Tell me what you know."

Ram shook himself free. "Not yet, sweetheart. I'll tell you when I learn something definite."

"Ram, wait!" It was too late. He was already gone.

Ram was shown into Fielding's office immediately. "What have you learned?" Fielding asked without preamble.

Ram stretched his legs out in front of himself, his hands tented before him. "For one thing, Phoebe knows nothing about the amulet or its disappearance. I can't vouch for her father until I find him. Phoebe's house was broken into again last night. It's unsafe for her to remain alone, and I've taken steps to protect her."

Fielding searched Ram's face. "Prudent of you. What steps have you taken? Do you require help?"

Ram cleared his throat. "I've moved Phoebe into my townhouse."

Fielding's eyes bulged. "You what? Your assignment has taken a rather strange turn. Would you care to explain?"

"You're going to hear it anyway, so I may as well tell you myself. Phoebe is my wife. We were married four years ago and became estranged shortly afterward. No one is to know that, however. Everyone will believe Phoebe and I were just recently married, and that's all the explanation you're going to get."

Stunned, Fielding blew out a breath. "This is a fine kettle of fish, Braxton. How is this going to affect your assignment? Do you want to beg off?"

"Not at all. I told you I'd recover the amulet, and I always keep my word."

"This is rather amusing," Fielding chuckled. "A man has no need to seduce his own wife."

"You don't know Phoebe," Ram said with an answering grin. "We'd been estranged for years. Seducing her wasn't easy, nor was obtaining information. However, we both got what we wanted. I was forced to divulge my association with the Foreign Office."

"I see," Fielding said, stroking his chin. "I'm not sure I like the idea of your wife knowing you're working for us, but as long as you recover the amulet, I suppose it doesn't matter. Am I to assume you and your wife have reconciled?"

Ram gave a bitter laugh. "I wouldn't go that far. There's resentment on both sides. I'm not sure we can overcome the unpleasantness in our past. I'm not even sure I want to. Despite my unfortunate marriage, I've done what I've pleased, gone where I wanted without a wife nagging me. I have no grounds for complaint."

"I find it interesting that you didn't petition the courts for an annulment," Fielding mused.

"Yes, well, it never seemed important. That's all I have to report. I do have a lead or two, though both are slim at best. I'll let you know how reliable they are after I've had time to investigate."

"Good luck," Fielding said. "Time is running out. If the amulet isn't returned to the Egyptian emissary soon, I fear England will lose face."

Ram left Fielding's office in a thoughtful mood. He decided not to return home immediately, for he knew what would happen if he did. He couldn't afford to let Phoebe get under his skin again. He stopped at an employment agency to hire a maid, then decided to visit Crocker's gambling hall. His body was clamoring for diversion, and Crocker's sounded just the thing.

Crocker's proved boring. Not even the fact that he was winning at cards distracted him. He played for hours, until he felt reasonably certain that Phoebe was tucked in her bed and sound asleep. He was scooping his winnings from the table when Luc found him.

"Never say the bridegroom is looking for outside diversions so soon," Luc laughed.

"Stow it, Westmore," Ram replied curtly.

"Leaving already? I'm on my way to Madam Bella's. Would you care to join me?"

Ram thought it a good idea until he was struck by an image of Phoebe stretched out naked in his bed. The picture was so erotic, so arousing, that he was relieved his coat covered the bulge stretching his breeches.

"Are you coming with me or not, Braxton?"

Ram wanted to say yes, but the word that came out of his lips was an emphatic "No."

Luc's elegant brows shot upward. "Are you sure?"

Ram shook his head no and said yes. What in the hell was wrong with him?

"You look a bit confused, Braxton. Is your Phoebe getting to you? If I didn't know better, I'd say you were becoming enamored."

"Hardly," Ram scoffed. *Was Westmore right?* "I feel like getting foxed, my friend. I have several bottles of excellent brandy in my wine cellar. Care to join me?"

"What about your wife?"

"What about her? She's tucked up all nice and cozy in her bed, I hardly think we'll bother her."

"I was looking for erotic diversion to stimulate my jaded senses tonight, and getting foxed isn't exactly my first choice, but why not?" Luc gestured toward the door. "After you, my friend."

Rather than face Ram at dinner, Phoebe had requested a tray in her room and then a bath. The food was delicious; she'd eaten every bite while servants set up the tub in her room and filled it. After Ram had left, she'd unpacked her clothing and laid out a nightgown and wrapper. After the servants filled the tub and left a fluffy towel and scented soap for her use, Phoebe undressed and sank into the deliciously hot water.

While she bathed and washed her hair, she listened for Ram's footsteps, for she didn't want him to find her in a vulnerable position. Ram was a womanizer, and womanizers didn't care where they found their pleasure. He had made love to her last night as if he cared, and she knew as surely as she drew breath that he had every reason to hold her in contempt.

Rising from the tub, Phoebe dried off, donned her nightgown and wrapper and rang for the servants to carry out the tub.

"Is there anything else you require, milady?" Porter asked as the servants removed the tub.

"No, thank you, Porter. Has His Lordship returned yet?"

"No, milady. Shall I tell him you inquired after him when he returns?"

"No!" Phoebe softened her tone. "That won't be necessary. Good night, Porter."

"Good night, milady."

Despite her exhaustion, sleep eluded Phoebe. Images of Ram with another woman flashed through her mind. She knew he was still the same sexual predator she had married and hoped to change. What a fool she'd been.

Phoebe had just started to doze when she heard the faint sound of laughter. Ram? She listened for his footsteps, but they failed to materialize. Overcome with curiosity, she rose, donned her wrapper and opened the door. Did Ram have a woman below stairs? She knew better than to believe he would remain celibate while she was living with him. Did she really want to witness his infidelity?

Yes. Light from the hall lamp guided her down the staircase. Once she reached the foyer, she followed the buzz of sound and bursts of laughter to the study. The door was ajar, and she peeked inside. She saw Ram sitting behind the desk and Lord Westmore reclining in a chair opposite him. Two empty bottles rested on the desktop between them.

Deciding that a cautious retreat was called for, Phoebe backed away.

"Don't go, Phoebe," Ram drawled in a voice laced with amusement. "Join us."

Phoebe froze. "I . . . can't. You have company, and I'm not properly dressed."

She watched in trepidation as Ram rose, swayed and clutched the desk for support. *He's foxed!* Phoebe realized. Whirling on her heel, she fled.

"Is she always so skittish?" Luc asked.

"Only when she's with me," Ram answered.

Walking somewhat unsteadily, he wended his

way to the sideboard and returned with a full bottle. "I saved the best for last."

They drank in companionable silence for a time; then Luc said, "The situation you've gotten yourself into grows more entertaining by the minute. How did you convince Phoebe to come live with you?"

"It wasn't easy, but she realized it was for her own good. The announcement of our marriage will appear in the morning edition of the *Times*. The news is going to shock the *ton*."

"It sure as hell shocked me."

"I suppose I should introduce Phoebe to society."

Luc snapped his fingers. "I know! I'll ask my sister to give a ball in your honor. How does two weeks from Saturday sound?"

"I don't want to put Lady Belcher to any trouble," Ram said.

"Are you kidding? Maryann will be delighted. She's always looking for an excuse to give a party, and her adoring husband doesn't have the balls to deny her. I'll talk to her and get back to you." He staggered to his feet. "It's time I left. Another drink will put me flat on my back. Don't bother seeing me out, I know the way."

Ram finished off the bottle, then slowly made his way to his room. Dudley, his valet, was asleep in a chair, waiting for his return. Ram shook him awake and sent him off to bed. Then he undressed, washed, cleaned his teeth and collapsed naked on the bed. He was asleep within minutes, but awoke an hour later in a state of desperate need.

An erotic dream about Phoebe had brought him from a deep sleep to full arousal. Groaning, he flopped over on his stomach. It didn't help. He should have gone with Westmore to Madam Bella's and slaked his lust with one of her accomplished courtesans. Unable to find sleep again, he rose, donned a robe and briefly thought about returning to the study and uncorking another bottle.

The thought of Phoebe sleeping peacefully in the room adjoining his sent that notion fleeing. He wove his way to the connecting door and stared at it, as if he couldn't quite decide what to do. If he hadn't been foxed, the idea he was entertaining would have died an early death. But his befuddled brain and his aroused body clamored for attention and would not be denied.

Ram's hand paused but a moment on the doorknob before he opened the door and stepped inside. The soft cadence of Phoebe's breathing, combined with the curvy outline of her body under the sheet, brought his cock jerking upward beneath his robe. Stifling a groan, he wove an unsteady path toward the bed and stared down at his sleeping wife.

Moonlight became her, Ram thought, admiring her innocent beauty in the silvery glow streaming through the window. He stifled a snort of laughter at that thought. Phoebe might be many things, but she wasn't innocent. That didn't matter. Neither was he. He'd never allowed himself to care about another woman after Phoebe, never looked farther than his next sexual encounter. His defensive walls were strong, and thus far he had done an excellent job of guarding his heart.

Phoebe stirred, and suddenly Ram felt as if he were attuned to her, body and soul. He was sensitive to her scent, subtle yet arousing, to the smallest shift of her body, to the heat emanating from her. Her body called to his on a primal level, and he responded.

* * *

Phoebe awakened to the sure knowledge that she wasn't alone. She was lying on her side, facing the wall, but she sensed Ram behind her. Her body thrilled at his sexual vitality at the same time as she shrank away from it. She could smell his arousal, feel the sharp intensity of his gaze. The energy in the room had abruptly changed from benign to charged.

Turning slowly, she opened her eyes and stared up at him. His hand was poised in midair, as if he'd been reaching out to touch her. "What do you want?"

He leaned toward her, and the spicy smell of brandy wafted over her. When he wove from side to side, she realized he was inebriated. "You're foxed!"

A lopsided grin lifted the corners of his mouth. "Not too foxed to know what I want or what I'm doing. You're my wife, Phoebe."

Phoebe gave a ragged sigh. "We'll discuss that point tomorrow. Go back to bed, Ram."

Ignoring her, Ram settled on the edge of the bed, his shimmering emerald gaze so intense, she felt impaled by it. "Are you going to deny us what we both want?" Ram asked, his words slurring together.

Another sigh. "It's late, Ram. I'm tired."

Reaching out, he smoothed a finger along her cheek, continuing down her throat to the top button on her nightgown. He released the button, then the second and third. Leaning forward, he brushed his lips across the pale skin of her upper breasts, licking a scorching path into her cleavage. Phoebe uttered a feeble protest and tried to pull the edges of her nightgown together, but Ram seemed determined to bare more of her as he yanked the thin material off her shoulders, exposing her breasts.

Phoebe felt her nipples harden and tried not to think about Ram's hungry gaze devouring her. A flush began at her waist and spread slowly upward to her hairline. How easy it was for Ram to seduce her with a mere look and a single touch. She stiffened when he stretched out beside her.

If she didn't keep her wits about her, she'd be welcoming him into her heart, and that would be disastrous. A man who loved as indiscriminately as Ram broke hearts on a daily basis, and she didn't want to add hers to the discarded pile after she'd learned to live without him.

When Ram took her breast into his hands and brought his mouth down to taste her nipple, her resolve began to crumble. If she didn't do or say something to defuse the explosive situation, she'd lose the will to resist.

"I'm not going to become your lover, Ram. I'm in your home because you insisted upon it, and because I need your help finding Father and clearing his name. Our becoming lovers will only confuse the issue."

He reared back and stared at her, a befuddled expression on his face. "You're my wife."

"Your estranged wife. We agreed not to muddle things by becoming intimate. When I leave this time, you can't pretend surprise, for you knew from the onset that this is a temporary arrangement. I need to find my father before something terrible happens to him. I don't care about the amulet; it was never ours to begin with."

No answer was forthcoming.

"Ram, did you hear me? We're not going to make love. I'm going to go to sleep, and I suggest you do the same."

Phoebe was becoming angry. How dare Ram ignore her! Rising on her elbow, she punched him in the shoulder. When he failed to react, she punched him again. She thought she heard him groan, but when she peered down into his face, she realized he was sleeping. What she'd mistaken for a groan was a snore.

He'd fallen asleep in the middle of a conversation! Foxed or not, she wanted him out of her bed, but accomplishing the deed would be no easy task. He was too heavy, and she was too weary to spare the energy. Sighing wearily, Phoebe turned her back to him and promptly fell asleep.

The sun was peeping over the horizon when Ram awakened the following morning, surprised to find himself in Phoebe's bed. The when and why of how he'd arrived in her bed escaped him. Had they made love? He knew he'd imbibed too freely last night, but he couldn't imagine forgetting something like that. Even though he was lying atop the blanket, she was snuggled against him, and his arm was curled around her. His body thrummed with excitement when he considered what might have taken place last night in Phoebe's bed.

He tried to remember what had happened. The last thing he recalled was stripping off his clothes and falling into bed, his own bed. He had no idea what had transpired after that, and his head hurt too badly to delve deeper into his memory. He was in Phoebe's bed and she was in his arms and that was all that mattered. He began to relax, savoring the feeling of warm female flesh against his mildly aroused body.

Ram knew the moment Phoebe awakened, for he felt her stiffen in his arms. "What are you doing?"

"Holding you. Shall we make love again?"

"Again! You must have been drunker than I thought if you believe we made love last night. You came into my room, we argued, and you fell asleep. You were too heavy for me to move so I let you stay. It's as simple as that."

Somehow Ram doubted it was as simple as Phoebe made it sound. "I fell asleep before making love?"

Enjoying his discomfiture, Phoebe said, "You fell asleep while I was talking. Now that you are awake, you may leave."

"That's a first," Ram muttered, attempting to rise without letting Phoebe know how much his head hurt. Though he imbibed regularly, he rarely exceeded his limit. *Never again*, he vowed as he moved very carefully toward his room.

"Tonight we'll make up for my lack," he said in parting.

"The only thing we're going to do together is find my father," Phoebe retorted. "If you don't meet my expectations on that score, I'll be forced to rely on David for help. At least I know *he* cares about Father."

"You try me sorely," Ram mumbled. "Something tells me you're going to make me very sorry I took this assignment."

Chapter Eight

The health of the prisoner locked in the cramped room hadn't improved. Sir Thompson was still weak and confused, his mind still unclear about times and events after weeks of relentless badgering by his captor.

"I can't get anything out of him that makes sense," Watts informed his employer. "The bastard's lost his wits. Either that or he's smarter than we gave him credit for."

A sharp curse left his employer's mouth. "Damn him! He's forcing my hand. Now it's time for devious methods."

Watts smiled, revealing a mouthful of rotting teeth. "Torture?"

"He's too frail for that. I've no choice but to go after the daughter. We'll need help. Someone who won't ask questions. Do you have a friend in need of blunt?"

Connie Mason

"Aye, that I do," Watts said. "Benny would kill his own mother for a shilling."

"Excellent. Bring him here. I'll return later and outline my plan."

Phoebe lacked the energy to get out of bed and face the new day. Ram had changed the fabric of her life, and she wasn't sure she wanted to know what the next hours would bring. A knock on her door and a voice she didn't recognize caught her attention.

"My lady, may I come in? Lord Braxton said you were awake. I've brought your morning chocolate."

"Come in," Phoebe answered.

The door opened and a plump young woman with rosy cheeks and a button nose stepped inside. She set the tray on a table and bobbed a curtsey. "I'm Abby, your new maid. His Lordship hired me yesterday. I hope I please you, my lady."

Since Phoebe had never had a personal maid, she was certain Abby would do. "I'm sure we'll rub along quite well together, Abby." She glanced at the tray. "What have you brought me besides chocolate?"

Abby whipped the cloth from the tray. "Cook sent up a sweet roll to hold you over till breakfast. I hope that meets with your approval."

"They look delicious. Thank cook for me."

"I can lay out your clothes while you eat," Abby offered. "His Lordship requests that you meet him in the foyer in an hour. He wants to introduce you to the staff."

Phoebe stifled a groan. She didn't want to become entrenched in Ram's household. "Thank you, Abby. Would you kindly fetch some hot water from the kitchen?"

Abby bobbed another curtsey and hurried off. In a pensive mood, Phoebe sipped her chocolate, surprised that Ram had remembered how much she loved it. She had just drained her cup and eaten the last of her roll when Abby returned with the hot water. After a quick sponge-off, Phoebe let Abby help her dress and arrange her hair. She couldn't recall when she'd felt so pampered.

When Phoebe descended the stairs a short time later, she saw the staff lined up in the foyer, their faces expectant as they awaited her. Ram was there, too, looking pale but handsome as always. He strode to the staircase when she reached the bottom and offered his hand. Heat flashed up her arm as she placed her hand in his, and she tried to pull it away. He gave her a strange look and tightened his grip, then began the introductions.

Phoebe knew she'd never keep the names straight, but she made a valiant effort to smile and repeat each moniker, from Porter, the butler, to Babs, the lowliest kitchen helper. Phoebe suffered a pang of guilt at their enthusiastic greetings, and wondered what they would think of her when she disappeared from Ram's life.

Ram dismissed the staff with a wave of his hand. "You've already met Wilson, my coachman. You can meet the gardener and stableman later."

"You have a lot of servants for one person. Can members of the *ton* do nothing for themselves?"

"Less than nothing," Ram allowed. "We're a pampered lot, sweetheart. Are you pleased with your maid?"

"Of course; why wouldn't I be? I hope you'll find a place for her in your household after I'm gone."

Ram's answer was forestalled when the brass

139

doorknocker announced a visitor. "Don't bother, Porter," Ram said, "I'll get it."

Phoebe turned toward the morning room to take breakfast, but a voice she recognized brought her spinning around.

"David!"

Ignoring Phoebe, Phillips rounded on Ram, waving the morning *Times* in his face. "You bastard! You're going to break her heart!"

"Please come inside and let me explain," Phoebe said.

"What makes you think I'll break Phoebe's heart?" Ram asked.

Phillips stormed inside, slamming the door behind him. "I was the man she turned to after she found the good sense to leave you. She was bereft, inconsolable. She was lucky to escape you that time. How did you convince her to marry you? It's the last thing I expected from you, Braxton. You can have any woman you want. Why Phoebe?"

"David, this isn't what it seems," Phoebe tried to explain.

Ram's arm curled possessively around Phoebe's waist. "We were just going in to breakfast, Phillips. Will you join us?"

"I've already eaten," Phillips growled.

"I'm sure a cup of coffee or tea wouldn't go amiss. Come along or not, it's up to you," Ram said, guiding Phoebe down the hallway to the morning room.

"Yes, do come, David," Phoebe urged. "I'm sure I can explain everything to your satisfaction."

Breakfast was already laid out on the sideboard when they reached the sunny room overlooking the garden. Ram seated Phoebe, then motioned Phillips into a chair opposite her. "We will serve ourselves," Ram said dismissively to the two footmen standing at attention.

Phoebe helped herself to a rasher of bacon, eggs, kidneys and toasted bread. She poured tea into her cup and concentrated on her food.

"I don't see how you can eat at a time like this," Phillips berated her. He cast a sidelong glance at Ram, then whispered, "Have you forgotten your father?"

"Lord Braxton knows everything, David."

David blanched. "You told him? Are you insane?"

"I had no choice," Phoebe argued. "Ram suspected something was amiss. He's agreed to help us."

"You may have just written your father's death warrant," Phillips sputtered.

"Don't be so negative, David. This has gone on too long; we've reached the point where we need outside help."

Her answer did nothing to placate Phillips. "Kindly explain your reason for marrying a man of Braxton's reputation. I wouldn't be surprised if he betrays his vows before the ink is dry on the marriage papers."

"It's time to reveal the truth, love," Ram drawled. "Do you want to tell him or shall I?"

"Tell me what?" Phillips asked, his gaze shifting from Ram to Phoebe.

Phoebe sucked in a steadying breath. "I'll tell him. He deserves to hear it from me."

"Very well, my love, but make it short."

"Braxton and I were married four years ago, before I left England."

David shot to his feet. "Never say it's true!"

"Please sit down, David." He plopped heavily into his chair. "It's true," Phoebe continued. "I thought I could change Ram after we were wed, but you proved me wrong. I expected Ram to obtain an annulment after I left, but I assumed incorrectly. I had no idea we were still married until he showed up at my door."

Phillips rose, clutching the edge of the table, his face mottled, his knuckles white. "Has the bastard demanded marital relations?"

"It wasn't like that, David. Ram insisted I move into his townhouse for my own protection. After the break-ins and the attack upon my person, he feared for my safety. We're not . . . intimate."

She glanced at Ram and ground her teeth when she saw his raised eyebrows and amused expression.

"I can't believe you've been stringing me along all these years," Phillips said icily. "I hoped to marry you, and you didn't even have the decency to tell me you were already wed to Braxton. I find that contemptible, Phoebe. I find *you* contemptible."

Ram left his chair in a blur of motion. In the blink of an eye he had Phillips backed up against the wall, pinned there by his rough hands, impaled by his hard stare.

"One more derogatory remark about my wife and I won't be responsible for my actions. I could snap your neck with the turn of my wrist, without a whit of remorse. Porter will escort you out; I strongly advise that you refrain from darkening my doorstep again."

Phoebe rushed to David's defense. "Release him, Ram! David didn't mean anything. We've shocked him, and he was merely lashing out. I understand his anger. I should have told him about us years ago."

As if on cue, Porter appeared in the doorway. Ram released his grip and Phillips sagged against the wall. "You're going to be sorry for this affront, Braxton."

"I doubt it," Ram drawled. "Porter, you may see our guest out."

"This way, sir," Porter said, grasping Phillips's arm.

Phillips shook free of his grip. "Are you going to let Braxton interfere with our friendship, Phoebe? You need me. Our relationship has been a good one over the years."

"Your relationship with Phoebe ended the day I reclaimed her," Ram said with quiet menace. "What she did with you in the past has no bearing on how she will conduct herself in the future. I intend to be the only man Phoebe welcomes in her bed. Is that understood?"

Phoebe's face flamed with embarrassment. "Ram, how could you? David is my friend."

"Get out of here, Phillips!" Ram said in a voice laced with menace. "Phoebe has me now, she doesn't need you."

"I'll be in touch," Phoebe promised as Porter escorted Phillips to the door.

"Like hell!" Ram roared, turning on Phoebe. "You're to have nothing more to do with him, is that clear?"

"You can't tell me what to do, Lord Braxton! Ours isn't a real marriage. Why are you acting like a jealous husband?"

Ram's eyes narrowed as he took stock of what had just occurred. Was he acting like a jealous hus-

143

band? Damn right he was. Just the thought of Phoebe and Phillips engaged in intimate relations stoked an uncontrollable rage inside him. Teeth clenched, jaw taut, he knew he had to leave before he did or said something he'd regret later.

Nonetheless, he couldn't prevent himself from speaking his mind. "Jealousy has nothing to do with it. I don't trust Phillips. He deliberately destroyed our marriage when he realized we were becoming close."

"You don't know that. David believed you would hurt me and set out to prove it. You can't blame him for your shortcomings. Besides, he has been relentless in his search for Father. I couldn't have managed without him."

"You've got *me* now. Forget Phillips. I won't have my wife cavorting with another man."

"I don't have you, Ram. I never did."

"You're wrong. You never gave me a chance to prove myself. Neither of us will ever know what could have been. Why did you leave me, Phoebe?"

"It doesn't matter."

"It does to me. You're responsible for my plunge into debauchery."

Phoebe gave an unladylike snort. "You were well on your way to perdition long before we met. How long would you have stayed with me after you took my innocence? Would you have left me in the country while you continued your lecherous ways in London?"

Spitting out a curse, Ram grasped Phoebe's arm and propelled her from the room. "It's time for us to talk. Privately. These accusations about what you perceived I did must stop. I've waited four years for this confrontation and I want the truth, Phoebe. No hedging, no lies."

"Where are we going?"

"To my room. You're going to talk and I'm going to listen. Then I'm going to talk and you'd damn well better listen."

His jaw set, Ram dragged a wildly protesting Phoebe to his room, slamming the door behind them. "Sit down."

"I'd rather stand."

"Suit yourself." He paced before her. "You may begin by telling me what happened after our wedding night. I was sleeping so heavily I didn't know you were gone until you returned and announced your intention to sail to Egypt to join your father. You left immediately, without a word of explanation."

"Are you sure you want to know? What good will it serve?"

"It will bring me peace of mind. How deeply was Phillips involved?"

"David was merely trying to protect me. He had no idea we had wed when he arrived that morning. He still believed I was sailing to Egypt with him. When he learned I intended to remain in England, with you, he tried to change my mind. I never told him we were married."

"What did he say to influence you against me?"

"When David learned I wasn't sailing to Egypt with him because I didn't want to leave you, he told me you weren't capable of remaining faithful to one woman. To convince me, he introduced me to the barmaid and the widow who were sharing your affections."

Astounded, Ram asked, "When did all this happen? Things couldn't have been better between us on our wedding night. I know I pleased you; you certainly pleased me."

"I awakened early and went to the kitchen to prepare breakfast. You were still sleeping, and I didn't have the heart to awaken you. David arrived shortly afterward. When I told him he would be sailing without me, he said there were two women he wanted me to meet."

"The barmaid and the widow," Ram said, his lip curling with derision. "They were my past, you were my future. You should have trusted me. I know Phillips wanted you and would have stopped at nothing to separate us, but that was despicable."

"He was concerned for me," Phoebe maintained. "I had reservations from the onset about our relationship, but then you asked me to marry you and I was deliriously happy. I thought your proposal meant you loved me as much as I loved you. I was aware of your reputation as a rake and a womanizer, but I believed you would remain faithful to our vows. David saved me from a world of heartache."

Ram shook his head. "You couldn't have loved me, Phoebe. Had your emotions been deeply engaged, you would have given me a chance to prove myself. You reacted recklessly to something I had already relegated to my past. You ruined what could have been a wonderful future together."

"So I'm to blame," Phoebe said mockingly.

Disdain curled his upper lip. Contempt frosted his green eyes. Bitterness radiated from his tall, elegant form.

"You and your precious David Phillips."

Could Ram be telling the truth? Phoebe wondered. Had she done him a grave injustice? What if he was spinning more of his lies? Too much time had passed for them to retrieve what had been lost

146

to distance and time. There would always be distrust between them. And resentment.

"If I was wrong, I made a grave miscalculation, but I refuse to believe David is the kind of malicious man you make him out to be. You're understandably bitter, and I don't blame you. I can return to my house on Mount Street if my presence disturbs you."

Ram halted in front of her, his face only inches away. "Your presence does indeed disturb me. Too damn much," he grumbled. "I can't seem to get you out of my blood. The sexual energy we generate explodes whenever we're together. I know you feel it too."

"I . . . don't know what you mean."

He stroked her cheek. "Liar." His hand drifted along the curve of her throat, continuing downward to her left breast. "Your heart is racing. We still possess the ability to stir one another's blood."

Oh, yes, her blood was stirring all right. Ram was a master at seduction. His words alone made her heart pound, and his touch sent molten heat coursing through her veins. Unconsciously she moved closer, pressing her breast against the torrid warmth of his palm. She allowed herself a moment to savor the feelings he aroused in her before she calmly removed his hand.

"Are you afraid of me, Phoebe? Do you fear how I make you feel? There's no shame in feeling pleasure. Marriage gives us the right to make love whenever we please."

He sent her a ravenous look that stole her breath, and for a timeless moment she could neither speak nor move. Then, without volition, her gaze slipped down to the rampant bulge in his trousers. His body was fiercely rigid, aggressively male, needy. A

Connie Mason

wordless sound escaped her throat, and her gaze flew upward to the burning hunger in his eyes. His desire was blatantly exposed in their verdant depths.

"Our marriage is a sham; our love died a long time ago," Phoebe whispered.

Curling a hand around her nape, he brought her closer. "Is this a sham?" He kissed her, his mouth closing over hers, his tongue probing ruthlessly. He drank from her mouth until her knees trembled. He lifted her then and set her upon the bed, his eyes never leaving hers as he pushed her down and lifted her skirts to her waist.

She shoved ineffectually against his chest, her voice rising in panic. "We can't. It's broad daylight. What if my maid comes in?"

Ram glanced at the door, then moved quickly to lock it. He was back in an instant, his gaze traveling the length of her exposed legs, from her trim ankles to her thighs and beyond. Phoebe shuddered and tried to shove her skirts back in place, but Ram wouldn't allow it.

Grasping her hand, he placed it over his sex. "My cock is hard for you, love. I want to shove myself inside you and take you fast and rough. I want you naked. I want to feel your skin against mine. I want to give you so much pleasure you'll always remember what we could have had together had you not listened to Phillips. Does he make you scream his name? Does he please you as well as I?"

Her hand fell away as if burned. "This conversation is pointless. Surely you don't intend to make love now."

He turned her around and attacked the buttons on the back of her gown. His voice was low, strident, ragged with need. "Oh, yes, Phoebe, I do. You never gave me the chance to get you out of my blood. Despite everything, I still desire you." He tugged her gown down her arms and turned her to face him. "I can't explain how or why, but you brought excitement back into my jaded life, and I intend to take advantage of it."

"For how long?" Phoebe asked. "Until another woman catches your attention?"

He stripped off her gown and tossed it aside. "Let's wait and see where this takes us. We're together, we're still married, and I need you. Isn't that enough for now?"

She lowered her lashes, then her head. He caught her chin with his forefinger, drawing her gaze back to his.

"Look at me, sweetheart."

Their gazes met and clung. "Right now you're the only woman in my life."

He lowered his head and found her lips. They were soft, lush, sweetly provocative. Warm, wet, seductive. He was no saint. He took what he wanted when he wanted, and he wanted Phoebe. He cradled her chin, tasting her, savoring her, then ravaging her mouth with his tongue.

His lips feathered over her neck, his fingers followed, taking the straps of her chemise with them as they skimmed her shoulders. In a matter of moments her petticoat and shift were gone. Seconds seemed like eons as he spread her legs and looked his fill. He knew the moment she caught fire by the way her body flushed and writhed beneath his intimate gaze. Then she reached for him, tugging his coat down over his shoulders.

"Damn you, Braxton . . . so arrogant, so sure of yourself! Has any woman ever denied you?"

"Not that I can recall." His gaze returned to her

moist center. "You're beautiful. I remember how shy you were on our wedding night." He lowered his head and brushed a kiss between her legs.

Phoebe gasped, her body arching upward. "Don't do that!"

He grinned at her. "You mean this?" He gripped her hips and set his tongue to her softness, flicking it against a spot so sensitive, she jerked and cried out. Then she felt the lap and probe of his tongue; the intimate caress sent her senses spiraling. Her nerves tightened and her skin tingled.

"Hold that thought, love," he said as he moved away and stripped off his clothes. Then he was back, his kisses searing her lips, her throat, the hollow there, tasting the firmness of her breasts, suckling her nipples until they rose proud and defiant into the wet heat of his mouth.

Immersed in the throes of ecstasy, Phoebe arched her back when he parted her thighs, buried his face in the vee betwixt them and stroked her cleft intimately with his tongue. Then he entered her, probing deep. Her hand flew to her lips to stifle the cry gurgling in her throat as hot blood rushed to the swollen petals of her sex. Groaning his encouragement, Ram grasped her curvy bottom in both hands and lifted, thrusting his tongue deep into her honeyed warmth.

Thrashing her head from side to side, Phoebe let out a long, piercing wail, buffeted by emotions both raw and frightening. She shivered, writhed, trembled, then shattered and cried out his name. Pressing his advantage, he rose and buried his throbbing cock inside her, thrusting and withdrawing with fierce, ravenous strokes. As she clutched his shoulders, her sated body reawakened, rising up to meet his, taking all he had to give and begging for more.

"Can you come again, sweetheart?"

Beyond speech, Phoebe felt the fire rekindling. His hand slid down between her thighs, his feather-light touch dancing upon the sensitive nub sheltered within dewy folds of pink flesh. The feeling was so vivid, so splintering, she nearly jumped out of her skin.

Fire exploded in her brain and her soul took flight. She came with him. Flew where he flew. In the dim reaches of her mind she heard Ram's shout, felt his body stiffen and the warm rush of his seed bathing her womb.

"I could stay inside you forever," Ram breathed harshly against her ear as he fought for breath.

He pulled out, stretched himself beside her and turned her into his arms. Phoebe sighed. She felt cherished, as if she belonged there, but she knew it was an illusion. Ram was very good at this sort of thing. She suspected he made every woman he made love to feel just like she did.

"What are you thinking, love?"

Several heartbeats later she said, "That those countless women you've bedded were lucky. Your reputation is well earned, my lord."

"We're good together. We don't have to end it after we've found your father."

"Can you promise we'll be together forever?"

Phoebe's hopes plummeted. Ram took so much time answering, she knew she had crossed a forbidden boundary. Ram didn't want a permanent wife. He only wanted her until another woman caught his eye.

"You don't want a wife," she said sadly. "I'd stifle you. I want more than you are willing to give, Braxton. I'd demand your love, your fidelity, your trust. I'd want to be the only woman in your life."

He raised his eyes and met hers. "You're right, but by God, I *do* desire you."

His answer hurt but didn't shock. "Did you really mean what you said about the barmaid and the widow?"

"I spoke the truth—that's all I'm going to say on the subject. How I conducted my life after you ran off is another matter. How many lovers did you have during our years apart?"

"None."

"None? Excuse me, what about Phillips?"

Phoebe's lips thinned. "Not David, not anyone, and that's all I'm going to say on the subject. Shouldn't you be leaving?"

Leaving was the last thing Ram wanted to do. He'd rather stay in bed, holding Phoebe in his arms and loving her again. Possessiveness rose strong inside him. She was his. He had claimed and branded her. She had surrendered and he had taken, giving everything but his heart in return.

How many women had he made love to?

Hundreds.

How many women made him crazy with need? Made him ache with a simple caress?

No one but Phoebe.

He recognized the danger but was powerless to prevent Phoebe from destroying the entire facade he had built after she had left him.

"Are you trying to get rid of me?"

"I intended to visit the dressmaker today, and it's growing late. You want me properly attired for Lady Belcher's ball, don't you?"

He placed his hand on her breast in a lingering caress. "Are you in a great hurry?"

"I . . . yes. Abby is probably waiting for me in the foyer. I . . . never had a personal maid before."

"You never gave me a chance to give you one," he reminded her. He stared at her lips, swollen and moist from his kisses, and knew he had to taste her again. His mouth swooped down and claimed hers.

Her lips were wantonly lush and supple. They softened beneath his and opened to accept the bold thrust of his tongue. He was almost to the point of no return when Phoebe broke off the kiss and pushed him away.

"Not again, Ram. You've exhausted me, and the day has just begun. Besides, if you intend to track down my father, you'd best get going. Dallying in bed with me isn't going to find him."

"I suppose you're right," Ram said regretfully. "Do you know where Phillips lives?"

"Why? You're not going to engage him in another fight, are you? Leave David alone. I've hurt him terribly."

"I'm not going to challenge Phillips," Ram assured her. "I want to hear how much or how little he knows about your father's disappearance. He was the last person to see him, wasn't he? We have few clues to go on, Phoebe. It's imperative that I question Phillips."

"I'm sure David knows nothing more than I do, but if you promise not to use force, I'll direct you to his lodging."

Ram's eyes darkened with barely suppressed anger. "I won't hurt your precious David."

She ignored his jibe. "He has rented a room at the Fin and Feather. Do you know where it is?"

"I do." Uncoiling his long body, he rose and stretched. "I'll try to return to take supper with you, but don't count on me. I intend to prowl a few of the more nefarious taverns along the waterfront for information. It's amazing what one can learn in low places."

He pulled on his clothing, threw Phoebe a kiss and left, albeit reluctantly. He'd much rather stay and show Phoebe a few more ways to make love. He'd hardly just begun.

After a hearty breakfast, Ram ordered his horse brought around and rode to the Fin and Feather to speak with Phillips. He intended to investigate the other man's daily habits. Ram didn't believe Phillips was as innocent as he pretended.

The Fin and Feather, situated in a shabby but respectable part of town, was nearly empty when Ram entered. Ram had been there a few times with Westmore and Bathurst, looking for the kind of amusement their clubs couldn't provide.

Ram ordered a pint of ale from the barmaid and asked a few discreet questions about Phillips. The barmaid told him she had seen Phillips leave earlier that morning, and that he hadn't returned.

"Does Mr. Phillips have many friends?" Ram asked.

The barmaid tossed her mass of unkempt blond curls and held out her hand. "How badly do ye want to know, ducks?"

Ram delved into his purse, removed a half crown and dropped it into the barmaid's hand. "Has your memory improved?"

"Aye, that it has. Mr. Phillips takes his meals here, but I ain't never seen him with anyone. He's a real prim and proper gentleman, he is. An E . . . gyp . . . tologist, whatever that is."

That wasn't precisely what Ram had wanted or expected to hear. Maybe Phoebe was right about Phillips and he was seeking answers in the wrong places.

Disappointed, he finished his ale and continued on to London Pool to question the longshoremen about unusual happenings the day Sir Thompson was abducted. He'd catch Phillips another time.

Chapter Nine

"Come back for me in three hours," Phoebe told Wilson as he handed her down from the carriage. "Spend the time however you wish. Fittings can be endless, and I'm sure your time can be better spent."

"Are you sure, milady?" Wilson asked. "I don't mind waiting."

"Quite sure," Phoebe said.

"Well, then, I don't mind enjoying a pint or two while I'm waiting, but I'll be parked at the curb when you're ready to leave."

Phoebe waved Wilson off as she let herself into the shop Ram had recommended. She had never visited this particular shop before because it was too expensive. Phoebe had to admit that her wardrobe, but for the two recent additions, was hopelessly outdated. Still, she was determined to purchase just enough to satisfy Ram during her stay with him. She didn't want to be beholden to him after they parted.

A birdlike woman with fluttering hands and sharp blue eyes greeted Phoebe at the door. She sniffed disdainfully as her sweeping gaze took in Phoebe's less than fashionable appearance.

"I am Madame LeBeau. One of my assistants will be here directly to help you," she said with a dismissive sniff. "We have a few readymade frocks on hand. They're not up to the standard of our custom-made gowns but less taxing on the pocketbook, which I'm sure you'll appreciate."

Phoebe found Madame LeBeau's condescension annoying but couldn't fault the woman for assuming she couldn't afford the best. She had never been one to indulge in extravagances. Being a commoner, Phoebe had never felt the need to keep up with the *ton*, but she couldn't help handing Madame LeBeau a mild put-down.

"My husband told me you were the best modiste in town and urged me to commission a wardrobe from your establishment. Of course, Braxton could be mistaken."

Madame turned a sickly shade of green. "Braxton? *Lord* Braxton? The Earl of Braxton?"

"The same. I'm Lady Phoebe Braxton, the earl's countess."

"Oh, dear, how remiss of me not to have known. I did hear Braxton had wed." Her gaze slid down to Phoebe's middle. "Quite sudden, wasn't it?"

"We've known one another for years," Phoebe replied. "If you're busy, I'll take my custom elsewhere."

"Oh, no, milady, please forgive my lapse of etiquette. How may I help you?"

"I'm in need of a ball gown, several day gowns,

petticoats, nightwear and all the accoutrements. I've been out of the country, and my wardrobe needs refurbishing. I'll need the ball gown and at least two other gowns within a fortnight. Is that possible?"

Madame clapped her hands and immediately two young assistants appeared from a back room. "Please take Lady Braxton into the fitting room and make her comfortable. I'll be in directly with fashion dolls and an assortment of materials."

Smiling to herself, Phoebe followed the two tittering girls into a curtained alcove littered with fabric remnants. She was offered tea, and when she accepted, the two assistants hurried off to accommodate her. Phoebe sank into a comfortable chair to await the proprietress. When female voices drifted to her from the front of the shop, she couldn't help eavesdropping. What she heard made her sit up and take notice.

"Isn't that Braxton tethering his mount to the hitching post outside the shop, Deborah?"

"Indeed," Deborah sighed. "Such a handsome rogue. Too bad about Bathurst. I can't imagine what he saw in Lady Olivia. But at least Braxton and Westmore are still in circulation."

"Haven't you seen today's *Times*, Pamela? Braxton has taken a bride. No one seems to know where or when he met Miss Phoebe Thompson, but it's the most delicious piece of gossip so far this season. They say she's a commoner. Can you imagine?"

"Never say it's true, Deborah! How will we ever manage without Braxton? He's the best lover I've ever had. Aside from Westmore and Bathurst, of course."

Pamela's voice held a hint of mirth. "You don't seriously believe Braxton will remain faithful, do

you? Really, dear Deborah, that's asking a bit much
of the man. And I for one am glad he's a libertine.
Doubtless he married for an heir, though why he
would wed a commoner is beyond me. Once his
wife is increasing, I predict he'll settle her in the
country and return to town posthaste. Braxton isn't
capable of confining himself to one woman."

"How fortunate for us," Deborah tittered. "Shall
we wager on which of us finds her way into his bed
first?"

Phoebe didn't hear the reply, for Madame Le-
Beau chose that moment to greet the two women.

"Lady Winthorpe, your gown is ready. One of my
assistants will fetch it for you. Lady Gardner, how
may I help you?"

"Nothing for me today, madame. I'm here with
Lady Winthorpe. We're taking tea together later."

Shortly after that exchange, madame bustled into
the alcove, her arms overflowing with fabric sam-
ples and fashion dolls. Pleasurably immersed in the
world of fashion, Phoebe was startled when the
curtain opened and Ram stepped through the opening.

"Ramsey! What are you doing here?"

"I hit a temporary roadblock and thought I'd
drop by and see how you're coming with your
wardrobe. I'm fairly good with colors and pat-
terns."

"I'm sure you are," Phoebe said dryly.

"Lord Braxton, how good to see you again," madame said enthusiastically.

Ram sent madame a warning look and cleared
his throat. "Yes, well, shall we get on with my
wife's fitting, madame?"

Phoebe didn't need a load of bricks to fall on her
to realize that Ram was a frequent patron of Ma-

dame LeBeau's establishment. Doubtless he had purchased clothing for his mistresses here, which gave her another reason to doubt Ram's ability to remain faithful to her. Obviously, Lady Winthorpe and Lady Gardner were just two of his countless lovers. There must have been dozens before and as many after they were wed.

"Pay attention, Phoebe," Ram said.

Phoebe channeled her concentration on the bolts of material spread out before her, storing Lady Winthorpe's and Lady Gardner's remarks in a corner of her mind for future reference.

Many hours later, a grateful Madame LeBeau promised delivery of a ball gown, two morning gowns and appropriate lingerie in a fortnight. Three walking dresses and two more day gowns were to follow in quick succession. Phoebe had protested such extravagance, but Ram was adamant. He even insisted on taking her to the shoemaker and having her measured for slippers to match the gowns and two pairs of walking boots.

Afterward, Ram tied his horse to the back of the carriage and rode home with her.

"What kind of a roadblock did you encounter?" Phoebe asked as she settled back against the squabs. "Did you see David?"

"No, he wasn't in. Nor did I learn anything about his habits. He seems to have few friends."

"David has been out of the country for four years," Phoebe reminded him. "What can you expect? I suggest you look elsewhere for Father's abductor."

"Perhaps you're right," Ram muttered without conviction.

"By the way," Phoebe said, "while I was in the

161

fitting room I overheard a conversation between two of your paramours."

"What makes you think they were my paramours?"

"They spoke glowingly of your sexual prowess. Perhaps you recognize their names. Lady Winthorpe and Lady Gardner."

"Pamela and Deborah," Ram muttered. "They're merely acquaintances I—"

"—bedded," Phoebe finished.

"I never said I was a saint."

"I'm sorry, Braxton, I have no right to pry. We're merely living together for convenience."

"As you say," Ram replied, slanting her an amused look. "I'll see you home, and then I'm off to the docks. Someone has to have seen what happened the day your father disappeared."

"I'll come with you," Phoebe offered with an eagerness that lit her face.

"Not this time. London Pool is a rough-and-tumble place. I don't want you there. I promise you'll be the first to know if I learn anything of value."

Though she didn't like it, Phoebe accepted Ram's edict, and he handed her down from the coach and escorted her to the front door. She watched him ride off, her thoughts returning to the conversation she'd overheard at Madame LeBeau's shop. If she had had hopes of making her marriage work, what she'd heard today would have killed them. A man like Braxton, whose sexual appetite was legend, wouldn't be content with one woman. Four years had changed nothing about him.

Sighing regretfully, Phoebe was about to enter the door that a footman held open for her when a young lad darted from behind some shrubbery, thrust a note into her hands and ran off.

"Shall I catch him for you, milady?" the footman asked.

"No, let him go," Phoebe answered as she stared at the grubby note.

Phoebe hurried up to her room. Intuition told her the note was from her father's kidnapper, and her heart pounded with anxiety.

With shaking hands she unfolded the missive and read the words scrawled across the page. Her suspicions proved correct. It was indeed from her father's abductor. She was instructed to go to the west entrance of Hyde Park tomorrow at two o'clock in the afternoon to await information about her father, and warned to tell no one about the note or its contents.

Phoebe reread the note twice, then tore it into tiny pieces and deposited them in the hearth. She didn't like keeping information of this kind from Ram, but in this case she had no alternative.

Ram returned home shortly before the supper hour. He bathed, dressed and joined Phoebe in the drawing room. He went directly to the sideboard, filled a snifter with brandy and bolted it down in one gulp. When he turned to greet Phoebe, his face was grim.

"What happened?" Phoebe asked.

"Not much." He sounded frustrated. "It just doesn't make sense. How could your father just disappear into thin air? I think I'll call on Phillips again tomorrow. The man knows more than he's willing to admit."

"You're wrong about him, Ram."

Ram plopped down on the sofa beside her. "I've been wrong before, but this time I think I'm right.

Can you tell me what Phillips has been doing since his return from Egypt?"

Phoebe glanced at Ram, then looked away. She felt guilty about concealing the contents of the note from him and feared her eyes would give her away. Ignoring his question about David, Phoebe said, "What are you going to do now? We have no leads, no clues to Father's whereabouts."

Ram's answer was forestalled when Porter arrived to announce dinner. Ram escorted her into the dining room and waited until they had almost finished eating before broaching the subject again. "Is there anything more you can tell me about the amulet and your father's abduction? Something you may have forgotten?"

Phoebe's gaze slid away from his. "Why would I keep anything from you?"

His eyes narrowed suspiciously, Ram stared at the top of Phoebe's lowered head. "Why indeed?" A long pause ensued; then Ram asked, "What is it, Phoebe? Something is going on in that complex mind of yours. What aren't you telling me?"

Phoebe made herself look into Ram's eyes, keeping her expression purposely blank. "You're imagining things, Ram. Why would I keep anything from you when I desperately need your help?"

"Why indeed? Shall we retire to the study and resume the conversation over coffee?"

Being alone with Ram was the last thing Phoebe wanted. He had a way of getting the truth from her, and he already suspected she was hiding something.

"I'm tired, Ram. Besides, this conversation is going nowhere."

Ram didn't know exactly what bothered him about Phoebe tonight, but something definitely did.

She was lying; the proof was in her eyes. She'd avoided looking at him all evening. Did it have something to do with her encounter with two of his former lovers? He felt compelled to explain. Those casual encounters had meant nothing to him. She knew he hadn't lived like a hermit these past four years.

"Surely not that tired," Ram persisted as he helped her from the chair and folded her arm beneath his. "We'll take coffee in the study, Porter," he instructed the butler.

The study was Ram's favorite room. Its comfortable leather chairs, wood furniture, dark velvet drapes and large fireplace suited his masculinity; it was where he felt most at home. He seated Phoebe and pulled up a chair beside her, stretching his long legs out toward the fire. He stared at the flames in brooding silence until Porter served the coffee and departed.

"You're awfully quiet tonight," Ram said as he stirred cream into his coffee.

"I told you, I'm tired. Fittings exhaust me. I don't see why I needed so many gowns. Father and I will probably return to Egypt after this is all over, and those fancy gowns will be useless to me."

"My wife should dress in a style befitting her rank."

She looked away. "You said you learned nothing from the longshoremen today," she said, abruptly changing the subject. "Time is running out."

Phoebe was so adamantly opposed to the notion that Phillips was involved in her father's abduction that Ram had decided beforehand not to tell her what he'd learned at the docks. Of all the men he'd spoken to, only one recalled seeing men matching Phillips's and Thompson's descriptions debark

165

from the *Egyptian Star* the day it arrived. The long-shoreman remembered seeing Phillips approach a rough-looking thug who had been lurking near the docks.

That information was enough to renew Ram's suspicion of Phillips. Tomorrow he intended to confront the man and force the truth from him.

"Don't give up yet," Ram said. "The government is as anxious to find the amulet as you are to find your father. We won't let it rest."

Ram watched Phoebe sip her coffee as he gathered his thoughts. After a long pause, he asked, "Are you still upset about what happened at Madame LeBeau's? Deborah and Pamela mean nothing to me. I saw no reason to deny myself after you left me."

"I'm not upset. What you did after we parted is none of my concern. I still don't understand why you didn't obtain an annulment. I *did* abandon you, after all."

"Let it alone, Phoebe," Ram said.

Shrugging, she rose. Ram leaped to his feet. "I'll escort you to your room."

"That's not necessary. I know the way."

Ram's persistence won out. He grasped Phoebe's arm, felt her tremble and knew he affected her in the same way she affected him. His hand touched her cheek as he bent his head to taste her lips. He didn't try to hide his desire, his need. He kissed her until they were both breathless, until Phoebe broke free and stepped back.

"This isn't a good idea, my lord."

Ram grinned. "It's the best idea I've had all day." He pushed himself against her, letting her feel his rampant erection.

His lips brushed her cheek, then grazed the long

line of her throat while his hands roamed over her body. Phoebe groaned. Those wicked, wanton hands knew too well how to make her shiver, shudder, how to touch, where to caress. He made her hunger for more, made her want with a frightening level of desperation. He was a master of seduction and she his willing plaything.

If he didn't stop touching and kissing her, she'd soon be begging him to take it further, proving her weakness.

"Don't touch me like that, Ram."

His hand closed over her breast. "You mean like this? Your breasts are perfect, sweetheart. I love touching them."

The low, sexy timbre of his voice did nothing to reinforce her resolve. Her breasts were swollen and aching, and he had yet to touch her bare flesh. One hand closed possessively over her stomach, kneading provocatively. She moaned and shifted closer against him. Her nipples tingled; her stomach was a tight knot of need.

His hand slid down, pressing her skirts between her thighs as he rubbed his hand against her, slowly, deliberately, until she thought she'd go mad.

"These damn clothes are a nuisance," Ram growled. Without waiting for her permission, he unfastened her bodice and slid it down her shoulders, taking her chemise with it.

"Not here!" Phoebe cried. "Not now." Every time he made love to her, he left her exposed and emotionally vulnerable.

"Here," Ram said, swinging her into his arms and lowering her to the soft carpet before the hearth. "Now. I worked up a huge appetite watching you disrobe at Madame LeBeau's today. You can't say you don't want me."

He flipped up her skirts and shoved them above her hips, then pulled her beneath him. Parting her thighs, he touched her, cupped her, and then slid one long finger deep into her softness.

An inarticulate sound gurgled in her throat and her lids dropped in involuntary reaction as she clutched his shoulders.

He stroked, reaching deep. She gasped and squirmed. He caressed her intimately until she was writhing and frantic. Suddenly his hand was gone, free to unfasten his trousers. Then she felt his hardened length probing against her tender core. He was fully erect, iron-hard and thick. He pushed in and she gasped, tightened, then eased to allow him entrance. Her body welcomed him, softening, yielding, hot and slick. Anchoring her fingers behind his neck, she gripped his flanks with her thighs and tilted her hips to take more of him.

With one quick thrust, he seated himself fully, embedded within her lush heat. Caught in a net of spiraling pleasure, Ram felt bound to Phoebe as never before. This wasn't supposed to happen. He wouldn't *let* it happen. He felt ridiculously exposed—vulnerable. He wanted to believe his only link with Phoebe was mutual lust but knew it was much more.

Shaking off his disturbing thoughts, Ram set a frantic pace of thrust and withdrawal. Lowering his head, he took a pert nipple into his mouth, sucking and teasing, losing himself in the texture and taste of her. She had gone limp against him; he could feel her heart fluttering wildly.

She uttered a sound like a soft moan in the back of her throat, making him hotter, harder, moving him to greater abandon. His lids fell, his jaw locked, fighting the need to empty himself immediately.

"I'll wait for you," he panted into her ear. But he wasn't certain he could wait. Her moans, writhing and panting made him surge anew, his pleasure honed to excruciating sharpness.

"Ram!"

His name resonated in his ears as she came apart in his arms. He followed swiftly, convulsing strongly as he poured himself inside her.

Phoebe came slowly to her senses, her body thrumming, abruptly aware that Ram was removing her clothes, tossing them hither and yon.

"What are you doing?"

"Undressing you. We're going to go more slowly next time."

Panic rendered her speechless as Ram lifted her onto her feet and swept her up into his arms. It wasn't until he strode toward the door that Phoebe found her voice.

"Are you mad? I can't leave the room without my clothing. What will the servants think?"

"It's late; they're probably in bed by now."

"What about Porter?"

"He knows better than to look."

She pounded on his chest. "Put me down. I won't be humiliated like this."

He set her down long enough to snatch up her gown and drape it around her before sweeping her into his arms again and striding out the door. To Phoebe's relief, Porter was nowhere in sight and they reached Ram's room without mishap. He deposited her on the bed, quickly stripped and joined her.

Gathering her into his arms, he said, "This is

much nicer than the floor." Then he began to make slow, deliberate love to her. Resistance fled as wave after wave of passion flowed through her, filling her and carrying her away. She returned his kisses, opening her mouth for his tongue.

When his mouth slid from hers to devour her throat and breasts, she arched her body and moaned his name. When his lips continued downward over silken flesh, she welcomed his intimate caress as he spread her thighs and diligently plied his tongue to her heated core. A heartbeat later, he flipped her onto her stomach and raised her hips.

He moved closer, gripping her hips with steely fingers. Straddling her calves, he pressed the blunt head of his erection between her thighs, probing her swollen flesh. Then his palms curved over her bottom, lightly caressing before tracing down her thighs. Tormented beyond endurance, she braced her backside against him and wriggled invitingly.

Laughing softly, he held her steady and surged inside, claiming his ownership in the most basic way. He drew back and filled her again. Then he began a steady rhythm of thrust and withdrawal that drove her toward sweet oblivion.

Braced on her hands and knees, her body rocked with each forward thrust of his loins. She tried to gain purchase, but his legs were rigid columns, unmovable, giving not an inch. He plumbed her depths, driving her higher and higher, igniting an inferno that burned out of control.

He filled her again and again, his hips rocking hers, his hands closing about her naked breasts, pounding into her, harder, faster, deeper. Heat spread from her neck to where they were joined. Fire flamed and spasms of white-hot sensation erupted through her. She cried out, aware of his hands holding her in place, and of his hot seed scalding her. She felt his climax shudder through him, felt him surrender everything to her as he called out her name and joined her in that place where only lovers dwelt.

Ram's heart beat an erratic tattoo as he savored the indescribable sensation. No other woman had ever moved him as powerfully as Phoebe.

And that frightened the hell out of him.

Phoebe awakened the following morning in Ram's bed, tired but content. Then she remembered what she had deliberately withheld from him. Had she told him she was to meet with her father's abductor today, he would have insisted on accompanying her, and that would have led to disastrous complications. Somehow she had to sneak away without anyone knowing. Glancing at the empty place beside her in the bed, Phoebe vaguely recalled Ram rising early and telling her he'd be gone most of the day.

Glancing at the clock on the mantel, she was startled to see she had slept away the morning. She rose, donned her robe and rang for Abby. The maid appeared a few minutes later, bearing a tray with chocolate and sweet buns fresh from the oven.

"Lord Braxton said to let you sleep as long as you liked," Abby said as she placed the tray on the nightstand.

"I'd like a bath, Abby," Phoebe requested as she sipped the chocolate and nibbled at the bun.

"His Lordship thought you would want a bath when you awakened. The water is already heated and the tub ready to be carried up. I'll see to it while you finish your chocolate."

Phoebe didn't argue as she ate the bun and

drained the last drop of chocolate from the cup. It wasn't long before Abby returned, followed by a line of servants bearing a tub and buckets of water.

Phoebe didn't linger in the tub. She washed and dressed quickly, sat impatiently while Abby fashioned her hair into an attractive style, then went downstairs. A substantial breakfast had been laid out on the sideboard in the morning room, and Phoebe ate ravenously, surprised at her appetite. She kept herself busy until one-thirty, then informed Porter that she was going for a walk in the park.

"I'll fetch Abby to accompany you."

"There's no need," Phoebe said dismissively. "You can ask her to fetch my spencer, however."

Porter's disapproval was apparent as he went off to find Abby. The maid returned a short time later carrying Phoebe's spencer. "You shouldn't go out alone, milady," Abby chided.

"It's all right, Abby. Nothing is going to happen to me. I'm a married lady, and I can go about alone if I choose." Having said that, she sailed out the door.

Once Phoebe rounded the corner, she hailed a passing hackney and directed the driver to the west entrance of Hyde Park. After a brief ride, the hackney deposited her at her destination. She paid the driver and he drove off.

Hyde Park was bustling with activity at this time of day, but hardly anyone gave her a second glance as she lingered near the entrance. A frisson of apprehension slid down her spine, and she spun around. She saw nothing to warrant suspicion and turned her attention elsewhere, ignoring the prickly sensation at the back of her neck. Glancing around, she noted that she was now standing alone near the entrance. Everyone else had proceeded inside the park.

She heard a sound behind her and turned. But before she knew what was happening, a hand had closed over her mouth and she was being dragged toward a closed coach that had been pulled up to the curb. Her arms flailed wildly, and she dug in her heels, but to no avail. Her captor tossed her into the dark interior, leaped in behind her and slammed the door. Immediately the coach jerked forward.

Phoebe opened her mouth to scream, but a harsh voice close to her ear warned, "Be quiet. I'm taking you to yer father." Before she realized what was happening, a blindfold was tied over her eyes.

"Why are you doing this?" Phoebe asked in a quivering voice. "I would have gone along peaceably had I known I was being taken to see Father."

"I couldn't take the chance," the man growled. "I was paid to do a job and I ain't one to leave things to happenstance."

"Where are we going?"

"I just told you. Sit back and enjoy the ride."

"May I take off the blindfold?"

"No. You ain't supposed to know where ye're going."

Her nerves jangling, Phoebe perched on the edge of the seat and took stock of her situation. Blindfolded as she was, she had no idea in which direction they were traveling. The one thing she could do, however, was to listen carefully and hope she'd hear something she'd be able to identify later.

The coach clattered over a bridge, and she committed that fact to memory.

The ride seemed interminable. Phoebe wondered if Ram had returned home and missed her. Would he look for her? Would he even care? She almost laughed aloud at that thought. Of course he'd care, if for no other reason than because he wanted the amulet. She knew he'd be angry, for he had warned her before about going out alone.

Then the coach made a sharp right turn and a few minutes later slowed and drew to a halt.

"We're here," her captor growled.

He opened the door and gave her an ungentle shove. She stumbled as she stepped out but caught herself. Then she heard a door hinge groan and stumbled again over what she assumed was a threshold. She felt the change of atmosphere and realized she was inside a dwelling of some kind. Driven by anxiety, she whipped off the blindfold and waited for her eyes to adjust to the dim light.

The figure of a man came into focus. He was big and brawny, dressed in the rough clothing of a longshoreman.

"Who are you? Where is my father?" Phoebe demanded.

"You can call me Watts. Follow me."

Watts opened a door, and Phoebe followed him into a darkened room that held a cot and little else. Peering through the gloom, Phoebe saw a wasted figure lying beneath a single blanket. With a cry of dismay, she flung herself toward her father.

Chapter Ten

Dropping to her knees, Phoebe grasped her father's hand and called his name. Sir Thompson turned his head, his eyes widening when he saw Phoebe bending over him.

"Phoebe? Daughter? Is it really you?"

"It's me, Father," Phoebe choked out. "What have they done to you?"

"Dear God, I prayed you would be kept out of this. Have they hurt you?"

Tenderly Phoebe brushed a strand of damp hair from his forehead. "I'm fine, Father. Do you know who abducted you? Is Watts working alone?"

"Watts merely follows orders, I'm sure someone else is in charge. Unfortunately, I've not seen the man. I . . . I've been ill."

"What's wrong with you?"

"Malaria. I suffered my first attack after you left Egypt. Nasty business, that. The sea voyage seemed to relieve the symptoms, but they returned after I was abducted and brought here. I've been out of my head a good deal of the time since my captivity. My dear child, I never wanted to involve you in any of this."

Sir Thompson was becoming agitated, and Phoebe sought to soothe him. "Be easy, Father. I became involved the moment you disappeared. I rue the day we found the amulet. Why won't they believe you don't have it?"

"Lean closer," Sir Thompson whispered.

Phoebe bent low to hear her father's whispered words.

"During the voyage to England, I discovered the amulet inside a vase I had packed in my trunk. I have no idea how it got there, but I intended to turn it over to the proper authorities so it could be returned to the Egyptian government."

Shocked, Phoebe could only stare at her father. "You don't know how it got there?"

"Indeed not. I'm not a thief, daughter. I knew when we recovered it from the tomb that the Egyptians wouldn't let such a valuable artifact leave the country. I gave it to David, and he promptly relinquished it to the proper authorities. That's the last I saw of it until it turned up in my trunk."

Remembering Ram's suspicions, Phoebe asked, "Do you think David placed it in your trunk?"

"Never! David is my trusted assistant; he's no more a thief than I am."

"Then who?"

Thompson shrugged. "I don't know. Did you find it when you unpacked my things?"

Fearing to tell him about the break-ins lest he become more agitated than he already was, Phoebe said, "I searched the trunk thoroughly when I unpacked it. The amulet wasn't there."

Thompson forced a weak grin. "I hid it well. You'll find it inside my shaving kit, beneath the soap in my shaving mug. I want you to take it to the authorities. I suspect the Egyptian government is eager to have it returned."

Phoebe stared at him as if he had just sprouted horns. "I can't do that! These men mean business. They'll kill you if I don't give them the amulet."

"Heed me well, daughter. I'm old and sick. What happens to me doesn't matter. What does matter is my reputation. Take the amulet to the Foreign Office and tell the authorities what happened."

"What if Watts won't release me?"

"He will if you tell him you're ready to cooperate. Once you retrieve the amulet, take it directly to the Foreign Office."

"What are you two whispering about?" Watts asked harshly. "Get yer father to tell you where he hid the amulet and you'll both be released as soon as it's in my possession."

Phoebe whirled to confront Watts. "Can't you see my father is ill? I demand that you release us at once."

"Ye're in no position to demand anything, milady," Watts growled. "Get the old man to tell you where he hid the bauble and all will be well."

"Who are you working for? Who is behind Father's abduction?"

"Never mind. Just do as I say."

"Phoebe, remember what I said," Sir Thompson hissed beneath his breath.

"Leave us alone," Phoebe ordered. "I wish to speak with my father in private."

"Take yer time; no one's leaving until we get what we want."

"We? Who else is in this with you?" Phoebe asked. Her question went unanswered as the door closed behind Watts.

"It's no use, Phoebe, he won't tell you a thing."

"We have to escape, Father. Can you walk?"

He tried to rise but fell back against the mattress, apparently too weak to move. Phoebe watched helplessly as he began shaking so hard his teeth rattled.

"Father, are you all right?"

"It's the malaria, daughter. It will pass."

"Has Watts provided medicine for your ailment?"

Thompson shook his head. "I don't think so. I've been out of my head much of the time."

"I can't let you suffer, Father. I'm going to do what they want. I'll tell Watts I'm ready to meet his demands."

Thompson grasped her arm with surprising strength. "No, Phoebe, you can't do that. You must do as I say."

"They'll kill you."

"Once it's known that the amulet has been returned to the government, I'll be of no further use to my abductors."

"I fear for your life," Phoebe said on a sob.

"I'm willing to take that risk. Promise, Phoebe; promise you won't give in to their demands."

He was trembling, and sweating so profusely Phoebe didn't have the heart to add to his distress, so she gave her promise, though she knew she wouldn't keep it.

Her heart heavy with fear, Phoebe watched over her father as he fell into a fitful sleep. He needed medicine, and quickly. She'd do anything to see him well again, even break her promise to her father and betray Ram's trust. Phoebe tiptoed to the door and turned the knob. It was locked. She rapped on the door, quietly at first, then more vigorously. No answer was forthcoming.

How long did Watts intend to keep her under lock and key? Didn't he realize Ram would raise a hue and cry when her abduction was discovered?

"Watts comes and goes," Sir Thompson said from the cot. "I believe he leaves to meet with the man who paid him to abduct me."

"I didn't mean to awaken you," Phoebe said, returning to his side. "Do they feed you regularly?"

"They haven't starved me, but I have little appetite." He patted the cot. "Sit here and talk to me, daughter." Phoebe perched on the edge of the cot and took his frail hand in hers. "I never should have remained behind in Egypt," he lamented. "I should have returned to England with you, but there were so many loose ends to tie up before I could leave."

"Thank God David was there with you," Phoebe said.

"David was a great help to me. He handled everything after I became ill. I couldn't have managed without him."

"I'll find the best doctor for you once you're released," Phoebe vowed. "Perhaps Lord Braxton will recommend his own physician."

Thompson gave her a puzzled look. "Lord Braxton? Nice chap. Didn't he court you at one time?"

Phoebe realized the time had come to tell her father the truth about her and Ram. He was bound to find out sooner or later.

"This might not be the best time, Father, but there's something you should know about Braxton and me. Something that happened a long time ago."

"Dear child, you can tell me anything. Did you think I wouldn't understand?"

"No, it's not that . . . it's just that I was ashamed of what I did. You see," she began, "I'd decided not to join you in Egypt four years ago. I'd fallen in love with Braxton and believed that he returned my love. I should have known he couldn't remain faithful, but I was young and impulsive and had stars in my eyes."

"Falling in love isn't a bad thing, Phoebe. I assume you got over him, for you arrived in Egypt with David as planned."

Taking a deep breath, Phoebe said, "I married Braxton, Father. I married him one day and left him the next. I neither saw nor heard from him again until I returned to London. I naturally assumed he'd had our marriage annulled, but I was mistaken. We're still married."

"You got married and never told me?" Thompson said, astounded. "Did David know?"

"No, but he does now."

"No wonder you refused to wed him. He must have been devastated when he found out. Did Braxton tell you why he never sought an annulment?"

"No. I was shocked when he called on me in London. He appeared at the house I rented a few weeks after you disappeared."

"There's more to this story than you're telling me, isn't there, Phoebe?"

Phoebe released a sigh. "I'm sorry, Father; this is all so complicated. That blasted amulet has turned our lives upside down. The house was broken into twice, and I was accosted in Vauxhall Pleasure Gardens."

"Dear God! I'm sorry, Phoebe. I never thought

they would come after you. Continue your story, my dear. Where does Braxton fit into all this?"

"Braxton worked for the government during the war. When an Egyptian envoy arrived in London and notified the Foreign Office that the amulet was missing, they contacted Braxton and asked him to find the missing artifact. You, of course, were the prime suspect, and he was to get to you through me."

Phoebe had no intention of telling her father that Ram had been ordered to seduce her. She'd known from the beginning that Ram would never have contacted her unless he had an ulterior motive.

"Why did you leave Braxton if you loved him?" Thompson asked. "I understand none of this, Phoebe."

"David came to my rescue. He showed me how naïve I was to believe Braxton would remain faithful. Braxton had more than one lover in the village and doubtless a mistress or two in London."

"But he married *you*, my dear," Thompson chided gently.

"Men like Braxton don't know how to remain faithful. He would have left after he tired of me. I couldn't bear it, Father. I had to get away as quickly as possible. I left Ram the morning after our"—she blushed and looked away—"our wedding night. David and I left for Portsmouth immediately. We boarded a ship a few days later. That's the last I heard from Ram until I returned to London."

"How do you feel about him now?"

"Nothing has changed. Ram is still a womanizer and a rake. He has gone through half the women of the *ton* and is working on those he missed. The rogue never met a woman he didn't like," she groused.

"You still love him." It was more of a statement than a question.

"I'm . . . not sure. I moved in with him, but only because he forced me to. He didn't want me living alone after the break-ins. He now believes we are innocent, that we didn't steal the amulet."

"Are you going to tell him what we discussed today? He can help you return the amulet to the proper authorities."

Phoebe had no intention of telling Ram she knew where to find the amulet. He would take possession of it for the government, and she couldn't let that happen. Her father's welfare came first.

Phoebe was saved from answering her father's question when Watts entered the room.

"Brought you something to eat and drink," he said as he placed a tray of bread and cheese and mugs of ale on the table.

Phoebe gave the tray a disdainful look. "My father needs some nourishing beef broth."

"I ain't paid to cook," Watts sneered. "Eat or not, it makes me no difference."

Phoebe immediately picked up on the word "paid." "Who paid you? Who are you working for?"

"I ain't no blabbermouth, either. If my employer wants you to know, he'll tell you himself."

He turned to leave.

"Wait! When are you going to let me go?"

"You ain't going nowhere until the old man tells you where he's hidden the amulet."

"I wish to speak to your . . . employer."

"He'll show up when he's good and ready."

The door shut and the key turned in the lock. Phoebe stared at the door several pensive moments

before turning back to her father. "Have you any idea who hired Watts?"

"I've seen no one but Watts. Sit down and eat, daughter. Someone should take advantage of the food."

"I'll share it with you," Phoebe said, approaching the table.

Thompson shook his head. "I'm not hungry."

After much cajoling, Phoebe finally persuaded her father to drink the ale and eat a small piece of cheese. Then he lay back on the bed and fell into a fitful sleep. Phoebe pulled up a chair and sat by his side, listening to his harsh breathing. With nothing to occupy her time, her thoughts turned to Ram.

Last night in Ram's arms had been pure magic. He had the power to compel her body to want him, to make her burn with need. His ability to seduce and beguile was honed to perfection. He was irresistible when he set his mind to seduction.

Phoebe knew that what she intended to do would infuriate Ram, but her mind was made up. Her father would always come first with her. She would retrieve the amulet, give it to Watts and take her father home to recuperate. Once he was well enough to return to Egypt on another expedition, she would go with him, for she couldn't face Ram once she betrayed him . . . again.

"What are they doing in there?" the man in the room with Watts asked.

"Just talking," Watts replied. "I think the old man told his daughter what we want to know. I heard them whispering together."

"Excellent," the other man replied, rubbing his hands together. "I knew I was right to bring her here."

"Do you want to question her?"

"No. You handle it. Make her realize her father's life is in jeopardy if she doesn't comply with our demands. If she tells you where to find the amulet, go get it. But I suspect she's as stubborn as her father and will insist on retrieving it herself. Should that occur, have Benny drive her to her destination, then return here immediately once she gives him the gem."

"What about Thompson?"

"I have no reason to kill him once I have what I want. You and Benny can disappear, and he can find his own way back to London. I suggest that you both stay out of sight for a while. I'm counting on you, Watts. Don't disappoint me."

"Benny won't be back with the coach till morning."

"It's just as well. That will give the daughter time to consider the consequences should she fail to do as she's told. Bring the amulet to me tomorrow night at the Rusty Fox."

"What if the woman refuses? The old man won't tell us a damn thing."

"She won't refuse." He gave Watts a hard look. "The amulet is worthless to you should you decide to keep it. Not a fence in the country will touch it. I wouldn't be able to get rid of it myself if a private buyer on the Continent wasn't waiting for it."

"Don't worry, you'll get the bauble. If what you say is true about the government wanting it, it ain't worth the trouble."

"Just remember that. Until tomorrow night, Watts."

Ram returned home to find Phoebe missing and the household in a dither. The frantic butler reported that Phoebe had left earlier that day and hadn't returned.

Warning bells went off in Ram's head. "Did she say where she was going?"

"For a walk, milord. I tried to discourage her from going out alone, but she wouldn't listen." He assumed a woeful expression. "I should have insisted. Forgive me, milord."

"It's not your fault, Porter. I know how stubborn Phoebe can be," Ram said distractedly.

"I wonder . . ." Porter mused, stroking his chin.

"If you know something, Porter, tell me immediately."

"One of the footmen reported that a street urchin delivered a note to Lady Braxton yesterday."

Ram stiffened. "Why wasn't I told?"

"I didn't know myself until today. Since Lady Braxton seemed unconcerned, the footman simply dismissed the incident. I'll discharge him immediately."

"A reprimand will do," Ram said. "I'm sure he'll think twice before forgetting to mention something that could be important."

Fear rode Ram as he ascended the stairs. Phoebe was in danger, he could feel it in his bones. Why hadn't he set a guard on her? Impulsive and independent minded, Phoebe acted first and thought later. Why hadn't she told him about the message? All the while she'd made love with him, she'd kept a secret that could have placed her in grave danger. She hadn't trusted him four years ago and she didn't trust him now.

The one thing that could send Phoebe into the jaws of danger was a message from her father's abductor. What in God's name had she gotten herself into?

A thorough search of Phoebe's room turned up not even the slightest hint of her whereabouts. Glancing out the window, he saw the last rays of daylight fade into darkness and knew he'd go mad if he didn't do something. Fear prowled through him. His first inclination was to tear the city apart with his bare hands, but a calmer head prevailed.

Ram charged from the room, yelling for Porter as he ran down the stairs. Porter met him in the foyer.

"I'm going to the dock area to inquire about Lady Braxton, Porter. Someone has to know something about Phoebe's disappearance, and the taverns seem the most likely places to start looking. Send a footman to find me if something turns up here."

Unfortunately, Ram's search led nowhere. His subtle questions gained him nothing but impatient stares and rebuffs. It was the wee hours of the morning when Ram returned home. Porter was waiting up for him. The butler roused himself from the bench where he had been dozing.

"Any news, milord?"

"No, nothing," Ram said tautly. "It's as if the earth opened up and swallowed her. There's nothing more I can do till morning. Get some sleep, Porter."

Ram's steps dragged as he climbed the stairs. The thought of someone harming Phoebe called forth all the fury in his soul. When he'd first heard that Phoebe had returned to England, he'd wanted to see her hurt as badly as she had wounded him, but the need to inflict hurt had been sacrificed to a more urgent need. Ram wasn't quite sure what that need was, but he'd figure it out later, once Phoebe was back where she belonged.

That thought brought on another. Where *did* Phoebe belong?

His first inclination was that she belonged in his arms, in his bed. His next thought was darker, deeper. Would he ever be able to trust her? Life had a way of repeating itself. Phoebe didn't want to be married to him any more than he wanted a wife. Therein lay his dilemma. Even a libertine like he recognized the strong emotional bond that existed between them. For many years the only feeling he'd allow himself had been erotic pleasure. Superficial though it was, it had been enough for him.

He'd fashioned his life on hedonistic pleasures, pursuits such as womanizing, drinking and gambling. Then Phoebe had reentered his life and turned it upside down. He had loved her desperately once and had been willing to devote the rest of his life to their marriage and the family they would create together.

Ram lay down on the bed fully clothed and closed his eyes, but Phoebe's image kept intruding. He realized their differences no longer mattered. Only Phoebe mattered. He had to find her, if only to wring her foolish little neck.

Phoebe awoke to daylight, cramped from dozing in an uncomfortable chair. She glanced at her father and saw that he was still sleeping. Reaching out, she gently touched his forehead. He was feverish, his thinning hair plastered limply against his brow.

During the long night she'd been aware of his fitful tossing and knew in the deepest part of her heart that she couldn't let him suffer. Her promise to him had been made under duress; she'd do what her conscience directed. The amulet was just a cold, inanimate object, but her father's life was precious.

Walking resolutely to the door, Phoebe rapped lightly so as not to awaken her father. "Mr. Watts. Open the door. I have something to say to you."

The door opened. Clutching her reticule, Phoebe tried to step through, but Watts stopped her. "Please, Mr. Watts, I don't want to awaken Father. Can we speak privately?"

Watts considered her request, then let her pass. "Did yer father tell you where to find the amulet?"

"Close the door. I don't want Father to hear us."

Watts closed the door and leaned against it, watching Phoebe through narrowed lids. "Well? Have you decided yer father's life is more important than the amulet?"

Phoebe looked him straight in the eye. "That's exactly what I've decided."

"All right, talk. Tell me where it is and I'll fetch it."

Phoebe wasn't stupid. She wasn't going to give Watts more information than he needed. He wasn't the kind of man who inspired trust. "No. I'll get it myself, but you must first promise to release Father once the amulet is in your hands."

"My employer ain't interested in taking yer lives. You'll be free to go once the amulet is delivered."

"How do I know you're telling the truth?"

"Well, now, you'll just have to trust me, won't you?"

Phoebe had to believe him or she'd go mad wondering if she was doing the right thing. What she planned to do would disappoint her father. And deceiving Ram bothered her more than she cared to admit. Once her husband learned she'd handed the amulet over to the enemy, there would be hell to pay.

But even if he turned her and her father over to the authorities, they'd be better off than they were now. She was certain she and her father could explain everything to the satisfaction of both England and Egypt. Surely the authorities would recognize the truth, wouldn't they?

"Very well, I'll get the amulet and return here with it. Once you have it, you are to return Father and me to London."

"I'll do it. Tell me where to find the amulet."

"No. It's my way or no way."

"I ain't sure my employer is going to like this," Watts said.

"He wants the amulet, doesn't he?"

"We'll compromise," Watts said cagily. "Benny will be here with the coach soon. He'll take you where you need to go. When you retrieve the amulet, bring it to me. Once it's in my hand, yer father will be released."

Phoebe didn't like the sound of that. She could not depend on the word of a criminal without a conscience. "No, that won't do."

"Take it or leave it, lady."

"My husband will have your guts for garters. You *do* know who he is, don't you?"

"The Earl of Braxton. My employer doesn't seem concerned, so why should I? Just remember, yer father will suffer if you try to outwit us. The old man can die in that room for all I care."

"Don't worry. I'm not going to place my father's life at risk. I know I'm dealing with heartless criminals who care nothing for human life."

The door to the cottage opened, terminating their discussion.

"Here's Benny," Watts said. "Ye're just in time. The wench has decided to cooperate."

Benny, even more rough and unkempt then Watts, leered at Phoebe. "What did you have to do to her to make her see things our way?"

"Nothing," Watts replied. "Orders are she's not to be touched. Remember that."

"Shame," Benny complained, eyeing Phoebe greedily. "She's a pretty little thing. What am I supposed to do with her?"

"Take her wherever she directs you and wait until she places the amulet in your hands. Then ye're to bring it to me."

"What about her?" Benny asked, gesturing toward Phoebe. "Should I bring her back with me?"

"That won't be necessary. Once we have what we want, she's of no further use to us."

"What about my father?" Phoebe cried. "You promised to release him."

"I said he'd be free to go, didn't I?" Watts groused. "Go with Benny. He'll take you wherever you say. But if you try anything funny, you'll suffer for it."

Phoebe hated to leave her father behind, but she had no choice. Watts wouldn't release him until the amulet was in his possession. There *was* something she could do, however. She intended to return with Benny to make certain Watts kept his word, even if she had to force her way into the coach.

"I'm ready," Phoebe announced.

"Wait!" Watts said, whipping out a cloth from his pocket. "First the blindfold."

A frisson of fear slid down Phoebe's spine. "Why is it necessary to blindfold me?"

"Like I said before, I ain't leaving nothing to chance."

Chafing with impatience, Phoebe allowed Watts to blindfold her and guide her out the door and into the coach. Once the coach rattled off, she whipped the blindfold off. She saw nothing but darkness. The leather shades had been pulled down and securely fastened. Though she worked on them the better part of an hour, they remained firmly in place.

Suddenly the coach slowed to a stop and Benny flung open the door.

"We've reached the city limits," he said. "Where am I to take you?"

Phoebe glanced out the door and saw the Tower rising in the distance. She attempted to get her bearings, but Benny's bulky form moved in front of her, blocking her view. She did, however, manage to see a signpost indicating the name of the village they had just passed through.

"Mount Street," Phoebe directed. "Number thirty-two."

The door slammed shut and Benny returned to the driver's box. Then the coach jolted back onto the road.

Phoebe's nerves were on edge by the time the coach pulled up in front of the house on Mount Street. So many things could go wrong. What if the amulet wasn't where her father said it was? He was ill and confused, and his mind wasn't working properly. There were still so many unanswered questions. How had the amulet appeared in her father's trunk in the first place?

Her father hadn't taken it.

But someone had.

Who?

Chapter Eleven

The coach rolled to a stop a short distance down the block from her house on Mount Street. She stumbled down to the sidewalk without help. Benny caught her elbow and growled a warning.

"Don't try anything funny. I'll be here waiting for you when you return. If you ain't out in a reasonable time, I'll come after you."

Phoebe pulled from his grasp. "Don't worry. I'm not about to abandon my father. Just make sure you and Watts keep your part of the bargain."

Phoebe strode briskly toward her house, aware that she was about to betray both Ram and her country. But it couldn't be helped. She couldn't allow her father to become a pawn in this dangerous game.

The front gate gave a warning creak as she pushed it open. She stepped through and stopped abruptly. Oh, God, she had forgotten! The man lounging near the front steps came to attention, his stance confrontational. Phoebe knew immediately who he was. Why hadn't she remembered that Ram had hired Bow Street Runners to keep an eye on the house?

Summoning a smile, Phoebe forced herself to relax as she approached the Runner. "Good day. I'm glad to see you are following my husband's orders."

Her words seemed to do little to allay the man's suspicion. "Your husband?"

"The Earl of Braxton. I'm Lady Braxton."

The Runner removed his hat. "I'm Slaughter, milady. Is there something I can do for you?"

"No, thank you. I've come to collect some personal items I left behind."

Slaughter glanced behind her. "Is Lord Braxton with you?"

Thinking quickly, Phoebe said, "No, I came alone. My husband is otherwise engaged."

Slaughter's dark brows rose sharply upward. "How did you get here? I didn't hear a conveyance stop in front of the house."

"Are you questioning my veracity, Mr. Slaughter?"

Slaughter became immediately apologetic. "Forgive me, milady, I mean no disrespect. I'm just trying to do my job." He stood aside to let her pass.

Phoebe had to brace her shaking legs as she swept past Slaughter. She turned once before entering the house and found him staring at her with a puzzled look. Then she quickly closed the door behind her, leaning against it until her nerves calmed. She couldn't fail now.

Once the door closed, another man stepped out from behind a bank of bushes beside the front entrance.

"You heard, Akers?" Slaughter asked. Akers nodded. "What do you make of it?"

"Something is amiss," Akers said. "Best we apprise Lord Braxton and let him decide."

"I'll fetch His Lordship," Slaughter said. "If Lady Braxton attempts to leave, try to stall her until he arrives."

Phoebe spent a few minutes meandering from room to room. Everything was just as she'd left it when Ram had removed her to his townhouse, except for the layer of dust that covered the furniture. She wandered into the study, wincing at the empty shelves. She knew the artifacts were safe in the museum, but she missed them.

Concentrating on her mission, Phoebe ascended the stairs. When she glanced inside her old room, images of her and Ram making love on the bed teased the edges of her memory. After today, Ram would never again look upon her with passion and admiration. Once her father was safe, she would tell Ram what she had done. She owed him that much. She didn't know how she could bear his disappointment in her or his contempt, but somehow she would survive.

Shaking those disheartening thoughts from her head, Phoebe closed the door on the memories her bedroom held and proceeded to the room that had been reserved for her father.

Phoebe recalled unpacking her father's shaving mug, but wasn't sure where she had put it. The washstand would be the logical place, and she looked there first. She found his razor and strop but no mug. She took her time wandering the room, opening drawers and peering inside. She wasn't worried about Benny coming to fetch her, for she

195

felt certain he would keep his distance once he spied the Bow Street Runner.

When the drawers failed to yield the elusive shaving mug, Phoebe moved on to the wardrobe. She spied the mug immediately. It sat on a shelf beside a few other personal items. Relief washed over her as she hugged the mug to her breast. When her nerves settled, she removed the brush and peered inside. She saw nothing but hardened soap.

Phoebe smiled at her father's cunning. No one would think to look beneath the soap for the valuable artifact. She wanted to make sure, however, that the amulet was where it was supposed to be before returning to the coach. Phoebe carried the mug downstairs to the kitchen, intending to fetch a knife to pry out the soap.

Meanwhile, back at his townhouse, Ram prowled his study, his mood dark. Where could Phoebe be? Early this morning he'd set Bow Street Runners on her trail and was waiting for a report. He'd also sent for Luc, for if ever he needed a friend, it was now.

A discreet knock sounded on the door. "Come in," Ram growled.

Porter stood in the opening. "Lord Westmore is here, milord."

Luc swept past Porter, stopping abruptly when he saw the look on Ram's face. "My God, what's happened?"

"I think Phoebe has been abducted by the same men who kidnapped her father."

"Bloody hell! How long has she been gone?"

"She disappeared yesterday. I'm at my wit's end, Westmore. If I get my hands on the bastard who did this, I'll kill him."

"Calm down, Braxton. If you think about it, you'll realize that Phoebe's abductors aren't bent on murder. If they were, Sir Thompson would already be dead. They want the amulet."

"Phoebe doesn't have it. Neither does Sir Thompson."

"Are you sure?"

"About Phoebe, yes. About Thompson, I'm taking Phoebe's word for it."

"How can I help?"

"I'm waiting for the Bow Street Runners I hired to report back to me. I don't know where to begin my search, Luc, and it's killing me."

"You care for her, don't you?"

"Lord knows I tried not to. I have every reason to loathe and distrust her, but I can't. David Phillips is responsible for what happened between us. I—"

The door opened. "Forgive me, milord, but a Bow Street Runner is here and I thought you'd want to see him straightaway."

"Yes, yes, show him in."

Porter stood aside, allowing a short, nondescript man to sidle past him.

"Did you learn anything, Markly?" Ram asked without preamble.

"I located the hackney driver who picked up your wife and took her to her destination."

Ram frowned. If Phoebe had hired a hackney, that meant she hadn't been abducted. It didn't make sense. "Where did the hackney take her?"

"To Hyde Park, milord. But then we lost her trail. It's as if she disappeared off the face of the earth."

"Are you sure about this?"

"Aye. I placed all my available men on the case,

and they came up with no leads after Lady Braxton was deposited at Hyde Park."

Luc strode out the door. "I'll cover the park, Ram. Someone had to have seen her."

"Shall my men continue the search?" Markly asked.

"Yes, yes, of course. Someone has to have seen something. No matter what it costs, I want my wife found."

Markly nodded and withdrew. Ram went immediately to the sideboard and poured himself a large brandy. With shaking hands, he tossed it back without really tasting it. How could he have let Phoebe be abducted when he had vowed to protect her? How could this have happened?

"Milord, someone—" Porter's words ended abruptly when a man barged into the room.

"Slaughter, is something amiss at the house?"

"I'm not sure, milord, but Akers and I thought you should know."

"Know what? Spit it out, man."

"Lady Braxton is at the house on Mount Street even as we speak. She said she had come to collect some personal items she had forgotten, but something just didn't ring true. I came as fast as I could."

"Porter, have my horse brought around!" Ram shouted. "Did my wife say what she wanted at the house?" Ram asked as Slaughter raced to keep up with him.

"No. I spoke with her briefly but didn't inquire. I thought it prudent to get here as fast as I could."

"You did exactly right, Slaughter. There'll be a nice bonus in this for you and Akers. My wife has been missing since yesterday."

*   *   *

Phoebe placed the mug on a high shelf with some dishes and went to the drawer where the knives were stored. She was rummaging around for a knife when she heard the front door open and shut and footsteps approaching. Benny had said he would fetch her if she took too long, but she doubted he would risk an encounter with the Runner. More likely it was Slaughter.

Phoebe was wrong on both counts. Her heart nearly stopped when the kitchen door flew inward and Ram stepped through the opening. One look at his fierce expression was enough to send fear lancing through her.

"Where have you been?" he roared. "I've been worried sick. No lies, Phoebe. Only the truth this time."

"I . . . I . . ." Words failed her. What could she say? Telling Ram her real purpose was out of the question. He would do his duty to his country and return the amulet to the government, and her father would die.

"You knew all along where the amulet was, didn't you? You came here to fetch it."

"No, I . . . I . . ."

Impaling her with a hard look, he repeated, "Where have you been?"

"I can't tell you."

"Give me the amulet; I know you have it."

Desperation made her voice tremble. "I can't, Ram. I . . . don't have it." Her tongue stumbled over the lie, but she bravely stood her ground before Ram's implacable anger.

"Lies! All lies! I should have known a leopard doesn't change its spots. Let me guess where you've been. Ah, yes, conspiring with those who want the amulet for their own personal gain."

"That's not true!"

"What is the truth? I know a note was delivered to you. Who was it from?"

Phoebe couldn't risk telling the truth; perhaps half-truths would do. "The note was from Father's abductors. They offered to take me to him."

Ram gave a snort of disbelief. "Why would they do that?"

Phoebe shrugged. "I'm not sure. Perhaps to prove that he is alive."

"Is he?"

"He is, but he's desperately ill with malaria and in need of medical attention."

"Then they let you go, did they?" Ram said with scathing mockery. "Why didn't you let me know you were here? Do I look like a fool? You and your father made a deal with the men who want the amulet, and you've come to fetch it. I'm going to ask you one more time, Phoebe. Give me the artifact."

Phoebe shook her head. "I can't give you what I don't have."

Ram snorted in disbelief. "Very well, have it your way. Tell me where to find your father and I promise no harm will come to him."

"I can't."

Ram's fingers tightened on her shoulders. "You can and you will."

"You don't understand! I was blindfolded. I have no idea where I was taken."

He rolled his eyes. "Why don't I believe you?"

Phoebe's heart plummeted. If she hoped to save her father's life, she had no choice but to lie to the man she had never stopped loving. She cast a surreptitious glance at the shaving mug resting inconspicuously on the shelf and suppressed a groan of disappointment. She had come so close. If Ram hadn't walked in on her, the amulet would be on its way to Watts and his employer. And her father would be free.

"You do realize, don't you, that I intend to order a thorough search of the house," Ram informed her.

A brief nod was all Phoebe could manage. Deliberately she refrained from glancing at the mug. It looked so innocuous, she doubted anyone would suspect it contained anything of value.

"Slaughter!" Ram shouted. The Bow Street Runner appeared immediately.

"Aye, milord."

"I want the house searched from top to bottom. Hire as many men as you need; nothing is to be overlooked."

"What are we looking for?"

Ram turned to Phoebe. "Describe it to him."

Phoebe hesitated but a moment. "A gold amulet in the form of a starburst with a large ruby in its center. It's very old and very valuable."

"If it's here, we'll find it," Slaughter said confidently.

Phoebe prayed they would fail. Unless Ram put her under lock and key, she would recover the artifact, and pray that her father's abductors would contact her again.

"We're leaving," Ram said after Slaughter withdrew.

"Where are we going?"

"Home. You won't be given the opportunity to betray me or your country again."

"Hello! What's going on?"

David Phillips's voice carried to them from the doorway.

Connie Mason

"I should have known you'd be involved," Ram bit out.

"Involved in what?" David asked innocently. "I just happened to be passing and noticed the commotion."

Phoebe wanted to rush to David and beg for his help, but something in Ram's expression stopped her.

"Are you saying you didn't know Phoebe was missing?"

David's eyes widened. "Missing? Are you all right, Phoebe? What happened?"

"I saw Father. He's ill."

"You saw him? Where is he?"

"I don't know. I was blindfolded and had no idea where I was being taken."

"Did he reveal the location of the amulet?"

Phoebe wanted to tell David everything, but not with Ram listening. "Father didn't steal the amulet." That, at least, was the truth.

"Excuse us, Phillips," Ram said. "We were just leaving."

Phoebe saw a brief flicker of anger in David's eyes, but it was gone so quickly, she thought she had imagined it.

"May I call on you, Phoebe? There are matters concerning your father's disappearance I need to discuss with you."

"No!" Ram answered, forestalling Phoebe's reply. "Phoebe won't be receiving visitors anytime soon."

"Why are you angry with her?" David asked.

Anger didn't begin to describe what Ram was feeling. Dismay, disgust, disappointment, rage, hurt . . . all these and more coursed through him. Phoebe had destroyed a tenuous relationship that in time could have become the basis for a strong marriage. His feelings for his wife had begun to return, but once again she had betrayed his trust. Did she have no heart? No, she didn't, for greediness had devoured it long ago. Obviously, Phoebe and her father wanted the amulet for the wealth it would bring them.

"Let's just say I can't trust her," Ram said. "I wanted to protect Phoebe, but clearly she doesn't need protection."

"Let her go," David argued. "I'll take care of her."

Phillips's offer did nothing to allay Ram's rage. Phillips might have been Phoebe's lover, but Ram vowed that the man would never have her in his bed again.

"Phoebe is coming home with me," Ram growled, pushing her out the door.

"Do I have no say in this?" Phoebe asked, digging in her heels.

"No," Ram bit out. "You'll do as I say until you decide to tell the truth." He glanced at Phillips, realized he was lingering behind and prodded him through the door. "You have no reason to be here, Phillips. Slaughter will escort you out."

Slaughter, who had been hovering nearby, appeared almost instantly. "I was keeping an eye on him, milord. Don't know how he got past me." He sent Phillips a stern look. "If you'll follow me, sir, I'll see you to the door."

Phillips preceded Slaughter out the door, glancing once over his shoulder to send Phoebe an encouraging smile.

"I almost believed you when you said Phillips wasn't your lover," Ram muttered, shaking his head. "Obviously, you're full of lies. I no longer know what to believe."

Grasping her arm, he guided her through the house and out the front door.

"How did you know I was here?" Phoebe asked.

"Slaughter thought your coming here alone was odd and reported it to me. I came as soon as I was informed."

They had just walked out the gate when Ram placed a restraining hand on her arm. "Who is that?"

"To whom are you referring?" Phoebe asked with feigned innocence.

"That man walking away from us. All I can see is his back, but he must have been loitering nearby. He's climbing into the coach parked down the street and driving off."

Phoebe shrugged. "What makes you think he looks suspicious? He could have been visiting someone nearby."

Ram didn't think so but decided not to belabor the point. He knew Phoebe hadn't spoken a truthful word since he'd walked in on her today, so why should he expect the truth from her now?

"We'll have to ride double," Ram said, lifting Phoebe into the saddle and mounting behind her. "But make no mistake, Phoebe, you're going to tell me the truth sooner or later. I'll accept nothing less from you."

The man in the hooded cloak entered the cottage in a foul mood. He rounded on Watts and Benny the moment he spied them.

"Fools! Can't you do anything right? Why didn't you get rid of the Bow Street Runners before-hand?"

"We didn't know they were there, and the woman didn't see fit to tell us," Watts explained. "Don't blame us."

"What do you want us to do now?" Benny asked. "Maybe we should put some pressure on the old man."

"How is Thompson?"

"About the same," Watts answered.

"Are his ramblings making sense yet?"

Watts shrugged. "No more than usual. He's sleeping a lot."

"We're going to have to be more forceful. We need him to lead us to the amulet. His daughter is no good to us now. Braxton probably won't let her out of his sight. Blast and damn! Nothing has gone right. Who would have thought the old man would be so stubborn?"

"You want me to torture him?" Watts asked eagerly.

The other man grimaced. "Torture's not the answer. The old goat isn't likely to survive it. We need to move him to another location. His daughter is smart; she might remember something about this place and tell Braxton. I'll let you know as soon as I find a safe place to take Thompson. Meanwhile, try questioning him again. You know where to reach me should you learn anything."

Phoebe felt as if her world had crumbled beneath her. Ram was treating her like a stranger. With cold courtesy he'd escorted her to her room, then left her there to stew. Her unwillingness to tell the truth had earned her nothing but his contempt. Unfortunately, betraying Ram hadn't helped her father, for she'd failed to retrieve the amulet.

What was she going to do now?

Connie Mason

She longed to confide in Ram, but confession was unlikely to help her father. She had failed him and failed Ram. She needed to return to the house and retrieve the amulet as soon as possible. She had seen Benny hightailing it back to Watts, and by now their employer must know his plan had gone awry. Would her father suffer for her failure?

Her disconsolate thoughts ended abruptly when Ram entered the room and slammed the door behind him. Her pulse surged. Tension coiled into her limbs, but she stood her ground. She was no coward.

"What are you going to do to me?"

"Nothing, as long as you tell the truth." He glared at her. "Do you even know the meaning of the word?"

"Of course I do."

Ram rolled his eyes. "Suppose we start at the beginning. Where were you last night?"

"I told you. With my father."

"So far so good. What did he do with the amulet?"

"He didn't steal it."

"Phoebe, I'm losing patience. That's not what I asked."

Phoebe's lips compressed into a stubborn line. "Ask me something else."

"Is Phillips involved?"

Phoebe sent him a puzzled look. "Why would you think that? David is definitely not involved in any of this."

He reached for her, his grip unrelenting. "What were you doing at the house on Mount Street?"

"Gathering some personal belongings I had left behind."

"Damn you! Why didn't you let me know you

206

were all right? Do you have any idea how frantic I've been?"

Phoebe was caught off guard by the note of desperation in his voice. It sounded as if Ram actually cared for her, but she found it difficult to credit such a thing. "I'm sorry."

"Sorry isn't good enough, Phoebe," Ram grated. "The simple truth is all I ask."

Phoebe stared at him. Did she dare? Maybe she could tell him some truths, give him enough to make him trust her, at least long enough to end her confinement.

"I'm waiting, Phoebe."

"What will you do to me if I remain silent? Beat me? Turn me over to the authorities? What, Ram?"

"I'm hoping you'll be sensible so none of those alternatives are necessary."

Phoebe gnawed her lower lip. She was torn, wanting Ram's trust but fearing the consequences of confiding in him. If only David were here to advise her. *He* would understand.

"Just answer one question, Ram," Phoebe said. "How far would you go to save a loved one?"

"That's unfair."

"It's entirely fair."

"I hoped you would trust me enough to let me help you."

"If you had the amulet, would you return it to its rightful owners, even if it meant the death of a loved one?"

He hesitated but a moment. "It would be the right thing to do."

"Not if it means losing my father. Now do you understand?"

"I've always understood, Phoebe, but my duty is to my country."

Phoebe refused to look at him. "I know that. Just as I know I can't sacrifice Father for a bauble."

"A very valuable bauble, Phoebe. International relationships are at stake. Tell me where to find your father and I will take care of everything."

"I don't know. I was blindfolded."

"What do you remember? What smells or sounds do you recall?"

Phoebe searched her brain for answers. Could Ram really rescue her father? If such a thing were possible, there would be no reason to lie to him.

"I recall crossing a bridge as we left the city," Phoebe said. "We traveled for close to an hour, then made a sharp right turn onto a rutted lane."

"Anything else?"

"Epping," Phoebe said, excitement coloring her words. "I saw a road sign. The cottage where Father is being held is near the village of Epping."

"If I promise to return your father to you unharmed, will you confide in me? Will you tell me where to find the amulet?"

She wanted to, desperately, but thought it best to err on the side of caution. Ram couldn't guarantee her father's safety. Only she could do that. Her father's life depended upon keeping the amulet out of the government's hands.

"I can't, Ram. Don't ask that of me."

"Consider this. Until your father's abductors are brought to justice, your life is in danger. You have information they want, and they'll stop at nothing to get it. You leave me no choice but to confine you to the house."

"I don't have what they want," Phoebe protested. Dear God, the situation was getting more complicated by the minute.

"But you know where it can be found."

Phoebe grappled with her conscience but found no sure answers to her dilemma. Being confined to the house was a devastating turn of events. She could neither receive messages from Watts and his employer nor recover the amulet. A tear slid down her cheek.

Suddenly she was in Ram's arms, her head buried against his chest as she sobbed uncontrollably. She hadn't meant for it to happen, but the tears wouldn't stop. At length she became aware that Ram was speaking to her, his voice fraught with emotion.

"Damn you! I was devastated when I learned you had vanished. My imagination ran rampant, and I blamed myself for failing to protect you." He gave a bitter laugh. "Never once did I think you had left of your own accord, or that you had conspired against me. You managed to draw me into your lies from the day we met."

He lifted her tear-stained face and stared into her eyes. "What am I going to do with you, Phoebe? Even now, knowing how deceitful you are, all I want is to make love to you."

The lump in Phoebe's throat grew. She swallowed hard and gave him a wobbly smile. "Why would it be wrong?"

"Making love wouldn't solve a damn thing."

Maybe not, Phoebe thought, *but it couldn't make things any worse than they were now.* She lowered her gaze, fearing Ram would read her thoughts and despise her for them. But obviously, Ram's thoughts paralleled hers, for his arms tightened around her, pulling her more deeply into his embrace.

"God help me, for I can't help myself," he

groaned, and his mouth descended on hers.

Ram's heart was racing, his blood pumping hot and heavy, and he ached with urgency. This shouldn't be happening, but his body seemed to have a will of its own. He kissed her hard, his tongue delving into her mouth in a mindless explosion of passion.

He'd been so relieved to find her unharmed that it was difficult to sustain his anger. He wanted to shake her until her teeth rattled, to make her promise never to lie to him again, but despite his anger, a thread of something basic and elemental prevented his temper from surging out of control. He recognized it now as need, need to make love to his wife. To protect her from those who would harm her.

"You're mine, Phoebe," he groaned against her lips. "You have always been mine. Never forget that. No one else's, mine. No matter how far you flee, nothing will ever change that."

He couldn't help himself. The moment her mouth softened against his, he lost control. Phoebe might not love him, and he wasn't certain he loved her, but he damn sure wanted her and she wanted him.

His hand slid between her legs, finding her through the layers of her clothing. As she gasped into his mouth, her hips rocked against his. His body clenched in frustration. Bloody hell! He wanted nothing between him and Phoebe.

Biting back a curse, he spun her around and began attacking the buttons marching down her back. Her gown fluttered away, and she stood before him in nothing but her gauzy shift.

He attempted to sweep her into his arms and carry her to bed, but Phoebe shook her head and backed away. "Wait. I do want to make love with you, but first tell me if it will change anything. Would you still return the amulet to the government if you had it in your possession?"

Ram went still, his expression guarded. "Making love to you has nothing to do with the amulet, or the lies you've told me. It's for me—for us. I want you regardless of what you've done or haven't done."

Chapter Twelve

Phoebe couldn't find the strength to deny Ram. He was the only man she'd ever loved, the only man she'd ever wanted. He thought her a liar, didn't trust her, but he still wanted her.

His hands were on her breasts, shaping and molding them through the linen of her shift. He wedged his knee between her thighs and propelled her backward toward the bed. Catching her lip between her teeth, Phoebe arched against him and felt her nipples swell against his palms. Suddenly his hands fell away, and moments later her shift was gone and she was lying flat on her back, sprawled across the bed in wanton abandon.

Eyes narrowed, she watched him undress, catching her breath at the sight of his arousal springing powerfully from the curly nest at the base of his belly. Then he was beside her, the heady male scent of him filling her senses. The hard texture of his skin, the coarse hair on his chest, the very maleness of him was enormously arousing.

His hands moved over her, leisurely at first, touching her with familiar assurance, sending delicious little tremors through her. Sexual excitement throbbed inside her, turning her blood to liquid heat as he found her most sensitive places.

He kissed her endlessly, his tongue sweeping her mouth again and again, as though he were trying to lose himself in her. Her lips, her breasts, her nipples, the insides of her thighs—nothing went unattended. The only sound competing with her tiny gasps of pleasure was the increasing fury of the rain beating against the windows.

But the fury couldn't compare with what she felt when Ram brushed his thumb across the sensitive nub between her legs, increasing the pressure with each caress. Fire seared through her veins, coiled in her belly, rode between her legs.

"Ram!"

"You're so passionate, Phoebe," Ram murmured. "I love the way your body weeps for me. Will you let me make love to you?"

Her breath came out in a rush. She nodded wordlessly, the only response she could manage, but it seemed enough for him.

Phoebe's brain shut down when Ram lifted her bottom in his hands and gave her his mouth. She screamed, her hands clutching him as he aroused her with his mouth, his teeth, his tongue. Her body moved independent of her mind, her hips thrusting into his intimate caress as his hot breath seared her.

He eased a finger inside her and she screamed again, so close to the peak she could feel it building and building deep inside her. She was quaking, nearly frantic. She arched her back, fisted her hands in his hair and shattered. She couldn't stop the sensation and willingly gave herself up to the ebb and flow of her climax. It lifted her and carried her away as he pushed her farther than she had ever gone before, leaving her limp and satiated.

"Now it's my turn," Ram said, moving over her.

With a shout of satisfaction, he came into her hard, deep, raising her bottom so she could take all of him. Immediately he was seized by a bewildering sensation of losing his balance, his focus; he was certain of nothing but a confusing swirl of emotions. Being inside Phoebe was pure heaven. When her long legs went around his flanks and drew him even deeper, he nearly lost what little control he had left. Phoebe's power over him was an awesome thing.

Thrusting hard, withdrawing, pushing deeper, he drove her until he felt tension rebuilding inside her. He smiled, proud of his ability to restore the passion so recently spent. Then he looked down where they were joined, saw himself embedded in her softness and began to tremble, fearing he wouldn't be able to wait. He gritted his teeth and held on, thanking God and all the angels when Phoebe's muscles clenched around him and he felt her stiffen with her first contraction.

He shouted to the heavens and tumbled right over the edge. His body continued stroking her, drawing out the pulsing heat of her climax and his. Then he buried his face in her neck, withholding the words he didn't dare utter.

Phoebe's throat ached with love, with yearning, and all the things she wanted to say but knew Ram wouldn't believe. She wished this moment would never end, but of course it did. And with it came reality. Reaching up, she laid her palm against his lean jaw. He met her gaze, his eyes slightly narrowed.

"What happens now, Ram?"

"I don't know. Our destiny lies in your hands. If you don't trust me, we have no future together."

Phoebe groaned. His words proved that there was virtually no hope for them. All they shared was passion. Once she got her hands on the amulet, she would use it to free her father, and Ram couldn't accept that. What did she care about relationships between countries when all she had in the world was her father? Why couldn't Ram understand that?

"It seems we are at an impasse," Phoebe sighed. "If I had the amulet, I would use it to free Father."

Ram's sigh was even deeper than Phoebe's. "I know, and I'm sorry." He rolled away from her and climbed out of bed. "Rest, Phoebe, you look exhausted." He began to dress. "I'll send a tray up to you later."

She yawned. "Where are you going?"

"Does it matter?"

She yawned again. "I suppose not. Am I a prisoner?"

"Not really. Feel free to go anywhere in the house you'd like. But you'll not be allowed to leave without a Bow Street Runner or myself in attendance."

Phoebe opened her mouth to protest but couldn't find the energy; she was already half asleep. Her arguments would have to wait.

Porter was waiting for Ram at the bottom of the stairs.

"Lord Westmore attends you in your study, milord. He said not to bother you, that he'd wait until you came down."

"Thank you, Porter. I'll see him directly."

"You look like hell," Luc said when Ram entered the study. "Porter said you'd found Phoebe. Since it's raining outside, I decided I might as well wait to learn the details." He raised his glass. "Damn good whiskey."

"I prefer brandy," Ram said, moving to the sideboard.

"Do you want to tell me where your wife has been?"

Glass in hand, Ram seated himself across from Luc and rested his head against the back of the chair. "It's damn complicated, Westmore. Phoebe said her father's abductors contacted her and took her to see him."

"For what purpose?"

"I'm not sure. Nothing adds up. Phoebe thought they wanted to prove to her that her father was alive and well."

"Was he?"

"Alive, but according to Phoebe, not well. She says he has malaria and needs medical attention." He stared morosely into his glass. "I found her at the house on Mount Street. I'm convinced Thompson told her where he had hidden the amulet and she went to fetch it."

Luc's eyes shone with excitement. "Do you have it?"

"No. Phoebe denies knowledge of its location, and she insists Thompson didn't steal it." He drank deeply from his glass, swallowed and grimaced. "She's lying. What in bloody hell am I going to do? Nothing I've said thus far has convinced her to trust me to find her father."

"Are you sure Phoebe and her father aren't conspiring together to sell the amulet for personal gain?" Luc asked. "Can you believe anything Phoebe says?"

"When I first encountered her in the house on Mount Street I thought just as you did, but now I believe she is genuinely concerned for her father."

"I don't envy you, my friend," Luc said. "What are you going to do?"

"Attempt to find Phoebe's father."

"How can I help?"

"Come with me. Two heads are better than one. Phoebe said she was blindfolded, but she was able to provide some pertinent clues. With luck, we can locate the cottage and free Thompson."

"If indeed he is a prisoner," Luc speculated.

"That's the theory I'm going on right now. Until I prove otherwise, I prefer to believe that Thompson isn't involved in the theft. It's difficult to believe that a man whose whole life has been devoted to studying antiquities would steal one. I know him, and he doesn't strike me as a greedy man."

"Whatever you do, count me in," Luc said.

"Thank you. Nothing can be accomplished in the dark, however. We'll leave in the morning. Come by first thing. We'll take my carriage. If Thompson is as ill as Phoebe said, we may have need of it."

"What about Lady Braxton?"

"What about her?"

"She'll probably want to come with us."

Ram's jaw hardened. "I'm not going to tell her what we're about."

Luc rose. "You know what's best. I hope you and Phoebe still plan to attend Maryann's bash Saturday night. After I convinced her to give a ball in honor of your marriage, she'd be devastated if the guests of honor failed to attend."

"We'll be there," Ram said. "With luck, I'll have

found Thompson and the amulet will be in my possession by then."

After Luc took his leave, Ram remained in his study, staring pensively out the window, watching darkness swallow what remained of daylight. He didn't know that Phoebe had entered the room until she cleared her throat. He jumped and spun around to find her standing close enough to touch him.

"I thought you were sleeping," he said.

"I napped a bit. Was that Lord Westmore I saw leaving?"

"Yes. He's a frequent visitor. Are you hungry?"

"I didn't eat much yesterday and nothing today."

"I was going to send something up to you, but as long as you're awake, we'll dine together."

He pulled the bell cord and Porter appeared shortly. "Tell cook we'll dine in thirty minutes, Porter. We'll eat informally here in the study. Please send someone to lay a fire. It's chilly tonight. Does that meet with your approval, Phoebe?"

"Yes, of course," Phoebe said.

A tense silence ensued as servants moved about laying a fire and setting up trays for their meal. Phoebe chewed her bottom lip, wondering what Ram was thinking. His anger had been formidable earlier today, but he'd also seemed relieved to see her. Had he really been worried about her?

"What are you thinking?" Ram asked once they were alone.

"Wondering what *you're* thinking," she shot back. "Am I really confined to the house?"

Ram's hard expression told her the answer even before he spoke. "That's the way it has to be, Phoebe. You're going to be watched every minute of every day. It's for your own protection."

"I don't need protecting."

"Don't you? Had I protected you properly, you wouldn't have been abducted off the street. That is what happened, isn't it?"

"Not exactly. I was supposed to meet someone at Hyde Park. My contact was to give me information about Father, and I hoped to convince the man to release him."

"But you *were* abducted, were you not?"

"I . . . suppose. But I'm glad. I got to see Father and judge his condition for myself."

"He told you where he'd hidden the amulet," Ram guessed, "and you promised to fetch it and give it to his abductors."

"Father didn't steal it."

"That's not the issue, Phoebe, and you know it."

"What is the issue?" Phoebe pressed.

Ram sighed. "We've been over this time and again. England's relationship with Egypt is at stake."

"Don't people count?" Phoebe challenged.

"You still don't trust me, do you? I'll do everything in my power for your father. Just tell me where to find the amulet so it can be returned to Egypt."

"You think Father stole it. He's no thief."

"Tell me who did steal it. Maybe then I'll believe you."

"What makes you think Father knows anything about the amulet?"

"Logic, Phoebe. I've figured everything out except . . ." He paused.

"Except what?"

"I'm not sure whether Sir Thompson has really been abducted or if he's a player in the plot to sell the amulet to the highest bidder."

220

"You wouldn't know the truth if it struck you in the face," Phoebe charged.

Ram's answer was forestalled when servants arrived bearing their dinner. With her lips clamped tightly together, Phoebe watched in seething silence as plates of roasted pheasant, creamed vegetables, glazed potatoes and fresh bread and butter were placed before them. Her stomach rumbled at the delicious smells wafting up to her.

Hunger took the place of anger, but it returned when Ram said, "I've never lied to you."

"Have you not? You wedded me under false pretenses. You never did intend to settle down, did you?"

"That was my intention when we married."

"What about the barmaid and the widow?"

"They were in my past. Phillips found them in order to discredit me. He knew we were becoming close and feared you would refuse to travel to Egypt with him. Why didn't you tell him or your father we were wed?"

"I was hurt and disillusioned."

"Had you loved me, you wouldn't have run off without giving me a chance to defend myself. It was months before I could get my life back on track, and it took far longer than that to forget you. For the first time in my life I was in love."

He took a deep breath before continuing. "The humiliation of being abandoned left a raw place inside me, so I told no one about our marriage. Meanwhile, I lost myself in sensual pleasure and dissolution, denying myself nothing. Women were mine for the taking, and I took voraciously. I gambled, drank and became known about town for my roguish ways. And all because of you, Phoebe."

"Ram, I . . . I'm sorry for judging you harshly.

221

David was my friend; I believed he was trying to protect me from a lifetime of hurt."

"What's done is done. We can't call back the past, but we can look forward to the future." He regarded her solemnly, his eyes darkly probing. "Do you want a future with me, Phoebe?"

Do I? Phoebe wondered. She loved Ram, had always loved him, but she loved her father too, and having to choose between them was tearing her apart. After years of thinking about the cowardly way she had fled after their hasty marriage, Phoebe had come to the conclusion that she had been wrong to judge Ram without hearing him out. It was true she had let David influence her, but she had trusted him then and still trusted him.

"I think our marriage could work," Phoebe whispered, "once this is behind us."

Ram didn't know what to say to that. "Eat before your food gets cold. We'll talk later."

Phoebe picked at her pheasant but found it difficult to swallow. Why hadn't Ram answered her? She set her fork down and glared at him. "No, we'll talk now. Do you want to be married to me?"

His expression softened. "I want you. I love making love to you." A ghost of a smile played over his lips, a sad smile. "But unless there is truth between us, there can be no marriage."

Phoebe swallowed past the lump in her throat, overjoyed and disheartened at the same time. She wanted Ram to love her unconditionally, but she supposed that was asking too much. She had done nothing to earn his trust.

"I've never stopped loving you," she said, her voice barely audible.

Ram stiffened, his disbelief palpable. "Another lie, Phoebe?"

"It's true. I think I regretted leaving you the moment the ship left England. But it was too late. I accepted responsibility for what I had done and tried to move on with my life."

"Rehashing past mistakes is doing neither of us any good. Our future must be built on trust. Are you willing to meet me halfway?"

Yes. "I . . . can't. I know what you want, but I can't give it to you."

His expression hardened. "Forget about recovering the amulet for anyone other than the government. I'm not letting you out of my sight."

A discreet knock sounded on the door. Ram gave permission to enter, and Porter stepped into the room. "Mr. Slaughter is here to see you, milord."

Ram rose. "Have him wait in the foyer. I'll see him directly." Porter withdrew.

"Mr. Slaughter, the Bow Street Runner?"

"Yes. Finish your meal; I'll be right back."

Ram hurried off. If Slaughter had found the amulet, he could put an end to this.

"Slaughter, did you find it?"

"No, milord. We tore the place apart but found nothing like Her Ladyship described."

"Bloody hell."

"Shall we keep looking?"

"I could have sworn the damn thing was hidden in that house. How thorough was your search?"

"We even pried bricks from the fireplace."

Ram pushed impatient fingers through his hair. "No sense searching further unless you can think of something you forgot. Continue to watch the house, and report back to me if anything unusual occurs."

Slaughter took his leave, and Ram returned to the study. Phoebe's dinner still sat before her virtually untouched. "I thought you were hungry."

"What did Mr. Slaughter want?"

"They didn't find it, Phoebe."

Incredible relief surged through her. She sent him a look that said, *I told you so*.

"I'm not the fool you think me, Phoebe. I know that you know where the amulet is hidden." He stomped off.

"Where are you going?"

"Out. Don't wait up."

"Ram, please don't be angry with me."

"I'm not angry, Phoebe. I'm beyond that. Good night."

The stunning finality of Ram's words was heart-rending. Nothing could mend the rift between them now. She had closed the door on happiness with Ram as firmly as he had closed the door to the study. With heavy heart, she rose to her feet and left the room. She was truly alone now, with only herself to depend upon. Somehow, some way, she had to escape Ram's scrutiny long enough to recover the amulet and free her father.

Ram really didn't have anywhere to go. He just didn't feel like being alone with Phoebe right now. Her stubbornness defeated him. She said she loved him. *Bah!* Her lies wouldn't work this time. Just because she made love like an angel didn't mean he'd let her stomp on his heart. Why in bloody hell had she come back into his life again?

Ram reached the foyer and shouted for Porter. The butler appeared moments later, somewhat disheveled but still dignified. "You called, milord?"

"Have another bedchamber made up for me."

"Another bedchamber, milord?"

"Are you hard of hearing, Porter?" Realizing he

had been unnecessarily harsh, Ram said, "Forgive me, Porter. I shouldn't take out my frustrations on you. Just see to the room, please."

"Right away, milord."

Ram strode into the drawing room and poured himself a measure of brandy from a decanter on the sideboard. When he heard footsteps, he glanced over his shoulder and caught a glimpse of Phoebe ascending the staircase. Since he preferred the study to any other room in his townhouse, he returned to his favorite retreat and plopped down in a chair before the hearth. He closed his eyes. Phoebe's scent still lingered in the air.

How sweetly she had made love with him. How wonderfully alive she made him feel. No matter where their lives took them, he would never forget her. Quite possibly he loved her. Due to present circumstances, he might never be able to plumb the depths of their relationship.

Damn duty. Damn king and country, Ram silently swore.

"Here you are, milord. The green room has been prepared for you," Porter said from the doorway.

"Thank you. Good night, Porter."

"Good night, milord."

Ram finished his brandy and trudged up the stairs to the green room. He couldn't trust himself to sleep beside Phoebe tonight. Lack of trust might have severed the fragile bond between them, but he still wanted her. Who would believe that Lord Braxton, one of the infamous rogues of London, had discovered a heart? He knew exactly how Bathurst had felt when he'd met his Olivia. Slightly off balance, he supposed, and somewhat confused, and angry for allowing himself to be pulled into a silken web of deceit. Olivia the highwayman and Phoebe the thief; they were two of a kind. He wondered what fate awaited poor Westmore.

Ram was having breakfast when Viscount Westmore arrived early the following morning. He was shown into the morning room, where Ram was having breakfast.

"Did you get any sleep last night?" Luc asked, eyeing the circles beneath Ram's eyes.

"Not much. Have you eaten?"

"Yes. Are you ready?"

Ram tossed down his napkin. "My carriage is being brought around even as we speak. Let's go."

"Where are you going?"

Two pairs of eyes swung around to the doorway. "You're up early, Phoebe."

"I've always been an early riser. Where are you and Lord Westmore off to at this hour?"

"Business," Ram muttered.

"Indeed," Westmore added. "My sister is looking forward to meeting you at the ball Saturday next."

Phoebe's gaze sought Ram's. "Are we still going?"

"Of course. I wouldn't want to disappoint Lady Belcher after she's gone to so much trouble on our account. Shall we go, Westmore?"

Ram's carriage was waiting at the curb. "Get in; I'll drive," Luc said. "You look somewhat rattled. You and Phoebe need to settle your differences."

"Easier said than done," Ram muttered.

They drove northeast in the direction of Epping. When they rattled across a bridge spanning a stream, Ram knew they were headed in the right direction.

"Look for a sharp right turn onto a rutted lane," Ram said, recalling Phoebe's directions.

The carriage continued on for a time, Ram's uncertainty growing as they neared the village of Epping and there was no sign of the lane Phoebe had described. Then he saw it, the sharp right turn.

"There it is!" he shouted. Luc drew rein.

"We shouldn't storm up there without a plan."

"You're right as usual, Westmore. Let's look for a place to hide the carriage and proceed the rest of the way on foot. Do you have your gun?"

Luc patted his coat pocket. "Right here."

Luc pulled the carriage into a clearing beneath the lofty branches of an oak tree.

"Follow me," Ram said as he leaped to the ground and moved cautiously down the rutted lane. "There it is." He pointed to a small cottage dead ahead. "Let's circle around to the back and have a look."

"The shutters are closed," Luc noted.

"Do you hear anything?" Ram whispered, crouching beneath a window.

"It's too quiet," Luc replied. "I'm going to try the latch."

He reached for the latch and found it secured from the inside.

"Maybe the front door is unlocked," Ram said hopefully.

Hugging the wall and ducking beneath the shuttered windows, they inched their way to the front of the cottage. Cautiously, Ram approached the front door and tried the latch. It wasn't locked, and he threw the door wide.

"Empty," Ram said, moving aside to make room for Luc to enter.

"There's another door," Luc said. "Probably leads to a bedroom." Both men started forward.

227

"Bloody hell," Ram sputtered. "Either we're too late or this isn't the right place."

"Nothing here but a rumpled bed, a table and a chair," Luc said with barely disguised disgust.

Ram pulled back the covers and searched beneath the dirty gray sheets.

Luc slanted him a curious glance. "What are you looking for?"

"I don't know. A clue, I suppose. Anything to prove that Thompson was here. There's nothing," he said, clearly disappointed. "Let's get out of here."

"Hold on," Luc said, reaching beneath the bed for a shiny object he'd spied amid the rolls of dust. "What's this?"

Ram reached for the object in Luc's hand. "Let me see." Grasping the object, he held it up by its gold chain. "A pocket watch." Turning it over, he read the inscription and gave a hoot of elation. " 'Tis Thompson's watch. See here," he said, pointing out the lettering on the back. "It bears his initials."

"So he *was* here," Luc said. "I wonder . . . Was he a prisoner or an accomplice?"

Ram's sharp gaze settled on a glass sitting on the table. He picked it up and held it up to the light, noting the brown residue staining the bottom. Bringing it to his nose, he took a deep whiff.

"What is it?" Luc asked.

"My guess is laudanum. I doubt that Thompson left here under his own power."

Clutching the watch in his hand, Ram stormed from the cottage. Luc followed close on his heels. They returned to the carriage and retraced their route back to London.

"Do you think Phoebe was telling the truth?" Luc asked.

"About her father being ill, yes, I suppose so. But I'd bet my last farthing she could lead me to the amulet if she wanted to."

When they reached Ram's townhouse, Luc took his leave.

"Keep me posted, Braxton. Summon me if you need me."

Ram nodded and entered the house, loath to tell Phoebe what he had found. He was given scant time to procrastinate, for Phoebe met him at the door.

"You didn't find him!" she lamented.

"I don't know what—"

"Don't lie, Ram. I know you and Westmore went to look for Father. Did you find the cottage? I tried to remember every detail but—"

"We found the cottage," Ram said, deciding that lying would serve no purpose. Phoebe was too astute to be put off by lies or half-truths. "Your father was gone when we got there. The cottage was deserted. All we found was this," he said, dangling the watch by its golden chain.

"Father's watch!" Phoebe cried, reaching for it. Ram relinquished it instantly.

Phoebe's legs started to buckle, but Ram caught her. "All is lost," she wailed. "I will never find Father now." Furious, she pushed him away. "It's your fault! If not for your interference, Father's captors would have the amulet and Father would be free. Damn you! I hate you!"

"Phoebe," Ram cajoled. "Be reasonable. All is not lost yet. Obviously, your father is still alive. Sooner or later his captors will try to contact you.

You'll be watched every minute. I swear no harm will come to you."

"Do you think I care about that? How can I give them what they want if I'm confined to the house? All you've ever cared about is the amulet. Human life means nothing to you. *I* mean nothing to you. I'm just a means to an end. Admit it, Ram; we never would have crossed paths if not for the amulet."

"You may be right, Phoebe, but fate brought us together for a reason. Tell me where to find the amulet and we'll work together to find your father."

Phoebe backed away, her expression fraught with anguish. "No. I want nothing to do with you and your promises. I don't need your help. In fact," she said, storming past him, "I don't need *you*. Good-bye, my lord."

She didn't get far. Ram reached out and snagged her around the waist. "You're not going anywhere, Phoebe. You have something I want, and I intend to get it."

"We'll see about that," Phoebe said, spinning away.

Chapter Thirteen

"You look ever so lovely, milady," Abby said, putting the finishing touches on Phoebe's hair. "His Lordship will be proud of you."

Phoebe's mass of shiny black curls had been piled atop her head and held in place by jeweled pins, a gift from her father on her eighteenth birthday. They were the only pieces of jewelry she owned.

"Stand up so I can fasten the back of your gown," Abby instructed.

Dutifully, Phoebe stood, smoothing the folds of emerald silk skirt over her shapely hips. The bodice was cut fashionably low, revealing the rounded tops of her breasts and a good deal more cleavage than she would have liked. The dressmaker had assured her the style was all the rage, and Ram had agreed.

Abby had just finished fastening Phoebe's gown

when the door opened and Ram strolled inside. "Are you ready?"

"Doesn't she look fetching, milord?" Abby asked, beaming proudly.

"Indeed," Ram agreed. "You may go, Abby. And don't wait up. In fact, take the evening off. I'll act the lady's maid tonight."

Phoebe wanted to protest but decided to hold her tongue until they were alone. Abby draped a shawl around Phoebe's shoulders and withdrew. The moment the door closed behind the maid, Phoebe lit into him.

"How dare you dismiss my maid without consulting me!"

"This is still my home and Abby is my employee."

His gaze traveled over her slowly, his eyes kindling with approval. "Abby was right. You do look fetching." He touched her throat. "Have you no jewelry? The gown is lovely, but it lacks sparkle. Perhaps you can find some use for these," he said, removing a velvet pouch from his pocket.

"What is it?"

"You're my countess; it wouldn't do for you to appear in public without an impressive piece of jewelry or two. I have a reputation to uphold."

Phoebe inhaled sharply when Ram removed a diamond and emerald necklace from the pouch and dangled it before her eyes.

"You're giving me this? It . . . it's . . . words can't describe it. I've never seen anything so lovely in my life."

Ram stepped behind her and fastened the necklace around her neck. Resting his hands lightly on her shoulders, he turned her toward the pier mirror standing in the corner.

"Your ears look bare," he said, gently touching

one earlobe. "Perhaps these will help." He delved into the pouch again and pulled out a pair of emerald and diamond earrings dangling from golden posts. "They're yours to keep no matter what the future holds for us."

"Why are you doing this?"

Something unreadable flashed in Ram's eyes. "I told you. I don't want my peers to think I'm a miserly husband. And one other thing—it would help my image if we appeared a happy couple tonight. Everyone assumes ours is a love match."

"Why would they assume that?"

"Our marriage was sudden and unexpected; nothing short of love would fell one of the Rogues of London. The *ton* naturally assume I fell hard, like my friend Bathurst did for his Olivia."

"We both know the truth, don't we," Phoebe said dryly. "I don't know why we're continuing this charade."

"Yes, you do. Whether you like it or not, I'm still responsible for you. I intend to protect you until this is over. Shall we go?"

Disdaining an argument, Phoebe fastened the earrings to her lobes and nodded. As Ram preceded her to the door, she couldn't help admiring how elegant he looked. She knew that he would cause more of a stir among the women tonight than she would among the men. Ramsey Dunsmore was that kind of man.

Ram ushered her out the door and down the stairs to the waiting coach bearing the Braxton crest. There was a bit of a chill tonight and a touch of rain in the air, and she pulled her shawl tightly about her to ward off the dampness.

"About tonight," Ram said as the coach pulled

away from the curb. "I intend to stay with you the entire time. Don't even think about slipping away. I said I would protect you and so I shall."

"Protect me from what?" Phoebe challenged.

"Not what, whom," Ram replied. "You're not safe until the amulet is found and returned to the Egyptian government. I intend to make damn sure there will be no more abductions."

A tense silence ensued as they joined the line of coaches waiting to unload passengers at the elegant Belcher mansion. When their turn came, the coachman let down the stairs and held the door open while Ram climbed down and assisted Phoebe.

The crush of people was daunting to Phoebe, who had never attended a London ball. The few house parties she had been to in the country had not been nearly so grand. And in Egypt, she and her father did not mingle with the close-knit society of English aristocrats and businessmen living there. Her life had been simple and uncomplicated before she returned to England and Ram turned up at her door.

"Don't be nervous," Ram whispered as they moved toward the receiving line.

"There you are," Luc said, looking vastly relieved as he spied them near the door. "Maryann wants you and Phoebe in the receiving line with her and Belcher."

He deftly moved them forward, until they stood beside a handsome couple whom he introduced as his sister and brother-in-law, Lord and Lady Belcher.

"So you're the woman who won Braxton's heart," Lady Belcher said with a twinkle as she grasped Phoebe's hand. "I wish his good fortune would rub off on my brother."

"Forget it, Maryann," Luc laughed. "I'm not going to walk down the same path as Braxton and Bathurst."

"I'm pleased to meet you, my lady," Phoebe said, returning Maryann's smile. " 'Tis most gracious of you to honor us with a ball."

"Maryann doesn't need an excuse to give a party," Lord Belcher said, smiling fondly at his wife.

Phoebe took her place beside Ram as people whose names she would never remember filed past. Never had she felt more conspicuous or ill at ease. Not just the men but also the women were sizing her up, as if measuring her shortfalls. Some of the women seemed openly derisive of her lack of noble birth, and she could tell by the way they ogled Ram that they hoped he would turn out to be anything but a devoted husband.

Phoebe's legs were ready to give out when the line thinned and strains of music could be heard coming from the ballroom.

"Finally," Maryann said, stretching the tightness in her back. "You two go off and enjoy yourselves while I make sure things are going smoothly in the kitchen."

Lord Belcher excused himself and went off to mingle. Ram ushered Phoebe up the stairs to the ballroom and swept her onto the dance floor. She went naturally into his arms. She adored dancing but had had little opportunity during the last several years. She stumbled once, then quickly caught the rhythm and followed Ram's lead.

He was an excellent dancer, just as she'd guessed he would be. Rogues instinctively knew what women liked and went out of their way to please them. It was part of their nature.

Phoebe danced with several partners as the evening progressed, from aging noblemen to young dandies, aware that Ram's gaze followed her everywhere. She was surprised to find jealousy gnawing at her when he led several ladies of the *ton* out onto the dance floor.

The evening wore on. It was nearly time for the midnight buffet when Phoebe felt the sudden need for a breath of fresh air. Heat from hundreds of candles, together with body odor disguised by perfume, was making her light-headed and nauseous. She headed for the ladies' retiring room on wobbly legs.

Ram appeared before her, his face etched with concern. "Where are you going?"

"To the ladies' retiring room. Do you mind?"

He stepped aside to let her pass. "Not at all. I'll escort you. Don't be long. It's almost time for supper."

"On second thought, some fresh air sounds better. I'm feeling a little faint."

Ram tucked her arm in his. "The veranda it is. It is rather stifling in here."

They skirted the dance floor and had almost reached the wide veranda doors that had been opened to admit the night breezes when a footman intercepted them.

"Lord Braxton, Lord Fielding wishes a word with you in the library."

"Fielding? I didn't realize he was here. Very well, tell him I'll see him directly." The footman bowed off.

"What does Lord Fielding want with you?" Phoebe asked.

"I don't know, but it must be important. Wait here for me, I'll be right back."

"Ram, I really do need some air. I . . . don't feel well."

Grasping Phoebe's hand, Ram pulled her through the crowd toward Westmore, who was conversing with a group of his peers.

"Excuse the interruption, gentlemen, but I'd like a private word with Lord Westmore."

Luc made his excuses and joined Ram and Phoebe, his brows raised in question. "What's amiss, Braxton?"

"Will you escort Phoebe onto the veranda? I dare not leave her alone, and Lord Fielding has summoned me to the library. Was he invited tonight?"

"I don't know, but I can ask Maryann."

"Don't bother. Just keep an eye on Phoebe while I'm gone. She's feeling a little faint."

"Go meet Fielding. I'll see to Phoebe."

"No one has to 'see' to me," Phoebe said. "I'm perfectly capable of taking care of myself."

"Phoebe," Ram warned, "don't fight me on this. I told you how it was going to be. Go with Westmore."

Spinning on her heel, Phoebe flounced off. Luc shrugged and followed. Phoebe had just disappeared through the door when Maryann, accompanied by a petite blonde, intercepted him.

"Luc, there you are. You remember Lady Caroline, don't you?"

Ever the courtier, Luc bowed and kissed Lady Caroline's outstretched hand. "How nice to see you again, my lady."

"They're playing a waltz, Luc, and Caroline doesn't seem to have a partner," Maryann hinted broadly.

Luc cast an anxious glance toward the veranda.

"Perhaps the next dance, Lady Caroline. You see, I—"

"Luc!" Maryann reprimanded. "How unlike you. Don't disappoint Caroline."

"I understand," Caroline said, obviously embarrassed. "If Lord Westmore is unwilling . . ."

Luc stifled a groan. Disappointing a lady, especially one as beautiful as Caroline, was not something he wished to do. Besides, what harm could befall Phoebe on the veranda with other couples about?

He offered his hand to Caroline and led her onto the dance floor.

A ghost of a smile played over Phoebe's lips when she peeked through the open door and saw that Westmore had abandoned her for a young, blond beauty. Good. She wanted to be alone anyway. Her stomach really was churning and her head spinning. So many things were going through her mind. Why had Ram given her jewelry when their marriage was just a scam? He didn't intend to stay married to her any more than she intended to remain his wife.

"Lady Braxton, you look unwell. Shall I find your husband and send him to you?"

Phoebe caught her bottom lip with her teeth, trapping a moan between her lips. *Of all the rotten luck.*

"We were introduced earlier this evening. I'm Lady Winthorpe, an old . . . acquaintance of Lord Braxton."

A former mistress, Phoebe thought. "I'm fine, Lady Winthorpe, thank you for your concern. I assure you my husband knows where to find me."

Lady Winthorpe gave Phoebe a sly smile. "Is this your first lovers' spat?"

Phoebe wouldn't give the other woman the satisfaction of knowing how badly her marriage was going. "Lord Braxton and I have not quarreled. I simply found myself in need of a breath of air."

"You do look pale, my dear. How far along are you?"

Inwardly, Phoebe groaned. "I'm not in the family way, if that's what you're implying."

"Really? We all thought . . . well, knowing Braxton, we naturally assumed . . ." She let the sentence dangle, then shrugged. "What else was one to think? Braxton's low opinion of marriage is legendary. He'll stray, you know."

"Pamela, there you are. Come inside, they're playing another waltz and you promised this dance to me."

Pamela smiled up at the handsome young lord and offered her hand. "Of course, Gladstone, how could I have forgotten? I'm sure Lady Braxton will excuse me."

"Gladly," Phoebe intoned dryly.

The only other couple on the veranda followed them inside, leaving Phoebe blessedly alone. She walked to the end of the balcony and gazed up at the stars twinkling in the dark sky. If only she could be as carefree as those stars. She didn't want to be here tonight. She should be out looking for her father, not pretending to enjoy herself at a society function that meant nothing to her.

"Phoebe."

Her name was no more than a whisper. Had she imagined it?

"Phoebe."

There it was again. Not her imagination. "Where are you?" she said.

"Look down."

Phoebe gazed downward and saw nothing but a neat row of bushes surrounding the veranda.

A head popped up. "Here."

Disbelief colored her words. "David! What are you doing here?"

"I heard about the ball and came in hopes of finding you alone. I need to talk to you, but your husband keeps you too well guarded. It's about your father."

Phoebe's hopes soared. "We can't talk here. Ram or his friend Westmore might come looking for me."

"I've thought of that. There's a carriage house behind the mansion. We could be alone there."

Phoebe hesitated, but David's next words convinced her. "I've found your father."

"I'll be right there." She found a set of steps and descended. David met her at the bottom.

"This way," he said, grasping her hand and pulling her away from the circle of light streaming through the windows.

Difficult though it was, Phoebe withheld her questions as they fled through the night. She was elated at the prospect of contacting her father's abductors and negotiating for his return.

The carriage house was dark and deserted; all the grooms were tending to the guests and their equipages. Phoebe followed David inside.

"Where is Father?" she asked without preamble. "Is he well? How did you find him?"

"Well, I didn't actually find him," David stammered.

"You lied to me?"

"No, not at all. A man named Watts contacted me."

"Why you?"

"Since I'm Andrew's assistant, I was the logical choice after you became unavailable to them."

"What did Watts want?"

"You know what he wants, Phoebe. Watts said your father revealed the location of the amulet to you. Do you have it?"

"If you think Father stole the amulet, you're wrong. He found it concealed in an artifact he'd packed in his trunk and intended to turn it over to the authorities when he reached England. He swore he had no idea how the artifact got into his personal belongings."

"You don't have to convince me, dear." His voice had an edge to it that made Phoebe doubt his sincerity. She couldn't recall ever feeling that way about David before.

He grasped her shoulders, his fingers digging into her flesh. "Where is it? Never say you gave it to the authorities."

"David, what are you doing?"

"I want the amulet, Phoebe. Do you have it? Have you already disposed of it?"

"David, you're hurting me. What's wrong with you? You know I'd never give the amulet to the authorities if it meant placing Father's life in jeopardy."

David must have realized he was frightening Phoebe, for his grip eased and his voice gentled. "Forgive me, Phoebe. I'm worried about Andrew. Watts is growing impatient, and I fear your father will suffer for the delay. Tell me where to find the amulet and I'll use it to secure your father's freedom."

Phoebe had no idea why she hesitated. She trusted David, didn't she? He wouldn't lie to her, would he?

"Is it still in the house on Mount Street?" David persisted.

Meanwhile, Ram and Lord Fielding were concluding their business in the library.

"Time is running out," Fielding warned. "The Egyptian envoy is sailing to Egypt in a fortnight. If he doesn't have the amulet in his possession when he leaves English soil, it could mean an end to diplomatic relations with that country. Our business interests will suffer and trade agreements will not be renewed."

"I understand," Ram said. "Tell the envoy he'll have the amulet in his possession before he departs."

They parted on that note, and Ram returned to the ballroom. He scanned the crowded dance floor for Phoebe and Westmore and failed to find them. He was turning toward the veranda when he spotted Westmore. Waving wildly, Westmore started in his direction.

"Thank God you're here," Luc said, panic in his voice.

Ram's heart pounded with dread. He was sure he wasn't going to like what Westmore was about to say. "Where's Phoebe?"

"I'm sorry, Braxton. It wasn't my fault. Maryann insisted that I dance with one of her friends, and I couldn't refuse."

"Where's Phoebe?" Ram repeated, clenching his teeth.

"She went out on the veranda without me. When I went to fetch her after the dance ended, she was gone. I was going to inform you first and then search the house. I thought she might have gone into the ladies' retiring room, but Maryann checked and said she wasn't there."

Ram cursed beneath his breath. "You search the house, I'll take the grounds."

"There's not much out there save for a carriage house," Luc flung over his shoulder as he rushed off.

Ram exited through the veranda doors and descended the steps to the ground. He found a path of sorts and hurried along it. No light shone through the carriage house windows, but he decided to investigate anyway. As he approached the open door, voices drifted to him from the interior.

"I don't have the amulet, David, but I know where to find it. It's among Father's belongings in the house on Mount Street. Ram interrupted me before I could recover it. I lied to him about it. He wants to return the amulet to the Egyptian government, and I can't let that happen. He doesn't seem to understand that a man's life is at stake."

"I understand," David said. His voice tautened. "You can confide in me, Phoebe. I want to help you. Tell me where to find it."

Still Phoebe hesitated. David seemed less concerned about her father than about recovering the amulet.

Grasping her shoulders, he gave her a vigorous shake. "Damn you, Phoebe, why are you being so obstinate?"

Ram followed the low hum of voices until he saw the dim outline of two figures: a man and a woman. He couldn't see the man's face, but he suspected it was David Phillips, and he knew that the woman was Phoebe. "Take your hands off my wife!"

"Ram!" Phoebe knew there was really going to be hell to pay now.

"Damn your stubborn hide, Phoebe," David hissed.

Ram sprinted forward to rescue Phoebe, his rage uncontrollable. Phillips was manhandling his wife, and Ram was going to smash his face in.

Apparently, David knew he was in danger, for he made a swift decision. He shoved Phoebe so hard she fell backward, stumbled against Ram and took him with her to the ground. They fell in a tangle of arms and legs, allowing David to slip past them and out the door. By the time Ram had found his footing and helped Phoebe to her feet, David was gone.

"What were you doing out here with Phillips?" Ram roared.

"David is worried about Father. He wanted to know if I'd heard anything from his abductors." *Almost the truth.*

"How did he know where to find you?"

"He'd heard about the ball and hoped for a private word with me. It's a sad state of affairs when I can't speak to old friends."

"It's a sad state of affairs when one's wife spews nothing but lies." He grasped her arm and dragged her off. "We're making our excuses to our host and hostess and leaving."

Ram was seething with rage as he dragged Phoebe back to the veranda and into the ballroom. Luc was waiting for him.

"Thank God you found her. Are you all right, Lady Braxton?"

"She's fine," Ram said tersely, "but I'm taking her home. Where is your sister?"

"Maryann and Belcher are partaking of the buffet," Luc said. "Shall I get them for you?"

"No, don't bother. Make our excuses for us and tell them something unforeseen called us away. I'll send an apology around tomorrow."

Grasping Phoebe's elbow with a firm hand, he escorted her from the ballroom and ushered her into their waiting coach.

"Dammit, Phoebe, what am I going to do with you?" he said after instructing Wilson to take them home. "Why do you trust Phillips and not me?"

"David has my father's best interests at heart. He cares about Father."

"I'm convinced that Phillips's interest in the amulet has nothing to do with your father. I pray you did not tell him where to find it."

"I . . . don't know where it is."

The coach rolled to a stop before their townhouse. Ram stepped to the ground and lifted Phoebe out before Wilson came around to help. He set her on her feet, placed his hand in the small of her back and propelled her forward. A footman opened the door. Ram picked up a candle from the hall table and ushered her toward the stairs.

Once they were in their room, he set the candle down and slammed the door shut. Phoebe walked behind the screen and began to undress. Ram followed.

"Turn around," he growled, aware that she couldn't unfasten her gown without help.

"Leave me alone, Ram. I can't take any more badgering tonight."

Ram stiffened. "Did Phillips badger you?"

Phoebe hesitated for the space of a heartbeat. "No! Are you satisfied?"

"Did you give him the information he sought?"

"I told him nothing he didn't already know. He

said a man named Watts contacted him. Watts told David that time is running out for Father."

"It's running out for everyone," Ram said. "The Egyptian envoy is sailing to Egypt in a fortnight, and diplomatic relations will suffer if he doesn't return with the amulet."

"Father is suffering, too."

Ram grasped her shoulders. "Listen to me. Fielding came up with a plan. I don't like it, but it's all we have right now. We both know I have to give the amulet to the authorities once it's in my possession, and though I will do everything in my power to protect your father, I can't guarantee his safety."

"That's what I've been trying to tell you all along. That's why I must take the amulet to Father's abductors." She clapped her hands. "I'm so glad you finally understand."

"I understand, but that's not the issue. I cannot allow the amulet to fall into the wrong hands. Here's Fielding's plan. You'll be released from confinement and allowed to come and go as you please, but either Fielding's men or I will monitor your movements. Once the abductors contact you, you're to agree to an exchange. You'll be followed to where the exchange is to take place, and we'll take it from there."

Phoebe looked unconvinced. "What if they don't contact me?"

"They will. They're getting desperate."

"What's the catch? What aren't you telling me?"

"You must tell me where to find the amulet."

Phoebe paled. "So many things could go wrong. The amulet is all I have to bargain with."

"I won't let anything happen to you, love."

"I'm not worried about myself. It's Father I'm concerned about."

He dragged her against him, his eyes softly pleading. "I said I'd do my utmost to protect you and your father, and so I shall. Believe me when I say I don't want anything to happen to either of you."

Tilting her chin, he gazed into her misty blue eyes for the space of a heartbeat, then lowered his mouth to hers. Her lips trembled beneath his and he deepened the kiss, willing her to trust him, to believe in him. His tongue swept inside her mouth. The soft answering flick of her tongue was an aphrodisiac, making him instantly hard. The slight movement of her body against his was all the encouragement he needed. His arms tightened around her as he deftly moved her toward the bed.

They fell in a tangle of arms and legs and flying skirts. She burrowed against his chest, but he wouldn't let her hide. Raising her chin, he kissed her again and again, the sweetness of her mouth drawing him deeper and deeper into the bottomless pit of desire.

No matter how angry she made him, no matter how often she lied, he still wanted her. "Witch," he murmured against her mouth.

He undressed her quickly, efficiently, like a man who knew what he wanted and wasted no time going after it. Then he removed his own clothing and came down beside her.

Phoebe breathed deeply, breasts rising and falling quickly, turning into him, pressing her heated body against his damp, glistening chest.

"Why can't I hate you?" she whispered on a ragged sigh.

"For the same reason I can't hate you." His hand threaded into her hair. "Make love to me."

Rising on her elbow, she regarded him through slumberous eyes, then slowly, oh so slowly, lowered her head and took his flat male nipple into her mouth. He yelped in surprise when she bit down softly, then laved it with her tongue.

"Witch," he repeated as his hands glided down the delicious planes of her back, molding her closer. Then, sliding his hands further, he cupped the firm mounds of her bottom and lifted her atop him.

She offered him her mouth anew; rapaciously he claimed it, plundering, ravishing it deeply. "I'm dying," he said when he finally came up for air. The candle on the table flickered in a sudden draught, and her blue eyes seemed to catch the flame and throw it back at him, setting him on fire.

His mind went blank when she slid down his body, took his erection in her hand and lowered her head, flicking her tongue over the throbbing head. He lurched upward and gasped, "Now I really am dying."

She pushed him back down, plying her mouth and tongue with surprising expertise, down his rigid length and back, swirling her tongue across the dewy tip. He was breathing hard, his heart pumping furiously. He let her have her way until his toes curled and he was moments away from climax. Then he grasped her waist and flipped her on her back, penetrating her hard and fast. She raised her hips to meet his thrusts as he kissed the underside of her breasts, her tender nipples, her mouth. He kissed her until he felt her sheath contracting against his hardened length and madness claimed him.

It was too much. He shuddered and quaked and threw his head back and shouted. He was but dimly aware when she heaved up against him in the throes of her own climax. He didn't stop pumping until he felt her go limp beneath him. Then he pulled out and fell beside her in a boneless heap.

"That was as close to heaven as I'm likely to get," he gasped.

When they had both caught their breath, she turned to him. "This doesn't change anything, Ram. You haven't convinced me that you and Lord Fielding can protect my father. Until you convince me of that, my lips are sealed."

"You're one stubborn woman, Phoebe, but I account myself capable of dealing with you. Before this night is over, there will be no more secrets between us."

Chapter Fourteen

Ram was too sure of himself . . . and of her, Phoebe reflected. She had decisions to make and needed all her wits about her. The plan Ram had presented to her seemed sound, but so much could go wrong. Perhaps, she thought, it was time to seek his help.

"What are you thinking, Phoebe?" Ram asked.

"About what you told me. Can you promise that nothing will happen to Father if I agree to Lord Fielding's terms?"

"I'll do my damnedest to keep him safe."

"I'm tired, Ram. Tired of shouldering the burden alone. That's why I wanted to confide in David. I trust him."

"You've placed your trust in the wrong person," Ram said.

"I'm sorry you feel that way about David."

"Do you trust me enough to confide in me?"

"Maybe. Once this is over and Father is safe, will there be an amicable parting of ways? I don't want us to be enemies. Chances are we'll never cross paths again, and I don't want you to go through life hating me."

His stillness unsettled her. What was he thinking?

"Our parting isn't inevitable, Phoebe."

"Yes, it is. I doomed our marriage before it had a chance to flourish. There is no reason for us to stay married once the amulet is recovered. We both know why we're together, and it's not for love."

"What do you intend to do?"

"When this is over, Father will need time to recuperate from his illness. I don't know if he plans another trip to Egypt in the future, but if he does, I intend to accompany him."

"With Phillips?" Ram bit out.

"David is Father's assistant and friend."

"You're a fool to believe that!" Ram blasted.

"Once we divorce—"

"There will be no divorce," Ram said sharply, dragging her into his arms.

"Why not?"

He sent her a measured look. "Being married will protect me from husband-hunting debs and their mamas."

"And you'll be free to continue your debauched ways," Phoebe added.

Ram did not contradict her assessment of his character, though he didn't consider himself the same man he had been before Phoebe reentered his life. Something had changed. Seduction was still his game, but the only woman he wanted to seduce was Phoebe. What in God's name had she done to him?

"What makes you think I wish to return to my previous lifestyle? Why do you believe one woman isn't enough for me? Give me some credit, Phoebe. I haven't strayed since we reunited, have I?"

"You were on a mission and I was your prey, Ram. Once your assignment ends, you'll grow bored with me. My way is best."

"Our future together, or lack of one, depends on you." A lengthy silence ensued. Then Ram asked, "Are you ready to tell me what I want to know?"

As ready as she'd ever be, Phoebe supposed. "Very well. Father found the amulet concealed in an artifact in his trunk while still aboard the ship carrying him to England. He had no idea how it got there and intended to return it to the proper authorities as soon he debarked."

"Go on," Ram said tersely.

"Father wanted to keep the amulet safe, so he hid it beneath the soap in his shaving mug. I found the mug, but you interrupted me before I could remove the amulet."

"Where is the mug now?"

"On a shelf in the kitchen."

"Thank you, Phoebe. You've done the right thing."

"Have I? I'm not sure of that. What I am sure of, however, is that I can no longer handle this on my own. Please help me, Ram."

"That's all I've ever wanted to do, love."

He lifted her chin and kissed her, his tongue delving deep to capture her sweetness. Then he made tender, unhurried love to her, slowly building her passion until she was writhing beneath him, eagerly opening herself to his mouth and tongue. Then he positioned himself above her and drove his erection

253

inside her, pumping them both to a shuddering climax.

"Go to sleep, love," Ram said as he dropped down beside her and fitted her into the curve of his body. "And try not to worry. I won't let anything happen to your father."

Phoebe was still praying that she had done the right thing when sleep claimed her.

Phoebe awakened late the following morning, disappointed to find Ram gone and his side of the bed cold. Abby entered the bedroom a few minutes later. She set down the tray she was carrying and pulled back the drapes to let in the sunshine.

"I heard you stirring," Abby explained as she bustled about the room.

"Have you seen Lord Braxton this morning?"

"He left the house early, milady. He said to let you sleep as long as you wished."

"I'd like a bath, Abby."

"I'll see to it, milady," Abby said, hurrying off.

Phoebe nibbled on a bun and drank a cup of tea, more than a little upset at Ram for leaving her behind. She knew without being told that he had gone to the house on Mount Street for the amulet and wondered why he hadn't waited for her. Did he not trust her? Had she done the right thing?

A sudden thought occurred to her. Perhaps she should have asked David's opinion before revealing the amulet's location to Ram. David was concerned about her father and deserved to know what was going on. By the time the bathtub had been set up and filled, Phoebe had come to a decision. Once she had bathed and dressed, she would go to David and tell him what she had done. He wouldn't be happy about it, but she felt obligated to tell him about the plan that Ram and Fielding had concocted to rescue her father.

Thirty minutes later Phoebe descended the stairs. By some miracle no one was about, even the footman was missing.

Phoebe opened the door and quietly let herself out. She hurried through the gate and down the street, hailing the first passing hackney she saw. After a quick look behind her to make sure she wasn't being followed, she gave directions to the driver and settled back against the dingy squabs.

As luck would have it, she found David in the common room of the Fin and Feather, eating breakfast. He surged to his feet when he saw her, a stunned expression on his face.

"Phoebe! What are you doing here?" He glanced behind her. "Are you alone?"

"I need to talk to you, David. In private."

"Come up to my room. It's the only place we can be alone. Were you followed?"

"No one saw me leave."

He grasped her hand and pulled her up the stairs. "I'm surprised Braxton let you out of his sight."

They reached the top landing; David propelled her down the hallway and opened the door to his room. She stepped inside and began to have second thoughts the moment the door closed behind her.

"What is this all about, Phoebe? Has something happened?"

Phoebe sighed. "You could say that. I told him, David."

"Told whom? What are you talking about?"

"Ram. I told him where to find the amulet. He believes that Father didn't steal it, that someone placed it in his trunk before he left Egypt."

"Damn you!" The veins in David's neck bulged,

his anger escalating to unreasonable rage. "How could you have been so stupid? Do you care nothing for your father? You know what's going to happen now, don't you?"

"Of course. The amulet will be returned to the Egyptians. Braxton has a plan to rescue Father," Phoebe explained.

"That's unlikely to happen without the amulet. Andrew's abductors are going to be livid. Your father is in grave danger. You need the amulet to free him."

"We need help, David. We can't do this by ourselves."

"Had you told me where to find the amulet, your father would already be free."

"It's too late for regrets. What's done is done."

David's eyes narrowed. "Tell me about this plan Braxton and Fielding have concocted."

"They believe Father's abductors will try to contact me again. I'm to make myself visible to them. What they won't know is that Fielding's agents will be watching me. When I'm contacted, I'm to agree to exchange the amulet for Father. Once a time and place is agreed upon, Fielding's agents will take over."

"Clever," David said without enthusiasm. "You do know, don't you, that you are being used as bait. Braxton's disregard for you appalls me. My opinion of him is even lower than my original estimation, if that's possible."

Phoebe regarded him coolly. "You misjudge Ram."

"How can one misjudge a dedicated rogue? Nothing has changed, Phoebe. Braxton is the same man he was four years ago. He cares nothing for you. He wants you with him for one reason and one reason only. He wants the amulet, and you're the key to recovering it."

Phoebe swallowed hard. David could be right. She had already considered that possibility.

"Don't tell me you've fallen for him," David said incredulously. "I thought you were smarter that that."

"Of course I haven't," Phoebe lied. "Once Father is free, Ram and I will part ways. Father will need a long period of recuperation before we can even think about returning to Egypt."

Phillips was quiet a long time, his eyes resting speculatively on Phoebe. Suddenly his gaze slid away, his mouth curving into a sly smile. "We don't need Braxton to rescue your father." He leaned close. "We can do it on our own."

Phoebe could hardly credit his words. "What do you mean?"

"I know where Andrew is being held. We don't have to depend on subterfuge or risk our lives to rescue him."

"Why didn't you tell me this before?"

"You surprised me. Hearing that Braxton has the amulet left me dazed."

"When did you learn where my father is? How?" Phoebe asked.

"Last night, after I left you at the carriage house. Do you think Braxton is the only one who has men out looking for your father? I've been conducting my own search. Last night one of my hirelings encountered a man named Benny at a grog shop. Benny was deep in his cups, and he bragged that he was about to come into a large amount of blunt.

"In the course of the conversation he let slip that he and a friend were holding a man captive; a man

Connie Mason

they intended to exchange for an item of considerable value."

"Father," Phoebe guessed.

"My man followed Benny to a dilapidated tenement in the East End. He brought the information back to me late last night."

"We have to tell Ram," Phoebe said. "We'll need his help."

"No, Phoebe. We most definitely *can't* tell Braxton."

"Why not? Surely you don't intend to burst into a nest of vipers and make demands, do you? Not only would that be unwise but dangerous."

David grasped her hands; his voice was harsh with tension, and with something Phoebe couldn't identify. "Listen, Phoebe. My man learned that Andrew is often left on his own in a locked room. We can do this without help. Why bring Braxton and the Foreign Office into this? They'll just muck things up."

Phoebe wasn't convinced. Something didn't ring true, but this was David she was talking to. David would do nothing to jeopardize her father's life.

"You do agree that my way is best, don't you, Phoebe?" David prodded.

"I . . . I suppose, but Ram isn't going to like it."

"Once Andrew is free, you can tell Braxton to go to the devil. Are you with me?"

"Of course," Phoebe said, grasping at this unexpected chance to free her father. "I'm willing to do anything to help Father. You're a good friend, David."

"We should leave immediately. I suspect this is the first place Braxton will look when he finds you missing. Just give me a moment to write a note to . . . my hireling."

258

Phoebe waited by the door while Phillips dashed off a note and sealed it. When he finished, he propelled Phoebe out the door and down the stairs.

"Wait here," Phillips said. "I need to speak to the innkeeper about delivering my message."

Phoebe watched as David spoke earnestly to the innkeeper, then placed a coin in his hand. He returned moments later and ushered her outside. Before long he had hailed a hackney and they were rattling toward the East End.

Thirty minutes later the hackney rolled to a stop. "Are you sure this is the right address?" Phoebe asked, eyeing the run-down building with misgiving.

"This is it. Come along."

David paid the driver and ushered Phoebe up the stairs to the front door.

"What if Watts and Benny are inside? Shouldn't you make sure first?"

"How do you propose I do that?"

The first seeds of doubt took root in Phoebe's mind. "Perhaps we should summon help. Your plan is unrealistic. I wasn't thinking clearly when I agreed to it. We're only two people, David, and both of us unarmed. What if we encounter trouble?"

David's expression hardened as his hand clamped around her arm. "I'm armed, Phoebe, and you're not going anywhere. You agreed to this; now stop being difficult."

She tried to twist free, but David's grip was relentless. "David, what's wrong with you? Let me go."

"No, Phoebe. I've come too far, risked too much. We're playing this out to the end."

"Playing what out? You're frightening me."

He opened the door and pushed her inside. "Up the stairs. Hurry."

"Where's Father?"

"You're going to see him very soon, that I promise."

Phoebe supposed his words were meant to make her feel better but they only added to her fears. Suddenly she didn't know David anymore. Even his features had changed. His eyes were cold, without a spark of warmth, and his expression had a hard edge to it that she hadn't noticed before.

Phillips stopped before a closed door, rapped sharply twice, paused, then rapped three times more. The door opened a crack, then widened to allow them entry. Phoebe dug in her heels. "No! What's the meaning of this, David?"

He shoved her hard, sending her through the door and into Watts's arms.

She flung herself away. "Don't touch me!"

"Why did you bring her here?" Watts asked. "Do you have the amulet? I'd sure like a look at it. Must be something, to have so many people chasing after it."

The truth was finally beginning to dawn on Phoebe. The man she trusted most had betrayed her and her father. Her eyes blazing with fury, she rounded on him. "How could you? Ram was right all along. You're involved in father's abduction, aren't you? I trusted you, David. How could you turn against us like this?"

"Blunt, Phoebe. Being your father's assistant doesn't pay well. I'm tired of seeing all that wealth slip through my fingers. I want the lifestyle Braxton and those like him enjoy. For once in my life I want to spend money without worrying about creditors hounding me."

"You know it will be difficult to sell the amulet, don't you?"

"Not at all, my dear. I plan to sell it to a private collector for his own enjoyment. The arrangements have already been made. As soon as the piece is in my possession, I intend to sail to France and place it in the hands of the prospective buyer."

"It's too late, David. Doubtless Ram has already retrieved the amulet."

Before David could reply, a series of knocks sounded on the door. Watts opened it, and Benny stepped inside.

"Do you have news, Benny?"

"Aye," Benny said. "Braxton went to the house on Mount Street. He was inside but a short time and returned home. He's there now."

"You had Ram watched!" Phoebe charged.

David sent her a smug grin. "As it turned out, it was a good thing. I'm not one to leave anything to chance." He rubbed his hands together. "You'll soon find out how little your husband values you."

"What do you mean? What are you plotting now?"

"The note I wrote before leaving my lodgings was addressed to Braxton. I informed him that you had joined your father in captivity, and that the amulet could gain your release."

Phoebe's heart plummeted. She knew what Ram's answer to David's demands would be. Doubtless he had already taken the amulet to Lord Fielding, but if he hadn't, David's ultimatum would go unheeded. The amulet was important to England.

"Ram won't agree to your demands," she warned.

"We'll see," David said with supreme confidence.

"Where's my father? Or were you lying about that, too?"

"Bring her to Thompson," David ordered Watts.

Grasping her arm, Watts dragged her toward a closed door. He unlocked it, flung it open and shoved her inside. Phoebe stumbled into the room and her father's arms.

"Enjoy your reunion," Watts said as he slammed and locked the door.

"Phoebe! My God, what are you doing here?" Sir Thompson cried. "Did you do as I asked? Did you turn the amulet over to the authorities?"

"I told Ram where to find it. He'll see that it reaches the right hands." She searched his face. "You're looking better. Have you taken medicine for your ailment?"

"No, daughter. The attack seems to be almost over. I'm still weak, but recovering." He led her to a chair. "Sit down and tell me what's going on. I've been so confused these past weeks."

"David did it, Father. He stole the amulet and hid it in your trunk. I suspect he planted it in your belongings so you would be blamed for the theft in the event it was discovered. He probably planned to retrieve it during the long sea voyage, but you found it first and foiled his plan. He arranged for your abduction and everything else since then."

Andrew plopped down on the bed, his mouth working wordlessly. It was a full minute before his voice returned. "I can't believe it's true, Phoebe. Not David. I'd trust him with my life."

Phoebe knelt at his feet and grasped one hand in both of hers. "We were both wrong, Father. Something changed the David we once knew. He's not the same man. I don't know what's going to happen to us. Ram will never agree to give the amulet to David."

"Look at me, daughter." She lifted her face. "Do you trust Braxton?"

She gave him a wobbly smile. "I do, Father."

"Then trust him to find a way out of this."

Meanwhile, Ram had located the shaving mug. It was exactly where Phoebe had said it would be. If she hadn't lied, he'd find the long-sought amulet hidden in the bottom of the mug. Fielding would be pleased, and England would avoid embarrassment.

But at what cost? Ram wondered. How in blazes was he going to find Phoebe's father when he didn't have a clue where to look? He didn't like the idea of using Phoebe as bait but saw no other alternative. He would have to trust Fielding's men to keep Phoebe safe, but he still didn't like it.

Grasping the mug tightly, Ram rapped it sharply on the edge of the shelf. It shattered in his hand, and he caught the oilskin packet that dropped out before it hit the floor.

Finally, he reflected, holding the packet reverently in his hand. He was finally going to see what all the fuss was about. Carefully he unfolded the oilskin and drew out the amulet. The breath caught in his throat as he stared into the flawless, blood-red core of the largest ruby he had ever seen. Set into the center of a golden starburst, it was as large as a robin's egg. Ram couldn't even guess at its value, for the piece was beyond priceless. He couldn't blame the Egyptian government for demanding its return.

With shaking hands he replaced it in its oilskin

wrapper and slipped it into his pocket. He knew he should take it immediately to Fielding, but he wanted to show it to Phoebe first. Phoebe had seen it before, but only briefly and from a distance. Since the amulet had brought them together, he felt strongly that she should, at the very least, hold it in her hand, if only for a moment.

The Bow Street Runners were waiting for him at the front door. "Did you find what you were looking for, milord?" Akers asked. "Slaughter and I searched the house from top to bottom and found nothing."

"I did indeed find what I was seeking. Unless you knew where to look, you would not have found it," Ram said. "Don't blame yourselves."

"That's generous of you, milord," Slaughter said. "Do you have further orders for us?"

"Not at the present. There's no longer a need to guard the house. Send your bill to my solicitor. If by chance I have need of you again, I'll send for you."

Ram returned to his townhouse. The moment he bounded into the foyer and greeted Porter, he felt the tension around him and knew something was wrong. His jubilant mood turned into alarm when he saw Porter looking positively undone.

Ram said the first thing that came into his head. "Where's Phoebe?"

Porter cleared his throat. " 'Tis my fault, milord. I don't know how Lady Braxton left without being seen. Abby reported Lady Braxton missing about mid-morning. No one is certain how long she'd been gone before her absence was noticed."

"Bloody hell!" Ram spat.

"I sent several footmen out looking for her," Porter added, "but she hasn't been found. I'm sorry, milord. It seems Lady Braxton has a tendency to disappear at will."

A chill settled around Ram's heart. Where in blazes had Phoebe gone this time? Had she been abducted again? Why had she left the house before he could arrange for protection? She knew how the plan was to work, yet she had deliberately placed herself in danger before all the safeguards were in place. What in the hell was going on?

"There's more," Porter said. His chin wobbled and he appeared on the verge of tears. "This came moments ago."

Ram regarded the folded note Porter held out to him and recoiled. He didn't want to take it, knew without being told, the news was bad. His hands were shaking as he took the note from Porter. He read it through once, muttered a string of curses, then read it again.

"Who brought this?"

"A street urchin, milord," Porter said. "He's in the kitchen filling his belly. I thought you might want to question him."

"You did exactly right," Ram said, striding off to the kitchen.

He found the lad stuffing fruit tart into his mouth and washing it down with milk. The boy saw Ram, apparently recognized quality when he saw it and leaped to his feet.

"You're the lad who brought the note around," Ram said.

The boy wiped his mouth on his sleeve and nodded. "Aye, milord. Thank ye for the food." He edged toward the door. "I'd best be off now."

"Not so fast, boy. Who gave you the note? Can you describe the man who paid you to deliver it?"

"Oh, aye, milord. It were the innkeeper at the

Fin and Feather. Gave me a shilling to bring it here, he did."

"Give the lad another shilling and send him on his way," Ram said as he passed Porter, who was hovering in the doorway.

"May I be of help, milord?" Porter called after him. No answer was forthcoming.

Ram took the stairs two at a time, entered his bedchamber and slammed the door behind him. He was literally quaking as he collapsed into a chair and reread the note. The words were brief and to the point. Phoebe had been taken hostage. If he wanted to see her alive, he was to keep the amulet out of government hands and await further orders. The note wasn't signed, but Ram was sure it had come from David Phillips, who he knew was lodged at the Fin and Feather.

Duty warred with fear for Phoebe. How could he give Fielding the amulet when it might cost Phoebe her life? Now he knew precisely how Phoebe had felt when she'd learned that the amulet was needed to preserve her father's life.

The hell with duty, he decided. He would use the amulet as he saw fit, and that was to save Phoebe's life. His face set in harsh lines, Ram stormed down the stairs and ordered his horse brought around, pacing impatiently until the groom arrived. Then he mounted swiftly and charged off down the street.

When Ram reached the Fin and Feather, he tossed the reins to a young lad lounging nearby and strode inside. The innkeeper hurried over to greet him.

"What can I do for you, milord? I've some decent brandy, if you'd care to sample a glass."

Ram opened his purse, removed a golden crown

and flashed it before the innkeeper's eyes. "All I require is information, good sir. Was a lady here earlier today with David Phillips?"

The innkeeper stared at the gold piece and licked his lips. "I didn't see her come in, but I saw her leave with Mr. Phillips."

"Was she . . . did she seem reluctant? As if she was being forced to accompany him?"

"Oh, no, milord, she seemed quite willing. She even waited while Mr. Phillips arranged with me to have a message delivered."

Ram didn't want to believe what he was hearing. If he did, it would mean that both Phoebe and David were involved in the theft of the amulet.

No, he refused to believe it. She had told him where to find the amulet, hadn't she? Nothing made sense. But what else could he think?

No, he still refused to believe it of her. Somehow Phillips had tricked her. He had to believe that or he'd go mad. "Thank you," Ram said, placing the coin in the innkeeper's palm. "One more thing. Would you be so kind as to let me know when Mr. Phillips returns? Direct the messenger to Lord Braxton. My townhouse is located on Park Lane. Number twenty-four."

"I don't want no trouble, milord."

"The lady is my wife. There will be more trouble than you can handle if you don't do as I request," Ram said in a voice suddenly gone cold.

The change in Ram's tone must have convinced the man, for the innkeeper quickly assured Ram he would send a messenger the moment Mr. Phillips returned to his lodgings.

Ram returned home, disheartened to learn that no further communication had arrived from Phillips. He knew he should report to Fielding, and he knew as well that his superior would demand that he return the amulet. If Ram kept the amulet and used it to bargain for Phoebe's life, he could be charged with treason. His dilemma was solved by simple logic. He would need Fielding's help to rescue Phoebe.

Chapter Fifteen

A short detour took Ram to the headquarters of the Bow Street Runners. He was admitted into the director's office immediately.

"I want to hire your best investigators," Ram said without preamble.

"Akers and Slaughter said you dismissed them. Has something else come up that demands our services?"

"Indeed it has," Ram said grimly. "My wife has been abducted again, and I want to find the man responsible. Cost is no object. There will be a bonus for the man who brings the information I seek."

Ram went on to describe both Phillips and Phoebe, wishing he'd thought to ask Phoebe for the description of the two men named Watts and Benny.

"I'll have men out scouring the city within an hour, milord," the director assured him. "Where can you be reached with our findings?"

"At my home. I have one more call to make, but it shouldn't take long."

Ram took his leave. He didn't know if hiring Runners would produce results, but he was desperate. His assumption was that Phillips would be known at a saloon, inn or grog shop in the neighborhood where Phoebe and her father were being held captive. Phoebe's abductors had to be purchasing their food somewhere, and the most likely place was a public inn or saloon. He had no idea if Phillips did the purchasing or if his lackeys did, but he prayed Phillips had done so on at least one occasion.

Lord Fielding was in a dither when Ram arrived.

"I was just about to send for you, Braxton," he said.

"What happened?"

"An Egyptian official arrived today. His ship docked early this morning. He went to the king and demanded the immediate return of the amulet. The king is furious. All hell will break loose if we don't recover that amulet soon."

Ram's hand went to his pocket, where the amulet was resting safely. He had the means to end the controversy now and restore his country's integrity, but at the risk of Phoebe's life. That was too much to ask.

"What's wrong, Braxton?" Fielding asked. "You look . . . odd. What's going on?"

"Phoebe's been abducted," Ram blurted out.

"Again? To what end?"

Briefly Ram considered his options. He could tell Fielding that he had the amulet or he could lie. He decided to skirt the issue for the time being.

"I've hired Runners to scour the city for information. Once I learn where Phoebe and her father are being held, I might need your help. I'll keep you informed."

Fielding searched Ram's face, his own expression wary. "What aren't you telling me, Braxton. Why was your wife abducted a second time? How can I commit men when you're keeping something from me?"

"Dammit, Fielding! Don't you understand? I refuse to place Phoebe's life at risk."

"I understand more than you think," Fielding said. "You have the amulet, don't you? Personal feelings have no place here. You had a job to do. I regret that your emotions became involved, but there can be only one outcome." He held out his hand. "I want the amulet, Braxton. Need I say more?"

Ram's mouth hardened. "You're asking me to abandon my wife, and I can't do that."

"You accepted the assignment," Fielding pointed out. "You have never shirked your duty or compromised your honor before, and I don't expect you to begin now."

"You're a hard man, Fielding."

"In my business, I have to be. Do you have any idea who stole the amulet and abducted your wife and father-in-law?"

"I do indeed. David Phillips, Sir Thompson's assistant."

Ram's shoulders slumped as he stared into Fielding's implacable visage. He knew what he had to do, but still he resisted. But Fielding would not back down. He had made it quite clear that Ram would be brought up on charges if he failed to comply, and either way, Fielding would end up with the gem.

271

Connie Mason

Producing the amulet for Fielding was the most difficult thing Ram had ever done. With great reluctance he removed it from his pocket.

"I've seen you in action, Braxton, and feel confident you'll find your wife," Fielding said, releasing Ram from his inertia.

Surrendering to the inevitable, Ram placed the amulet in Fielding's hand. Fielding immediately unwrapped it, his eyes widening at the sight of the priceless gem.

"Good Lord, what an amazing piece. Priceless—utterly priceless. I knew I could count on you, Braxton. Inform me of Phillips's demands as soon as you hear, and I'll place my best men at your disposal."

"I'll let you know if and when I need help," Ram said. "Don't do anything until you hear from me. Having too many men working on the case could endanger Phoebe's life."

"Very well, if that's what you want. You did the right thing, Braxton," Fielding said as Ram headed for the door.

"Doing the right thing isn't helping Phoebe," Ram muttered as he took his leave.

Ram returned home, hoping that word had arrived from Phoebe's abductors. Porter met him at the door.

"Has a message arrived for me?" Ram asked.

"No word yet, milord," Porter said. "But Lord Westmore is waiting for you in the study."

"How like Westmore to show up when I need him most," Ram said as he strode briskly into the room.

Luc rose to greet him. "You look like you've lost your best friend. I take it your investigation isn't going smoothly."

"Nothing is going smoothly."

"Is the amulet still missing?"

"The amulet is where it belongs, but my wife is gone again."

"You found the artifact?"

"Yes, and I took it to Fielding. That blasted amulet is the only bargaining tool I had, and I gave it up," he lamented. "Now I have nothing with which to bargain for Phoebe's release."

"What are you going to do?"

"Bow Street Runners are scouring the city as we speak, and Fielding has promised help should I need it. I'm waiting to hear from Phillips. I expect he'll tell me where the exchange is to take place."

"But you don't have the amulet," Luc pointed out.

"I'm hoping Phillips doesn't know that. Phoebe may have told him I took possession of it, but he doesn't know I gave it to Fielding."

A brief knock came on the door seconds before it opened. "Milord, you have a visitor," Porter said.

A rather small, nondescript man stepped around Porter. It was Slaughter.

"We have information on the man you described, milord," Slaughter said.

"Thank God! Out with it, man. Have you found where my wife is being held?"

"Not exactly, but we've pinpointed a neighborhood in the East End near the docks. A man answering Phillips's description bought food at the Hoof and Horn today. It's located near the docks."

"Good work," Ram crowed. "At least we have a starting place. Let's go."

"I'm going with you," Luc said.

Ram removed a pistol from his desk drawer. His expression was grim as he loaded and primed it.

Then he placed it in his pocket and nodded to Luc. "I'm ready."

"My carriage is outside."

Porter met them at the door. "A message just arrived for you, milord."

Ram's hand was shaking as he plucked the folded sheet of paper from Porter's fingers.

"Is it from Phillips?" Luc asked.

"I'll soon find out." He unfolded the note and quickly read the contents.

"I'm supposed to ride in Rotten Row in Hyde Park at precisely ten tomorrow morning. Someone will contact me and I'm to give him the amulet."

"What about Lady Braxton and her father? Is no mention made of them?"

"According to the note, they'll be released after the amulet has been delivered." He flung the note across the room. "Bloody hell, as if I trust Phillips to do as he says! Come on. That doesn't give us much time."

Phoebe toyed with the food David had brought, pushing it around with her fork into an unappetizing glob. "This is terrible," she complained. "No wonder you haven't recovered your strength. Who could eat this slop?"

"Most of the time I had no appetite," Thompson reminded her. "This is a sight better than what I was given before they brought me to London."

Phoebe threw down her fork. "We've got to get out of here."

"How do you propose we do that?"

She walked to the window and pressed her forehead against the wooden shutters. She felt a breath of refreshing air seep through the cracks and inhaled deeply. "I don't know. The door is locked and the window shutters nailed in place. I can't see much through the cracks."

"Where are we?" her father asked. "I was pretty much out of it when they took me from the cottage. At times I can smell the river, and there is another smell I can't identify."

"We're near the docks. You smell the river and the stench of poverty." She shuddered. "I pity the people forced to live here. How will Ram find us in such a place?"

Her face was etched with anguish as a sudden thought occurred to her. "What if Ram doesn't care what happens to us? He already has the amulet."

"You don't believe that," Andrew chided.

Her expression steadied and her eyes glinted with purpose. "We have to rescue ourselves, Father."

She returned to the table and sat down in the rickety chair, her brow creased in thought as she took stock of their resources. The room held a bed, a small scarred table, two chairs and a screen shielding a commode. Escape didn't look promising. Placing her elbows on the table, she rested her chin between her palms and considered her options. Giving up was not one of them.

She knew Ram was loyal to his country, and that he would never place the amulet in the hands of thieves, no matter what the cost to him personally. Would David kill them if Ram refused to meet his demands? She didn't know; she had never seen this side of David before.

Phoebe couldn't help blaming herself just a little for the abrupt change in David's personality. He had claimed to be in love with her and wanted to marry her. Had her refusal been somehow responsible for his change of character? Or had she failed to see his mercenary bent? Her thoughts delved back several years, to the morning after her marriage to Ram. Had David not placed doubts in her mind about Ram, she would not have left the man she loved. Why hadn't she seen through David's deception? How could she have been so naïve?

Consumed by anger, she pounded her fist on the table. "How could David do this to us, Father?"

The table wobbled, then tilted to one side. Phoebe leaned back and stared thoughtfully at the thick table leg, which was bent at an unnatural angle. Excitement tore through her. "Help me turn the table onto its top, Father."

"What are you thinking, daughter?"

"I'll tell you after I have a look at the table leg."

It wasn't a large table, and between them they upended it easily. "Look here!" Phoebe cried. "The leg has a large crack near its base. It wouldn't take much to break it off."

Andrew gave her a startled look. "For what purpose?"

Phoebe dearly loved her father, but he wasn't very imaginative. "Somehow we have to convince Watts to open the door. I'll hide behind it and slam the table leg into him when he steps through."

"What if Watts isn't alone?"

"I heard the outer door close right after David brought in our food, so I assume he's out making arrangements for the exchange. That means Watts is alone."

"You always were resourceful, daughter. Shall we try to break the leg away from the table? If we both put our weight on it, it should snap easily enough."

The table leg was more solid than it appeared. It took their combined strength to loosen it further, and several tugs before the leg snapped with a loud crack, sending Phoebe flying. She landed on her bottom.

"Are you all right, Phoebe?"

She picked herself up off the floor and rubbed her bottom. "I'm fine. We did it!"

Andrew hefted the table leg in his hands. "It's pretty solid. It's going to make a fine weapon. But I should be the one wielding it."

Phoebe shook her head. "You're too weak; I'll do it. Now, how are we going to lure David's henchman into the room?"

"I can pretend I'm ill," Andrew suggested. "When Watts comes in to investigate, you swing your club. Or we can wait until someone brings breakfast in the morning."

"No, we can't wait that long. It should be growing dark, and that could aid us in our escape. We have to do it soon."

"Pray there's only one of them out there when we make our move," Andrew said fervently.

Ram and Luc entered the Hoof and Horn and approached the innkeeper, a slovenly man who wore a stained apron stretched over his large belly. He answered Ram's questions readily enough once his palm was greased.

"Aye, I seen the man," he said after Ram described David Phillips. "I only seen him once, though. He came in earlier today to purchase food. A goodly amount it was, too."

"Was anyone with him?"

"No, not that I saw."

"Has anyone else purchased food from you in large amounts in the past few days?"

The innkeeper scratched a bald place on his

head. "Aye. A man named Benny. He's real friendly with one of my barmaids."

Ram's hopes soared. If Benny had told the barmaid something of importance, it would help the search considerably. "I'd like to speak to the barmaid."

"Suit yerself, Yer Lordship," the innkeeper said. "I'll send Sadie out." He scurried into the back reaches of the dingy inn.

A length of time passed before a blowsy blonde with straggly hair and large breasts sashayed out. "Nathan said ye wanted to see me, Yer Lordship." She gave him a coy smile. "If ye be wanting a bit of bedsport, I'm yer woman."

"All I'm wanting is information, Sadie. I'll make it worth your while."

Sadie gave him a wary look. "Wot kind of information?"

"I understand you're on friendly terms with Benny."

"Wot's the bloke done?"

"He keeps the wrong friends. Do you know where he lives?"

She cocked her head and shrugged. "He never said. We didn't spend much time talking, if ye get my drift."

"Will this help you remember?" Ram pulled a shiny coin from his purse and tossed it to her. She caught it handily, and the coin disappeared down her cleavage.

"Benny and a friend rented rooms nearby," she said.

"Is that all?"

"I said I didn't know much."

Sadie's reticence made Ram believe she was deliberately withholding information.

"Is that all, milord?" Her gaze slid over him with bold perusal. "Sure ye won't change yer mind about that bedsport?"

"Not today, Sadie."

"Wot about yer friend?" she asked, turning her avid gaze on Luc.

Luc gracefully declined. Sadie shrugged and flounced off.

"That's not much to go on," Luc said.

"At least we know they're in the neighborhood," Ram allowed. "That's enough for me. Since I no longer have the amulet to bargain with, we need all the help we can get."

"Did you *have* to give it to Fielding?"

"He left me no choice," Ram bit out. "Let's go. We've a lot of ground to cover."

Sadie peeked around the corner and motioned for the man behind her to remain hidden.

"What are they saying?" Benny hissed.

"Something about an amulet," Sadie whispered. Instantly alert, Benny asked, "What about it?"

She shrugged. "His Lordship gave it to a man named Fielding. Is it important?"

"Not to me, but it is to a man I know. Are they gone yet?"

"They're still talking," Sadie said. "Why are they looking for ye, Benny?"

"It's a long story. I think it's time to visit my sister in the country, but first I gotta warn my friends."

"Ye'll come back, won't ye?"

He patted her ample bottom. "Ye can bet on it, Sadie, girl. Give us a kiss and I'll be off."

After a wet, groping kiss, Benny scooted out the back door and disappeared down a dark alley. Rats scurried out of his way and his shoes made squishing sounds as he trod over foul-smelling garbage. He made a right turn and entered the rear door of a dilapidated building that had been boarded up and appeared uninhabited.

The stairs creaked as he made his way to the second floor, cursing the cockroaches and furry animals that scattered in his wake. He initiated a pattern of quick raps upon the door and hissed, "It's Benny. Let me in. There's trouble."

The door opened immediately. "It's about time you showed up," David Phillips complained. "What's this trouble you're talking about?"

"I just came from the Hoof and Horn. Lord Braxton was there, asking questions. Just wanted ye to know I ain't sticking around."

Phillips grasped a handful of Benny's jacket. "Did you see him?"

"Aye, I saw him. Sadie put him off our trail. There's something else ye should know."

"What is it?"

"That amulet you were hoping to get yer hands on—well, forget it. Braxton doesn't have it."

Phillips gave Benny a vicious shake. "I thought you said he went directly home after he recovered the amulet."

"He did, but I didn't stick around after that. I figured you'd want to know right away he'd gone to Mount Street, and assumed you would handle it from there."

Phillips's face turned an ugly shade of red. "My note had to be waiting for him when he returned home. The bastard deliberately ignored my warning. Phoebe was right. Braxton cares more about his country than he does his wife."

"What are you gonna do?" Watts asked.

"Braxton is going to pay. I'm taking the woman

and getting out while I can. There is a ship anchored in the river, waiting to take me across the channel to France. I planned to leave tomorrow, but tonight will do just as well."

"What about the old man?" Watts asked.

"Leave him. He's no longer important."

"Whatever ye're going to do, you'd best do it fast," Benny advised. He reached for the door latch. "I'm leaving. Good luck."

Watts reached out to stop him.

"Let him go," Phillips said. "He'll just get in our way." He pulled a pistol from his pocket, made sure it was loaded and stuffed it into his waistband. "Get Phoebe."

Phoebe pressed her ear to the door, trying to make sense of the mumbling she heard. "Someone just left," she told her father. "I heard the door open and close. I think there's only one person out there now. It's time to put our plan to work. Lie down on the bed, Father, and pretend you're sick. I'm going to raise a ruckus until someone comes to investigate."

She began to yell and pound on the door. "Help! Father is ill! Please help him!" She continued screaming and pounding until she heard a key turn in the lock. Grasping the table leg firmly in her hands, she pressed herself against the wall, raised it over her head and tensed.

"What the hell is going on in here?" Watts growled as he poked his head into the room. He saw Sir Thompson lying on the bed and stepped inside. "What's wrong with him?"

Those were his last words before the table leg smashed down on his head. He made a slow spiral to the ground and lay still.

"I hope I didn't kill him," Phoebe said as she dropped her weapon and knelt beside the hulking Watts.

"You didn't hit him hard enough to kill him," Andrew assured her. "Let's get out of here, daughter."

"Where do you think you're going?"

David Phillips stood in the open doorway, his pistol aimed at Andrew's middle. Phoebe's heart nearly stopped. She had made a mistake, possibly a fatal one. Refusing to admit defeat, she glared defiantly at David.

"That was clever of you, Phoebe, but your little caper didn't work." He glanced down at Watts and shook his head. "I suspect he's not going to be happy when he awakens." He made a jerking motion toward the door. "Move. You're coming with me."

"Where are we going?"

"Far away."

"I can't believe you're behind this, David," Andrew chided. "I'm grievously disappointed in you. You were my assistant, my friend and confidant. I trusted you."

"You always were a trusting soul, Andrew. I've been stealing artifacts and valuables from tombs for years and sending them to a private collector in France. I've a tidy sum of money waiting for me across the channel. I coveted the amulet the moment I saw it. Its great value would have set me up for life."

Andrew's eyes filled with sadness. "I pity you, David."

"Save your pity for someone in need of it." He grasped Phoebe's wrist. "Come along, Phoebe."

Phoebe dug in her heels. "I'm not going anywhere with you. Neither is Father."

"I don't want your father. But if you value his life, you'll do as I say."

"Take me instead," Andrew said.

"No. I want to make Braxton suffer for what he did."

Phoebe went still. "What did he do?"

"He robbed me of the chance to become wealthy beyond my wildest dreams. He cares nothing for you, my dear. But you've always known that, haven't you?"

"Whatever are you talking about?"

"Despite my warning, despite the threat to your life, Braxton gave the amulet to Lord Fielding. So you see, Phoebe, Braxton's actions prove your worthlessness to him. He cares nothing about you."

Pain. Dear God, the pain was unbearable. She'd known from the beginning what Ram's choice would be if he were forced to choose between her and duty to his country. She had known she would come in a distant second, so why should it hurt so badly?

Numbed by David's hurtful words, Phoebe couldn't think, couldn't move. It was as if she were frozen in time, pummeled by the knowledge of Ram's disregard for her. She couldn't find the strength to resist when David's grip tightened around her wrist and he started to drag her away.

Suddenly Watts moaned and sat up, holding his head. "What the hell happened?"

"Phoebe knocked you out. Get up; I need you."

"You bitch!" Watts said, shaking his fist at her.

"Stow it, Watts," Phillips said. "Phoebe and I are leaving. Stay here with the old man. Don't let him leave until tomorrow morning. Then I suggest you disappear from the London scene for a while. Take the blunt I gave you and find digs elsewhere."

"You're going to let Father go?" Phoebe said, finally finding her voice.

"I don't need the old man." Then he pulled her from the room and forced her toward the back stairs. They emerged in the alley behind the building.

"Where are you taking me?"

"Across the channel."

"Why? The amulet is lost to you—why not let me go?"

"I wasn't lying when I said I wanted you, Phoebe. I hoped to marry you. Why do you think I was stealing artifacts?"

"I don't know; you tell me."

"I expected to overcome your stubbornness one day and make you my wife. I needed money to provide for you."

"Stolen money," she spat. "Didn't you think I'd find out what you were up to?"

"None of that matters now. We're going to be together forever. I'll get what I've always wanted, and Braxton will finally get what's coming to him. Your husband is a possessive man. Losing you will gnaw at him the rest of his life."

Phoebe gave a snort of laughter. "You're mad. Braxton will simply write me off and move on to the next woman."

"I don't think so, Phoebe. Like I said, Braxton is a possessive man. I've seen the way he looks at you."

Phillips pushed her ahead of him into a narrow space between two buildings. "We're almost there."

"Where?"

"The docks and the packet ship that's going to carry us across the channel."

They emerged from the passage. It was full dark now, and a mist had rolled in from the river. David must have heard the voices at the same time as Phoebe did, for he pulled her back into the shadows and clapped a hand over her mouth. The voices grew louder; Phoebe struck out wildly in an attempt to free herself.

"Dammit, be still," he growled into her ear. "I'll shoot anyone who interferes."

Two men paused beneath the dim glow of a gaslight. Phoebe saw their faces clearly and let out a little whimper.

"I neglected to tell you Braxton was prowling about," Phillips hissed against her ear. "If the bastard was alone, I'd shoot him."

Phoebe managed to work his hand away from her mouth and let out a piercing scream. A sharp, stinging blow to her head cut it off, and she spiraled down . . . down . . . down into a black void.

"Did you hear something?" Ram asked, pulling Luc to a halt. "Was that a scream?"

"Sounded like a cat to me."

"Maybe," Ram said uncertainly. "It came from behind us. I'm going back to have a look."

"Wait for me." In the misty darkness they did not see the two figures crouched in the narrow alley as they hurried past.

"I don't see anything," Luc said. "Maybe the scream came from inside one of the buildings."

Ram sincerely hoped not. It would take hours to search all the buildings in the vicinity. A muscle clenched in his jaw. If Phillips hurt Phoebe, the bastard would regret it.

285

"Did you see that?" Luc cried, pointing to a nearby building. "Someone just ran out of the building as if the devil were on his tail. Wonder what he's up to. Shall we investigate?"

They reached the building in question and paused at the bottom of the stairs. "It looks deserted," Luc said.

"Just the kind of place Phillips might pick to hide his prisoners. I'm going inside."

Ram sprinted up the stairs and reached for the nearest latch, but the door opened before he touched it. A man staggered out and nearly fell into his arms.

"Help me, kind sir," the man gasped. "My daughter . . ."

"Sir Thompson? Is that you?"

Andrew raised his head, recognized Ram and collapsed against him. Ram eased him down onto the steps and knelt beside him.

"Where is Phoebe?"

"Let the man catch his breath," Luc advised. "He's nearly done in."

"Let me talk," Andrew said. "I must tell you . . ."

"Tell me what?" Ram asked impatiently.

"He took Phoebe away."

"Phillips?"

Andrew nodded. "He knew you were closing in on him. One of his henchmen reported that you were asking questions at the Hoof and Horn, and that you gave the amulet to Fielding. David was angry and vowed to make you pay. Watts was supposed to keep me confined until tomorrow, but the coward fled soon after David left."

"Sadie," Luc spat. "I guess we spoke too freely. She must have gone straight to Benny with the information."

"Andrew, do you know where Phillips has taken Phoebe?" Ram asked.

Andrew clutched Ram's lapels with trembling hands. "I don't know. He said something about taking her far away. Find her, Braxton." Then his eyes rolled back in his head and he swooned.

"He's reached the end of his endurance," Luc observed. "The poor devil's gone through a terrible ordeal. You can tell he's been ill just by looking at him."

"Take him to the Hoof and Horn," Ram said. "Once he's revived, bring him to my townhouse and tell Porter to summon my physician. Can you manage without help?"

"I'll be fine," Luc said. "He's already starting to stir. What are you going to do?"

Determination darkened his features and hardened his voice. "Find my wife."

Chapter Sixteen

"Wake up, damn you, wake up!"

Phoebe's head lolled from side to side as she tried to escape the hissing sound against her ear. Her temples pounded and her skull felt as if it were about to explode. She felt herself being boosted to her feet and slowly opened her eyes.

"Wake up, Phoebe."

David Phillips loomed over her, his face barely visible in the encompassing darkness. What she did see wasn't comforting. His expression was fierce; his pale eyes gleamed with madness.

"You hit me," Phoebe accused. "How could you? I thought you cared for me."

"My own needs come first. Can you stand up?"

"Why did you hit me?"

"I was afraid you'd alert Braxton. I hit you to keep you quiet." He peered around the corner of the building. "The coast is clear; we can proceed."

"Proceed where?"

"I arranged for a packet to carry us to France. It's moored out in the river."

"I'm not going anywhere with you."

"I think this will change your mind," Phillips said, ramming the barrel of his pistol into her back.

"You won't shoot me, David," Phoebe said. "We've been friends too long."

"Maybe, maybe not, but I *will* kill Braxton if he finds us before we board that ship, so I advise you to follow my instructions." He prodded her with the gun. "Let's go."

Phoebe knew better than to doubt David. His threat to kill Ram was very real. In order to escape arrest and prosecution, David needed to leave England. What she couldn't understand was his reason for taking her with him.

"Let me go, David. I'll only hinder your escape."

"Shut up, Phoebe. I need to reach that rowboat tied to the pier, and you're my protection. Braxton won't stop me as long as I have you."

"You're wrong, David. Ram will find a way."

"Just keep walking. If you think you can appeal to the ship's captain for help, you're mistaken. I'm paying the man enough to keep him from getting nosy."

The wild look in David's eyes and the gun pressing against her spine warned Phoebe against attempting an escape. David was desperate, and maybe a little mad. There was no telling what he would do. But she wouldn't give up. Her brain worked furiously to find a way out of this coil.

Ram charged down the street, trying to recall what Andrew had said about Phillips's ultimate destination. Had there been a clue in the few disjointed words he'd spoken? He remembered Andrew saying that Phillips was taking Phoebe far away, but that could mean anywhere on this earth.

A grim smile stretched his lips as the one logical answer emerged. The docks were nearby, and Phillips needed to leave the country in order to escape prosecution. Ram's gaze focused on the docks and the river beyond. Lengthening his stride, he ran in that direction.

He saw them before they saw him and ducked behind a stack of barrels. They were hurrying toward a small rowboat tied up to a pier. From Ram's vantage point it didn't appear as if Phoebe was protesting overmuch, but he knew from experience that drawing conclusions about Phoebe was unwise. He also knew that he had to stop Phillips before he forced Phoebe into the rowboat.

Stepping out from behind a barrel, Ram sprinted down the pier toward Phillips and Phoebe. Phillips must have heard his pounding footsteps, for he spun around, bringing Phoebe in front of him.

"I see you, Braxton. Stop where you are."

"Let Phoebe go!"

"Not on your life."

"He's got a gun, Ram!" Phoebe warned.

"Shut up," Phillips growled into her ear.

"Your fight is with me, leave Phoebe out of it," Ram shouted. "Release her and I'll let you go."

"Like hell you will! You don't care about Phoebe. If you did, you would have agreed to my demands. But no, you gave the amulet to Fielding."

Ram took a subtle step forward.

"Stop right there, Braxton. I've got a gun. If you value her life at all, you'll stay where you are."

Ram spit out a curse, his gaze fastening on Phoebe. He could see nothing but the pale oval of

291

her face in the swirling fog and darkness. "Are you all right, Phoebe?"

"I'm fine!"

"Heed my warning, Phillips," Ram said. "You have one bullet in that gun. If you shoot Phoebe, I may let you live, but only long enough to regret it."

"I'll take my chances."

All the while Ram and David were arguing, Phoebe's thoughts skittered hither and yon, searching for a way to foil David.

When he started dragging her toward the rowboat, she didn't resist. She could see Ram moving slowly toward them and willed him to be patient.

"Quit dragging your feet," David growled. "When we reach the boat, you're going to get into it."

Pretending compliance, Phoebe girded herself for what she intended to do next, and it certainly wasn't getting into that rowboat. She was marshaling her strength to spin around and attack David when a dozen men materialized from the mist behind Ram. Were they David's accomplices? While Ram seemed surprised to see them, he didn't appear particularly worried.

Ram couldn't believe what he was seeing. Fielding! And he had brought a dozen agents with him.

"You didn't think I'd let you do this alone, did you?" Fielding said, sidling up to join Ram. "We've got him cornered."

"He's armed and desperate," Ram said. "I'm afraid he'll hurt Phoebe."

"You're outnumbered, Phillips," Fielding yelled. "Let Lady Braxton go and give up peacefully."

"You've forced my hand," Phillips replied. "I've

got nothing to lose now. If I die, I'm taking Phoebe with me."

Over the horrible roaring in his ears, Ram had the presence of mind to shout, "Phoebe, can you swim?"

Phoebe feared she had misheard Ram. Now wasn't the time to worry about her ability to swim. The gun pressing against her spine and David's desperation were much more immediate concerns.

"Get into the boat, Phoebe," David ordered. "Now. Don't do anything foolish. I meant it—I've nothing to lose."

The pressure of cold metal against her back was a grim reminder of her grave situation. She realized now that the men who had appeared through the fog were there to help Ram, but as long as she remained David's hostage, there was little they could do.

With a jolt of insight, Ram's puzzling words began to make sense.

"Untie the boat and hand me the rope," David directed.

Phoebe studied the rope attached to a metal ring embedded in the pier and bent to untie it. David grasped the rope to hold the boat in place and prodded her forward. "Get into the boat."

Phoebe pretended to obey, but at the last minute she sucked in a breath, hurled herself into the river and sank down, down, down, her skirts billowing around her. Her feet touched the bottom, and she propelled herself upward. As her head broke the surface, she heard David shout, "You won't take me!" Then he hit the water.

Her skirts pulled her down a second time. She pushed upward again and her head bobbed above

the water. She couldn't see David, but Ram was
swimming strongly toward her. Then she caught a
brief glimpse of Fielding's men spreading out along
the pier, searching the swirling dark water for David.

Numb with cold, Phoebe's body felt like lead and
she could barely move her limbs. Had Ram not
reached her when he did, she seriously doubted she
could have stayed afloat. She had never tried to
swim while fully clothed before.

"I've got you," Ram said as he towed her toward
shore. "Relax."

"David—"

"Forget him. There's a good chance he drowned.
If he swims ashore, Fielding's men will find him."

Ram reached the riverbank and dragged her,
coughing and sputtering, onto dry land. When she
tried to stand, she was shaking so hard her legs
buckled under her. Ram swept her into his arms
and carried her up the steep incline. Fielding was
on hand to meet them.

"Take your wife home and warm her up," Fielding advised. "We'll finish here." He patted Phoebe
on the shoulder. "That was clever of you, Lady
Braxton. If Phillips is alive, we'll find him."

"Milord, over here!"

Phoebe turned her head toward the voice and
saw Ram's coachman, standing near the coach,
waving frantically at them.

"Wilson!" Ram called. "How did you know
where to find me?"

"Lord Westmore, milord. He said you would
need transportation home and directed me here."

"There'll be a bonus in this for you, Wilson,"
Ram said as he handed Phoebe into the conveyance.

"I'm c-c-c-cold," Phoebe stuttered as the coach lurched off down the street.

Ram reached for the folded blanket resting on the seat and wrapped it around her. "We'll be home soon."

"W-w-w-we can't leave until we f-f-f-find Father."

"Your father is safe, sweetheart. We found him, or rather, he found us. Westmore took him to my townhouse and summoned a physician to treat him. He appeared unhurt."

Phoebe winced and cried out when he pushed her wet hair from her face.

"What is it? Are you hurt?"

"David hit me with the butt of his pistol to keep me quiet."

"He won't hurt anyone again," Ram said through gritted teeth. "The river current can be treacherous. If he doesn't drown, Fielding's men will find him."

The blanket didn't help much. Phoebe felt chilled clear through to her bones. Luckily, they reached the townhouse quickly. Ram jumped to the ground the moment the coach rolled to a stop and lifted Phoebe out.

"I can walk, Ram."

Ram ignored her as Wilson scurried before them to make sure there was no delay in opening the door. He needn't have worried for the door opened at his first knock, allowing Ram to sweep past the footman.

"I want a bath prepared for Lady Braxton," Ram called as he swept past Porter and up the stairs. "And bring plenty of hot water."

Ram sat Phoebe in a chair and went immediately to stoke the fire. She was still shivering when he returned. "Stand up. We need to get you out of those wet clothes."

"I w-w-w-want to see Father."

"Later." He pulled her to her feet, stripped the blanket from her quivering form and quickly and efficiently removed her clothing. Then he tucked her into bed and piled blankets on top of her.

Abby arrived along with the servants bearing the tub and hot water. "How can I help?" she asked, wringing her hands.

"I can handle it, Abby," Ram said. "Hot broth and tea for your mistress would be welcome, however."

She curtsied and hurried off.

Ram arranged the bar of fragrant soap and stack of towels near the tub. When all was in readiness, he returned to the bed. "Your bath is ready, Phoebe."

"Not now, Ram," Phoebe pleaded. "I'm just beginning to warm up."

"The bath will do you good, sweetheart. You've the stench of the river on you." He pulled away the blankets and scooped her into his arms. When he lowered her into the water, she gave a blissful sigh. While she soaked, he stripped off his own wet clothes and donned a heavy robe. Then he knelt beside the tub, took up the cloth and soap and applied it diligently to her shivering flesh. Soon a warm glow suffused her body. Phoebe wondered if it was due to the warm water or Ram's ministrations.

"Almost done," Ram said as he soaped her hair and scrubbed gently. Then he picked up a bucket of water and held it above her head. "Close your eyes."

Phoebe sputtered as water cascaded over her.

Dashing soapy water from her face, she opened her eyes just as Ram dropped the robe and stepped into the tub.

"What are you doing?"

"Warming myself," he said with a shiver. He settled down behind her, fitting her into the vee between his legs.

His flesh was chilled, and she felt immediate remorse for thinking only of herself. She started to rise. "Forgive me for being so thoughtless. You saved my life. I know how to swim, but my skirts were dragging me down. You must be frozen. The tub is all yours."

She stepped out of the tub before he could stop her and wrapped herself in a thick towel. Then she sat on a bench before the fire to dry her hair.

Ram's gaze roamed hungrily over Phoebe as she dried her lustrous dark hair. Firelight burnished it with a halo of red, giving the silken strands a life of their own. The towel had slipped, baring one gleaming shoulder, allowing him a tantalizing glimpse of a rose-tipped breast.

Her shiny hair made his palms tingle to touch it.

Her flushed skin made him ache to caress every glowing inch.

A tremor passed through him. He had almost lost her. Her strength amazed him. Phillips had put her through hell, and she had triumphed over his evil machinations. The pulsing need to make love to her slammed into him. He wanted to feel her skin pressed intimately against his, explore the sweetness of her mouth and taste her passion.

Driven by need, Ram washed quickly and surged to his feet. Grabbing a towel, he crossed to the hearth and sat down beside Phoebe.

"Are you warm yet?" His voice rolled over her like thick honey.

"Not quite. Are you?"

A predatory gleam lit his eyes. "We'll both be warm soon . . . very soon."

Turning her into his arms, he tilted her chin up and stared into her face a long, suspenseful moment before his lips came down hard on hers. She opened her mouth to him as his hand came up to anchor itself in her hair, holding her still for his marauding lips and tongue.

Phoebe sank into the kiss, so happy to be in Ram's arms she forgot everything but the need to be one with him again. Later she would think about the future and whether she and Ram actually had one together. For now, nothing mattered but the heat of his body, the hunger coursing through her and the fiery grip of desire that clenched her insides.

The towel slid away from her body, made unnecessary by the heat their bodies were generating. His kiss deepened, and her arms came up to circle his neck, all inhibitions vanquished in the torrid flames of passion. She had no desire to flee, only to experience every nuance of his loving. Her tongue met his in a delicate, sensual dance. She felt him shudder and moan, and the fires of her passion spiraled higher.

His hand roamed up her body to cup her breast. His thumb circled her nipple; Phoebe gave a gurgle of pleasure as raw sensation rippled through her. His breathing grew harsh and heavy as his fingers kneaded and caressed, gently pressing and squeezing her nipple until it hardened into a taut, aching bud.

He pressed her down on the bench and leaned

over her, kissing the pink tip, then taking it into his mouth, suckling as eagerly as a babe at its mother's breast. Heat flowed between her legs, increasing with each tug of his mouth upon her. Her breath caught on a gasp when his mouth left her breast and continued downward to her dewy center. His fingers opened her, and he settled his mouth in precisely the right spot. She arched into his intimate caress and cried out his name, ecstasy incinerating her body.

He laved, teased and nibbled, his tongue swirling against her while his hands explored her, moving over her stomach and thighs and between them. She was melting, literally dissolving. His mouth and hands were driving her into a frenzy of sexual need.

Sliding his hands beneath her, he lifted her higher, relentlessly stilling the movement of her hips, giving no quarter, demanding nothing less than total surrender. With an anguished cry she gave him what he wanted, shattering violently. Her body was still vibrating with the force of her climax when Ram picked her up and carried her to the bed.

"I'm warm now, Ram, really warm," she said breathlessly.

"You're going to get a whole lot warmer, sweetheart."

Her gaze locked with his as he entered her, filling her with the force of his powerful need . . . dragging her back into the arms of ecstasy. Immediately her body spasmed, her inner muscles clasping him as he drove into her again and again, sending her spiraling out of control.

They reached their climax simultaneously, giving and taking everything from each other. His seed surged deep inside her and she welcomed it . . . for it might be the last time they would be together like this.

Ram watched Phoebe sleep. He had bedded countless women after she had left him, but none of those brief encounters had been as satisfying as what he had just experienced with Phoebe. What was it that made Phoebe special?

Phoebe had done a great deal of maturing during the years they were apart, and had learned the hard way that David Phillips's machinations had been the cause of their estrangement. Phillips had lied and connived to take Phoebe away from him, and he'd succeeded. If only Phoebe had not been so trusting; if only she'd seen through Phillips's lies.

Not that Ram was entirely blameless for their split. He hadn't been the model of propriety, and his reputation even then had been less than pristine. But he had fallen hard for Phoebe and married her with the intention of remaining faithful. Unfortunately, his good intentions were never put to the test. He wasn't allowed the opportunity to become the husband Phoebe wanted.

The longer Ram stared at Phoebe, the more he wondered what their future held. When he thought of life without Phoebe, an empty feeling settled in the center of his chest . . . something like a terrible longing, an ache, a desire to keep her with him always.

Did Phoebe want the same thing? Had their four-year estrangement pulled them too far apart to recapture what they had once shared? Perhaps their love had been an illusion . . . a spur-of-the-moment lust that had ended in marriage because Phoebe refused to bed him without a ring on her finger.

When Phoebe stirred, Ram sighed regretfully

and eased out of bed. If he didn't leave immediately, he would make love to her again, and as much as he wanted that, it wasn't in her best interests right now. Phoebe needed rest after the ordeal Phillips had put her through.

Ram pulled on his trousers and shirt and went downstairs in search of food. Porter met him at the foot of the stairs.

"My stomach is touching my backbone, Porter. See if you can find me something to eat."

"Cook kept dinner warm, milord. I'll fetch it for you straightaway."

"Has Sir Thompson been made comfortable?"

"He ate and went straight to sleep after Dr. Bellows left. The doctor left an infusion of the bark from the cinchona tree. Quinine, I believe it's called. He said Sir Thompson would recover with rest and a nourishing diet."

"Thank you, Porter. I'll eat in the study."

"Shall I send Abby up with Lady Braxton's broth?"

"My wife is sleeping. I believe rest will do her more good than food right now."

Ram continued on to his study. He ate heartily of the roast capon with vegetables, meat pie and apple tart that Porter brought. Replete, he sat back with his hands folded over his stomach, evaluating his relationship with Phoebe. Before he returned to bed, he had arrived at a decision. Right or wrong, he would let Phoebe decide their future. If she found marriage to him intolerable, he would let her go. But there would be no divorce. Their marriage was permanent and would remain that way.

Ram awoke before Phoebe the next morning. He rose and dressed and left the room without awakening her. He was eager to learn David Phillips's fate and planned to visit Fielding immediately after breakfast. Westmore arrived while he was finishing his coffee.

"Have you eaten, Westmore?"

"Yes, but I'll have coffee," Luc said.

After Luc's coffee arrived, Ram dismissed the footman so they could speak in private.

"You're here early."

"I couldn't wait any longer. How is Phoebe?" Luc asked, going straight to the heart of the matter. "I returned to the docks after I saw to Sir Thompson, but you and Phoebe had already left. Fielding and his agents were still there, looking for Phillips. He told me what had happened."

"Phoebe is fine," Ram returned. "Her dip in the river chilled her to the bone but did no permanent damage. A hot bath worked wonders. She's still sleeping."

"How is Sir Thompson this morning? I left as soon as the physician arrived."

"According to Dr. Bellows, Andrew is on the road to recovery. Thank you for what you did for him. And for sending the coach."

"You would have done the same for me. What are your plans?"

"I plan to call on Lord Fielding this morning. I'm hopeful that he'll tell me Phillips is either in custody or dead. I'd hate to think the bastard got away."

"Fielding seemed to think he drowned, but I didn't stick around to find out."

Ram threw down his napkin. "No time like the present to learn the bastard's fate."

"I'll catch up with you later," Luc said. "I'm off to Tattersalls to look at a new hunter."

They parted at the front steps.

*   *   *

Phoebe yawned and stretched and rang for Abby, feeling surprisingly well in spite of her harrowing ordeal the previous day.

"How do you feel, milady?" Abby asked solicitously.

"Fine, thank you. Do you know which room my father was given?"

"The one across the hall from yours, milady. I heard Porter say he's up and taking breakfast in the morning room."

"He's up?" Phoebe asked with surprise. "He must be feeling well if he's up and about. Has Lord Braxton breakfasted yet?"

"He's already eaten and left," Abby said. "He was on his way out with Lord Westmore when I passed him in the foyer a short time ago."

Phoebe frowned. Where was Ram off to so early this morning? Did his haste have to do with David? Still frowning, she quickly dressed and went downstairs to join her father. Andrew's eyes lit up when he saw her, and he opened his arms to give her a hug.

"Porter assured me that Lord Braxton had brought you home last night, and that you appeared well, but I was still concerned."

"I was worried about you, too, Father. You seem greatly recovered today."

"The medicine the doctor left worked wonders. Were I given the quinine immediately, it would not have taken me so long to recover." He paused, then asked, "What happened to David?"

"I don't know. We never knew the real David, Father. We trusted him, and he betrayed us."

"How did Braxton find you?"

Phoebe helped herself from the sideboard before

answering. "It's a long story, Father." Over the course of breakfast she recounted the story of her rescue.

"You actually leaped into the river?" Andrew asked when she told him the harrowing details of her plunge into the water.

"It was the only way. As long as David held me hostage, Ram and Lord Fielding's men could do nothing without jeopardizing my life. David was desperate; he threatened to kill me. I wouldn't have thought to leap into the river if Ram hadn't asked me if I could swim."

"What did David do after you jumped?"

"He followed me into the water. I have no idea what happened after that. Ram towed me to shore and brought me home."

"David is no longer our worry," Andrew said. "The amulet has been returned to the Egyptians, and we are of no further use to David. You have nothing but happiness with Braxton to look forward to."

Phoebe placed her fork on her empty plate and pushed it away. "I'm not sure my future lies with Ram, Father. I hurt him badly when I walked away from our marriage. Rather than place my trust in Ram, I believed David's lies. I doubt Ram will ever forgive me for the blow I dealt his pride."

"But . . . but . . . you're together now. What happened years ago is water under the bridge."

"Ram insisted that I move into his townhouse so he could protect me," Phoebe explained. "He took his obligation to me seriously. Since I no longer need protection, he'll want to return to his former life—one unencumbered by a wife."

"Did he tell you that?"

"He doesn't have to. You don't know, because

you had no access to newspapers during your captivity, but the gossip columns reported Lord Braxton's amorous exploits in detail. Ram and Lord Westmore are commonly referred to as the notorious Rogues of London."

"Men can change, Phoebe. Do you love Braxton?"

A subdued silence ensued. Finally, Phoebe said, "With all my heart. But until I hear Ram say he loves me, I see no hope for us."

"That saddens me, daughter. I've always hoped that you would find happiness with a man worthy of your love. You're too young and attractive to waste your life crawling about in tombs."

"You need an assistant you can trust, Father. Do you plan to return to Egypt once your health is restored?"

"I haven't thought that far ahead. If you recall, I was offered a teaching position at the university and turned it down to return to Egypt. If it's still available, this might be a good time to accept. But first, a sojourn in the country sounds just the thing after my harrowing ordeal."

Phoebe clapped her hands. "What a wonderful idea. We'll leave immediately. We can stay at an inn while we look over rental properties."

"I didn't mean you, Phoebe. Your place is here with your husband."

"I wouldn't think of letting you go alone. Besides," she said, avoiding his eyes, "I planned to move back to the house on Mount Street as soon you were up to it, but your idea is much better."

"Are you sure of this, daughter? Braxton isn't going to like it."

"I've thought of nothing else since I awakened

this morning. Until Ram proves that he wants a wife, I'm better off without him."

"Don't you think you're being a trifle hard on him?"

"I'm being harder on myself; I'm sure of my love for Ram. He tried to mask his contempt the day he called on me after our four-year separation, but I wasn't fooled. The look in his eyes told me exactly how low I stood in his regard. He wanted vengeance for what I had done to him after our hasty marriage. He actually believed that you and I had conspired to steal the amulet."

"But he doesn't think that now."

"Maybe not, but he still doesn't trust me."

"Don't do anything rash, Phoebe. Talk to Braxton first."

"I intend to, Father, but I'm not going to beg for his love. Unless he tells me he loves me and wants a wife, I'm prepared to bow out of his life."

Chapter Seventeen

"What do you mean, you don't know what happened to him?" Ram shouted when Lord Fielding told him Phillips hadn't been found.

"Calm down, Braxton. My men are still out there looking for him, but the consensus is that he drowned. No one saw him rise to the top after he plunged into the river, and there were a dozen pairs of eyes looking for him."

"Unless his body is found, you won't know for sure."

"If he was swept out to sea by the current, his body will never be found."

"We can only hope," Ram muttered, not at all pleased by this news.

"The king asked me to extend his gratitude to you. Without your help, the case might never have been solved. The Egyptian government has been pacified, and all is well."

Fielding's words did little to placate Ram. He'd wanted to hear that Phillips was in custody, or that he was dead and therefore no threat to anyone.

"If you're worried that Phillips will pop up and harm you or your wife, I sincerely doubt that you have any cause for concern. Even if he were alive, he would have no reason to remain in England. My agents have been investigating Phillips since you first voiced your doubts about him. He has a small fortune gained from the sale of stolen artifacts waiting for him in France. If he's alive, he's probably crossing the channel as we speak."

It was going to take more than conjecture to convince Ram that Phillips was headed for France, but belaboring the point with Fielding would accomplish nothing. Ram intended to maintain vigilance until he was assured that Phillips was no longer a threat to Phoebe. Vengeance was a powerful motivator. It could fill a man's soul with blackness and change the direction of his life . . . as it had his.

As Ram rode home, he thought about Phoebe and the unresolved issues dangling between them. Their marriage was in serious jeopardy, that much he knew. He had no idea what Phoebe wanted in regard to their future.

His own emotions were as muddled as Phoebe's appeared to be. Being with her again had reminded him why he had wed her in the first place. The qualities he had found appealing in her hadn't changed.

He wanted her, and he loved to make love to her, but the kind of life he had lived these past four years was not conducive to marriage. He readily admitted to being a rogue, whose indiscretions were legend.

Was he ready to settle down and be a husband? He thought he was.

Did he love Phoebe enough to be the kind of husband she wanted? The answer to that question was harder, more complex.

Exactly what was love?

Could he look Phoebe in the eye, tell her he forgave her for the hurtful way she had abandoned him and mean it?

He hoped so.

Was he ready to forget the past, give up his dissolute life and forge a future with Phoebe?

Could he risk telling Phoebe what was in his heart if his feelings weren't reciprocated? He had forced her to move into his townhouse, seduced her into sharing his bed, distrusted her, accused her of theft and used his well-honed seductive powers on her.

She had too many reasons to hate him.

Ram reached his townhouse without resolving even one of the problems worrying him. He went directly to his study and rang for Porter.

"Where is Lady Braxton?" Ram asked when Porter appeared.

"With her father, milord."

"How is Sir Thompson?"

"Better. He took breakfast in the morning room with Lady Braxton," Porter informed him. "I believe he's resting now."

"Please fetch my wife for me."

"I'm here, Ram," Phoebe said, entering through the open door.

He waved Porter away as Phoebe settled into a chair.

"Porter said your father is up and about this morning."

A smile dimpled her cheek. "He's definitely on the road to recovery."

309

"What are his plans? He's welcome to live here with us if he so desires. He should take time to rest and recuperate before deciding if he wants to return to Egypt."

"Father's plans are still up in the air." She looked down at her folded hands. "I thought we'd spend some time in the country. He's thinking of accepting a position at the university, but nothing is definite."

"I suppose we could repair to my ancestral estate. A little peace and quiet in our lives would be welcome. The London season won't start for a couple of months, so it's a perfect time to leave."

Phoebe's unwavering gaze met his. "Does the London season mean so much to you?"

The question startled Ram. In the past, he wouldn't have dreamed of missing a season in town. London was a beehive of activity. It proliferated with the gambling hells, bordellos and ballrooms that he and his friends frequented. Where coming home before dawn and rising before three in the afternoon was unheard of among the *ton*. Where he had his choice of women, married and unwed, to tempt his jaded appetite.

Ram's hesitation was telling. It spoke volumes about the way he preferred to live his life. Phoebe knew she couldn't compete with the pleasures to be had in decadent London.

"I hadn't really thought much about where we would live," Ram said after a lengthy pause. "I assumed London holds the same appeal for you as it does for me. I wouldn't want to live away from London forever."

Phoebe digested that, then asked, "What role am I to play in your life?"

"You're my wife," Ram said, as if that explained everything.

Phoebe took a deep breath and let it out slowly. "Do you want a wife?"

Ram sent her a measuring look. "What are you trying to say?"

"I simply want to know what's in your heart, and if there is room in it for me."

"I know we have unresolved issues but—"

Phoebe plunged directly to the heart of the matter. "Those issues are long-standing ones. You don't trust me. My behavior four years ago still haunts our relationship today. Have you forgiven me for abandoning you?" When he hesitated, Phoebe said, "The truth, Ram. We should at least have that between us."

"It's taken a long time, but I can honestly say I understand how Phillips swayed your opinion of me."

"But do you forgive me?"

"Why are you pursuing this, Phoebe? Why can't we just build on what we have and forget the past?"

A tear leaked from the corner of her eye. This conversation was going exactly as she'd expected. "The past just doesn't disappear. It will always be there."

"I forgive you, Phoebe. I think I forgave you a long time ago, once we both realized it was Phillips's interference that turned you against me." Another long pause. "As long as we're being honest, answer one question for me. Why did you leave me without giving me the opportunity to prove myself a worthy husband? Didn't you love me enough?"

Another tear trekked down her cheek. "I did love you, Ram. I've regretted leaving you ever since. The sin was mine, and I suffered for it. You say you forgive me, but do you trust me? There has to be trust for a marriage to prosper."

"Trust works both ways. Do you trust me?"

"How can I not? 'Tis due to you that my father is alive." Unflinchingly, she looked him in the eye. "I do wonder, however . . ."

"What? What do you wonder?"

"Why did you gave the amulet to Lord Fielding when you knew it would jeopardize my life? David said you cared more for king and country than you did me."

It was obvious from the stunned look on Ram's face that he hadn't expected that question. It was also apparent that he didn't have the answer Phoebe wanted to hear.

"You don't have to answer that, Ram."

"You wanted the truth and you're going to get it. I did consider using the amulet to bargain for your life, but I had to do what my conscience demanded."

"Thank you for that honest answer." She stared unwaveringly into his eyes. "Do you love me, Ram?"

"I care for you a great deal. We're good together."

"In bed, you mean."

"Why are you being so difficult? Most marriages don't have that much."

"If I'm being difficult, it's because I'm trying to make the best decision possible for both of us."

"I'm capable of making my own decisions."

"Given our tumultuous past, can you honestly say you will never want another woman?"

Ram surged to his feet. "This is beyond ridiculous, Phoebe. I refuse to sit here and be quizzed like a damn child. Trust is your issue, not mine.

Perhaps we should wait a few days to discuss our future."

Phoebe rose. "I doubt that anything will change." She blew out a breath. "It was foolish of me to hope for words you obviously don't feel."

Ram's heart plummeted. What in bloody hell was wrong with him? Why couldn't he say the words Phoebe seemed to need? The answer came winging to him from out of the past. Another betrayal would utterly destroy him. If Phoebe abandoned him as she had four years before, he simply couldn't bear it. There would always be the fear that the slightest provocation would send her fleeing.

God knew he hadn't led an exemplary life, but Phoebe had to share the blame for the way he had conducted himself in the past.

"Phoebe, I . . ." The words lodged in his throat. He felt them in his heart but didn't have the courage to say them. That way led to heartache. In time, perhaps, he would unburden his heart and tell her how he felt, but not until he was sure she returned his feelings.

"Father and I are leaving."

Stunned, Ram stared at her. "Leaving? Where will you go?"

"The countryside holds great appeal to Father."

"If you truly feel it necessary, you can go to my country estate. I can clear up things here and join you in a few days."

"No, Ram. I'm making this a clean break. I'm not going to your country estate."

Ram's mouth thinned. "Are you sure that's what you want?"

"Very sure."

"Don't expect me to beg you to stay, Phoebe. I've

never begged a woman in my life and don't intend to start now. I *will* say, however, that I don't want you to leave; I believe we can make this marriage work. What happens next is up to you."

Tell me you love me, Phoebe silently implored.

Silence.

"Very well, Phoebe, if that's your decision, so be it. I'll arrange for funds to be deposited in your name in the Bank of London. Spend the money as you see fit."

"That's not necessary."

"It's very necessary."

"You're bitter."

He shook his head. "Not bitter; outraged. You're doing it again, Phoebe. You're abandoning me, just like you did four years ago. At least tell me where you're going."

"I'll . . . think about it," Phoebe replied. She turned toward the door. Ram reached her before she opened it.

Grasping her wrist, he pulled her against him, his eyes glittering like shards of green glass. He stared at her lips for the space of a heartbeat, then anchored his hands in her hair and tilted her face up to his. He tried to put into the kiss everything his lack of words failed to convey: that she was making a huge mistake.

He deepened the kiss; his tongue delved into the sweetness of her mouth, tasting, teasing, beguiling. He felt her shudder, felt her sink into the kiss and melt against him. A jolt of satisfaction surged through him. Phoebe wasn't immune to him. Their passion was explosive. Why couldn't passion satisfy her? Why didn't she realize he wasn't sure enough of her feelings to trust her with his heart?

She had trampled on it once; he feared she would destroy it if she betrayed him again.

The kiss took on a life of its own. Ram could no longer control his response to her taste, to the pressure of her body melding with his as he fell deeper into the sensual spell drawing them together. This felt so right, so good; he couldn't stop himself.

His fingers speared through her hair, scattering pins. The dark mass tumbled down and he held it, savoring the feel of the heavy silk sliding through his fingers. He groaned against her lips, his hands trailing down, skimming the sensitive skin of her throat. Then his lips left hers to follow the path of his fingers.

Phoebe placed her hands on his chest and pushed, but he was as unmovable as a rock. "Ram, stop. I can't think when you're kissing me."

"Don't think. Just feel. Deny it all you want, but the passion we share is too powerful to be ignored."

His lips returned to hers as his hands closed over her breasts, kneading, caressing, until they were swollen and aching. But she wanted more than passion from him. She wanted assurances, meaningful words to appease her insecure heart.

She knew she should stop him, but she followed her heart instead of her mind as he stripped her gown from her, freeing one shoulder then the other, murmuring things she desperately wanted to believe. How many women had heard the same words from Ram? Her mind was in so much turmoil, she was barely aware when he jerked her chemise up and over her head.

She moved restlessly against him, felt his erection rigid against her stomach. She tried to shift away, but he caught her hips and held her captive between his spread legs.

"I just told you I was leaving you, Ram. Why are you doing this?"

The stark planes of his face appeared as if hewn from granite, and there was a hint of steel in his voice. "When you're making love with another man, I want you to remember me—remember this."

As if I could forget, Phoebe thought. Besides, it was a moot point, for there would never be another man. Ram already owned her heart.

She glanced at his face and saw something primitive behind the hard mask of his reserve. She could read nothing in his expression save desire. If love existed, he kept it well guarded.

His passion, however, was blatantly apparent. The heat of his body washed over her in undulating waves. And then his passion exploded. Gentleness was forgotten as his expression became fierce, almost austere. His eyes took on a predatory gleam that was almost shocking in its intensity.

This was a side of Ram she hadn't seen before. This was the legendary rogue, the seducer and the unrepentant rake whose exploits were well documented in the gossip columns.

God, she wanted him.

While she was still mentally counting all the reasons she shouldn't be doing this, Ram lowered her to the thick rug before the hearth and followed her down. His weight was gone for a moment, and when he returned he was as naked as she.

"No man will ever satisfy you like I do," he murmured as he spread her thighs with his knees and thrust his hand between them to test her readiness.

His fingers came away wet.

Phoebe flushed; the scent of her arousal was blatant proof of the power Ram held over her. She tried to avoid his mouth as it came down to claim hers, but he grasped her chin between hard fingers and held it in place, kissing her with a rough possessiveness that stole her breath.

His hands and mouth were everywhere; no part of her body was left untouched as he kissed, caressed and suckled. Then he was inside her, hips thrusting powerfully, driving her mad with heady pleasure. The violence of his passion broke over her like a fierce summer storm, wild, intense, turbulent. She was caught up in the violence of his passion, sucked into the swirling vortex, tossed hither and yon, then soaring into the eye of the tempest.

She heard herself scream, felt the searing heat of climax, then plunged in flaming pieces back to an imperfect world, where Ram was waiting for her. His breathing was harsh, his skin glistening with sweat. She lay quiescent in his arms, fearing to speak lest she break the fragile thread that bound them.

"Do you still want to leave?" Ram asked as he rolled away from her.

"Can you promise me forever?"

"I can promise you passion. I can promise you'll never want for anything."

"Can you promise me love?"

"As much as it is within me to give."

She searched his face, trying to read his thoughts. What she saw sent her spirits plummeting. "You don't trust me. You fear I'm going to abandon you again."

Ram reared away. "Dammit, Phoebe, why should I trust you? If you trusted *me*, you wouldn't be asking these questions."

Phoebe sat up and reached for her clothes. "It will take a few days to make travel arrangements, but Father and I should be gone by the end of the week."

Surging to his feet, he gathered up her garments and tossed them at her. His expression was forged of stone, his mouth a grim slash across his face. He knew that if he spoke he would lose control of his temper. He wanted to lash out, to say hurtful things he knew he would regret later.

Ram dressed quickly, looking anywhere but at Phoebe as she donned her clothing. He didn't speak until he had gained control of his temper. Parting was Phoebe's decision, not his; he had done all he could to prevent it.

Everything except tell her you love her, he chided himself. He had tried, but a tiny part of him that refused to lay his heart at her feet to be trampled upon. How did he know another David Phillips wouldn't appear and convince her to leave him?

"I doubt we'll see much of one another before you leave, so I'll bid you farewell now," Ram said coolly.

Phoebe's lips parted in a silent farewell as he stormed off.

Ram's emotions were strung as taut as a bowstring when he encountered Andrew in the foyer.

"May I have a word with you, my lord?" Andrew asked. "I have yet to thank you for saving Phoebe's life."

"Will the morning room do? The study is . . . occupied at the moment."

He strode into the morning room, glancing back once to make sure Andrew was following him. "I could ring for tea, if you'd like," he said, motioning the older man into a chair.

"That won't be necessary. I won't take up much

Seduced by a Rogue

of your time. Phoebe and I owe you a great deal. Is there any way I can repay you?"

"Seeing you and Phoebe alive and well is all the payment I require. You *are* feeling better, aren't you?"

"Indeed." Andrew beamed. "Thanks to your timely intervention."

Ram glanced at his watch.

"I hope you're not in any great hurry," Andrew said. "I'd like a word with you. About Phoebe."

Ram sighed and sat down, wanting to get this over with. "What about Phoebe?"

"Have you spoken with her?"

"On more than one occasion."

"Then you know she plans to leave you."

He summoned a bitter smile. "That comes as no surprise. Did Phoebe tell you anything about our history together?"

Andrew nodded solemnly. "She told me everything and even admitted she was at fault. She loves you." Andrew held up his hand when Ram made a scoffing sound deep in his throat. "At one time I'd hoped Phoebe and David would wed, but as the years passed it became increasingly clear that she had no wish to do so."

"Forgive me for doubting you, Andrew, but your daughter wouldn't abandon our marriage if she loved me." He paused to marshal his thoughts. "Phoebe doubts I can be the kind of husband she wants. Since she refuses to let me prove myself, I have no choice but to accept her decision."

Andrew adjusted his spectacles. "I'm sorry to hear you say that. I thought . . . Ah, well, both you and Phoebe are past the age to accept advice, no matter how well-meaning. I suspect we'll be leaving soon. But before we go, just tell me one thing."

Ram braced himself, for he knew what was coming. This was Phoebe's father, after all.

"Do you love Phoebe? Have you ever loved her?"

"That's two questions. I will, however, answer both. I wouldn't have married Phoebe if I didn't love her. Until I met her, I was headed for perdition. She steadied me and gave my life purpose."

He cleared his throat. "I wanted Phoebe in my bed, but she wouldn't have me without a ring on her finger. I respected her for that and was ecstatic when she accepted my proposal. It may have been a spur-of-the-moment decision, but I took my vows seriously. I knew marriage was the only way to keep Phoebe from sailing to Egypt."

"She never told me," Andrew said.

"Unfortunately, my reputation as a rakehell had preceded me, and David Phillips took advantage of it. Whatever he told Phoebe turned her against me. She left without an explanation."

"So you've held a grudge against her all these years."

"I couldn't help it. I felt humiliated. My pride had been wounded. I didn't apply for an annulment, because it pleased me to think Phoebe would run afoul of the law if she tried to marry while she still had a husband. As for my feelings now, I can only say there is no other woman in my life at this time. If Phoebe wants a declaration of love, she will have to prove I can trust her first."

"I understand your bitterness, but correct me if I'm wrong—haven't you and Phoebe been living as husband and wife these past weeks? There should have been a commitment before you began an intimate relationship."

Ram's shoulders stiffened. He was the aggrieved

party, not Phoebe. "Need I remind you that it was Phoebe's decision to leave?"

"I'm just trying to understand."

Ram shrugged. "So am I. Do you have any idea where you'll go? Phoebe said she'd let me know, but I'd rather you told me now. I offered the use of my country estate, but she refused."

"Phoebe has her mother's stubbornness. We decided to spend some time away from London and settled on Cambridge. I know the area well. We'll stay at the Prince Edward Inn until we find a suitable rental. I was offered a teaching position at the university, and living nearby will give me a chance to explore my options."

"Thank you for telling me," Ram said. "Now if you'll excuse me . . ."

"One moment, Lord Braxton."

Ram paused, his gaze narrowed on his father-in-law.

"Don't give up on Phoebe. Cutting all ties would be disastrous. Perhaps you'll come to realize you love Phoebe enough to open your heart to her and give her the words she needs to hear. It's the only way you'll win her."

Ram's reply was a curt nod. The next move, if there were to be one, would have to come from Phoebe.

Ram visited his solicitor later that day to arrange for a monthly stipend to be deposited in an account in Phoebe's name. The generous amount Ram mentioned raised the eyebrows of Mr. Hoskins, but he knew better than to question Lord Braxton. After concluding his business, Ram found himself in desperate need of strong drink and solitude, so he took himself off to White's.

After several brandies he decided peace and quiet wasn't what he needed after all and proceeded to Crocker's gambling hell, a favorite gathering place of the fashionable bucks and blades who shared his pursuit of pleasure and dissipation. But their chatter produced none of the usual camaraderie he'd enjoyed in the past. Before Phoebe had reentered his life, he would have regaled them with an erotic tale or two of his own.

As the night wore on, Ram felt no inclination to return home, despite his bone-deep weariness. Then he encountered Luc, and the night suddenly looked promising.

"I take it things aren't going well at home," Luc said.

"Phoebe is leaving me," Ram said sourly. "Good riddance, I say. Only a fool would want a woman who doesn't want him."

"You look in need of entertainment. I'm on my way to Madam Bella's. Care to join me?"

Ram slapped Luc on the back. "Lead the way."

Madam Bella's was nearly bursting at the seams with the usual crowd of men eager for diversion. Ram and Luc mingled for a while, then made their choices. Luc selected a buxom, dark-haired beauty while Ram settled for a redheaded vixen with eyes the color of agates. Her name was Fancy, and he had had her before.

Fancy took his hand and led him up the stairs, her firm, high bottom swaying provocatively beneath a deep green peignoir that left little to the imagination.

"Where have you been keeping yourself, Lord Braxton?" Fancy asked, tossing him a coy smile over her shoulder. "We've missed you."

"Busy," Ram muttered. For some unaccountable

reason, bedding Fancy was becoming less and less appealing. His eyes settled on her bouncing bottom, and it occurred to him that it was too broad.

"Here we are," Fancy purred, flinging open the door to her room.

Ram recoiled inwardly at the cloying smell of perfume and spent sex. Why hadn't he noticed it before? This wasn't the first time he'd been inside Fancy's room. If Fancy hadn't shut the door behind him, he might have made his excuses and fled. He sent a wistful look at the closed door, then returned his gaze to the woman posed provocatively beside the bed. In the brief moment he had looked away, she had stripped away her peignoir.

His first thought was that her breasts lacked firmness and her nipples were almost flat. He closed his eyes and pictured Phoebe's firm, round breasts and ripe nipples. When he opened his eyes again, Fancy was sprawled across the rumpled bed, her legs spread in wanton invitation. She crooked a finger and beckoned to him.

Ram took two steps forward and stopped. He couldn't do this. In the mood he was in, he would do neither Fancy nor himself any good. "I . . . can't."

"Don't be ridiculous," Fancy scoffed. "There's not a woman in London who wouldn't trade places with me right now. Your bedroom skills are legendary. I've experienced them on more than one occasion myself and know you to be a tireless lover, superb in every way."

Ram searched for an excuse that wouldn't tarnish his reputation too badly. "I . . . I'm married."

Fancy gave a hoot of laughter. "So are three-quarters of the men who frequent this establishment."

Ram backed away. "I just remembered a previous engagement."

He was mad. Totally, inexplicably mad!

"Wait!" Fancy cried, springing from the bed. "I know what's wrong. Every man experiences it a time or two during his lifetime. I know exactly what to do. You've always enjoyed my mouth on you."

She dropped to her knees before him, her nimble fingers unfastening the waistband and flap of his trousers. "Look at you," she crowed. "You're already hard."

When she reached inside for him, he grasped her wrist in an iron grip and removed her hand from his flesh. "I'm not a monk," he growled, viewing his erection with disgust. "But I don't happen to be in the right mood. Perhaps another time."

Ram fastened his trousers, then pulled a gold sovereign from his purse and flipped it to her. "For your trouble," he said as he beat a hasty retreat.

Fancy gave him a cocky grin. "It was no trouble at all, Your Lordship."

Ram sipped a brandy while he waited for Luc to appear. A full hour passed before his friend joined him.

"Can I use your spare bedroom, Westmore?" Ram asked.

Luc sent him a sharp look, but being the friend that he was, made no untoward comment. "Of course. I'm going home now."

Ram couldn't trust himself in his own townhouse while Phoebe still lived there. He knew he'd want to make love to her again and couldn't bear another rejection.

Chapter Eighteen

When Ram returned home to change clothes four days later, Porter informed him that Phoebe and her father had left earlier that morning. The dignified man's chin was wobbling and his eyes held a note of reproach when he presented Ram a note on a silver salver.

"From Her Ladyship," Porter said.

With great reluctance Ram took the folded paper, stuffed it in his pocket and stormed into his study. He went immediately to the sideboard and filled a glass to the brim with brandy. He tossed it back in one gulp before turning his attention to Phoebe's missive. Her message was no more and no less than he expected.

She wished him happiness in whichever direction he chose to take his life and suggested that he seek a divorce through the courts. Cursing, Ram tossed the note in the fireplace and watched it go up in flames. There would be no divorce. Not now, not ever.

With Phoebe out of the picture, Ram resumed his former lifestyle. He charged headlong into the diverse entertainments London had to offer, frequenting the dark and seamy haunts that had suited him so well in the past. No gambling hell was too uncivilized, no dockside saloon too wild. Dissipation wasn't difficult to achieve for a reprobate like him, and he did his best to live up to his reputation.

Unfortunately, his heart wasn't in it. Though he was seen strolling in Vauxhall Pleasure Gardens with a different woman on his arm every night, he bedded none of them. Nonetheless, he continued to go to Covent Garden, where prostitutes were easily had. And he flirted outrageously with the orange girls at the opera house and was seen returning home roaring drunk in the wee hours.

The gossip columnists couldn't get enough of Lord Braxton's antics. Items concerning Lord B's scandalous behavior began appearing regularly in the *London Times*. One particular columnist went so far as to hint that Lady B was expecting the requisite heir and had been sent to Lord B's country estate to await the birth, leaving Lord B free to return to his decadent ways. A wager had been placed in White's betting books concerning the date of birth, implying that the only reason Lord B had been caught in the parson's trap was because he had gotten Lady B with child.

Ram paid little heed to the gossip and did nothing to stop it. Lord Westmore seemed to be the only person able to have a serious conversation with him, and even then, certain subjects were off limits.

Ram sank deeper and deeper into debauchery.

He had nearly hit bottom when a letter arrived from Sir Thompson. Phoebe's father wrote that he had rented a house at the end of a quiet lane not far from the university and mentioned the house number and street. Thompson went on to say he and Phoebe were well, but that Phoebe appeared melancholy and unhappy.

After reading the letter, Ram had no inclination to go to his club. He sat in his study brooding, his anger at Phoebe unquenchable. If she was unhappy, it was entirely her own fault. That night, however, he did venture out, and if he was a little wilder in his pursuits than usual, he laid the blame at Phoebe's door.

Ram was sipping coffee and nursing a monumental headache the following morning when a strange foreboding slithered down his spine. Something dark and disturbing warned him that Phoebe needed him.

His unexpected caller that morning appeared at a most propitious time.

"A Mrs. Crowley is here to see you, milord," Porter announced.

It was Phoebe's housekeeper from Mount Street. "Show her in, Porter."

Mrs. Crowley bustled into the room, dipped a curtsey and was invited to sit down. The housekeeper settled into a chair and accepted a cup of tea.

"What can I do for you, Mrs. Crowley?"

"You said to let you know when my daughter had her babe and was ready to travel. Dan, Lottie's husband, is eager to move to the cottage you promised and take up his new position at your country estate." She sent him a worried look. "You do remember, don't you? You said there would be a position for me in your household as well."

"Indeed," Ram allowed, though concentrating was difficult. "I'll dash off a note to my overseer. He'll see that your family is settled into the cottage and will assign you positions."

Mrs. Crowley beamed. "Is Miss Phoebe . . . er . . . Lady Braxton well?"

A sudden notion popped into his head. Phoebe might not like it, but it would give him some peace of mind. He decided to sound Mrs. Crowley out before presenting his idea to her.

"Phoebe is in the country with her father."

Mrs. Crowley made a clucking sound in her throat. "Poor man; is he still ailing?"

"He's recovering, but Phoebe decided he shouldn't be alone. Would you consider going to Cambridge to be with Phoebe instead of accompanying your daughter and son-in-law to my estate?"

"Why, I would consider it an honor to serve your lady again," Mrs. Crowley said.

"Then it's settled. Does your family need transportation to Derbyshire?"

"No, they intend to travel in the same cart carrying the household goods."

"Very well. I shall send you to Cambridge in my carriage. Will thirty pounds a year and every other Sunday off suffice?"

Mrs. Crowley's eyes widened. "That's more than generous, milord." And indeed it was, for the yearly salary of a housekeeper seldom topped fourteen pounds.

"It's settled, then," Ram said. "Give me your direction and I'll send the coach around for you in the morning." He rose. "Please wait here while I write a short note to my overseer regarding your son-in-law and his new position."

Ram returned a few minutes later. "I have a favor to ask of you, Mrs. Crowley."

"Anything, milord."

"I'm worried about my wife. I want to be informed if anything out of the ordinary occurs."

"Like what, milord?"

"Can I trust you, Mrs. Crowley?"

The housekeeper bristled. "Of course. I'm sorry you have to ask."

Ram nodded in brief apology. "What I tell you is not to be shared with anyone. My wife and I are currently estranged, but her well-being is still my responsibility. A short time ago Phoebe was in danger and needed protection. I'm not sure the danger has passed. I know she would protest my interference, but I feel confident she won't object to you. I'm not asking you to spy on her, just report anything unusual. Will you do that? Can I depend on you?"

"I'm truly sorry that you and Lady Phoebe are having problems and sincerely hope you'll find a way to resolve them. I will do as you ask but will do nothing to hurt the dear girl."

"Hurting Phoebe is the last thing I want to do," Ram assured her.

"How will I contact you should I need to?"

"I've considered that. I'm acquainted with Cambridge; I attended the university during my youth. There's an innkeeper at the King and Crown Inn. His name is Higgins. Give him your letter and he'll see that it gets to me. I'm well-known to him."

Mrs. Crowley's eyes widened. "You really *are* worried, aren't you? Anything in particular I should watch for?"

"Not really. It's just a feeling I have. I'll rest much easier if you're with Phoebe during this . . . trying time."

After Mrs. Crowley departed, Ram hoped he wasn't overreacting. What could happen to Phoebe? Cambridge was a quiet and dignified university town, its residents reserved and scholarly.

Yet . . . something unformed and menacing nagged at the back of his mind. The feeling had begun after Phoebe left, and he had been running from it, refusing to acknowledge it as he raced down the path to perdition. He would feel better with Mrs. Crowley looking after Phoebe.

Why are you even bothering? a voice inside him whispered. Phoebe had made her position perfectly clear. She wanted nothing to do with him.

She does want something from you, that annoying voice reminded him. *Why can't you give it to her?*

The answer hadn't changed. He knew what she wanted from him, but the price was too dear.

Damn Phoebe for demanding more than he was willing to give.

Phoebe liked Cambridge but she missed Ram. She'd had more than enough free time to ponder her decision to leave him, to wonder if she'd been too hard on him. Perhaps he wasn't capable of saying what she wanted to hear. Even so, did she want a man incapable of expressing his feelings?

What if his feelings for her were uncertain? Or worse yet, what if lust was the sum of his emotions? She couldn't accept Ram on those terms. Eventually another woman would catch his eye and he would stray, and that would destroy her. Better to separate now, before he shattered her heart.

Seduced by a Rogue

Phoebe was surprised the day Mrs. Crowley showed up at her door. She welcomed the kindly housekeeper warmly and invited her into the parlor. Only then did it occur to her that there was only one way Mrs. Crowley could have known where to find her.

Her father had told Ram, and Ram had sent for Mrs. Crowley. Why?

"What brings you to Cambridge, Mrs. Crowley?" Phoebe asked.

"You, dearie . . . I mean, milady. My daughter and her family were ready to accept Lord Braxton's offer of employment, and I called at his townhouse to inform him. He asked if I'd like to serve you and your father in my old capacity. You don't have a housekeeper, do you?"

"No. We just recently moved here and I haven't had a chance yet to inquire at an employment agency." She sent Mrs. Crowley a wary look. "What did Lord Braxton tell you about our . . . living arrangement?"

"Not much. He said your father was recuperating in the country and that you accompanied him. He thought you might appreciate having someone you were familiar with in your employ."

Phoebe wasn't convinced that was all there was to it. How far was Ram willing to go to keep tabs on her?

"Don't worry about my salary," Mrs. Crowley continued. "Lord Braxton has taken care of it. I left my bags in the coach, but if you don't want me . . ."

After careful consideration, Phoebe decided she *did* want Mrs. Crowley, wanted her despite Ram's interference in her life. She gave the woman a hug and told her as much.

"Who have we here, daughter?"

Phoebe smiled as her father ambled into the room. "This is Mrs. Crowley, Father. She was my housekeeper on Mount Street."

"I cook, too," Mrs. Crowley added. "I can prepare the kind of nourishing meals Sir Thompson needs to regain his strength. He looks a mite peaked to me."

"I'm feeling much better," Andrew allowed, "but I shall look forward to those meals you promised. I'm sure they will be delicious."

"Did you come by public coach?" Phoebe asked.

"Lord Braxton was kind enough to offer me his coach."

"Lord Braxton sent you?" Andrew asked.

"Indeed he did."

"Instruct the coachman to bring in your bags, and I'll show him to the room you're to occupy," Phoebe said. "I think you'll like it. It's near the kitchen and rather large."

The moment Mrs. Crowley went to fetch the coachman, Phoebe turned to her father. "You told Ram where to find us, didn't you?"

"Ummm, I may have."

"Father . . ."

"Oh, very well, I wrote and gave him our direction. He's your husband and has a right to know. Are you unhappy with Mrs. Crowley? I thought it rather admirable of him to send someone trustworthy."

"I'd hoped Ram would honor my request not to interfere in my life," Phoebe groused.

Mrs. Crowley returned, putting a period to the conversation between Phoebe and her father. Phoebe showed her the way to her room and left her to unpack and settle in. When she returned to the small but comfortable parlor, Andrew had made a timely retreat.

As the days passed, Phoebe had many reasons to appreciate Mrs. Crowley. Not only did she do the shopping, which Phoebe detested, but cooked the nourishing meals she had promised and kept the house in order with the help of a housemaid that Phoebe had hired. Since their house was more a roomy cottage than a grand mansion, it was easily maintained. Without Ram, Phoebe found a simple life more palatable than a public one.

Her father had made a decent living for them and they had always lived comfortably, but Phoebe had never been one to wish for riches. It hadn't been Ram's fortune that had attracted her. She had fallen in love with the man himself.

One morning a few weeks after Mrs. Crowley arrived, she found Phoebe vomiting into the chamber pot. The housekeeper's knowing gaze slid over Phoebe's slim form, resting on her stomach. "How far along are you, dearie?"

"Oh, no," Phoebe denied, "it's not what you think. I'm sure the fish last night didn't agree with me. I've always had a problem digesting trout. But Father enjoys it, so I try to eat a little to please him."

The housekeeper sent her an appraising look. "If you say so. I'll go down to the kitchen and brew a pot of tea to settle your stomach."

The tea did the trick. Phoebe felt so good that afternoon, she took a brisk walk down to the pond at the edge of town and sat on her favorite rock to contemplate life and all its complexities. This was one of her favorite places; it was quiet and peaceful and far away from the town's bustle. She had discovered it on her very first walk through Cambridge and visited often.

*   *   *

After Phoebe left for her walk, Andrew joined Mrs. Crowley in the kitchen. It had become his habit to take breakfast in the cozy atmosphere the house-keeper had created in the sunny kitchen. This morning he had with him a stack of London news-papers that had arrived by post.

"I see your papers arrived, Sir Thompson," Mrs. Crowley said.

"Please, call me Andrew. Formalities aren't nec-essary in this household."

"Oh, dear," Mrs. Crowley said, flustered. "Are you sure?"

"Very sure."

"Then you must call me Annie."

They smiled at one another in mutual under-standing, and then Andrew began perusing the pa-pers while Mrs. Crowley prepared his breakfast.

"Good grief," he blustered. "This won't do at all."

"What is it, Andrew?"

He began riffling through the rest of the papers, growing paler as he read. "It's Braxton. Phoebe mustn't see this." He handed an offending news-print to the housekeeper to peruse.

Her eyes widened. "This isn't good."

"Whatever is Braxton thinking?" Andrew la-mented. "I was under the impression he hoped to reconcile with Phoebe, but if the gossip columns can be believed, he's going about it the wrong way."

"The poor misguided man," Mrs. Crowley clucked sympathetically. "He seemed so concerned about Lady Braxton when I spoke with him last. He asked me to . . ."

Andrew's attention sharpened. "To what?"

"I'm not at liberty to say," she demurred.

"I'm Phoebe's father; I have a right to know."

Mrs. Crowley debated long and hard and finally decided that he did indeed have a right to know. "Lord Braxton was worried about his wife. He asked me to keep an eye on things here and report anything out of the ordinary. I believe he has deep feelings for her."

"He has a funny way of showing it," Andrew grumbled. "Have you any ideas that might convince Phoebe to reconsider her decision to leave Braxton?"

"I believe circumstances will bring the dear girl around," Mrs. Crowley said cryptically.

Andrew snorted. "What kind of circumstances? My daughter is too stubborn for her own good."

"I . . . can't say."

"Annie, if circumstances exist, I need to know about them."

Casting a wary glance at the door, she leaned close and whispered, "I think Lady Braxton is increasing."

"What! Are you sure?"

"Reasonably sure."

"We need to inform Braxton. I'll post a letter to him today."

"I was thinking of doing the same thing. Write your letter and give it to me. I have a way of getting it to His Lordship faster than the post can." She placed a plate of eggs and several slices of toasted bread in front of him. "Eat your breakfast, Andrew. I'll just take these newspapers to your room before Lady Braxton sees them."

"Why don't you want me to see the newspapers?" Phoebe asked.

She'd been watching from the doorway, surprised to see Mrs. Crowley and her father with their heads together like conspirators.

Andrew looked utterly flummoxed, and Mrs. Crowley hid the papers behind her back.

"I wanted to read them first," Andrew blustered.

His quick thinking failed to appease Phoebe. She held out her hand. "May I see them, please?"

"Now, daughter, there's nothing in them you need to see."

His obvious reluctance firmed Phoebe's resolve. "The papers, Mrs. Crowley."

Andrew sighed. "Give them to her, Annie."

Annie? What was going on?

Reluctantly Mrs. Crowley handed the papers to Phoebe. Phoebe sat down beside her father to peruse them, wondering what they had found in them that would be offensive to her. It didn't take long to discover the cause for their concern. The gossip columns in the entire week's worth of newspapers were filled with Lord B's latest debauchery. The accounts of where and with whom he had been seen and his wild shenanigans must have set the *ton* on its ear. There was even mention of Lady B's retirement to the country, possibly to await the requisite heir.

Aware that her response to the articles was being closely monitored, Phoebe collected the papers and rose. "I believe I'll take these up to my room and read them in private."

"Oh, dear," Mrs. Crowley said as Phoebe disappeared through the door. "What do we do now?"

"I'm going to write that letter straightaway and send it off to Braxton."

"Don't mention our suspicions about her condition. That's something Phoebe should tell him. Just say he should come as soon as possible."

"Maybe he doesn't care anymore," Andrew worried. "If his exploits are any indication, he has enough to keep him occupied in London."

"Nevertheless, he deserves to know that Phoebe needs him. What he does about it should be his decision."

Though Ram tried to retain enthusiasm for his hedonistic pursuits, he was losing the desire to drink and carouse into the wee hours. Excessive amounts of alcohol created a fog in his head and kept him in a constant state of befuddlement. High-stakes gambling was eroding his fortune, and the ladies he squired were becoming impatient with the excuses he used to avoid performing sexually.

Ram had heard nothing from Mrs. Crowley since he'd dispatched her to Cambridge, and he assumed that Phoebe was doing well without him. Too bad he couldn't say the same about his own state of mind. Physically he was healthy, but mentally he was a wreck. Being abandoned twice by the same woman hurt.

This couldn't go on, Ram decided one cool, rainy morning as he sat in his study nursing a hangover. It suddenly dawned on him that he was on a course of self-destruction and that it had to stop. He rang for Porter and asked for tea.

"Tea, milord?"

"Tea, Porter, and bring me something to eat. I need to make some decisions and can't do it with my head buzzing and my stomach growling."

Porter grinned. "Does your decision to mend your ways have anything to do with Lady Braxton?"

"It has everything to do with Phoebe. And, Porter, on your way out, collect the empty bottles and

Connie Mason

get rid of them. I don't want any reminders of how I've wasted the past few weeks."

While Ram made plans to redirect his life, Andrew's letter was being received at the King and Crown for prompt delivery to His Lordship. A messenger was dispatched immediately.

Ram wasn't home when the messenger arrived. Porter told the man to wait in case there was an answer and sent him to the kitchen for food and refreshment. Ram returned home a short time later. Porter handed him a letter on a silver salver and informed him that the messenger from Cambridge was awaiting his reply. Ram read the letter, crumpled it in his hand and told Porter to pay the messenger and send him on his way, there would be no reply.

While Sir Andrew's letter was somewhat vague, it confirmed Ram's belief that Phoebe needed him. Within minutes he had sent his valet packing his bag and his groom racing for his carriage. By midmorning he was well on his way to Cambridge.

It was close to midnight when he located Phoebe's house. He took his bag and sent Wilson off to an inn with the carriage. He approached the dark house, his heart pounding as he climbed the front steps. He had no idea how his sudden appearance in the middle of the night would be greeted.

The door was locked, of course. He went around to the back, saw a light shining through the kitchen window and peeked inside. He saw Andrew standing at the stove, pouring hot milk into a cup. Ram rapped on the window. Startled, the old gentleman peered through the windowpane, recognized Ram and opened the back door.

"My word, you got here quickly."

338

"I came as soon as I received your letter. What's wrong with Phoebe?"

Andrew shook his head. "That's for Phoebe to tell you, but not tonight. It's late. Don't worry, she's fine. There's a spare bedroom upstairs—I'll show you the way."

Frustration gnawed at Ram. After summoning him, why wouldn't Andrew tell him what was wrong?

"What are you doing up at this hour?" Ram asked, choosing not to voice the question uppermost in his mind.

"I haven't slept well since becoming ill with malaria. Sometimes it helps to drink hot milk when I'm restless."

Andrew picked up the candle and lighted the way up the stairs. "This one is mine," he said, indicating a room on the right. He passed a closed door on the left and stopped before the second. "This is your room. Take the candle; I won't need it. Sleep well, Braxton. You can speak to Phoebe in the morning."

Ram entered the bedroom, set down his bag and placed the candle on the nightstand. Then he undressed and pulled on a robe he took from his bag.

Though exhausted from his long ride up from London, Ram couldn't relax. He walked to the window and stared distractedly at the distant stars twinkling in the moon-washed sky. His mind was incapable of thinking beyond the fact that a thin wall was all that separated him from Phoebe.

His deep feelings for his wife had become abundantly clear these past weeks. After much soul-searching, he had reached a decision that could clear the way for reconciliation. He simply could not, would not let Phoebe go. There was no way he could wash his hands of her and forget her.

His love for Phoebe had been there all the time despite his unwillingness to say the words. He had never stopped loving her, and it was time he told her. A declaration from him could change the course of their future. Fear of being hurt again and his damnable male pride had prevented him from baring his heart to her. But what was pride compared to endless years without the woman he loved? His aborted attempt to return to a life of debauchery proved how wrongheaded he had been.

The house was quiet. Ram glanced at the closed door, compelled by something stronger than mere desire. Guided by destiny, he opened the door and walked the short distance to Phoebe's room. Her door opened noiselessly beneath his touch and he stepped inside, careful to close the door behind him.

He approached the bed and stared down at her. An errant moonbeam touched her face, creating a halo around her head. Her glowing beauty mesmerized him, made him weak in the knees. Over the years his need for her might have dimmed, but it had never disappeared. Days and weeks might have passed without his thinking about her, but her memory was always lurking in the dark reaches of his mind. She was as lovely today as she had been the day he met her.

The scent of her sank into him, wreathed his senses. Her vulnerability called out to every primitive instinct he possessed. Instantly hard, instantly needy, he tossed off his robe and slid into bed beside her.

Immersed in layers of sleep, Phoebe had a sense of well-being she hadn't felt since leaving Ram's bed in London. The arms surrounding her felt very real, intensely comforting. Phantom hands teased her breasts, tweaked her nipples into hardness and slid down her stomach, tangling in the thatch of dark hair between her thighs.

She'd dreamt about Ram before, but never had it been as real as this. She could feel his breath tickling her ear, hear the rapid pounding of his heart. Layer by layer, sleep peeled away until nothing but raw awareness remained, and a joy so sharp it was like a physical pain.

Ram was here.

In her bed. Holding her in his arms.

How? Why?

Groaning, she turned into his arms. Looking into his shadowy face, she recognized the hardness that was an integral part of him, the strength that hinted at stubbornness, the blatantly sensual, heavy-lidded green eyes and tempting fulness of his lips.

She touched his mouth, couldn't help herself. She loved him, loved the way he looked, the way he moved, the way his body reacted to hers. Why couldn't he love her?

"Ram. What are you doing here? How did you get in?"

"Your father let me in. I couldn't stay away, Phoebe. You're mine. I can't let you go. Tell me you need me as desperately as I need you."

"I've always needed you, Ram, even when we were thousands of miles apart. I've never questioned *my* feelings, only yours."

"What will it take to bring you back to me?"

"I think you know."

"Pride is a powerful obstacle to surmount. When you left, I was hurt, disillusioned and angry. You

341

are the only woman who has ever rejected me. Not once, but twice."

Inwardly, Phoebe grinned. If ever a man was in need of a comeuppance, it was Ram.

"The grudge I held against you ate at me for four long years," he continued. "Then the opportunity for revenge fell into my lap, and I jumped at it." He sighed. "Unfortunately, things didn't work out as planned. I wanted to make you fall in love with me. I wanted you to suffer when I walked away. I never expected to fall in love with you all over again."

Phoebe's breath caught. She had waited forever for those words. "You love me?"

"I'm sorry I gave you reason to doubt me. I couldn't declare myself because I feared rejection. How could I say the words when I had no idea if you'd say them back?"

"I told you weeks ago that I loved you, but you refused to believe me."

"I was a fool."

"You really love me?" Phoebe repeated.

"Didn't I just say so?" He took a deep breath. "Will you be my wife, Phoebe?"

"I already am. Will you be my husband?"

His lips hovered scant inches from hers. "Always."

Chapter Nineteen

Ram kissed her, tasting her surrender, drinking deeply of it, savoring it. Nothing had ever tasted so sweet. Phoebe was his. No one was going to take her away. Nothing would ever come between them again. There would be good times and bad times, but they would be together come what may.

"Are you sure about this, Ram; very sure?" Phoebe asked, as if doubting his sincerity. "I read disturbing accounts of your carousing in the *London Times*. If they are to be believed, you're not ready to settle down."

"You shouldn't believe everything you read. 'Tis true I drank too much and gambled too freely and was seen out and about with various women, but I bedded none of them. They weren't you," he admitted sheepishly.

Still Phoebe held him at bay. "Are you sure you trust me?"

Connie Mason

"Absolutely," he said without hesitation. "Do you trust me, love? I need you to believe that I love you, and that we'll be together forever. Will you return home with me? Can we start afresh and not look back?"

"I want that more than anything."

"Then let me make love to you. We can make this marriage work as long as love exists between us."

"Oh, yes," she said breathlessly. "Make love to me before I wake up and discover this is a dream."

"This is no dream. I've never meant anything more in my life."

His embrace tightened as he kissed her, drawing his tongue along the seam of her lips, urging them to open to his sensual probing. He kissed her until she was giddy, and then he moved his lips slowly across her cheek and down her throat to the tender hollow where her pulse throbbed erratically.

Baring her shoulder, he kissed his way down her arm and along the curl of her fingers, then into her palm. Phoebe moved restlessly against him, her eagerness bringing a smile to his lips.

"Easy, sweetheart. I've barely begun."

With renewed fervor he handily dispensed with her nightgown and kissed her nipple, drawing it into his mouth with slow relish. His hands settled on her hips, his thumbs brushing her belly. Pleasure seared through her. She caught her breath and waited for him to continue, wondering where his hands and mouth would stray next.

He kissed her belly, and she reared upward into the caress as his tongue darted out to lick the dewiness of her skin. A tiny moan escaped her lips. Then his fingers delved downward into the dark thatch of curly hair, parting her tender folds to

344

probe and stroke. Spreading her thighs, he opened her and touched her with his tongue. Thought scattered, coherence flew out the window.

His tongue swirled against her, delved inside her. She moaned with rapture as his lips sipped at her. Her head fell back; ecstasy so irresistible that it was nearly agony sent chills racing down her spine. The heady scent of his arousal spurred hers, and she gave herself fully into his keeping.

He slid his hands beneath her and lifted her higher. Relentlessly his mouth followed the movement of her hips, giving no quarter, demanding total surrender.

She gave it with a cry that echoed through the charged silence of the room. She finished at last, and as she began to collapse, he settled his hips between her thighs and thrust powerfully, filling her with his need and dragging her back to ecstasy. Her legs clamped around his thighs. She spasmed in his arms, her muscles contracting around him as he plunged and withdrew, fully immersed now in his own drive to completion.

"Again, darling; come again." His voice was ragged, commanding.

She opened her eyes. His gaze met hers. She saw his beloved face and lost herself in the promise of his glittering green eyes. She would follow him to the ends of the earth were he to ask it of her.

They climaxed together; she gave him everything, the vow of forever inherent in her surrender. Crying out his name, she welcomed the gush of his seed, the heat and the wetness inside her.

Phoebe felt as if today were the first day of their lives. The past no longer existed. Ram had forgiven her past mistakes and she his, and they were both ready to move forward. She accepted that he had changed, and that he no longer intended to pursue a life of debauchery.

"I've never felt like this before," Ram said as he pulled out and settled down beside her. "I don't ever want to wake up without you in my arms. I want children with you. I never thought I'd yearn for a family, but loving you has turned my life around. Would you like children, sweetheart?"

Phoebe smiled, lightly touching her belly. She was fairly certain she was already carrying Ram's child but wanted to savor the knowledge, to hold it inside her another day before sharing it with Ram.

"I want *your* children, Ram."

He kissed her, sealing their pact. Then he loved her again, arousing her slowly, with great tenderness. And she loved him back, kissing and caressing with hands and mouth until he could stand it no longer and entered her in one slow, deep thrust. They reached the pinnacle together and soared to the stars, floating gently back to reality in each other's arms. Then they slept, wrapped in blissful contentment.

The sun had just poked through the dawn when Phoebe awakened. She turned to make sure she hadn't been dreaming Ram's appearance in her bed, and the sudden movement jolted her stomach. Nausea churned in her belly and she swallowed hard. The last thing she wanted was to be sick in front of Ram. Tea usually settled her stomach, and she hoped it would do the same today. She eased out of bed, washed quickly and dressed.

The household was still sleeping as she made her way to the kitchen. She found the tea in a canister and built a fire in the brick stove. Her stomach was still grinding with nausea when she poured water into a kettle and set it on the stove.

Unfortunately, the need to empty her stomach became too urgent to ignore. She fled out the back door and dry-heaved into the shrubbery. By the time she returned to the kitchen, the water was boiling. She measured water and tea in the teapot and munched on a dry biscuit while she waited for it to steep.

She drank the tea hot and strong and without cream. The tea, along with the biscuit, seemed to help, and once her stomach settled, she decided a walk would clear her head. Her favorite spot by the pond seemed to beckon her. Grabbing her shawl from a hook, she left the house and walked out into the brisk morning air, intending to return before she was missed.

Pleasure replaced her earlier malaise as she trod the sun-dappled path beneath a canopy of trees. The morning was glorious, the air brisk but the sun warm.

Phoebe found her favorite seat upon a flat rock and lifted her face to the sun. Everything in her world was right. Ram loved her, and his child grew beneath her heart. She couldn't wait to tell him.

She heard a rustling noise behind her and smiled. Ram must have awakened, found her gone and asked Mrs. Crowley where to find her. She could think of no more perfect place to tell him about their child. She turned to greet him, her smile widening.

The corners of her mouth wobbled, then turned down when David Phillips stepped into view. She leaped to her feet. "You! You're supposed to be dead."

"Sorry to disappoint you, Phoebe. I outwitted

Connie Mason

Fielding's goons by hiding beneath the pier until they left. The water was cold and I nearly froze, but I was far from dead."

"How did you know where to find me?"

"I knew you had left London. The gossip columns went on in great detail about Braxton's carousing while his wife was away. But I knew your husband couldn't stay away from you forever and simply watched and waited. I followed him when he left town. I wasn't surprised when he led me straight to you. The poor, besotted fool had no idea he was being followed. I waited outside the house, hoping to catch you alone, and my patience paid off."

"What are you doing in England? I understand you have an ill-gotten fortune waiting for you in France."

"Hardly a fortune. But I hope to add to it very soon."

David stood directly in her path, blocking her escape. Cautiously she began to work her way around him, but it was not to be. David grasped her arm, stopping her in her tracks.

"You're coming with me," he hissed.

Phoebe dug in her heels. "I'm not going anywhere with you. Ram and I are together again; we're going to make our marriage work."

David's laughter mocked her. "Braxton couldn't be faithful to you if he tried. He's too steeped in debauchery. One woman will never be enough for him."

He started dragging her toward the path. "I ran across Watts while I was hiding in London's underworld. He's waiting with a coach a short distance down the road."

"Why are you doing this?"

348

"I expected to collect enough money from the amulet to keep me in luxury for life. Braxton deprived me of that, so I've decided to hold you for ransom. I'm demanding ten thousand pounds for your release. Braxton is wealthy, ten thousand pounds is nothing to him."

"Ten thousand pounds! You're mad! Braxton will never agree to that."

"Time will tell. Once we reach our destination, Watts will see that the ransom note stating my demands is delivered."

Phoebe tried to twist free, to no avail. "Ram's no fool. He won't agree to your terms."

"We'll see. Come along. Protesting will do no good; one way or another, I intend to get what's coming to me."

"I'm sure you'll get exactly what you deserve," Phoebe said dryly. "You're no match for Ram. You'll pay for this."

"I doubt it. He'll have to find me first. I intend to travel the globe, to see sights other than the inside of a tomb."

"On stolen money?"

"I don't think of it that way. I earned every farthing."

Phoebe decided the time had come to play her trump card. "I'm expecting Ram's heir." Silence. "Did you hear me?"

David laughed. "A child! How delightful! You've just guaranteed that my demands will be met."

"Ram will hunt you down like the animal you are."

"Perhaps I should demand twenty thousand pounds," David mused. "The child you carry should be worth at least another ten."

* * *

Ram awakened shortly after Phoebe with an odd tingling in his chest. A premonition? Something was wrong; he sensed it immediately. It wasn't just his disappointment at waking up alone; it went deeper than that. This was a gut-grinding ache, a clear warning sign that had never failed him in the past.

Leaping from bed, he performed brief ablutions and dragged on his clothes. When he appeared in the kitchen, Mrs. Crowley was so startled to see him, she dropped the bread she had just taken out of the oven.

"Lord Braxton! When did you arrive?"

"Last night. Andrew let me in. Have you seen Phoebe this morning?"

"Isn't she in her room?"

"No. I just came from there."

Mrs. Crowley's eyebrows rose and a smile hovered on her lips.

"She must have awoken early," Ram continued. "I expected to find her in the kitchen."

"Lady Braxton sometimes takes an early morning walk before breakfast. I suspect you'll find her at her favorite place. I'll give you the direction, if you'd like."

Unable to dispel the curious foreboding needling him, Ram chafed with impatience as Mrs. Crowley gave him directions to the pond. He thanked her and left immediately. He found the path with little difficulty, paying scant heed to the coach parked nearby. Entering the cool shadows of the wood, he strolled briskly along the path. He heard the distant sound of voices and wondered if Phoebe's father had accompanied her. The harshness of the male voice soon disabused him of that notion.

Ram stopped short of where the path ended and

slipped behind a tree to spy on what was going on. Panic seared through him when he saw David Phillips with his hands on Phoebe.

Why wasn't the bastard dead?

Cautiously he crept closer, until he could hear what they were saying. Whatever Phillips was saying, Phoebe was vigorously protesting. Ram was going to wring the bastard's neck first and then put him behind bars where he belonged.

When he heard Phoebe say, "I'm expecting Ram's heir. Did you hear me? I'm with child," his breath ceased and his head began to spin. He fought for control and won. Why hadn't she told him? How long had she known? While his heart told him to charge forth and attack Phillips, his mind bespoke caution. He couldn't afford to act rashly; obviously, Phillips was unstable, and Ram feared he would hurt Phoebe and the child she carried.

My child.

Those two words swelled his heart with joy. He hunkered down against the tree to gather his thoughts and formulate a plan. Though Phillips had brandished no weapon, Ram wasn't sure he was unarmed. The man couldn't be in full possession of his mind if he intended to abduct Phoebe. If Phillips had had a lick of sense he would have left England. What in bloody hell did he want?

To Ram's dismay, the answer to that question came with Phillips's next words.

Ransom! Phillips intended to hold Phoebe for ransom. Then he recalled the coach waiting beside the road and realized it was there to carry Phoebe away.

Over my dead body, he thought, cursing his lack of foresight. He had left the house without a weapon. He didn't even have the pistol he usually carried while traveling, for he had left it in his coach

"I'm not going with you," Phoebe cried, digging in her heels.

Ram decided it was time to intervene. He stepped out from behind a tree into Phillips's path.

"Bloody hell!" Phillips gasped. "Where did you come from?"

"From your worst nightmare, Phillips. Let Phoebe go."

Then Ram's fears were realized when Phillips pulled a pistol from his pocket and thrust it into Phoebe's back. "I don't want to shoot Phoebe, but I will if you don't back off."

"Take me hostage instead. I'll write a note to my solicitor, instructing him to pay any amount you name. Phoebe can deliver it."

"I'm not stupid, Braxton. I can handle Phoebe, but you're a loose cannon." He started dragging Phoebe backward along the path. "Return to London to await instructions."

"If you hurt Phoebe . . ."

"I don't intend to hurt her—unless you disobey my instructions. Someone has to pay for the loss of the amulet. You cost me a small fortune, Braxton. Stand aside and let me pass."

Ram had no alternative but to obey Phillips. Endangering Phoebe's life was not an option.

"Don't worry, Phoebe, I won't let the bastard get away with this."

He watched helplessly as Phillips dragged Phoebe along the path, his pistol prodding ruthlessly into her soft flesh. Ram followed at a discreet distance, already planning his next move. He emerged from the wood in time to see Phillips force

Phoebe into the coach and follow her inside. Ram sprinted after them as Watts whipped the horses into motion.

Racing after the coach, Ram reached out to grasp the back rail as it picked up speed. Exerting superhuman effort, he dragged himself onto the tiger's perch, his chest heaving and his pulse pounding in his ears.

Clinging tenaciously to the perch, Ram prayed that Phillips wouldn't discover he had hitched a ride on the boot. He breathed deeply as he considered his dilemma. Should he climb over the roof to the driver's bench or let himself into the coach through the open window? There were pros and cons to both plans. If he attacked the driver, the man might lose control of the horses and cause a fatal accident. Letting himself in through the window might surprise Phillips, but Phoebe could be hurt if his pistol discharged, whether by accident or on purpose.

As the coach bolted over the bumpy road, Ram saw something that made his heart leap into his mouth. The door opened, and Phoebe leaned through the opening. Surely she didn't intend to jump, did she? He was about to shout a warning when Phillips dragged her back inside and closed the door.

Once his panic subsided, Ram knew he had to act swiftly. Phoebe was likely to do something foolish, something that could endanger her and their babe. Right or wrong, Ram's decision was to get rid of Watts first, take over the reins and deal with Phillips once he brought the horses to a stop.

Hoisting himself up and onto the roof, Ram slowly made his way toward Watts.

Meanwhile, Phoebe was making plans of her

Connie Mason

own. When she had opened the door and threatened to jump, David had dropped the pistol on the seat between them as he struggled to restrain her. Phoebe had no intention of jumping, however. The life of her unborn child was too precious to her. She had wanted to distract David, and she had succeeded.

"Don't try that again," David warned. "You're no good to me dead."

Phillips braced himself against the side of the coach with one hand and gripped Phoebe's wrist with the other, presenting her with the opportunity she had been waiting for. She lunged for the pistol with her free hand. David released her wrist instantly and grappled with her for the weapon.

A silent struggle ensued as the combatants bounced around in the bolting coach. Suddenly the pistol discharged, sending a bullet into the cushions.

Ram was slowly making his way toward Watts when he heard the explosion. He recognized the sound immediately, and a horrific image of Phoebe lying dead seared through him. Had Phillips shot her? Had the pistol discharged accidentally? Had Phoebe gained control of the pistol and shot Phillips? Nothing was impossible.

Frightened by the explosion, the horses bolted, nearly hurling Ram to the ground. Only his fierce tenacity saved him. He heard Watts cursing as he attempted to control the horses, but his inept handling was his undoing. He simply lacked experience as a coachman.

Abandoning his original plan, Ram grabbed the window ledge and swung himself through the opening. As luck would have it, he landed atop Phillips.

"Ram!" Phoebe screamed.

"Are you all right? I heard a gunshot."

"I'm fine."

Suddenly finding himself at a disadvantage, Phillips began struggling with Ram. But the uncurbed speed of the coach worked against him, allowing Ram to gain the upper hand. Ram fought desperately to subdue Phillips, fearing that the coach would overturn.

"Hang on, Phoebe," Ram warned as he landed a blow to Phillips's chin.

Then, with a sensation of horror, he felt the wheels hit a deep rut. The horses screamed as the coach veered sharply to one side. The door swung open and he braced himself to keep from falling through. Releasing Phillips, he reached for Phoebe and dragged her into his arms to cushion her against the jarring impact he knew was coming.

Tilting crazily, the coach slid along on two wheels, then toppled, scraping along the road until it came to an abrupt stop. All the while the coach lurched and tumbled, Ram anchored Phoebe to the cushions, his big body taking the brunt of the impact. The violent contact with the ground sent Phillips flying through the open door, and there was little Ram could do to stop him.

Somehow Ram managed to hang on to Phoebe, taking the worst of the battering. He didn't release her until the coach skidded to a shuddering halt, and Phoebe began to stir beneath him.

They were lying in a corner, crumpled together in a jumble of arms and legs. Cautiously Ram released Phoebe, sucking in a breath when a sharp pain jolted him. He knew immediately that at least one and maybe two of his ribs were cracked.

"Are you all right, Phoebe?" If he had sustained

an injury, chances were good that she had too.

"I'm shaken but fine otherwise."

"How fares our babe?"

Phoebe's hand flew to her stomach. "Nothing unusual seems to be happening."

"We need to get out of here. I'll have to climb out the window; the coach toppled over on the door side."

Wriggling through the window was no easy task, considering his injuries. He tried to stifle his groans but failed.

"You're hurt!" Phoebe cried.

"Not seriously." He bit back a moan as he pushed himself through the window onto the side of the coach. "A couple of cracked ribs. They'll heal."

He knelt beside the window and peered inside. "Lift up your arms and I'll pull you through."

"You'll hurt yourself."

"Phoebe, love, don't argue with me. Just do as I say. I need to find out what happened to Phillips and his cohort."

Phoebe raised her arms and Ram grasped them, biting his bottom lip to keep from groaning as he slowly lifted her from the overturned coach and swung her down to the ground. Then he slid off, landing on his feet beside her. They clung to one another for a moment, savoring the fact that they were both alive.

"Your legs are shaking, sweetheart," Ram said. "Sit down and pull yourself together while I search for Phillips."

He helped her to the side of the road and settled her beneath a shady tree. Then he went to survey the scene of the accident, holding his ribs in an effort to stop the grinding pain. He walked around the coach and found Watts; his lower legs were pinned beneath one of the wheels.

"Help me," Watts begged. "I think my legs are broken."

Ram regarded the wheel thoughtfully. "I can't lift the wheel and slide you out by myself."

Watts began to whimper. "It hurts like hell."

"Where's your partner in crime?"

"I don't know. Forget him. I can't stand the pain."

Closing his ears to Watts's pitiful cries, Ram went in search of Phillips. He recalled that Phillips had been flung through the door moments before the coach overturned, and he hoped to hell that the bastard hadn't escaped unscathed.

He started searching along the side of the road.

"Where are you going?" Phoebe called out.

"To find Phillips. He can't be too far from where the coach overturned."

Ram had walked but a short distance when he saw Phillips lying at the side of the road, his head flush against a tree trunk. Ram approached cautiously, then hastened forward when he realized Phillips was unconscious. He knelt beside him and checked his pulse. He was still breathing. It didn't take a sleuth to realize what had happened. Phillips must have hit his head on the tree when he was flung from the coach. Rummaging through his pockets, Ram found the pocketknife he always carried and returned to the coach.

"Did you find him?" Phoebe asked.

"Yes. He's alive but unconscious." He walked toward the horses, saw they were uninjured and cut their traces. Then he cut off a good-sized hunk of leather and returned to Phillips.

357

"What are you going to do?" Phoebe wanted to know.

"Use the leather traces to bind Phillips. It's a long trek back to town, and I don't want him getting away. Watts is pinned beneath the coach and in a bad way. We need to get him help. Can you walk?"

Bracing herself against the tree, Phoebe rose and walked to where Ram stood. "I'm fine."

He placed his arm around her waist, gave it an encouraging squeeze and led her down the road. "Good girl."

"Oh, I see David," Phoebe exclaimed. "He looks . . . pathetic."

"It will only take a moment to secure his hands and feet." They both became aware of a coach rattling toward them at the same time.

"Someone is coming!" Phoebe exclaimed.

"Good. That means we won't have to walk to town. Stand aside while I flag it down."

There was no need, however, for the coach rolled to a stop without being hailed. The door opened and Sir Andrew stepped down.

"Thank God we found you!" He opened his arms and Phoebe ran into them.

"How did you know?" Ram asked.

"Wilson arrived this morning shortly after you left. He was worried about you. He'd overheard Watts talking to the stableman early this morning."

"That's right, milord," Wilson concurred. "I'd gone to the stables to see to the horses and heard a man, said his name was Watts, talking to the stableman. Watts started to brag that a filthy rich London lord was going to pay him a bundle to get back something that belonged to him. I put two and two together and figured I'd best report what I heard."

"Good work," Ram said.

"You weren't at the pond when we checked," Andrew continued. "Signs of a struggle were everywhere. We returned to the coach, intending to alert the authorities. Then Wilson spied wheel tracks that looked fairly recent. Since we had no other lead, we followed. What happened?" he asked, pointing to the overturned coach.

"It's a long story," Phoebe said. "David Phillips is alive. He followed Ram to Cambridge. He was going to abduct me and hold me for ransom."

"Did he get away?"

Ram pointed to where Phillips lay sprawled on the ground. "He's unconscious. I was just about to bind his hands and feet when you arrived." He handed the leather strips to Wilson. "You may do the honors."

Wilson made short work of Phillips, leaving him trussed up like a Christmas goose.

"It's a miracle you and Phoebe weren't hurt. How did the coach overturn?" Andrew asked.

"The horses bolted and Watts couldn't handle them," Ram said. He thought it best not to mention the gun. "He is pinned beneath the coach. We were planning to walk to town and summon help, but the three of us should be able to lift the coach and pull him free."

"Ram's hurt," Phoebe said. "He needs medical attention."

"It's nothing, just a couple of broken ribs."

"I can bind your ribs, milord," Wilson offered.

"You can use my petticoat," Phoebe offered, turning her back and lifting her skirt to undo the tapes. Whipping the petticoat off, she handed it to Wilson, who immediately began tearing it into strips.

"Take off your coat and shirt, milord," Wilson directed.

"You're making too much of this," Ram complained.

"Do it for me," Phoebe whispered.

When it was put that way, Ram could not refuse Phoebe's request. He pulled off his coat and shirt and let Wilson attend to his injuries.

Once his ribs were tightly wrapped, the three men went to Watts's aid. He had passed out, which was a good thing. While Ram and Wilson lifted the wheel, Andrew pulled Watts out from beneath it. After a cursory examination, Wilson confirmed that Watts's right leg was broken.

Wilson found a sturdy piece of wood and bound the broken leg to it with a length of leather Ram had cut from the traces. Then Watts and Phillips, who was just starting to come around, were placed inside the coach.

Ram directed Wilson to take Phillips and Watts to town and turn them over to the magistrate. "There's no room for everyone in the coach, so Phoebe and I will wait here for your return. Sir Thompson will go with you and explain the situation to the magistrate."

Andrew climbed onto the driver's bench beside Wilson, and the coach rattled off. Ram took Phoebe's hand, seated her beneath a tree and sprawled out beside her.

"It's over, love; really over," he said. "Phillips will never interfere in our lives again."

He sent her a stern look. "Now let's talk about the babe you're carrying."

Chapter Twenty

Phoebe gave Ram a tremulous smile. "You know."

"I heard you tell Phillips you're carrying my child. Is it true?"

"I'm as certain as I can be."

He gave her a stern look. "Were you planning to tell me?"

"Yes, of course."

"When?"

"Today. When I returned to the house." A sudden thought occurred to her. "Did Mrs. Crowley write to you? She suspected I was increasing before I realized it myself."

"I did receive a letter from your father, but he said nothing about your condition. He simply stated that you needed me, and I came immediately."

"Mrs. Crowley must have told Father and he in turn decided it was something you should know."

She grew thoughtful. "Father and Mrs. Crowley have grown rather close of late. I wonder . . ."

"Forget them for a moment. Did you know you were carrying my child when you left London?"

Phoebe shook her head. "I had no idea. Believe me, I would never deprive you of your child."

"Would you have returned to me when you realized you were increasing?" Ram asked.

"Truthfully, I . . . don't know. Reading accounts of your debauchery in the newspapers was disheartening. But I would have told you about our babe and made arrangements for you to see him or her."

"My debauchery was wildly exaggerated. Those women weren't you."

"I believe you. The point is moot anyway. You're here and we're together. Our child is going to have a mother *and* a father."

"Thanks to your father," Ram added.

"Though I don't approve of his writing to you without my knowledge, I can't fault his good intentions. As it turned out, his interference brought us together. I love you so much, Ram. Having your child means more to me than you'll ever know. When I left four years ago, I entertained a secret hope that I carried your babe with me, but it was not to be."

"Forget those lost years, sweetheart. The rest of our life together begins today." He searched her face. "You look exhausted."

Phoebe sent him a reproachful look. "Whose fault is that?"

Ram grinned. "Mine, and I'm not a bit sorry. Lay your head on my shoulder and try to sleep. It could be a while before Wilson returns with the coach. This is a little-traveled road, I doubt anyone will pass this way anytime soon."

Phoebe laid her head on Ram's shoulder and closed·her eyes. She was tired and sore from being tumbled about inside the coach, though she kept that knowledge to herself. She didn't want Ram worrying unnecessarily. Within minutes she was asleep.

Ram kissed the top of Phoebe's head and held her comfortably against him. His ribs ached like the very devil, but things could have been worse. Phoebe could have lost their child. A shudder passed through him. If that had happened, he would have killed Phillips. He might kill him yet if Phoebe suffered belated effects from the accident.

Ram's eyes grew heavy. His mad dash up from London and the sleepless night that followed had severely drained him. And the wrenching pain from his broken ribs added to his discomfort. Everything that had happened the past two days combined to drag him down into the depths of sleep.

"Wake up, milord."

Ram jerked awake and immediately regretted it; the jarring movement aggravated his pain.

"Wilson! You've returned. I must have fallen asleep. How long have you been gone?"

"Outside of two hours, milord," Wilson said. "Sir Thompson did a credible job of explaining to the constable and seeing to the formalities. I returned as soon as I could."

The sound of voices awakened Phoebe, and she opened her eyes and sat up. "Is it time to leave?"

"Wilson just arrived, sweetheart." Ram started to rise, grasped his ribs and doubled over. Several long moments passed before he could draw a breath.

"Let me help you, milord," Wilson offered.

"I'm fine," Ram said, waving him away. "Help

Lady Braxton; she needs it more than I."

"I'm in better shape than you are," Phoebe contended, placing a supportive arm around Ram's waist.

Clinging to one another, they walked the short distance to the coach. Wilson closed the door behind them, climbed into the driver's box and set the horses into motion.

When they reached the cottage, Mrs. Crowley insisted on putting Phoebe to bed and inspecting Ram's ribs. Phoebe protested being shuttled off to bed, but Mrs. Crowley was adamant. Once Phoebe was safely tucked in, the housekeeper undid Ram's bindings, inspected his ribs and declared two of them broken. Then she smoothed on a healing salve and rebound them.

"Lunch is ready, milord. Shall I bring up a tray for you and Lady Braxton?"

"Just bring lunch for Phoebe," Ram said. "I should visit the constable to check on the prisoners."

"I'm not an invalid," Phoebe protested.

"All I ask is that you rest until dinnertime," Ram replied.

"His Lordship is right," Mrs. Crowley affirmed. "According to Andrew, you were badly shaken in the coach accident. A woman in your condition can't be too careful."

Ram placed a kiss on Phoebe's brow, then followed Mrs. Crowley out the door.

"Do you think she'll be all right?" Ram asked anxiously.

"There's nothing to indicate she'll lose the babe," the housekeeper replied. "She's not even badly bruised. I suspect she has you to thank for that. You have bruises aplenty."

buys his books. Nice work if you can get it is what I say. Anyway, I expect you don't want to have me nattering to you all afternoon, and even if you do I've got better things to do. Sister says you'll probably be discharged this evening so you can go to your own home and sleep in your own bed, which I'm sure you'll much prefer. Anyway, hope you feel better, here's a couple of newspapers.''

Dirk took the papers, glad to be left alone at last.

He first turned to see what The Great Zaganza had to say about his day. The Great Zaganza said, ''You are very fat and stupid and persistently wear a ridiculous hat which you should be ashamed of.''

He grunted slightly to himself about this, and turned to the horoscope in the other paper.

It said, ''Today is a day to enjoy home comforts.''

Yes, he thought, he would be glad to get back home. He was still strangely relieved about getting rid of his old fridge and looked forward to enjoying a new phase of fridge ownership with the spanking new model currently sitting in his kitchen at home.

There was the eagle to think about, but he would worry about that later, when he got home.

He turned to the front page to see if there was any interesting news.

"Better me than Phoebe. I'm the one who led Phillips to her and endangered her life. I can't believe I was so careless."

"Don't blame yourself, Braxton," Andrew said. "Phillips is a sly one. Sit down and eat something. You left the house this morning without breakfast. The constable can wait."

Ram didn't realize how hungry he was until he saw the tempting array of food Mrs. Crowley was placing before him.

Once he'd eaten his fill, he excused himself. "I shouldn't be long. Make sure Phoebe stays in bed."

The constable, a capable man who followed the law to the letter, listened intently to Ram's recitation of the events leading up to this morning's climactic capture of Watts and Phillips. After hearing the facts, he agreed to transport the prisoners to London, where they would be charged and tried by the highest court in the land.

"Fear not, milord, they won't escape," the constable declared. "They'll be carried off to London in chains."

"Watts can probably be moved in a day or two," Ram said. "He'll be charged as an accomplice. I expect to return to London tomorrow or the following day. Upon my return, I'll personally inform Lord Fielding of all that transpired here. I think that covers everything. I should be getting back to my wife."

"I'll take care of matters from this end," the constable said. "Good day to you, milord."

Phoebe was sleeping when Ram returned to the cottage. He undressed and lay down beside her, and within minutes was asleep himself.

* * *

Phoebe awakened to find Ram sound asleep beside her. She glanced out the window, surprised to see that the sun had sunk below the horizon. She must have slept for hours. When had Ram joined her? She eased out of bed so as not to awaken him, but the slight movement brought his eyes open at once.

"Where are you going?"

"I need to . . ."

"Oh."

She disappeared behind the screen and returned a few minutes later. "Did you see the constable?"

"Yes. He's going to deliver Phillips and Watts to Lord Fielding in London. Now I've finished what I set out to do and have no intention of working for the Foreign Office again." A slow grin, ripe with sexual promise, curved his lips. "Come back to bed."

Phoebe tossed her mane of dark hair. "You're going to have to wait, my lord decadence." She patted her stomach. "I'm hungry. Mrs. Crowley will have dinner on the table soon."

"I wouldn't think of depriving an expectant mother of sustenance," Ram teased as he climbed out of bed. "We'll go down together."

"There you are," Mrs. Crowley said when Ram and Phoebe appeared in the parlor arm in arm. "Dinner is almost ready. Find His Lordship something to drink, Andrew, while I take care of things in the kitchen."

"Will brandy do, Braxton?" Andrew asked, walking to the sideboard.

"Brandy will be fine," Ram replied.

"Father, you and Mrs. Crowley seem to be getting on rather well," Phoebe observed.

"Annie is a fine woman, daughter."

"She is, indeed," Phoebe allowed. "However . . ."

Mrs. Crowley poked her head into the parlor. "Come and eat before the food gets cold."

Andrew offered Phoebe his arm, and Ram followed close behind. Phoebe was somewhat surprised when the housekeeper joined them at the table, but somehow it seemed right. There was an undercurrent of something inexplicably sweet between her father and Mrs. Crowley, and she intended to find out exactly what was going on. Table conversation centered on David Phillips and the day's happenings, until Ram abruptly changed the subject.

"Phoebe and I will be leaving for London tomorrow or the day after, depending on her state of health. We'd like you to come and live with us, Andrew. There's plenty of room. We'll probably retire to my country estate soon to await the birth of our child. You're welcome to accompany us, Andrew. Or if you prefer, you can remain at our townhouse in London. It's your choice."

"I'm rather fond of Cambridge," Andrew said, sending Mrs. Crowley a secretive smile. "And this cottage suits me just fine. I'm seriously thinking of accepting a teaching position at the university. Besides, you two don't need me rambling about. You're almost newlyweds and need to be alone, and I still have some good years left to contribute to the study of Egyptology."

"Are you sure, Father?" Phoebe asked. "We'd love to have you."

"Very sure. Cambridge isn't all that far from London—we can visit often. I'll plan a long visit to Braxton Manor when the baby arrives."

"I suppose you'll be wanting to join your family

at Braxton Manor, Mrs. Crowley," Ram ventured. "I'll make all the arrangements for your travel."

The housekeeper and Andrew exchanged meaningful looks. "Annie is staying with me," Andrew said. "I couldn't manage without her."

"Is that your wish also, Mrs. Crowley?" Ram asked.

Mrs. Crowley dimpled prettily and patted Andrew's hand. "I wouldn't dream of leaving Andrew on his own."

"Father, is there something I should know?" Phoebe asked. "Have I missed something?"

Andrew gave Mrs. Crowley's hand a squeeze. "Annie and I are getting on in years. You have Braxton, and Annie's daughter has her family. Annie and I genuinely like and respect each other. I see no reason why we shouldn't take our relationship further."

"Nor do I," Ram said, suppressing a smile. "Do we have a wedding to anticipate?"

"Oh, my," Mrs. Crowley said. "It's far too soon for that."

"Do you have any objections, daughter?" Andrew asked.

"None, Father. You and Mrs. Crowley . . . Annie . . . have my blessing. I'm too happy to object to anything. My true love has been restored to me and everything is right in my world."

Ram must have taken her words as a sign, for he rose and extended his hand. "Shall we retire, wife?"

Phoebe placed her hand in Ram's, giving him her trust, her love, her heart and her soul.

By the time they reached their room, Ram and Phoebe were in a fever of desire. Phoebe went eagerly into his arms, offering her lips for his kisses and her body for him to worship. Ram undressed her with reverent hands, then proceeded to cherish every inch of her silken skin with lips and mouth and tongue.

When he rose up on his haunches and nudged her legs apart, she slid out from beneath him and pushed him down into the feather mattress. Smiling with kittenish delight, she teased him mercilessly with mouth and tongue, lavishing all the love in her heart upon him.

He let her have her way until his body thrummed and he was moments away from exploding. Then he pulled her beneath him and thrust inside, bringing them both to a shuddering climax. Afterward, he gathered her close in a tender embrace, sharing the tumultuous pleasure coursing through her body.

His loving had been heartbreakingly tender, bringing tears to Phoebe's eyes. She had wasted four years of her life and intended to make every moment of their remaining years together memorable.

This time they would have forever.

"Forever," Ram murmured, echoing her thoughts. "Mine forever."

Author's Note

Seduced by a Rogue is the second book of my Rogues of London series. The first book, *The Rogue and the Hellion*, was a June 2002 release. I hope you enjoy both of them.

My next release from Leisure is set in Scotland in the year 1428 during the reign of King James of Scotland. Blair MacArthur is in danger, and her dying father asks Graeme Campbell to wed her in order to protect her. *Bewitched* is the story of a healer, a faery woman who, according to family legend, will lose her special powers if she falls in love.

I hope you enjoy the exploits of my feisty heroine and brave hero. The last book of my Rogue series will follow in 2004.

You can reach me by e-mail at conmason@ aol.com or by mail at P.O. Box 3471, Holiday, FL 34690. Visit my website to read my current news-

Author's Note

letter, a brief description of my books, and to keep
abreast of all my scheduled reprints and reissues.
All My Romantic Best,
Connie Mason